DOCTORED DEATH

DOCTORED DEATH

A KENZIE KIRSCH MEDICAL THRILLER #2

P.D. WORKMAN

ISBN: 9781774681114 (IS Hardcover)

ISBN: 9781774681107 (IS Paperback)

ISBN: 9781774681121 (IS Large Print)

ISBN: 9781774681077 (KDP Paperback)

ISBN: 9781774681084 (Kindle)

ISBN: 9781774681091 (ePub)

pdworkman

ALSO BY P.D. WORKMAN

Kenzie Kirsch Medical Thrillers

Unlawful Harvest

Doctored Death

Dosed to Death (Coming soon)

Gentle Angel (Coming soon)

Zachary Goldman Mysteries

She Wore Mourning

His Hands Were Quiet

She Was Dying Anyway

He Was Walking Alone

They Thought He was Safe

He Was Not There

Her Work Was Everything

She Told a Lie

He Never Forgot

She Was At Risk

Parks Pat Mysteries

Out with the Sunset

Long Climb to the Top

Dark Water Under the Bridge

Immersed in the View (Coming Soon)

Skimming Over the Lake (Coming Soon)

Hazard of the Hills (Coming Soon)

Auntie Clem's Bakery

Gluten-Free Murder

Dairy-Free Death

Allergen-Free Assignation

Witch-Free Halloween (Halloween Short)

Dog-Free Dinner (Christmas Short)

Stirring Up Murder

Brewing Death

Coup de Glace

Sour Cherry Turnover

Apple-achian Treasure

Vegan Baked Alaska

Muffins Masks Murder

Tai Chi and Chai Tea

Santa Shortbread

Cold as Ice Cream

Changing Fortune Cookies

Hot on the Trail Mix

Recipes from Auntie Clem's Bakery

High-Tech Crime Solvers Series

Virtually Harmless

AND MORE AT PDWORKMAN.COM

To nurturers, both those in
lab coats and those in fur coats

1

Will awoke in a dark room. He couldn't remember where he was. He wasn't sure what had woken him up, but something was wrong. Something was definitely wrong. He sat up and looked around, straining his eyes in the darkness. His breathing was irregular and he had a difficult time swallowing. Was he sick? He must be sick. It looked something like a hospital room.

He needed to talk to someone and find out what was going on. He slid his feet out from under the covers and put them on the floor. It was carpeted rather than tiled like a hospital room normally was.

He realized as he slid out of the warm spot he'd occupied on the bed that he was wet.

Something was definitely wrong. A grown man didn't wet the bed.

His legs were wobbly and weak. He held on to the bed as he tried to push himself upright. The room lurched around him. He couldn't find his balance.

He needed to get help. Someone outside the room could help him. If he could just make it to the door and out into the hallway.

He felt for the wall to steady himself. He kept banging his legs against furniture as he made his way around the room. A couple of times, he fell to his knees and it was a struggle to get back up again. Eventually, he decided it was easier to crawl along the floor than it was to walk.

If he just knew where he was going.

He banged his head against something hard. It sent his brain spinning. Blackness gathered closer in to him. A warm trickle ran down his temple. As he lay on the carpet, giving in to the hopelessness of the situation, a line of light appeared across the room. It was too bright, making him squint. The line grew into an elongated rectangle. A partially open doorway?

Will was relieved. Someone was there. Someone had come to check on him and they would tell him what was wrong and help him back to bed where he could rest his head.

But it wasn't a nurse that came in to see to him. He felt a cold nose and warm snout against his hand and arm. A dog. It moved to his face and sniffed and breathed its warm breath on him, investigating his face, licking him in greeting and cleaning away the blood.

He murmured words to it. He didn't know the animal's name, but it brought him comfort to have another living being there with him. He wasn't alone.

The dog barked a couple of times. That would bring help. Then it lay down alongside him. It was warm and soft.

Will closed his eyes and breathed out.

2

K enzie was awakened by the insistent beeping of her clock. She reached over to turn it off, forcing her eyes open. Friday. And she had the weekend off, provided nothing untoward happened that required her at the Medical Examiner's office. One more day. Saturday she could sleep in. She sat up, hoping that would help to wake her enough to get her day going. She ran her fingers through her wildly curly dark hair to push it away from her face.

She felt the bed beside her to see if Zachary were there, but she knew he wouldn't be. It would have been more than rare for him to still be in bed when she woke up. It had only happened once or twice in the months Zachary had been sleeping there. After the assault, it had been different. His sleep patterns had become completely erratic and he was frequently unable to get out of bed or to keep from falling asleep where he sat on the couch or in front of the computer. But he was back to his normal routine, and that meant that he was up before she was. Sometimes hours before.

Kenzie pushed herself to her feet and staggered to the ensuite bathroom. She went to the bathroom and then started the shower. She rubbed her hands over her face and looked at herself in the mirror while she waited for the water to warm up. A cold shower might wake her up faster, but she preferred her creature comforts; she wasn't getting in until it started to steam.

After a quick shower, Kenzie tidied her spiraling hair into some order, put on her makeup, including the red lipstick that would have to be reapplied after breakfast. But she loved the way it looked, so she put it on anyway. She pulled on her usual work uniform. A blouse and slacks topped with a short blazer. Comfortable shoes, since she would be on her feet much of the day. Then she left the bedroom and went down the hall to the living room and kitchen area to see how her partner was.

"Morning, Zachary."

He didn't look up from his computer.

Kenzie hadn't picked Zachary Goldman for his looks. He was a small, slender man with close-cropped black hair. He had been feeling pretty good over the summer, but she thought he might be losing weight again. His cheeks, which had filled in since his last depressive cycle, looked a little thin and his eye sockets hollow. He hadn't shaved yet and might not. He frequently kept a scruffy three days' growth of beard. It made him look like a homeless man. Intentionally so. People looked away from him, discounted him, which made his surveillance jobs much easier.

The reason Kenzie was with him was because he was kind and cared about people and he made her laugh. He was also one of the few people she could discuss her job at the Medical Examiner's Office with. He was interested in the medical mysteries she helped to solve, not disgusted by them.

There weren't a lot of people she could look at autopsy photos with over dinner.

"Zachary." Kenzie leaned over his shoulder and gave him a peck on the cheek.

He gave a small start and looked at her. He smiled. "Oh, you're up." He stretched and massaged his neck. "I didn't hear you."

"Up and dressed and ready for breakfast," she pointed out, in case the private investigator didn't notice these clues. "Are you ready for something to eat?"

He stood. "Sorry, I didn't hear you in the shower or I would have put some coffee on."

"It won't take long." Kenzie picked up a couple of mugs from the side table, one empty and one half-full of lukewarm or cold coffee. Zachary was pretty good about keeping them away from his computer to prevent any accidental spills. Not so great at remembering to pick them up again later.

She carried them into the kitchen and, after dumping the one in the sink, put them into the dishwasher. She started the coffee maker and put a couple of pieces of bread into the toaster.

Zachary went to the fridge and got out the margarine and marmalade for her. They moved around each other, used to the flow of the morning routine. Kenzie put a granola bar in front of Zachary's chair. His meds made eating in the morning difficult, but he could usually manage one of the chocolate chip granola bars, and the doctor said that anything he could get down was better than nothing.

They both sat down once the coffee was finished brewing and the toast popped.

"How did you sleep?" Kenzie asked. She couldn't remember him getting up.

Zachary had a sip of the hot coffee and started to unwrap the granola bar. "Not the best night. Restless. But I got a few hours in."

"Good. I didn't hear you up."

He nodded. "I tried to be quiet. Don't like you to be tired at work."

"I know. But if you need me..."

He gave her a smile. The one he always gave when he was comparing her reaction to how his ex-wife Bridget would have treated him. Criticizing him from disturbing her beauty rest instead of inviting him to wake her up if he needed her. The bemused smile that said he wasn't sure he deserved to be treated so kindly.

Zachary broke off a corner of the granola bar and put it in his mouth. "Think you'll be busy today?"

"Things have been quiet lately. I just don't know if that means they are going to continue to be quiet or we are building up to something big."

"Hopefully quiet. But not too quiet. Enough that you won't be bored. But no mass murders."

"Exactly," Kenzie agreed, taking a couple of bites of her marmalade toast. "I don't think there's any need to worry about me getting bored. People aren't going to stop dying."

3

Kenzie arrived at the Medical Examiner's Office and went immediately to work, checking over any calls that had come in during the night and making sure that any remains which had been brought in while the night crew was on had been properly logged in and had all the necessary reports attached. She glanced over her email inbox and took a quick peek at Dr. Wiltshire's as well to make sure there was nothing hot that needed to be dealt with right away.

After squaring away those systems, she took a quick walk through the suite of rooms that comprised the Medical Examiner's Office, making sure that nothing was out of place. Dr. Wiltshire liked his desk left just-so. He didn't like to come in to find sticky notes or pink phone messages all over it, attempts by the police or other city employees to end-run the proper procedures and get their case in front of him next or ask questions outside of the proper protocol.

While there were proper procedures for everything, people were lazy and didn't always follow them. She and Dr. Wiltshire didn't want to end up with remains or tests not correctly logged in, or the opposite, disappearing without having been properly logged out. Dr. Wiltshire had seen it happen in other ME offices, and he ran a tight ship.

All of her housekeeping complete, Kenzie returned to her desk and started to sort incoming emails, responding where necessary, filing and printing lab reports that had come in, and forwarding messages to Dr. Wiltshire or other employees.

Dr. Wiltshire arrived, Starbucks cup in one hand and briefcase in the other. "Morning, Kenzie."

"Good morning, doctor. I've opened files for a couple of new arrivals. The John Doe that the police consulted you on last night. He's already in storage waiting for you. And we had a call from Champlain House. One of their residents was found deceased this morning. A Willis Cartwright. He is on his way in."

"Good. Any concerns?"

"No, I don't think so. Just an unattended death. He was in good health up until a couple of days ago. They had started running some tests but hadn't made any determination yet. He was eighty-seven."

Dr. Wiltshire nodded and sipped his travel cup of coffee. "I'll look at him after the John Doe, then. That is more pressing, since the police are hoping for an ID."

"Okay. The file is on your desk. I filled in what I could on the intake."

Since Dr. Wiltshire had attended the scene of death during the night, Kenzie didn't know all the details. He would need to fill in what he had observed and make sure that all police and witness statements were present and accounted for.

Kenzie hoped she would be able to scrub in for at least part of the postmortems. While much of her job at the ME's office was administrative, she was a fully qualified doctor and was trying to get enough experience to someday be a Medical Examiner herself.

There was a lot of paperwork to manage. Far from heralding the arrival of the paperless office, email had only served to amplify the amount of paper that flowed through the ME's office. There was a never-ending supply of lab reports, police reports, interoffice correspondence, and research that piled up on each file, in addition to what Dr. Wiltshire dictated during the postmortem or filled out on his computer as he evaluated each case.

But Kenzie managed to get it under control in time to assist on the postmortem of Willis Cartwright, the man from the seniors' independent living center.

Dr. Wiltshire had done the preliminaries and was gowned up. Kenzie picked up the file and added the report she had received from the nursing home concerning Cartwright's health and death. She summarized aloud to Dr. Wiltshire before donning the last of her protective gear.

"Mr. Willis Cartwright, age eighty-seven, was discovered dead in his room this morning at Champlain House. He was on the floor. He has a laceration on his head. They believe that he got up in the night, disoriented, and hit his head before passing out. The body was cold and there were no signs of life. Dr. Archibald was on site and declared him."

"Medications at the time of his death?"

"Blood pressure... NSAID... antidepressant."

"What was the blood pressure prescription?"

Kenzie summarized it for him. Dr. Wiltshire nodded. "You said this morning that his health had taken a downturn the last few days?"

"Staff had noticed an increase in confusion and emotional lability. He was having more problems than usual with getting around. Wasn't eating much at mealtimes. They thought maybe he was fighting a virus. It didn't appear to be anything serious."

"What was his mental acuity before this?"

Kenzie scanned the report from the nursing home for details. "He was in the independent living quarters. No significant cognitive issues." She turned the page. "They have a living skills sheet that they fill out to indicate what level of help the resident needs with each task. He is at the independent end for all of them, able to feed and wash himself, change his clothes. Needed some assistance with shaving. Had his pills pre-portioned for him."

Wiltshire nodded. "Anything else?"

"Not offhand. We can review it in more detail later, but it seems like this was unexpected. Other than his age being a factor."

"Well, let's see what we can find."

Kenzie put on her mask, face shield, and gloves and approached the table. Dr. Wiltshire pulled the cover down to Mr. Cartwright's navel.

"George washed the body earlier. He noted that the deceased had urinated, probably perimortem, since the clothing was not wet in the same areas as show lividity."

Kenzie translated this in her head to tell Zachary later if he asked for details on the autopsy. The urine had flowed to one area of Cartwright's clothing due to gravity. But the blood in his body had been pulled to another location by gravity after death. It was a good catch by George, showing that Cartwright wasn't just wet because his sphincters had released on death.

She and Dr. Wiltshire both examined the body closely, looking for anything notable. Kenzie pulled a magnifying lens over the wound on his temple. Since the blood had been washed off, it seemed to be an unremarkable wound, like a toddler might get from running into the table. A bandage or a kiss and he'd be on his way to exploring again. But that wasn't the case for Cartwright. His adventures had been permanently curtailed.

"Small laceration," she announced to Dr. Wiltshire and the digital recorder. She described it as thoroughly as she could as to size, shape, location, and color. She explored the wound, but it did not appear to be deep. It would have bled a good amount, being a scalp wound, but she would be surprised if it were the cause of death. She pressed the wound gently, feeling the skull underneath. "There is swelling under the laceration, but not a lot. I can't feel any fractures in the skull. Do we have x-rays?"

Dr. Wiltshire hit a button on the floor with his foot to bring the imaging up on the large view-screen, tapping it several times to get to the photo they wanted. Kenzie walked closer to the screen.

"I don't see any skull fractures."

"I concur."

They continued their examination of the body. When they were finished with the front and sides, they rolled him onto his stomach to examine his back. The lividity had been on his right side. Kenzie didn't see any blood settled into the back of the body. He had, possibly, curled up in a fetal position on the floor after hitting his head. He had not been lying on his back.

Dr. Wiltshire had removed the drape. He frowned and pointed to Cartwright's backside. "Looks like diaper rash," he said. "I thought the documents from the home indicated he was continent."

"Yes. They did." Kenzie walked over to the desk where she had left the file. She didn't touch it, but looked instead at the inventory sheet that George had filled out, which had not yet been inserted into the file. She ran her eyes down the list of clothing items. "Pajamas and briefs. No diaper."

Wiltshire frowned, thinking about that. He made an official note of it on the recording and they continued with their examination of the body.

When they turned him back over, Kenzie examined his hands and trimmed his nails, looking for any dirt or foreign substances. Cartwright's nails were well-manicured and clean. He didn't have any injuries on his hands. Dr. Wiltshire examined the man's lower half and replaced the drape folded across Cartwright's middle before calling Kenzie over to look at the man's legs. His shins and knees were considerably bruised. Several cuts looked relatively recent.

"What do you make of that?" Kenzie asked.

"I would say he's been walking into things."

"That supports the theory that he was disoriented. Maybe he walked into something in the dark?"

"A few of these might be from last night, but not all of them." Dr. Wiltshire pointed at the edges of some of the other bruises and examined the healing cuts. "I would say... they go back about a week? What do you think?"

Kenzie looked at the bruises. Some of them had fading edges, colors changing from blue and gray to green and yellow. She thought about her own experience with bruises and nodded. "Some people heal faster than others, but for a man of his age, I wouldn't expect him to heal that much in a couple of days. We can compare them to the reference texts."

Wiltshire nodded. "Let's take some pictures. You can compare them later. I'm pretty confident in my timeline."

In other words, Kenzie needed to educate herself, but Dr. Wiltshire had been on the job long enough to know his bruises. Kenzie nodded. They took a few pictures with a camera on an articulating arm that hung down from the ceiling. Wiltshire reviewed the images before moving on to make sure they were what he needed.

Once the gross examination of the body was complete, it was time to open him up. If the cause of death had been obvious, perhaps if the wound on his temple had been more serious, they might not have gone any farther. But so far, they had not come across anything that clearly indicated Cartwright's cause of death.

4

Kenzie took one more walk around the lab to make sure that everything was tidied up and put away. That would make it an easier start the next day. She wouldn't be on. There wouldn't be anyone there in the evening unless they had call-outs. If there were remains to be brought in, one of the staff would be on call to go in and deal with it. Anything that could wait for Kenzie's return on Monday would wait. Hopefully, it would be a quiet weekend.

Once she was sure that everything was taken care of, Kenzie grabbed her purse from her locked desk drawer and headed out to her car. She waved to the night guard.

"Good night, Dr. Kirsch," he called out to her. "Have a nice weekend."

"I plan to! You too!"

He would be working through the weekend, so he wasn't exactly going to be enjoying his leisure. Kenzie was glad for the protected parking garage under the building. She didn't have to leave her baby out on the street all day. The little red convertible would attract too much attention and she didn't want anyone trying to boost it because it looked like an easy target. A guarded parking garage under the police building was about as safe as it could get in town.

There were a couple of lights on in the house when she got home, so she anticipated that Zachary was home, not out on surveillance. Which was good; she didn't like him doing night jobs. Daytime surveillance didn't bother her, but knowing that he was out after dark watching some adulterer or corporate spy always made her anxious. She found it hard to go to sleep on nights he was out. But he didn't do a lot of night surveillance. When he didn't have a big case going on, he was doing skip tracing, insurance fraud, and many other small projects that provided him with a steady income. The adultery and corporate espionage jobs were still there, but most of them could be handled during the day. At night, people went home to their wives or their televisions and relaxed.

Kenzie pulled her car into the garage and pressed her clicker to shut the big door. She walked through the house door into the back mudroom, then into the kitchen.

"Hey, Kenzie," Zachary noticed her immediately. "How was your day?"

"Pretty good." Kenzie stretched and arched her back. The table had been set to the right height for Dr. Wiltshire, but he was a little taller than she was, and her upper back and shoulders were feeling the strain by the time they finished the post. "Glad to be home. All weekend. You have time off too, right?"

Zachary was looking down at his phone and didn't acknowledge the question. Kenzie waited for him to look back up. "This weekend?" Kenzie prompted, when he eventually looked back at her.

"Do I have time?" Zachary asked, filling in the question with what he figured he'd missed. "Yes. I took time off. We're good."

"Great. It will be nice to have some real time together."

Zachary nodded. It was something that Dr. B—Zachary's therapist, who was also running their couples therapy—had been pushing them to do. Make more time to spend together. Not just the frayed edges at the end of the day when they both happened to be home at the same time. Some real quality time to visit, go to a movie, visit friends, or whatever other arrangements they felt like making. And, of course, she was right. Kenzie had been a workaholic throughout school, focused on her goal, and she was dedicated to Dr. Wiltshire and the office. Since Zachary had moved in with Kenzie— he did still have his own apartment in case one of them needed some space —they had fallen into the bad habit of assuming they would have time to do things together, with both of them filling up their time with work, chores, errands, meals, and sleep, until there wasn't anything left for quality couple's time or dates.

"Why don't you go get changed?" Zachary suggested. "I'll... set the table. Did you want to cook tonight, or do you want to order in?"

Kenzie considered. "I have one of those deluxe frozen pizzas from the grocery store. Why don't we have that?"

"Okay. Do you want me to put it in?"

"No. You can get it out, but don't put it in the oven yet."

Zachary nodded absently, looking back down at his phone. Kenzie went to her room to change. She dumped her purse on her writing desk and changed out of her work clothes into some comfy loungewear for the evening. She was pretty sure that Zachary wasn't going to put the pizza in the oven, but he hadn't really acknowledged what she had said. She knew from his past attempts that he was perfectly capable of putting the pizza into the oven with the plastic wrap on. Or forgetting to set the temperature or the timer.

It wasn't that he was helpless, but cooking, even just heating up meals, was not his forte. The poor executive skills and distractibility that came with his ADHD and PTSD meant that completing multiple steps in a particular order and keeping track of several things at once was a challenge. He would have to be completely focused, and he just wasn't interested enough in meals for it to keep his focus. He would be thinking about whatever cases he was working on, or their relationship, or his family, or Bridget, or some other random thought that flitted through his brain, and the dinner and all the remaining steps it would take to complete the meal would be forgotten.

When she returned to the living room, Zachary was still looking at his phone and had not bothered to get the pizza out of the freezer. Which was fine with Kenzie. Better that than trying to figure out how to get melting plastic wrap off the pizza before it was too late. She set the oven temperature, put the unwrapped pizza in, and set a timer. She had learned not to judge Zachary by how easy a task was for her to complete. And in the same way, he could run circles around her in private investigation, remembering camera f-stops, and out-of-the-box thinking. And he was sensitive and quickly attuned to others' emotions, when Kenzie might chatter with someone for half an hour without realizing that they were upset about something.

Zachary slid his phone into his pants pocket and entered the kitchen to pull out plates and set the table.

"Are you talking to someone?" Kenzie asked. "What's up with the phone?"

"Oh. Sorry, were you talking to me? I was just..." Zachary made a motion to his pocket. "Rhys."

Kenzie nodded and smiled. Rhys Salter was a teen Zachary had met on an earlier case and had remained friends with. He was Black and selectively mute. While he enjoyed messaging with Zachary sometimes, it could be hard to interpret his gif messages or other pictures or brief words. He didn't just text sentences like Kenzie would, mirroring what she would have said aloud. His use of language was not linear and writing more than a word or two was a challenge. Zachary's intense focus on the phone at intervals made sense if he were trying to interpret Rhys's messages.

"Oh, I see. How is he?"

"Good, I think. It's been rough, but I think he's at school most days now. Hopefully keeping up with his classes."

Witnessing someone getting shot had set Rhys back significantly, bringing back to him the day when his beloved grandfather had been shot. He'd missed a lot of school but was getting settled back into the routine.

Zachary set the plates on the table, then stared at them blankly for a moment before moving to get glasses and cutlery. He filled a pitcher with water and put it in the center of the table. He looked at the settings, then at Kenzie. "Am I forgetting anything?"

"Looks good to me. Grab the napkin holder; I have a feeling the pizza is going to be messy."

He did so, setting the napkins on the table next to the pitcher. "Do you want anything else?"

"No." Kenzie knew she should probably cut up some fresh fruit and vegetables to go with the pizza, but it was the weekend, and she just wanted to chill, not to have to eat right. "You want to put something on TV?"

"After dinner," Zachary said firmly. "Dr. B said to focus on each other over meals. Not to be distracted by TV or other entertainment or devices."

Kenzie nodded. "All right. Good for you. Because you know I totally would have gone for eating in front of the TV today."

He looked pleased with the compliment. He glanced over at the stove. "How much longer until it's ready?"

The timer was counting down right in front of him. "Fifteen minutes. You want to clean up and get changed?"

His face flushed, maybe realizing that he'd been working all day in clothes that he'd probably been wearing most of the week. Fine, if he were pretending to be a homeless person to stay under the radar. Not so good if he wanted to get close to his girlfriend during and after supper. He pinched his shirt between his fingers and brought it up to his nose. "Sorry. Yeah. I'll throw these in the laundry."

Kenzie watched him hurry off to the bathroom for a quick shower and change. He wouldn't have time to shave off his stubble, but he could at least be clean and fresh in that length of time. While she waited for him, she would check her phone and review any personal emails she had received during the afternoon and maybe be able to check her social network accounts as well. At least one of them.

Zachary was back just after the timer sounded, his hair still damp, looking and smelling much better. He smiled at Kenzie and gave her a quick hug and kiss before she had a chance to cut the pizza into slices. She kissed him back, then squirmed away, knife in hand. "If you don't want to get cut, Romeo, you'd better back up and let me get my dinner. I'm starving."

Zachary grinned and sat down at the table to give her space to use the long blade to quickly cut the pizza into wedges. Kenzie put the sliced pizza on the table and grabbed a couple of slices to start out with. Zachary looked for the smallest slice and put it onto his plate. Kenzie took a bite of her first wedge.

"Did you eat any lunch?"

Zachary frowned and considered. He toyed with the slice for a moment. "I'm pretty sure I took a break."

"And ate?"

He pursed his lips. "Maybe."

"That's not good enough. Your body needs more than a granola bar and a slice of pizza in a day."

"I know. And I'm pretty sure I did." He looked at the platter of pizza that remained. "I'll have a second piece."

"You'd better."

He nodded and had a bite of pizza. Kenzie had another bite and swallowed. "Old guy we did a post on today, his nursing home said that his appetite hasn't been too good the last couple of days. And he had nothing in his stomach. *Nothing.*"

"You don't think they were starving him, do you?" Zachary's mind immediately jumped to elder neglect.

"No, I don't think so. They have a pretty good record. We get residents from there now and then, and we haven't seen any starvation cases."

Zachary nodded. "So what killed him?"

"We're not there yet. Have some slides to look at tomorrow, tests to be run at various labs. Nothing obvious, but the home said that he hadn't been well the last few days, and we did notice a couple of anomalies during that time. Not eating, bruises, just little things. Maybe he had a virus and just wasn't strong enough to fight it off. Although," she shrugged, "he seemed like he was in pretty good shape before it hit."

"Maybe a change to his meds?"

"Nope. He wasn't on a lot of different prescriptions. What he was on, he'd been on for a while. No changes that the home could point to in the last week or so. Just that he took poorly."

Zachary nodded thoughtfully. He took another small bite of the pizza and chewed slowly. He was only going to be half done his first slice in the time it took Kenzie to wolf down two.

"Other than that... We had a John Doe overnight. Dr. Wiltshire did that post by himself; I'll have to read his report when it comes back from transcription tomorrow. Monday, I mean."

"Where was he found? Was he mugged? No ID?"

"Homeless, I think. Found in an alley. No ID. Probably alcohol or drug overdose, or some secondary effect of drinking."

"Nobody knew him? It's not that big of a town. I'd think that anyone else out there, on the street, they'd know him. Or someone at the shelter. He must have gone there in the winter, at least."

That was one thing about Vermont that couldn't be said about warmer climes like Florida and California. The homeless didn't survive through the winter without help. Someone in the shelter or another service company would have run into him at some time or another. They would be able to give the John Doe a name, even if it were only a first name or a street name.

They didn't have the flourishing homeless problem that the warmer states dealt with.

"The police will do a canvass. I'm sure they'll find something."

"Yeah. They're bound to. So that's it? Just two today?"

"That's enough. We still have other work to do too. It isn't just doing two posts and then going home because there's nothing else to do."

5

K enzie and Zachary had fallen asleep in each other's arms. Kenzie awoke as Zachary's breathing got louder and he started squirming around and pushing her away from him.

He pushed his covers back, huffing hard as if they were restricting his ability to breathe. He murmured something over and over again but, like with most of his dream talk, she couldn't make out his words. She nudged his shoulder gently.

"Zachary. Zach, wake up."

He squirmed away from her touch, then flailed suddenly as if he were falling and jumped, all his muscles activating, holding himself as stiff as a board.

"Zachary. It's okay. Wake up."

He let his breath out and, at first, his muscles started to relax; then he began to whip his head back and forth, looking for an escape.

"You're safe," Kenzie told him. She reached over and fumbled for the switch on the lamp. She managed to click it on, and squeezed her eyes shut tightly at the sudden dazzling light. Zachary sat bolt upright.

"What was that?"

"It's okay. Just a dream."

Zachary looked around, but Kenzie wasn't sure whether he was truly awake.

"Zach. Are you awake?"

He rubbed his eyes and peered around. He didn't wear glasses, but he squinted as if everything around him was blurred. "We have to get them out," he told her. "We have to get them all out."

Kenzie knew which dream he was having. She blew her breath out slowly and kept her voice calm and soothing. "It's just a dream, Zachary. Everyone is okay. Everyone got out."

He cocked his head for a moment, unsure, trying to process her words. "They're all in there. They can't get out by themselves. They can't walk."

That was a new spin. When Zachary's house had gone up in flames when he was ten years old, his siblings had all been old enough to walk. They hadn't been strong enough to break the windows, but they had been able to walk. The firefighters had been able to rescue them, while Zachary remained trapped in the living room full of smoke and flames, sure that he and his entire family were all going to die. *Who couldn't walk?*

"Everyone is fine," Kenzie repeated. "Everyone got out."

Then his eyes finally focused on her. He looked at her, then at the lamp and at the room around him in confusion.

"You're safe," Kenzie said. "Everyone is fine. It was just a dream."

"Oh." He blinked. "A dream... I dreamt... the nursing home was on fire."

Kenzie raised her brows. "The nursing home? Because I was talking to you about Champlain House at supper today?"

"I don't know. I guess so."

Sometimes their conversations or worries about a case worked their way into Zachary's nightmares. It wasn't predictable, so there was no way to avoid it. They both enjoyed discussing crime and solving forensic clues, so they weren't likely to stop discussing anything that might trigger him.

Zachary ran his fingers through his stubbly hair. He rubbed his eyes with his palms. Kenzie reached over for the lamp.

"Okay now? Shall I turn this off?"

"Yeah. I'm fine."

Kenzie turned the light back off and then cuddled up to Zachary, hoping that he would be able to get back to sleep if they didn't spend too much time talking and focusing on the disturbing dream.

Zachary's dream had Kenzie thinking about the nursing home in the morning while she luxuriated under a hot shower. They had not found anything in the Cartwright case to make her think that they were not taking care of their residents properly and following all the rules and regulations they were bound by. If nothing showed up on the slides and lab tests that they had sent out, Dr. Wiltshire was inclined to write it off as simply heart failure. Possibly due to a virus. Even the most innocuous virus could be dangerous to someone who was old or had an otherwise compromised immune system.

All the paperwork that had come from Champlain House had been in order. It would have made her feel better if he had been discovered sooner, and not lain on the floor for half the night, but it wasn't a case where they were required to check on him every fifteen minutes. Until recently, he had not had any issues and therefore didn't have a bed alarm to alert the staff if he got up in the night. He'd been independent and that meant that they left him alone unless he pressed his call button for help.

There hadn't been any red flags. On the contrary, the facility had provided all the paper they were expected to and more. Willis Cartwright wasn't the first resident from Champlain House to make it to the morgue, and he wouldn't be the last. Being a senior care center, there would always be deaths at the home. Many of them would qualify as deaths that had occurred while in the care of a doctor and wouldn't even go through the Medical Examiner's Office.

While Zachary's dream had made Kenzie consider whether there were any issues at Champlain House, she didn't think that it was portentous. There wasn't going to be a fire at the nursing home. She knew exactly why Zachary dreamed about fire. There was no mystery in that.

6

Much of Saturday had been spent running errands and doing chores around the house. Things that got pushed to the wayside when Kenzie was working without breaks in her schedule. And while Zachary was pretty good about sharing her space and keeping his possessions to limited areas, there was still more cleaning and other chores to do with another person living in the house. Especially if he spent most of his time working from there rather than going back to his own apartment or out in the field.

"We should visit Lorne and Pat Sunday," Kenzie suggested to Zachary after turning off the vacuum cleaner. "We have the time; we should take advantage of it."

Zachary's eyes brightened. Lorne Peterson had been his foster father for a few weeks when he had first been put into foster care, and he was the only parent Zachary had kept in contact with. When Lorne had later separated from his wife and begun a relationship with Patrick Parker, it had been quite scandalous from what Kenzie could tell. But more than twenty years later, the two men were still living together and, for the most part, society accepted their partnership. For a lot of years, they had been Zachary's only family.

"I'm sure they'd be delighted," Zachary agreed. "I'll give them a call." He stopped and looked at her, something else in his expression that Kenzie couldn't read. "Unless..."

"What?" Maybe Lorne and Pat already had other plans Zachary was aware of.

"I just thought... I don't know when the last time you saw your parents was. Do you want to see one of them?"

Kenzie shook her head. "Not really."

"I don't want to keep you from your family."

"You're not. I talk to my mom on the phone and email her, but I really don't need a face-to-face visit. She's always so busy with all her causes. She would just try to get me involved in whatever she's working on right now. 'I'd love to see you, MacKenzie; you can help me to sort the clothes donated for the Kidney Foundation. And bring that young man of yours along to the Cancer Society fundraiser...'" Kenzie rolled her eyes. "Trust me, it's better to keep your distance."

"You're always so accommodating about seeing Lorne and Pat or one of my siblings, but we don't see your family. What about your dad?"

Kenzie groaned and shook her head. "No. Trust me. He's not your kind of person. I love spending time with Lorne or one of your sibs, but seeing my dad is not a holiday."

"Neither is Joss," Zachary pointed out.

Kenzie chuckled.

The first two siblings Zachary had been reunited with decades after the fire were Tyrrell and Heather, and they were both friendly and easy people to like. Kenzie enjoyed being with them and hearing their stories about when they had all been children, before the fire. Joss, on the other hand, was hard and acidic. She was challenging to get along with and kept everyone at a distance.

"Well... okay. But my answer is still no. I'd rather see Lorne and Pat than either of my parents."

Someday, she knew, she was going to have to introduce Zachary to her parents. They would all be gracious about it, but Kenzie didn't want to deal with her parents' questions about Zachary's suitability and stability. And she didn't want to have to explain her family dynamics to Zachary. She didn't really understand them herself. Their family was broken. Maybe not as badly as Zachary's, but Kenzie also didn't think there was any chance it could be put back together again. Amanda was gone. Her parents, while still friends, were divorced. And Kenzie had had as little to do with them as possible since uncovering the secrets they had been keeping about Amanda's last transplant.

Zachary nodded his understanding. He understood dysfunctional families. As far as Kenzie knew, he never had tried to find his biological parents. Neither had his siblings. And the two youngest siblings still hadn't made contact with Zachary.

"I'll call Mr. Peterson then, and make sure they're going to be around," Zachary agreed.

One of the few points of contention between Kenzie and Zachary was whose turn it was to drive when they went to visit Lorne and Pat. Zachary enjoyed highway driving. It was one of the few activities that tamed his hyperactive brain and anxiety and allowed him to just chill out and be in the zone. But he also drove much too fast for Kenzie's comfort.

With her little red convertible, she should have been the speed demon. But she wasn't. She occasionally allowed her baby to creep up over the posted speed limit by a few miles an hour, but she stayed within reasonable limits. Enough that she had never been cited for speeding and had only been pulled over once. The officer had been easy to charm and had let her off with a warning. Kenzie hadn't been pulled over since. Zachary didn't usually get caught, but he liked to fly. Kenzie was always sure he was going to get into an accident, but he seemed totally in control when he drove. Like a fighter pilot.

"You drove last time," Kenzie reminded him. "You said that I could drive the next trip."

Zachary looked for an argument. With Vermont's climate, he often pulled the 'weather' card, insisting that it was too cold to drive a convertible that distance. But the weather had been nice, and Kenzie's baby would enjoy getting out on the highway instead of being cramped up in city streets all day.

"You just had bodywork done," Zachary tried. "Out on the highway, if someone hits a bit of gravel…"

"I'm not afraid of a few dings and scratches. Most of them will buff right out."

"A windshield chip won't."

"I'm driving," Kenzie said firmly. She looked him in the eye.

Zachary shrugged and looked down, conceding as she knew he would. "Fine. You're right; I think it is your turn."

"It is," Kenzie asserted.

There was less leg room in the convertible than in Zachary's car, but neither of them had particularly long legs, so that wasn't an issue. Zachary settled himself in the passenger seat as Kenzie sat down and turned the key, bringing the engine roaring to life. She ignored his restlessness when they got out to the highway. He wanted to be at the wheel. Once or twice before, he had even proposed that they go in separate cars, just in case they needed to return home at different times. They both knew very well that convenience had nothing to do with it; he just wanted to drive. And once he had an idea in his head, it was hard to let it go.

"How did they sound?" Kenzie asked, trying to distract him. "Everything going good?"

"Sounds like it. Mr. Peterson—Lorne—said that they were going to try reducing Pat's antidepressants. See if he still needs them, or if a lower dose will work just as well."

"That's good. That sounds positive."

"Yeah. They wouldn't be doing that if they had any concerns. I think his depression was mostly situational. Losing a friend like that. Jose, and then Dimitri. Finding out that it was someone that he knew. That was tough on him."

"I can see why," Kenzie agreed. All things considered, Pat had fared pretty well. It was a lot to deal with all at once, and if he were able to keep stable at a lower dose or even without antidepressants, that was good news. Kenzie knew that both Lorne and Zachary had been concerned about him.

Zachary stared out the window now, his restlessness stilled, but, Kenzie worried, maybe now obsessing over his involvement in Jose's case and the dark paths it had led him down. Pat might have recovered from his loss, but Zachary hadn't been able to make as much headway against his demons. What had happened to him at the hands of the sadistic killer would be with him for a long time. Kenzie didn't know all the details, but she knew that those memories would always be in the shadows whenever she touched him.

"You okay?"

"Yeah. Fine."

Zachary took a few more minutes to pull his attention from the scenery racing past the window. He looked down at his phone and busied himself with checking his email or social networks.

"Anything exciting?" Kenzie prompted.

"No." Zachary tapped his screen. "Looks like your John Doe made it to the local news."

"Oh? What does it say?"

"Just that they are trying to identify him. They have a picture."

"It's too bad there wasn't anything identifiable on the body. Tattoos or implants. Something traceable."

"You think he was homeless?" Zachary stared down at his screen.

"That was what the police speculated."

Zachary made reverse pinching movements, zooming in on areas of the photograph. "He doesn't look homeless."

"You and I both know that you don't have to look homeless to be homeless."

"No. But he's... very clean and well-groomed."

"Well, we do that before we take a picture. Wash him, try to make him as presentable and lifelike as possible. It makes it easier for people to identify him."

Zachary still wasn't convinced. "You did his hair?"

"I wasn't involved. It must have been yesterday. But yes, we'd comb hair. Add a bit of makeup. Try to make him look natural."

"But you don't cut the hair."

"No. We don't change his look. You change someone's hairstyle, and it changes the shape of their face. We want to keep everything the same."

"His hair is shaped. Like a barber does. Not just cut one length."

Kenzie glanced sideways at Zachary. "He might have had a friend or family member do it. Or a freebie at one of those expo events, when they get service providers together."

"How about his teeth?"

"They were in good shape. But maybe he hasn't been homeless for long."

"Or maybe he's not homeless."

Kenzie shrugged. "Maybe," she agreed. "I can take another look tomorrow."

"Look at everything. How old his clothes are, what brands they are. His shoes especially. Teeth, nails, hair. Not just where he was found or how dirty his clothes were."

"Makes sense. If you're right, maybe the police are talking to the wrong people."

7

K enzie could see Zachary straightening up and becoming more engaged as they approached Lorne and Pat's home. He slid his phone away and put his hand on the armrest of the door, waiting for Kenzie to take the last few turns. There weren't very many people in Zachary's life that were so important to him. When Zachary got attached to someone, he got really attached.

Zachary was out of the door as soon as Kenzie pulled to a stop in front of the house. He held himself back then, waiting for her to get her seatbelt unlatched and pick up her purse. Always the gentleman, walking her up to the house instead of leaving her behind while he ran to the door, no matter how eager he was.

"I'm coming. Just give me a second."

Zachary nodded politely. They walked up to the house together. Zachary rang the bell, then, after a moment's hesitation, opened the door and let himself in. Lorne didn't greet them at the door as usual, so Zachary looked around the corner into the living room for him.

Lorne was sitting in his usual chair, but his foot resting on the footrest in front of him was encased in a cast.

"What's this? What happened?" Zachary asked, leaning over to give him a hug of greeting. His brows drew down and there was a deep crease between them.

"It's nothing. I'm fine. Just a little mishap," Lorne assured him.

"Nothing? They don't put casts on nothing. What did you break?"

"I broke a couple of metatarsals. They said a few weeks in a cast and it will heal up fine. Tell him, Kenzie."

Kenzie wasn't a podiatrist or orthopedist, but she had her MD. She nodded her agreement. "If it's just a hairline or a clean break, it will heal in no time. What did you do to it?"

"I just dropped something on it. It wasn't anything."

"I told you those Polish sausages would kill you," Pat called from the kitchen. "Now you've been warned!"

"Sausages?" Zachary repeated, a smile replacing his worried frown.

"A package of frozen sausages, yes," Lorne admitted, shaking his head ruefully. "They jumped out of the freezer at me, and I didn't get out of the way fast enough."

"I hope we're eating them tonight."

Lorne looked surprised. "Do you like Polish sausages?" They were always looking for special foods that would tempt Zachary to eat more despite his poor appetite. If one of Zachary's favorite foods was sausages, Kenzie was sure that Pat and Lorne would both know it already.

"I don't know." Zachary shrugged. "But it seems a fitting punishment for them breaking your foot."

Lorne laughed. Pat poked his head in through the doorway to the kitchen. "I think so too! In fact, they are on the menu tonight. I'm making a stew."

"Whatever it is, it sure smells good," Kenzie told him. The hearty, spicy aroma filled the house, so thick she could practically taste it. "I can't wait."

"Good. I've just got a few more veggies to chop, and then I can let it simmer and join you for a visit."

Zachary and Kenzie sat down. Zachary looked at Lorne's cast and shook his head again. "Why didn't you tell me you broke it? When did this happen?"

"Just like you tell me any time you run into trouble?" Lorne teased. "It was just last night. After you and I talked. Or I would have mentioned it when you called."

"Hmm. Maybe." Zachary wasn't convinced.

"I would have, because I knew you were coming and would give me a hard time if I didn't tell you ahead of time."

Lorne leaned back in his chair. His face was round and cheerful. If the broken bone were bothering him at all, he didn't give any sign of it. His fringe of hair was gradually turning white, but he still moved like a young man. Other than when he was trying to avoid ferocious Polish sausages, apparently.

"I left some pictures in my office. You want to go get them?" Lorne suggested.

Zachary nodded. He retrieved Lorne's latest photographic creations and the two of them put their heads together, discussing perspectives and composition and the various settings on the camera. One thing that Lorne had shared with Zachary was his love of photography. He had given Zachary his first camera when he was living with the Petersons and they had developed pictures together in Lorne's darkroom over the years. Even at the height of digital photography, the two of them still used analog cameras and developed their own pictures when they could. Zachary used digital cameras for his work, but analog for his art.

Pat joined them in a few minutes. He rolled his eyes at Kenzie as he sat down. "Just nod and pretend you understand."

Kenzie laughed. "Yep."

"So, how have things been with you?"

Kenzie settled into the conversation, sharing what she could with Pat. That was mostly personal stuff because, unlike Zachary, Pat and Lorne were not interested in the nitty-gritty of forensic pathology. So Kenzie said only that things were going well at work and left it at that.

8

They went home feeling full and contented. Zachary was more relaxed than usual, all talked out, his eyes fixed on the highway as it spooled out before them. Kenzie listened to the music on the radio and left him to his thoughts. She valued any time he wasn't visibly depressed or anxious. One reason she liked going to visit Lorne and Pat—besides their company and good food—was that Zachary was usually relaxed and happy after a visit.

Once home, they vegged in front of the TV, but both knew Kenzie needed to get to sleep to be up for her work without being cranky or tired on the job, so they headed to bed.

"It was a nice weekend," Kenzie said as they cuddled.

"It was," Zachary agreed. "Good to take time off and just do some things together. Dr. Boyle was right."

"I'm sure she'll be glad to hear it." Kenzie rubbed Zachary's back, feeling for the tension he carried in his shoulders and neck, gently prodding and massaging, trying to get him nice and relaxed so he would sleep.

"You had a good time too?" he asked in a worried tone.

"Yeah. I did. It was great."

He didn't say anything in response. Kenzie kneaded his shoulders, making him flinch when she hit a tender spot.

"What is it?" Kenzie asked.

"Nothing. I just worry about you going back to work. That it's stressful."

"Well... sometimes it's stressful, yes. But I don't really mind. I knew when I went into medicine that it was going to be a high-stress job. But at least where I am, I'm not working in the emergency room or in a kids' cancer ward. I can't really harm my patients."

"I'm sure they're dying to see you again."

Kenzie groaned. She could feel Zachary laughing.

"You don't need to worry, though. I enjoy my job. And Dr. Wiltshire is good about letting me get my hands into things so that I can move up the ladder and someday maybe have a morgue of my own."

"Just what every little girl dreams of."

Kenzie chuckled and molded her body against Zachary's back, holding him firmly. "I'll admit it isn't how I saw my life path when I was a little girl. I guess I thought I'd grow up to be like my mother. A socialite, staying at home with a couple of kids, going to all the important fundraisers and events. But that never particularly excited me."

Zachary nodded. "Doesn't sound like you."

"No. She and I are... well, we're pretty different. I'm not saying that she's not doing something important. She is involved in a lot of very worthy causes. But it's not what I want to do. I like the challenge of medicine. I was one of the few girls who was excited about dissecting frogs in school. To actually see all an animal's insides. In person, not just a diagram in a textbook. To me, that was really interesting."

Zachary didn't respond with what his own experiences in life sciences at school had been like. No anecdotes about dissecting frogs and putting the kidneys down the shirt of the cute girl at the next lab bench. Nothing about being too sensitive to participate, or whether he had even been given the opportunity. Much of his time as a teen had been spent in institutional care, and Kenzie supposed they didn't like to put scalpels in the hands of kids with poor impulse control and behavioral problems.

"Everybody likes different things," Kenzie said drowsily, feeling herself starting to slip toward sleep. "The Medical Examiner's Office really is where I want to be."

Zachary said something in response, but Kenzie didn't catch what it was and couldn't remember in the morning.

Despite her assertions of the night before, Kenzie did feel a little stressed as she got ready for work Monday morning. Not because she didn't like it, just because she knew how busy Mondays could be, catching up with emails and requests that had come in over the weekend, knowing there was likely a backlog of bodies that would take the rest of the week to catch up on. There wasn't enough action to justify hiring more workers, which meant that sometimes they were overwhelmed when there was a spate of deaths.

But bodies kept, more or less, and they always caught up again eventually. Dr. Wiltshire was a good boss and Kenzie didn't dread going into work. It was just a Monday thing.

When she made it out to the kitchen for breakfast, Zachary already had everything prepared. The coffee was hot. Her toast had been buttered and was awaiting marmalade. The jar was just in front of Kenzie's plate. And there were a couple of articles that Zachary had printed off from his computer and left on the table for her, their John Doe's face prominent.

"I thought you might like to see those so you're up to speed by the time you get in," Zachary said. "And you were going to take a closer look at the body and his clothes to see if you think he really is homeless."

"I haven't forgotten." Kenzie sat down and began slathering marmalade on her toast. She skimmed through the articles, which were pretty generic, with just a few tidbits of information the reporters had managed to get ahold of. Tidbits that Kenzie already knew. She looked at John Doe's picture in the article. It was small, so she couldn't see all the details that Zachary had been looking at the day before, but she could see where he was coming from. Doe's hair did appear to have been shaped by a professional. His teeth didn't show in the picture, but he didn't have the shrunken cheeks that many of the homeless did, not just because they didn't eat enough, but because their teeth had rotted away due to poor oral hygiene or drug addiction. Doe's skin was relatively smooth and his pores small, even though he did have a five o'clock shadow.

But his whiskers were not long. It might have been just that, five o'clock shadow because it had been late in the day when he had died. Not because he had been on the streets and had failed to shave for several days or weeks.

"I'll look into it when I have a chance," Kenzie promised. She took a few more bites of her toast. "You look like you're having a pretty good morning. Sleep well?"

"Yeah, pretty good."

"Good. How's the calendar look this week?" Kenzie laid her phone down on the table and brought up her calendar app to look at their schedules for the week. Zachary had given her access to his electronic calendar so that she could look at both at the same time and they could adjust if there were any conflicts, which there rarely were. "Couples therapy Wednesday."

Zachary nodded. "And ice cream."

That had been Kenzie's suggestion. A reward for both of them for doing something difficult, especially when they couldn't always see progress from one appointment to the next. Like any kind of therapy or personal development, there were leaps forward and falls back. The falls could be discouraging.

"And ice cream, of course," Kenzie agreed with enthusiasm. Zachary gave a little smile and nod.

9

Kenzie did her preliminary walk-through of the office, ensuring that everything was in order for Dr. Wiltshire's arrival. She didn't have a chance to get through the email, but she hadn't seen any top priority flags, so what was there would wait until she had an opportunity to go through it. Several bodies had been checked in during the weekend. Apparently, people didn't stop dying just because Kenzie took a couple of days off. Dr. Wiltshire had performed one post on Sunday, but the rest had been left. Kenzie familiarized herself with the check-in sheets, and then returned to her public-facing workstation to process any requests for records or lab reports.

Dr. Wiltshire arrived with his Starbucks coffee as usual. He also had a wrapped muffin, which he placed on Kenzie's desk. She'd never asked him to buy her any baking on his Starbucks run. But every so often, he brought something anyway. Kenzie had noticed a pattern after a while. The days that he brought her treats were generally the days he anticipated to be busy or stressful. She didn't know if he even realized himself that was what he was doing. He brought her a treat to show her appreciation for her being there and being a diligent employee. Still, apparently the times his mind turned most to his appreciation were those days when he knew he would be putting her through the wringer.

So Kenzie was forewarned by the chocolate chocolate chip muffin. She smiled and greeted Dr. Wiltshire just like any other day.

"Good morning, doctor. How was your weekend?"

"Not bad, Kenzie. Nothing too urgent over the weekend, so I got a bit of a break. Played some golf yesterday."

"I didn't know you're a golfer."

"I'm really not," he confided. "But it was a nice day and I sensed that my wife wanted me out of the house. So... golf."

Kenzie smiled and nodded. Dr. Wiltshire rarely talked about his wife. She wasn't actually sure whether there was a Mrs. Wiltshire, or whether the doctor just invented her for his stories. There was no picture of a wife or children on his desk or anywhere in his office.

"I'm glad you had a good rest. We've got a few new bodies to be scheduled."

"Let's sit down in my office. I think this is going to take a little longer than usual today."

And it had. Kenzie intended to just give him a straight briefing on each of the remains that had been checked in, but he also wanted to know what doctors or police officers were on each of the cases and to evaluate what urgency would be assigned to each of their new guests. Kenzie made suggestions on each of the cases and they set up a schedule. Kenzie stacked the intake sheets in order and promised to add the lineup to Dr. Wiltshire's calendar so that he could stay on top of it.

"And if anyone calls to find out where their case is in the pile, you can speak to them with authority," he advised Kenzie. "No need to guess or pass it back to me. Let them know how many cases there are ahead of them and promise we'll get to it as soon as we are able."

"Sure," Kenzie agreed. Of course, everyone would want their case to be first on the list, but that wasn't the way it worked. Potential homicides needed to lead the pack. And the cases where there were religious practices to be adhered to if possible. They would make an effort to process any cases that had to be interred within a certain length of time when they needed to be.

On returning to her desk, Kenzie found a couple of law enforcement offi-cers waiting for her. She gave them the appropriate request forms to be filled out and started going methodically through her email inbox. Of course, there were a lot of requests to be processed and reports to be printed, reviewed, and filed. She had glanced at the email subjects on her phone a couple of times over the weekend to make sure she was not missing anything important, so she knew she could just start at the top and work her way down through the various emails.

She nodded when the law enforcement officers left their requests in her inbox, promising that she would get to them as soon as she could. Her laser printer was humming away, spitting out a constant stream of reports as she added them to the queue.

Kenzie opened one of the imaging files and was startled by what she saw. She looked up at the name of the patient again, just to make sure she had gotten it right, then sent it to the printer. She would have to wait for everything ahead of it to finish printing first, but Dr. Wiltshire would want to see it as soon as possible.

10

K enzie knocked on the door as she entered the surgical suite. Dr. Wiltshire looked up from his work, surprised to see her there.

"Kenzie. What's up?"

Kenzie took a moment to finish suiting up so that she wouldn't contaminate any evidence and took her printouts over to Dr. Wiltshire. "Sorry, I thought you would want to see this right away."

Wiltshire looked curious as he waited for Kenzie to tell him what she had.

"These are the brain slides for Willis Cartwright."

He looked at her for a moment, thinking back. "From the nursing home."

Kenzie nodded. "Right."

"There was no bleed at the site of the blow to the head. Everything appeared to be normal. A little shrinkage attributable to old age, but gross examination seemed to be unremarkable."

Kenzie stood beside him and showed him the image from the first slide.

Wiltshire's brows shot up. Kenzie saw his eyes do the same thing as she had initially done. Double-check the name of the patient at the top of the page.

"But Mr. Cartwright hadn't shown any overt symptoms."

"No."

"Well... those are clearly amyloid plaques and tau tangles."

Kenzie nodded her agreement and flipped to the next page. She held a couple of images side by side for Dr. Wiltshire. He chewed his lip and nodded.

"Well, there have been cases of amyloid plaques being found in the brains of people who showed no symptoms of Alzheimer's Disease before death."

"I've heard of that. And I guess... that's what we've got here. But does that mean that he did or did not have Alzheimer's Disease?"

"We'll need to discuss it in more detail with his doctor and the nursing staff. He may have shown mild symptoms. But if he didn't have any..." He shook his head as he mused over the problem. "I'm reluctant to say that a patient had Alzheimer's Disease if he showed no signs of dementia."

"Even with the size and number of these plaques and tangles?"

"If you brought me this brain with no other information, I would say that it is a patient who had advanced Alzheimer's Disease. But we have to realize that what we know about the human body is really just a freckle on the backside of science. We don't know more than we do know."

"So then... it's just an anomaly?"

"If you add up all of the anomalies in Alzheimer's Disease—or any disease—eventually you will have a new pattern. We may be able to use cases like this to find a way to protect people against the ravages of the disease. We may find something in this man's biology that could be used as a vaccine in the future. He appears to be resistant, in some way, to the progression of the disease. *If* we have the correct information from the nursing home and his family. And *if* this isn't a case of a sample being mislabeled or saved to the wrong file. We need to explore all of the possibilities before declaring this to be a case of a man being immune to the effects of amyloid plaques spreading throughout his brain."

Kenzie had her work cut out for her. She retrieved the slides from the Cartwright case and checked the label on the box in her own writing, as well as the individual bar codes on the slides. She put the slides under a microscope to view them directly. After adjusting the focus, she saw the same results as shown on the processed images.

That was pretty clear.

Just to be sure, Kenzie retrieved Cartwright's remains. She made another examination of the brain, which did not show the deterioration she would expect in a case of advanced Alzheimer's disease. She prepared additional slides of the brain tissue and took them directly to the microscope. There could be no doubt that Cartwright's brain was full of the amyloid plaques and tau tangles normally associated with Alzheimer's disease.

K enzie didn't usually do any fieldwork, so it was exciting to go to Champlain House to follow up on the Willis Cartwright case. She pictured herself as a private investigator like Zachary, going out to interview subjects and ferret out the truth. She was experienced in the lab work and in understanding and interpreting test results. Actually going out and talking to people about a case was something that she hadn't done in... well, since Amanda had died. She had succeeded in digging up the truth in that case, or as much of it as she could, but there had been serious and long-lasting consequences that she preferred not to think about.

She told herself that wasn't her fault. But it was going to take a lot of convincing, because she didn't believe it, even after all the intervening years.

She pushed thoughts of that long-past case aside and pulled into the parking lot of Champlain House. She managed to find a parking space marked for visitors and pulled in. If there weren't any free visitor slots, she would have taken one of the reserved places. She was, after all, there on official Medical Examiner business. But it was probably better not to get people's backs up the instant she arrived.

There was still a chill in the air as she got out of the car. She had hoped that it would warm up more during the day, but she suspected it wasn't going to get much warmer. It was early afternoon, the sun already on its descent. She loved fall in Vermont, with all its gorgeous riot of colors, but she was sorry to see the summer go.

The reception area of Champlain House was quiet and comfortable. Dark wood, well-upholstered furniture that didn't look like it got a lot of use, the ringer on the phone at the reception desk set to a low murmur so that it didn't echo all the way through the room. The older woman at the desk, maybe a nurse but maybe just an administrative clerk, gave her a warm smile as she approached.

"Good afternoon. How can I help you today?" Her eyes went quickly over Kenzie, evaluating her. She knew that Kenzie was not a regular visitor for one of the residents.

"My name is Kenzie Kirsch. I'm from the Medical Examiner's Office."

"Oh. And what can we do for you?"

"I would like to talk to anyone regularly involved in the care of Willis Cartwright."

"I see..." The woman, the name Delores imprinted on her name badge, didn't make a move toward the phone or computer keyboard. "Can I ask if there's something wrong?"

"I'm just following up on a death."

"I don't remember ever having a personal visit from the Medical Examiner's Office before."

Kenzie didn't want to say that it was out of the ordinary, which might make people defensive. But she wasn't about to say that it was commonly done either, which Delores would know was a lie if she had worked there for very long. There were deaths at Champlain House regularly, like there would be at any other nursing home, and they would know that most did not require an in-person visit from the ME.

"There were a few things in this case that we wanted to be sure of," she said vaguely. "So if I could talk to nurses, doctor, housekeeping...?"

"You don't have an appointment..."

"No. And I think Mr. Cartwright's family would probably like to hold his funeral sooner rather than later. Shall I tell them that you're holding up the ME's report?"

Delores didn't like that idea. She wrinkled her nose. "I don't know who you'll want to talk to. He was in our independent living center, so he didn't have dedicated nurses assigned to him. There was staff around if he needed assistance, but he was pretty self-sufficient."

Kenzie hadn't anticipated that Delores would know any details. She leaned forward on the counter, giving Delores a grateful smile. "That was what the report we received said. You knew Mr. Cartwright well?"

"I don't know about well, but... yes. Certainly. He was around and I knew him by name to say hello or have a conversation. He wasn't one of the troublemakers, you know, just a very pleasant old gentleman."

"And had he been having any trouble recently? The report we received said that they had started running some tests, because his behavior had changed."

"Changed? No, I don't know if I would say that," Delores shook her head. "He was having some trouble... but everybody does now and then. He might have had a bit of a bug. We were all very surprised to hear that he had passed away. He didn't seem sick."

Kenzie nodded. "What kinds of things was he having trouble with?"

"I don't know." Delores looked to each side as if she were afraid someone might overhear her gossiping. But there was no one else around. The lobby area was quiet and empty. "I'm not a nurse. Don't have the stomach for it. He'd... had some dizzy spells. Seemed disoriented. He forgot names or would start to say something and then forget where he was going with it." She shrugged. "We all do those things sometimes. It doesn't mean anything."

"But it was enough that his doctor had ordered some tests to be run."

Delores looked reluctant, but nodded. "Maybe he saw something that I didn't. He would have been privy to Mr. Cartwright's private medical information. I only saw him casually, and I didn't see much change from one day to the next."

"So I should talk to his doctor for sure. And that would be doctor...?"

"Dr. Able." Delores sighed, like she had been trying to protect him, but the cat was out of the bag now. "I suppose so."

"Is he in today or will I need to set up an appointment with him?"

Delores looked at the watch on her wrist with a pretty silver-chain strap. "He will be doing rounds this afternoon. I can't promise you that he'll have any time to talk to you, but he is around."

"Great. And if I could talk to any of the nursing and housekeeping staff that has contact with him."

"People need to do the work that they're here for. They don't really have the time to be dealing with inquiries." Delores shrugged as if Kenzie were being unreasonable.

"If I need longer than a few minutes, then I'll set up an appointment for them to come into my office. But I'm sure they'd rather talk to me here than to have to set something up separately. And, of course, the Cartwright family wants to be able to proceed with their arrangements in a reasonable time period. We don't want to keep putting this off. Eventually, they will get upset and start making waves. Maybe even go to the media about how Champlain House is holding things up and wondering if you're trying to hide something."

"We are not trying to hide anything!" Delores's face grew red. "We're a very good nursing home; we do a lot of good for the community. I won't have you throwing around aspersions."

"I didn't say I was going to cause you any problems. I said that eventually, the family is going to get upset that the investigation hasn't been completed and the remains are being held up. I don't think either of us wants to be in that situation."

D elores gave Kenzie a long, hard glare before finally breaking down. Of course, she didn't want the facility to garner any negative media attention just because she was being a diligent gatekeeper.

"I will let Dr. Able know that you are here. But don't be surprised if he reports back to the ME's office about how... overzealous you are being here."

Kenzie nodded and took a couple of steps back to allow Delores a semblance of privacy while she called the doctor. Delores's job was to help the family and friends who came to see their patients and keep any media or unwanted attention out. They didn't want people poking around and implying that they were not providing the best care possible. Anyone in the industry had to be aware of other facilities that had been exposed for substandard care. It was enough to scare even the best facilities. Walk in and find one patient complaining about falling down on the way to the bathroom, or the bad food, or saying that the staff was stealing from them, and it could be blown up into a three-ring circus.

But they were still answerable to their regulators and law enforcement. They couldn't just brush off an inquiry from the Medical Examiner.

"Dr. Able is just finishing up his rounds now," Delores said. "He will be fifteen or twenty minutes, and then he will see you in his office."

"Thank you," Kenzie acknowledged. Rather than asking whether she could talk to the other staff in the meantime, she chose one of the comfortable-looking pieces of furniture and sat down to wait, pulling out her phone to check her email. Things would go much better if the doctor were satisfied with Kenzie's professionalism and reasons for showing up at Champlain House. He could smooth the way for her to talk to the rest of the staff. Or he could make a big stink with the ME's office and try to get her pushed out.

There were a few emails in her work inbox that she could handle with a brief reply or file into one of her action folders. But most of it was stuff that she had to print out or would take a longer time to handle. Kenzie switched over to her personal email instead. There were a few emails from friends, mostly girlfriends that she liked to go out to eat with. There were a few emails from online acquaintances or men she had previously gone out with or who had tracked her down through one of her dating app profiles. She just deleted them. She had closed her profiles since getting more serious with Zachary, but that didn't stop people from tracking her down.

Zachary had sent her an email with a query about a couple of prescription medications and what they might be for. He could search them on the internet just as easily, but he liked to refer medical questions to her since it was an interest they shared. Kenzie would have more insight on why someone would be taking a certain combination of drugs. The internet might tell him the possibilities for each individual one, but two or three together gave a better picture of what condition the subject might be dealing with. Kenzie glanced over the names. He had inverted a couple of letters, but it was still obvious what he had intended. She clicked reply and thumbed out a quick answer.

Viagra and blood pressure. Is this a cheating spouse?

It was email rather than an instant messenger, so she wasn't expecting an immediate reply, but either he was already in his email or he had an alert set up for her reply.

Looks like it, unless he's selling them on the street.

Kenzie thought it unlikely that they had a very high street value. It looked like someone was taking his extra-curricular activities somewhere else.

"Miss Kirsch?"

Kenzie looked up at the man standing a few feet away from her. She hadn't even heard his approach. She glanced down at his shoes. Rather than the black dress shoes that she often saw doctors in, he was wearing white sneakers, like the nurses wore for long days on their feet.

"Yes." Kenzie stood and reached out her hand to him. "Are you Dr. Able?"

If he weren't, it was better to mistake a nurse for a doctor than vice versa.

"At your service." He smiled, "Ready, willing, and Able."

Kenzie laughed. She wondered how many times he had used that line. The nurses probably all rolled their eyes when they heard it. "It's very nice to meet you. Thank you for agreeing to see me; I know it isn't easy to make time for unexpected visitors."

"No, but if they were all as pretty as you, I would make the time." He smiled charmingly.

He'd hit a home run in the looks department. Several inches taller than Kenzie or Zachary, dark wavy hair, piercing blue eyes, and a ruggedly hand-some face and strong jaw. He was undoubtedly used to women falling victim to his charms. Looks *and* money and prestige.

"And it's Dr. Kirsch," Kenzie said. "With the Medical Examiner's Office."

His smile wavered. He released her hand and gave a more professional nod. "Of course. I'm sorry."

"I'd like to ask you a few questions about Willis Cartwright, if I could. You were his regular physician?"

"Willie was in pretty good shape." Able gestured in the direction they were to go and escorted Kenzie into one of the long, brightly-lit corridors. "He didn't need a lot of my attention."

"But you must have still seen him fairly regularly. Was he on any medications?"

"Just blood pressure," Able said proudly, as if it were due to his own excellent care of Cartwright. "Maybe the occasional painkiller for his joints or something to help the digestion along, but those are pretty common in old age. Not much anyone can do about that."

"Wow. Good for him. He must have really taken care of himself."

"Ex-army, from what I understand. That type likes to stay in shape. Very well-disciplined. Got his exercise, watched what he ate."

Kenzie nodded. "Yeah. I've seen a few. But then in the last few days before his death...?"

They entered Dr. Able's office. He sat down behind his large, dark desk and Kenzie sat in one of the visitor chairs, sitting forward on the edge of it so that she was closer to him.

"Yes. I thought he might be fighting a virus. Certainly not anything dangerous. I was as surprised as anyone when we found him down in his room."

"He'd had a fall?"

"Yes. I feel bad that it happened. We are very careful with our patients' health. If he'd been someone who regularly had falls or was out of his bed in the night, we would have had either a bed alarm or a fall alarm or both. But as it was, they did not know that he'd gotten out of bed and fallen in the night. We're very sorry that happened. But as we told his family, we could not have foreseen that would happen. He wasn't a habitual wanderer."

"He had experienced a couple of falls, though, hadn't he?"

Able considered for a moment before nodding. "Yes, minor. He wasn't hurt."

"And he had several bruises on his shins or knees that would suggest he'd been walking into things."

He shook his head. "I wasn't aware of that. Elderly people often bruise very easily. They might have been caused by very minor bumps. Hitting a knee when he sat down at the table, for example. Not even enough that he would remember it later. He didn't have any complaints about walking into things, bruises, or hurting himself."

"And the staff didn't know anything about them?"

"Not that I am aware."

"Speaking of what he could remember..."

Able looked at her steadily. Kenzie looked for any sign that he was keeping secrets. She couldn't see anything that would suggest deception. "Yes?"

"Mr. Cartwright had been displaying some memory problems? Dementia?"

"No, I certainly wouldn't go that far. He'd had a couple of episodes just in the week before he died when he had experienced some disorientation or confusion. But it wasn't that notable. I wouldn't classify it as dementia."

"But you were looking into it."

"Certainly. Even if we thought it was only being tired or a simple mistake, we were still following up to make sure that it wasn't the development of something more serious. I had set up some blood tests, brain imaging, cardiac just in case. So many systems can affect the brain... I thought it was simply being short on sleep or fighting a UTI, but was following up just to be sure."

Kenzie nodded. She made a few notes on her phone just to make sure she wouldn't forget anything when she returned to the office to write up a report on her findings at Champlain House.

"And nothing showed up in those tests?"

"No."

"And up until his last few days, no problems at all. You felt he was in good shape."

"I figured he would live to be a hundred, honestly. Or older. He wasn't even ready for managed care yet. He was here for the convenience of having professionals around, someone else making his meals, having a community of people of his age to do things with. It wasn't because he could no longer manage on his own. I'm sure he could have. Up until... the end."

"I'm sure you're wondering why I'm here."

He gazed at her. "It did occur to me."

"Mr. Cartwright's brain showed signs of advanced Alzheimer's Disease."

D r. Able's brows shot up. He leaned forward over his desk, staring at Kenzie. "What?"

Kenzie had brought several of the images with her. She assumed that working with seniors, Dr. Able would have at least a working knowledge of Alzheimer's Disease and its markers. She took a couple of pictures out of her slim briefcase and slid them across the desk to him.

He looked them over, frowning, and shook his head. "I think the samples must have gotten mixed up at your lab."

"That was our first thought too. But I prepared slides and examined them myself today. There is no doubt that the man in our morgue under the name of Willis Cartwright had extensive AD markers in his brain tissue."

"But that just can't be. That much damage... it takes years to develop and he would have shown signs."

"There are cases of Rapidly Developing Alzheimer's Disease."

"Rapidly Developing, yes. But overnight? No. This man," Able pointed at the images. "He wouldn't be able to function in our independent living center. I know the effects of Alzheimer's Disease, Dr. Kirsch, and I can assure you that Willie did not have it."

"You don't think that the symptoms you saw the last few days might have been signs of Alzheimer's Disease?"

"And he just got it last week?" Able's voice dripped with sarcasm. "He started showing symptoms last week and then was dead? Rapidly Developing AD takes weeks to months, not days, to kill."

Kenzie nodded slowly. The symptoms, then, were probably just what Able had initially thought. Cartwright fighting a virus. Something that might have been completely innocuous to someone else but had caused damage to his brain or heart that had resulted in his death. Nothing to do with the amyloid plaques.

"Let's say it's not AD," Kenzie said, following this train of thought. "Let's say it's something different. When did he start showing changes in behavior?"

"As I said, it was only a few days before he died. He had a couple of falls. Nothing serious. He would get dizzy or disoriented. Forgot people's names or the conversation you had just had with him. But that's all. It could have been vertigo from an ear infection."

"Yes. Except that we didn't find any sign of infection in his body. In fact, he was in pretty good shape, considering his age."

"And the fact that he was dead."

"And the fact that he was dead," Kenzie acknowledged. "He seemed to be strong and healthy. Other than the bruises, the blow to his head, and the brain pathology." She considered, trying to think of whether there was anything else she should ask Able about. "Oh. Can you tell me if he was continent?"

"Yes. Certainly. No issues there."

"And he didn't have much appetite the final few days."

Able shrugged. "Like a man with a virus. We weren't particularly worried about it. Like you said, he was apparently in good health and we figured he would rally and be feeling better again in no time."

"Yes, that's understandable. You had no way of knowing that there was anything wrong. We still aren't sure what it was that killed him."

"Not the fall? The blow to his head? That's what I was worried about."

"No. There was no hematoma. No clot. No concussion. Just a laceration."

"Well, thank you for that. I appreciate knowing that it wasn't the fall that killed him. Or the fact that it wasn't discovered until the morning."

"I wonder if I could talk to any of the nursing or housekeeping staff who are around today who are familiar with Mr. Cartwright? I won't take up a lot of their time, but it will be faster to deal with this and get Mr.

Cartwright's remains back to his family than if we have to go back and forth making appointments."

"I don't see how they're going to help you. I've already told you everything we know."

"I need to do a full investigation. If I can't find out anything else... that's fine. That will be the end of it."

He rolled his eyes, but nodded. "I'll take you to his unit, and you can discuss it with the staff. But please be... discreet. I don't want you upsetting the other residents. And I don't want there to be rumors that there is something strange or ominous about Willie's death. Sometimes people do die unexpectedly. Sometimes we can't find a reason or an explanation."

14

K enzie was escorted to the living unit where Mr. Cartwright had been housed. It was not locked or alarmed in any way. It was a pleasant, homey atmosphere. Clean, bright, open. They saw other residents coming and going as they pleased without any need for checkout. People took walks up and down the halls, dropped in on each other, played games, or watched TV in the common room they passed. Dr. Able took Kenzie to the nurse at the desk and introduced her, explaining in a low voice what Kenzie was there for.

"Mr. Cartwright?" Nurse Summers asked with a sad smile. "What a lovely gentleman he was. I was very sorry to see him go. It was a bit of a shock."

Kenzie nodded. "That's what I understood." She smiled and nodded at Dr. Able. "Thank you for your help."

He looked at her for a moment, then shrugged and left, heading back toward his office. Kenzie didn't want him hovering while she asked questions. She didn't need him monitoring her or feeding lines to the nurse to make sure she said the right thing.

Kenzie sighed. "I understand Mr. Cartwright went downhill pretty quickly?"

"Downhill? Who told you he went downhill? That's not what Dr. Able told you," Summers said accusingly, looking in the direction Dr. Able had gone.

"Not in so many words, no. But I understand he was forgetting things, disoriented, had lost his appetite... and then, of course, there was his sudden death. I'm pretty sure that all of that together counts as going downhill."

"You make it sound a lot worse than it was. Everybody forgets names now and then. It doesn't mean there is anything wrong. And his falling down and disorientation...? He was probably just fighting a virus. It happens. I fully expected that in a few days, he would be over it and would be right back to normal. His old self."

"So you don't think there was anything wrong."

"Not seriously, no. Now... I don't know what that means for his cause of death... but sometimes I think patients do just choose their own time."

"Do you mean suicide? Assisted death?"

"No!" Summer's voice climbed louder, and a few people stopped what they were doing and looked at her. She looked embarrassed and lowered her chin, looking down at the top of her desk at nothing in particular. She spoke more quietly, in an excessively reasonable tone. "I don't mean that he took something to cause his death or planned it out in any way. Just that sometimes, we have residents who... they know their time or they pick their time. They just decide that's when they are going to stop living... and they do."

Kenzie had heard this kind of thing before and thought it was a little suspect. She did not want to find out that they had an angel of death at the nursing home who was selectively ending its residents' lives, but that was the first thing that came to her mind. Not a supernatural reason. Someone who, with a vial of insulin or some other medication, was deliberately putting an end to the lives of those she chose.

Of course there were cases where the cause of death could not be determined, where they had to list it as 'sudden cardiac death' or 'natural causes incidental to age' or some other phrasing to satisfy the law. They couldn't always determine the exact cause of death. But that didn't mean that those people were simply choosing to die. She didn't believe that.

"I see," she told Summers, nodding wisely. It wouldn't do her any good to argue the point. She wanted to be able to continue with her investigation, not to get kicked out. "And those symptoms that Mr. Cartwright was having prior to his death, those were..."

"They were nothing, really. Just some minor changes that didn't mean anything. They happen as people get older. Knees start to wear out. Balance goes. People lose their appetites. It's all part of aging."

"Yes, I see. Do you think I could see his room?"

"It's already been cleaned out," Summers said doubtfully. "His personal effects have been turned over to his family. I don't think that there is anything in there that would help you. We've just refreshed it for the next resident. We have a waiting list, you know. We'll have someone else in there within a week."

"That's wonderful. I've always heard great things about Champlain House. It's quite the jewel for our little town."

"Yes," Summers nodded vigorously. "Nothing like the warehouses you see in the big city sometimes. I've worked places like that, and believe me, it is nothing like working at the House. We really are a close-knit family here. We care about our residents and we take exceptional care of them."

As long as that didn't involve a service to help them out the door at the end of their lives.

"I would still like to see his room and to talk to any of the staff who knew him. Just so I can wrap this up and say that I have pursued all appropriate avenues."

Nurse Summers still seemed reluctant, but she shrugged her broad shoulders. "I don't see any reason why not, if you want to waste your time."

Kenzie smiled her agreement. Summers pushed herself up out of her chair and walked around the counter to Kenzie. "It's just down here. Follow me."

She led Kenzie down the hall. Many of the doors had pictures or flowery wreaths on them, as well as the nameplates. Sometimes crayon pictures drawn by grandchildren or great-grandchildren, with scrawled expressions of love slapped onto them.

They arrived at a blank door. No decoration or personal effects. No nameplate. Nurse Summers paused for a moment, perhaps quelling the impulse to knock on the door to announce herself before going in. Maybe a gesture of respect, a second to acknowledge that the former occupant had moved on. A moment of grief. Then she turned the handle and pushed the door open smoothly. She reached for the light switch and turned it on, even though the room was still well-lit from the sunlight outside. The windows were large, giving the little room an airy feel despite how small it was.

But the room was cold and sterile. There was a bed, neatly made in white sheets and a light mint-green cotton blanket. The flooring was a low-pile carpet rather than the hard tile seen in a hospital. There was a small dresser, a TV, and a closet empty of all but a couple of folding chairs to be used when the occupant had visitors. There were, as Nurse Summers had explained, no personal items left over from Willie Cartwright's stay there.

Summers sighed and looked around, resting her hands on her hips. "This is it. Like I said... He was over there," she pointed at the carpet, halfway between the bed and the door. "Curled up on the floor with Lola. The blood on his face was dry. He was cool to the touch."

Kenzie frowned at this new revelation. "Lola?"

Summers gave a chuckle. "Not another of the residents, I assure you. Lola is a service dog. Emotional support. Makes a big difference to the residents here. Sitting and petting a dog is a very soothing, relaxing activity. Lowers blood pressure. We don't need to give out as many painkillers. She does wonders in seeking out the patients who need her the most and giving them attention."

"Oh, isn't that nice? Where is Lola now?"

"One of the staff took her over to the non-ambulatory unit." Summers looked at her watch. One of those fancy ones that counted steps. "She'll probably be back here in about fifteen minutes. I'll introduce you."

"It's nice that they can have an animal here. A lot of them probably had to give up pets before they could move in. And Lola stays here overnight?"

"Yes. She has a bed behind the desk, but more often than not, she goes and finds a patient to keep company."

Kenzie made a mental note to double-check Cartwright for any parasitic infections. Some, like toxoplasmosis, could be difficult to find if you were not looking for them. And toxo could, Kenzie knew, cause behavioral changes. Though she didn't think it could cause amyloid plaques.

"How long had Mr. Cartwright been a resident here?"

"Oh... I'm thinking it's about three years now? Not a newcomer. But not the longest, either. We have a few here who have been around for ten years or more."

"In this unit?"

"One of them. Mrs. Moses has been here for... twelve, I think."

"Wow. I guess she must like it here!"

Summers nodded and looked around. "Do you need to see anything else here?"

"What else was in the room when Mr. Cartwright died? Do you know what he hit his head on?"

"There were a few other things... a chair. There was an IV stand, because he hadn't been eating and we needed to make sure he stayed hydrated. We think that he hit his head on the corner of the dresser." Summers indicated the corner in question. "But otherwise... well, you know, he just had personal effects. Some pictures and medals on the wall. His clothing in the dresser. Maybe a book and some writing materials. He didn't have a lot of possessions. You really can't, in a room like this. It's hard for people when they come from a house crammed full of personal possessions to move into a room like this, where you have to fit everything you own into a little dresser." She looked again at the piece of furniture. "But Willie always had everything ship-shape in here. He wasn't one of those hoarders. Some residents, we have to clean their rooms out whenever they are not in there, because they'll just grab everything they can. Plastic forks. Presents from family. Books from the library. They feel like they have to have *things*. More things all the time."

"Someone said Mr. Cartwright had been in the army."

"Yes, that's right. He had medals up on the wall. And the way that he held himself, straight as a ruler, you knew he was military."

"Did he ever talk about what he had been through in the army? Had he ever been gassed? Attacked with a chemical or biological weapon?"

"No, he didn't talk about it. Not much."

"Sometimes the army experimented on the soldiers too. Giving them drugs or food or other experiences to see if it would improve their ability to fight."

"Oh, I don't think they ever did that to Willie. He never talked about anything like that. He was very loyal to the army."

15

Kenzie had to admit that there wasn't anything in the bedroom that would help her. She and Summers exited, and Summers pulled the door shut behind her. Kenzie thought she detected a slight relaxing of her shoulders, a sigh of relief. She didn't like being in that room, empty and bare of all decoration.

Kenzie nodded to a woman in a smock who was putting used linens and towels into a large wheeled bin. "Did she know Cartwright?"

Summers fumbled, not sure what to say. "I—I suppose so," she admitted. "But the housekeeping staff doesn't really have anything to do with the residents. They generally clean when the residents are out of the room, at meals, or participating in activities. They don't visit with them."

"I'd like to talk to her anyway."

Summers shrugged, looking baffled at the request. "Of course. If you think it will help."

Kenzie walked over to the little Hispanic woman and introduced herself. The woman's eyes immediately got big and round. "I am legal," she protested. "I have papers."

Her name tag said Maria.

"I'm not looking for papers, Maria. I just wanted to ask you about one of the men who lived here. One of the men who died."

"I just take care of the rooms. No medicine. I don't treat anyone."

"I understand." Kenzie nodded.

The woman still shook her head in protest. "I not have anything to do with Mr. Cartwright."

"Did you clean his room?"

"Yes."

"When he was alive? You worked here and cleaned his room sometimes?"

"Yes."

"That's all I want to talk to you about. I don't think that you did anything wrong. I just wanted to ask a few questions about his room. About whether you noticed anything strange the last week or two."

"Strange. How?" The woman cocked her head, mystified.

"I wonder if anything had changed. If you saw him do or say anything that was different than before. Or if he had anything in his room that he didn't before. Or if there was anything... anything at all that was different than last week."

"His bedsheets?"

"Yes... was there anything different about his bedsheets?"

"Well, he not wet the bed before. But at the end, he sick, then yes."

"He wet the bed the last week? And he never had before?"

She nodded her agreement.

"One time? More than one time?"

Maria thought about this, then held up three fingers. "Three times."

"Three times. And he never had before." Kenzie thought about the rash Dr. Wiltshire had noticed. "What about... was it ever dirty?" Kenzie wrinkled her nose to convey her meaning to Maria while trying to think of the Spanish word for feces.

Maria started to shake her head. Then she put her hand to her mouth. "Not the bed. But when I pick up his laundry, his pants... he had tried to wash them. In the sink, maybe. They were wet, and he did not get it all out."

"And he didn't wear diapers. Did anyone else know about this?"

Maria shook her head.

"You didn't tell anyone?"

"I thought... it is only once. He is an old man. Wait and see if it happens again."

Kenzie nodded. Two more symptoms to add to the last week of Cartwright's life. Both urinary and bowel incontinence. Symptoms of Alzheimer's Disease, or something else?

16

K enzie figured she had about worn out her welcome at Champlain House, having talked to everybody that she could. Others were not on shift, of course, but Kenzie figured the chances that they would have anything more to say than Kenzie had already heard was pretty low. She was getting pretty much the same information from everyone. Surprise that Mr. Cartwright had passed away, only minor concerns in the week before he died, certainly nothing that could have contributed to his death, other than the dizziness. Most thought that the cause of death had been the blow to his head. And Kenzie would have thought the same, except she had seen the state of Cartwright's brain. No bleeding in the brain due to the fall. Instead, tissue clogged with plaques and tau tangles. A very different picture from what they had expected.

She was just going up to the nursing station to thank Nurse Summers for her cooperation and that of the staff when Lola got back.

Kenzie had completely forgotten about the dog. She looked up to see a nurse with a shaggy mane of blond hair coming down the hall with a large, mostly brown German shepherd. Kenzie's mind went blank for a moment, thinking that the dog must belong to one of the patients, and then she remembered what she had already been told about Lola.

Lola had been curled up with Cartwright the night he died. She had apparently discovered him on the floor after his fall and had kept him company until after he had passed. Maybe they should have gotten a collie rather than a German shepherd. On TV, Lassie always went to get help and bring them back to anyone who was injured. If the dog had attracted attention instead of just curling up to go to sleep with the fallen man, would it have made any difference?

Kenzie smiled. She couldn't help but be attracted to the big dog walking down the hall toward her, mouth open in a broad doggy smile. "This must be Lola."

The nurse didn't know who Kenzie was, but smiled in return. "Yes, this is Lola." They walked up to her.

Kenzie immediately stooped down to offer her hand to the dog. "She's friendly?"

"Oh yes. She loves meeting new people," the nurse assured her. Her name tag said Ellie.

Lola proved Ellie's point, smelling Kenzie and then thrusting her snout and head under her hand to encourage Kenzie to pet her and scratch her ears.

"Oh, you are, aren't you? What a sweet girl," Kenzie cooed to the dog. "I'll bet everybody loves having you around here."

Ellie nodded. "She's very popular. Even people who are usually afraid of dogs don't usually have a problem with her; she's so well-behaved. She doesn't jump up or bark. She's just very quiet and friendly. She'll sit with someone for hours if she thinks they need it."

"She must be very patient."

"Yes. And intuitive. Dogs can tell things, you know, that we can't sense."

"I've heard of dogs that can sense low blood sugar or when someone is going to have a seizure."

Ellie joined Kenzie in scratching Lola's ears. Her tail waved back and forth in long, sweeping arcs, and she panted her appreciation.

"Yes. It's amazing what they can do. Lola hasn't even been trained as an emotional support animal; it just comes to her naturally. She always wants to take care of people. I think we're all her puppies here." Ellie grinned.

"Have you had her for long?"

"No, not long. The other units enjoy visits from her too. Even in the dementia unit, she's very good at soothing agitated patients, getting them to settle down."

Kenzie considered that. "Does she spend a lot of time with dementia patients?"

"A lot? No. We try to take her over there a couple times a week, maybe. She enjoys it, but she belongs here."

"You wouldn't say that she is more attracted to the dementia patients? That she is eager to spend more time with them?"

"No," Ellie shook her head slowly. She looked at Kenzie, her brows drawing down. She glanced around her. "Are you visiting someone today? I don't think we have met before."

"I'm doing some interviews. My name is Kenzie Kirsch, from the Medical Examiner's Office. I am following up with some questions on Willis Cartwright."

"Oh, poor Willie. I was very sad to see him go. He was such a nice man."

"Did Lola spend a lot of time with him?"

Ellie stared into the distance as she considered the question. Then she shook her head. "A lot? No, I wouldn't say a lot. They liked each other's company, but Lola didn't spend a lot more time with him than with anyone else."

"I remember something in the reports I received about Lola being with Mr. Cartwright when he died," Kenzie lied. It hadn't made it to the official reports; it had just been mentioned by Nurse Summers. But Kenzie didn't see any problem with fudging the source of her intel.

"I don't know if she was with him when he died," Ellie hedged. "But she was in there in the morning when he was found."

"You don't think she was with him when he died?"

"Well, no, I just don't know for sure. Maybe she was, or maybe she went in afterward. None of us knows exactly when he died. But she was in there in the morning when he was found. I guess... she wanted to keep him warm. She knew something was wrong."

"Has she done that before?"

"What do you mean?"

"You've had other deaths here. That's natural with a nursing home. People are not here because they are healthy and starting out on some new venture in their lives. They come here because they are getting older or have health problems. They are approaching the end of their lives."

"Well, yes. Of course that's true."

"I'm just wondering if there's any pattern. Has she shown any particular attention to someone who was dying or had just died before this?"

Ellie pushed a hank of blond hair back from her face. "I told you she doesn't have any special training. She wouldn't know someone was sick or dying."

"I just wondered if there was a pattern. Like you said, sometimes they can sense these things."

"No." Ellie looked away. "I don't know. I can't think if she's spent any more time than usual with someone who has been sick lately. I mean... everyone around here gets sick sometimes, even if they are in good shape like Mr. Cartwright."

"Have you had many deaths in this unit lately?"

"No more than usual. It is a nursing home. Usually, they are moved out of this unit as their health declines, so they don't die here."

Kenzie thought back to the cases they'd had come through the Medical Examiner's Office recently. There hadn't been any major influx. Most of the people who died at the nursing home were under a doctor's care at the time, so their deaths did not need to be investigated. She would have to go through the files to track down the last few deaths. Just to make sure there weren't any connections.

"Well, it's been very nice to meet Lola." Kenzie bent down and scratched the dog's ears vigorously, looking into her eyes. "She is a very nice girl."

17

I t had been a long day, and Kenzie was late getting home. She dropped off her files and notes at the ME's office before finally getting on her way. The night guards were on and the sky was dark. She hadn't intended to let the job keep her so late, but there wasn't much she could do about it.

She couldn't face the idea of having to cook a meal after the rest of the day, so she stopped off at a fast food place on the way home. It would probably have been healthier to go out to the all-you-can-eat buffet, which boasted a pretty good salad bar, but she couldn't bring herself to go out and deal with people around her. She was a social person, but sometimes even she needed to get away from everybody at the end of the day.

Except for Zachary, of course. He was going to be waiting for her at the house, assuming he was back from whatever work he had been doing, and he would want to know all about her case and why it had run so late.

She started scripting it in her head, justifying why she had been so late and hadn't bothered to call him.

After all, they were both grown adults, and neither was required to account to the other for every minute.

Then why did she feel like she had to justify it?

She thought about the couples sessions they'd had with Dr. Boyle and tried to put her finger on the problem. She was making assumptions about how Zachary would handle her being late, which wasn't fair to him. He hadn't been calling her, demanding to know why she'd been silent all day or when she was going to get in. He wasn't usually the type of person who jumped all over her for a variation in her schedule. So why was she feeling so defensive?

Maybe just because she was tired and hungry and hadn't yet sorted out her thoughts about the Cartwright case.

When she got to the house, the outside light was on, but she didn't see any lights on inside. It would be very strange for Zachary to be sitting in the dark if he were home.

Kenzie entered through the garage door and put the bag of food down on the table. The aroma of fried food had been filling the car and she was famished. She took a quick look around and turned on lights, which confirmed her impression. Zachary wasn't around. She pulled out her phone and dialed him while trying to open the food bag one-handedly. Not so easy with the way it was stapled shut.

The phone rang many times and she was preparing to hang up, not wanting to talk to his voicemail. There was a click and then Zachary's voice, sounding very far away.

"Hello?"

"It's Kenzie. I just got home. I've got food."

"Oh, good. You must have been busy today."

Kenzie strained to hear him. "Where are you? Are you on surveillance?"

"Just doing a little job. I was going to swing by my apartment on the way home... you should go ahead and eat without me."

"Really? I thought we were going to always try to be home and eat dinner together."

"When we can," Zachary agreed. "But you were working late and I've got this thing. I should have said something, I guess... I didn't know you were going to pick something up."

"It's not going to keep. Everything will just get soggy."

There was no answer. Kenzie tried to picture Zachary. Where was he? In his car? He was right, of course. He had no way of knowing she would pick up food for him. If it was anyone's fault that the food would go to waste, it was hers.

"How long will you be?"

"Uh... maybe an hour. Don't wait for me. I'm really not hungry anyway."

"You need to eat. You've been losing weight lately."

"Maybe a little. I'll try to have something when I get home."

"You are coming back here?" Kenzie asked.

There was a brief pause before Zachary answered. "Yes... I was planning to. That's okay?" Even though his voice was faint, she could hear the anxiety kick up another notch.

"Yes, of course. I want you to come back here. You said you were going back to your apartment and I just wanted to make sure you were still planning to come back after."

He blew out his breath noisily. "Yeah. About an hour, I think. I'll be there."

"Okay. See you then."

Kenzie waited to see if Zachary would hang up first, and when he didn't, she ended the call. Now he was going to be worrying half the night that she hadn't actually wanted him to come home, that she'd been hoping he was staying at his own apartment. Because... she didn't know what he would imagine. Because she was bored with him or angry at him? Because she wanted to see someone else? She was sure he could come up with a dozen scenarios to feed his fears that she didn't actually want to be with him anymore.

She sat down at the table to unpack the burgers. She had lost her appetite. Zachary not being home and her worry that something was going on with him had thrown her off. Though she'd asked, he hadn't verified whether he was on surveillance or doing something else. Usually, if he were going to be away when she got home, he gave her a heads-up and told her what was going on. But this time, he hadn't. He might have called her to tell her during the day and she had been too busy to answer. And she hadn't checked her email since she'd been waiting at Champlain House for Dr. Able.

Kenzie forced herself to eat anyway, checking her social networks and her email and glancing over the day's news to see if the world was ending yet. It wasn't like she needed to worry about keeping up her weight like Zachary did, but if she were going to be in a reasonable mood when he eventually got home, she needed to eat.

It was closer to two hours before Zachary returned. Kenzie was not happy about the delay. She was tired from her day and ready to head to bed, and he wasn't even home. Maybe she should have just told him to stay at his apartment so she could spend the evening how she wanted to and get a good solid sleep without being awakened by his nightmares.

But she immediately regretted the thought. She didn't like to think of him lying in his bed alone, fighting his demons. She wanted him to feel safe and to be comforted when he awoke from a nightmare.

"It's late," she said, keeping her tone neutral. "Were you working this whole time?"

He rubbed his forehead as if trying to erase the worry lines. "Yeah. Some work and some errands. When you work for yourself, there isn't anyone else to pass stuff off to."

Although he had been using his sister Heather as a consultant for some work, teaching her how to do skip tracing and some other basic detective work.

Zachary didn't have any shopping bags or boxes to indicate that he'd picked anything up. He could have been dropping something off, or he might have left whatever it was at his own apartment, but she thought his behavior seemed a little off.

That thought led her to segue to Cartwright's behavioral changes before he had died. Not because they were anything like Zachary's behaviors or she thought that he was going to drop dead. Just because she wondered how significant the changes had been and what they had meant.

Zachary joined Kenzie on the couch and put his arm around her tentatively. He pulled her close and kissed her cheek gently.

"It sounds like you had a long day. Dr. Wiltshire kept you? Was there an accident...?"

Other days when there had been a sudden influx of bodies from a traffic accident or some other tragedy, Kenzie and Dr. Wiltshire had stayed after hours to get a chunk of the work done without disrupting their usual workflow.

"No." Kenzie snuggled into him and closed her eyes, letting her body relax. "I was actually out doing detective work."

"Really?" Zachary was immediately interested. "What were you doing? If you can talk about it."

"Interviewing subjects at a care facility to get more information about the deceased. It's an interesting case and we need more information to sort it out."

"Isn't that usually the job of the police?"

"Yes and no. It isn't because we think it was a homicide; we're just trying to get background on his behavior and health before he died. Trying to solve all of the clues to put together the puzzle."

"Can you tell me anything about the case? Why is it hard to determine what happened, if you think it was natural causes?"

"Because the guy's brain pathology doesn't match what we were told about his behavior before his death."

"He was behaving erratically, but there wasn't any indication in the brain?" Zachary asked. Then he shook his head. "No... someone's behavior can change without being able to see any difference in the brain. But the opposite..." He looked at her, eyes sparkling in that way that they only did when he had an intriguing puzzle to solve. "You saw changes in the brain that should have affected his behavior."

Kenzie nodded, impressed that he had figured that out from the little she had said. "You nailed it. I thought you were tired!"

He smiled proudly, though he immediately tried to wipe it away. Always trying to keep his emotions hidden from the world. Kenzie pulled his head down toward her to kiss him. "There's nothing wrong with showing that you're proud of yourself."

He looked away from her. "No one likes a show-off."

She kissed him again. "I do. We both like solving mysteries, so why can't you show that you're happy about figuring my riddle out so quickly?"

He shrugged, but allowed another smile to cross his face again fleetingly. "So how did it go at the care center? Were you able to find anything out?"

"Some interesting stuff came up. I'm going to need to write up a report for Dr. Wiltshire tomorrow and... to see what I really got, I guess. Think it all through and see where it leads me. I know a few more tests that I'll want to run, and we might need to do some research, because what we're seeing doesn't really make sense."

"You ruled out human error?"

"Yeah. I made new slides and looked at them myself this morning.

There's no mistaking the brain pathology. But his behavior was normal, right up until a few days before his death, and even then, he only had mild symptoms. Symptoms that could have had other explanations."

"So was it this brain disease that killed him?"

"I don't know. Anything is possible. But if he was somehow resistant to the disease until the final stages... it could be significant. It could point the way for future medical study. Maybe a treatment or vaccination."

18

"What about you?" Kenzie turned the conversation back around to Zachary. "What case were you working on so late?"

"A few different things." His answer was uninformative.

"Did you make any progress on your adulterous husband?"

His brows went up, surprised.

"You sent me a question on his prescriptions," Kenzie reminded him.

"Oh, yeah. I forgot about that. Well... I never know whether a client will be happy to have it confirmed that a lover is fooling around on the side or devastated that they were right. Or both. It's never easy news to break."

"I can imagine. But if she knows what prescriptions were in his medicine cabinet, then she probably already has a pretty good idea."

"I don't think she really has much doubt. She just wants proof that she can see with her own eyes."

Kenzie grimaced. "I don't think I would want to see for myself. What does she want? Pictures of him with another woman? In the act?"

"I don't do pictures 'in the act.' Too dangerous and inflammatory. Pictures of him with another partner, going into a hotel or out at a restaurant or somewhere romantic. But if someone actually wants intimate photographs or videos, they'll have to find someone else. I'm not giving someone ammunition for blackmail or a manslaughter defense."

Kenzie nodded, impressed with the thought that he had put into the policy. "I don't think I would want to gather that kind of evidence, personally. Talk about awkward. And how do you get it without getting caught?" She pictured Zachary peering in a bedroom window with his camera to get a picture or masquerading as a waiter bringing them champagne and sneaking off a picture of the two culprits.

"Well, a hidden camera would be the best option. Remote operated or motion-triggered. But like I say, I don't do that."

"Good. You've gotten yourself into enough dangerous situations without that one to add to the list."

"I don't intentionally get into trouble."

"I hope not," Kenzie agreed. She knew that he was too impulsive and that he tended to jump in to help other people without thinking through the possible consequences to himself. All part of his ADHD. She stretched and nestled herself into his shoulder again. "Do you want to watch something before bed? I'm beat, but I could unwind for a bit longer."

"Sure." Zachary looked at the blank TV screen for a moment before looking for the remote, which was on his side of the couch. He stretched to reach it, then handed it to Kenzie.

"What do you want to watch?"

"Anything is fine. Whatever you want."

He looked over at his computer. He probably wanted to work while they watched, but that would be a bad idea. He would get caught up in work and not pay any attention to the show or to her, and when it was time to go to bed, he would be all wound up and would not be able to settle in to sleep for even the few hours that his brain would allow.

"Time for a break," Kenzie told him. "Some 'us' time."

He nodded and dragged his gaze back to the TV screen. He tilted his head to rest it against hers while she turned on the TV and browsed through the guide for something that would be acceptable to them both, eventually settling on a classic mystery show. How weird was it that they both worked in crime, yet that was what they watched to unwind together? Not a sitcom or soap or something to escape into, but more crime-solving TV. And some of it was pretty bad, if she were to admit the truth. Not even close to the way things played out in real life. And maybe that was why they liked it.

They watched for a few minutes. Kenzie thought that Zachary seemed distracted, but he didn't say anything and she didn't want to force him to reveal his thoughts if he wasn't ready to or it was nothing to do with her.

"Did you have anything to eat?"

"Uh..." Zachary's eyes were distant.

"Zachary. Food. You need food to keep your body running and to fuel your brain."

"I know."

"But you didn't eat anything tonight?"

"I might have picked something up."

"If you can't remember it, then you probably didn't."

"Well. Maybe not."

"Your burger is still on the table. Do you want that? We can zap it in the microwave for a couple of minutes. And there are fries."

He wrinkled his nose. "No."

"Are you nauseated or just not hungry?"

"Just not hungry."

"What about ice cream?"

He tilted his head slightly, a sign that he was considering it. She could often tempt him with ice cream when nothing else would work.

"I'll make you a sundae," Kenzie offered. "No—a banana split."

"You're just doing that to make me eat fruit."

"Whatever it takes."

He chuckled.

"So is that a yes?"

He shrugged and didn't say no, so Kenzie got up. "Let me know what happens," she said, indicating the TV. Though, of course, she knew how it was going to end. The plot was not complicated.

When she returned with his bowl of ice cream a couple of minutes later, Zachary was sitting with his head tipped back and his eyes closed. He startled at her touch and looked surprised by the banana split. He took it from her without comment and just poked at it with his spoon.

"Is everything okay?" Kenzie asked.

"Yeah."

"You're acting like you have something on your mind. Do you want to talk about it?"

"No. No, it's nothing. I'm fine."

"You remember what Dr. B said about 'it's fine'?"

He looked as if it took a great effort to drag his attention from the mound of ice cream to Kenzie's face. She waited, not feeding him any lines.

If she asked a question or told him what she thought was the problem, he would just accept her suggestion and not process his own feelings.

"I'm just... thinking about this case. And about... Bridget."

Kenzie's anger flared at the mention of Zachary's ex-wife. She hated that Bridget still had a hold over Zachary. That so much of his emotional real estate was invested in her.

It was vital for Kenzie to react to this revelation without judgment, but what she really wanted to do was to tell him to *get over it*. Bridget was out of his life. She had kicked him out physically and emotionally. She was strong and independent. She had a new partner and was pregnant with his baby. Twins, in fact. Bridget had moved on in her life and it was time for Zachary to do the same.

"What about Bridget?" she asked evenly. She had asked him to tell her his true feelings, not to just brush them off as something that didn't matter. If she really cared about his feelings, then she had to accept them for what they were and let him express himself.

"I'm just... I don't know. I'm worried about her. About how she's feeling. About the babies. If everything is going to be okay."

In fact, they knew that everything was not going to be okay. Both Bridget and the babies had some serious medical issues. Which made it that much harder for Zachary to move on. Leaving Bridget behind when she was healthy and happy with her own life was one thing. But letting her go to deal with her own problems, or to get help from Gordon, her parents, or the community, was unbearable. He had been obsessed with Bridget since he'd met her, and Kenzie expecting him to be able to let go of that obsession was unreasonable. He was doing his best in both individual and couples therapy, but leaving that part of his life behind was not something that would happen overnight. Or even in a year. The wins were incremental, so small that they were sometimes almost impossible to see.

She thought about Zachary's faraway voice when he had answered the phone that night. The number of rings it had taken to get through to him. How he hadn't answered her when she had asked him where he was. Was he stalking Bridget? Sitting in his car staring at her house because there was no other way for him to be part of her life?

"You're worried about her," Kenzie repeated back, hoping he would go on and analyze his own thoughts and feelings to get himself out of the rut.

"Yeah. I know, I shouldn't be thinking about her. She's not part of my life."

"You can't stop yourself from thinking about something. But you can try to think about something else. To distract yourself from Bridget and think about the things that you have more control over. The things that make you happy."

"Yes." He looked down at his ice cream and deliberately pushed his spoon down into the mound of ice cream, bananas, chocolate sauce, and whipped cream. He took a bite. "Being here with you. The way things are going in my life. Our future."

Kenzie nodded.

Zachary took another large bite of the ice cream. He wouldn't be able to keep it up. Even at the best of times, he wouldn't finish a whole bowl. A few more bites and he would be done.

"You should have some too," Zachary held the bowl toward her. "Didn't you bring a spoon for yourself? I can't eat all of this."

"Eat what you can." Kenzie rubbed Zachary's back, trying to help him relax. "Bridget and Gordon have their own life. They have their own trials and they need to work through them on their own."

"Yeah. Just like everyone else."

Zachary stared off into space, eyes cloudy. Gone. Kenzie could fight to get his attention back and to work through what was bothering him, but she didn't have the energy and she didn't want to hear anything else about Bridget. She pretended that they were both engaged in the mystery show on TV and let it go.

19

K enzie spent as much time as she could the next day going over her notes and thoughts that she had gathered at Champlain House the previous day, trying to put it together in a way that made sense. It was frustrating to see the pieces that did not seem to fit together correctly. Were they missing something, or did they not have the medical knowledge necessary to understand Cartwright's death?

In the afternoon when she had a bit more time, she began to go through the computer database and filing system to pull out the deaths that they had dealt with from the nursing home in the past weeks. Most of the nursing home deaths were considered attended deaths and therefore did not go through the ME's office. Kenzie was surprised when she started to compile the cases that they had dealt with to see how many there actually were.

Had there been an increase in deaths at Champlain House? Or were the numbers normal and she just hadn't realized how many there were before? To know for sure, she would have to go back through the database to previous years to see if there had been a change in the number or types of cases that had come through the office.

Kenzie started a simple table, trying to filter out all the noise. There was too much information on the files and she needed to distill it down to a few key points to look for commonalities. Beginning with name and cause of death.

There were no homicides. They were all either accidents or natural causes. They were old people living in a nursing home, not gang bangers or street kids. But writing down the causes of death didn't seem to produce any patterns.

Falls, strokes, dementia, respiratory issues. They were all very common in that population. There wasn't any connecting thread. No indication that the majority of them had contracted the virus that the staff thought Mr. Cartwright might have had. No spate of Alzheimer's Disease or another type of dementia. She had hoped to be able to spot the pattern immediately.

She started adding in sex and age and pre-existing conditions. There wasn't a field in the database that would allow extensive discussion of their symptoms in the days or weeks immediately preceding their deaths, so she would have to go to the files for those.

Dr. Wiltshire walked out of his office suite to Kenzie's desk. He looked over the notes she was making. "What are you working on?"

"Previous deaths from Chaplain House. Looking for any patterns."

"Ah. Finding anything?"

Kenzie sighed and pushed it away from her. "No. Nothing obvious. That doesn't mean there isn't anything, but I haven't spotted it yet."

"What is your hypothesis?"

"I don't have one particular working theory right now. I'm kind of pursuing several different directions. First, we have the Alzheimer's Disease or the non-Alzheimer's protein deposits. Alzheimer's itself can cause death when it becomes so advanced. He did have some minor symptoms the week or so before his death. Some of which his doctor was not aware of."

"Oh? What additional information did you find?"

"They didn't know about his continence issues. They knew he'd had a few falls, but weren't aware of the bruises on his legs that indicate he'd been walking into things. I'm not sure yet what else, but he was managing to mask some of his symptoms. I think there was more dementia than was indicated in the doctor's report."

"But still not enough to account for death due to Alzheimer's Disease."

"No." Kenzie pressed her lips together and thought about the possibilities. "Then there is the possibility that someone caused his death."

"Murder?"

"Angel of death, maybe? I don't know. Just something I thought of while I was there. Patients don't usually die in the independent living unit. They usually get transferred to another unit when their health declines. The dementia unit or advanced care. It's possible that someone has decided to spare residents from having to go through that and 'save' them before their condition gets serious enough for them to be transferred."

"Possible. Method?"

"I was looking for a pattern in the previous deaths, but I don't see one. Something like insulin would be quick, but difficult to detect. Since we would have to test for it within forty-eight hours and it isn't something we normally look for. But these last few patients," Kenzie looked at her notes. "They've had a wide variety of symptoms. Nothing that I could blame on a single poison or method."

"One of the problems with nursing home killings is separating out the natural deaths from the unnatural deaths. Nurses can be pretty good at hiding their methods, and you can't tell when you start which ones are related. Very difficult to establish a pattern. That's why most of them aren't discovered until they confess or are caught in the act."

"Great. So if it is an angel of death, good luck on figuring it out. I have another possibility, it's a bit of a long shot."

"Uh-huh?"

"There is a dog in the unit. She visits other units as well. Not a trained dog, just for emotional support. Likes to sit and get petted by the residents. Maybe seeks out the ones who are sad or declining. She was with Mr. Cartwright when his body was discovered."

"With him?"

"Curled up with his body, apparently."

Dr. Wiltshire squinted off into the distance like he was looking into the sun. "They should have included that detail in their report. And you think the dog might have had something to do with his death?"

"It's possible. I'm wondering about parasites. Even toxoplasmosis. That can get into the brain and affect behavior."

"Do dogs even get toxoplasmosis?"

Kenzie had looked it up that morning, curious. She had known that people could get it from cats but didn't know about other animals. "They can. If they eat something that is infected. They don't normally pass it on to humans like cats do. But if it was the right environment, close contact with an infected animal by someone with a compromised immune system.

Maybe someone who was already fighting another infection. It is theoretically possible."

"Or if they roll in infected dirt and then a resident pets them," Dr. Wiltshire suggested. "They get the parasite on their hands and then touch mouth or nose, or the particles become airborne and are breathed in. It's a possibility. Check the slides for any sign of toxoplasmosis. We can run blood and fecal tests." He gave a nod. "Those are all viable routes... Alzheimer's Disease would explain the amyloid plaques, but the brain pathology might just be an anomaly that has nothing to do with his death."

Kenzie nodded her agreement. It was a puzzling case. It would be easy to just write it off as 'natural death' or 'unknown causes,' but they liked to have reasons. It wasn't very satisfying to say they didn't know why someone had died. It didn't provide the same closure to family members. And if they were dealing with a case of a nurse or someone else at the care center putting residents out of their misery, then shrugging off an unexplained death could lead to the deaths of others.

20

_____

Kenzie sighed and put her project aside to work on the other things that were burning on her task list. She couldn't afford to spend so much time on just one case. People didn't stop dying just because she was still trying to figure out a previous case. She didn't have to wait for Dr. Wiltshire to tell her that. She would look at the Cartwright file again when she was fresh and the additional lab tests that they had requested had come in. It would be easier to sort things out if they had a bit more data. And if she were fresh, she might just have an insight or two that would help the case along. Until then, there was plenty else to be done.

Kenzie went to her inbox and started to print the various reports she had flagged earlier in the day.

She came across Dr. Wiltshire's transcribed postmortem for the John Doe and remembered her discussion with Zachary over the weekend. She opened the report and browsed through it. At least there was no mystery about the cause of death on that case. Kenzie took it with her to give to Dr. Wiltshire, but before going to his office, stopped to have a look at the personal belongings that had been carefully labeled and put to the side for the man's next of kin, if one were ever found. Kenzie opened the paper bag to look at the items, but did not take anything out. She frowned and thought about what Zachary had said, then went to talk to Dr. Wiltshire.

Kenzie poked her head in the door. Dr. Wiltshire was sitting at his desk, one elbow on the table, with his hand over his eyes, unmoving. It was late and he should probably have packed it in a couple of hours before.

"Can I interrupt you for a minute?" Kenzie asked tentatively.

He dropped his hand from his eyes, startled. "Kenzie. Are you still here?"

"Just finishing up a couple of things."

"We should both close up and head home. Get a good sleep tonight."

"Yeah. I just wanted to ask you about the John Doe." Kenzie entered Dr. Wiltshire's office and put the transcribed report on his desk in front of him.

"Of course. Sorry you couldn't be a part of this one, but it was pretty straightforward. Not much to learn from this one."

Kenzie nodded. She'd seen the blood alcohol results. There couldn't be much doubt about what had killed the man. The only question was how he had gotten so much alcohol down his throat before succumbing. "The thing is... I'm wondering if he was actually homeless."

"Well..." Wiltshire pushed up his glasses. "He was found in an alley. He was dead drunk—quite literally. Clothes soaked. Dirty. Unshaven. All of that says homeless to me."

"His clothes... I was just looking at them. They're not exactly what you would expect from a homeless guy."

"Oh? Why? Too expensive?"

"Well, not really high-end. But... trendy."

"And you don't think that a homeless man could be wearing something trendy? They get clothing donations. Whatever people clear out of their closets. He might have just had an eye for that style. Even homeless people can have good taste—or trendy taste—in clothes."

"Yeah. But looking at them, they're not stained or worn. Dirty from lying in the alley and having alcohol spilled all over them. Maybe got jumped or was rolled after he passed out."

Wiltshire frowned and tented his fingers, thinking about it. "Possible, I suppose," he admitted.

"His teeth were in good shape."

Wiltshire nodded. "If he was homeless, it was probably a recent development. He'd had good dental care. Fillings, no missing teeth, no gum disease."

"And his beard growth... doesn't look that extensive or unkempt in the pictures."

"With the way the young people grow beards these days, who can say? It was short by some of today's standards."

"Not tangled and dirty?"

"Dirty... not like some I've seen. Not full of food remains or bugs."

Kenzie shuddered at the thought.

Wiltshire smiled. "You wouldn't believe some of the things I've found living in unkempt beards."

"Ugh. Not before dinner." Kenzie had a strong stomach, but the suggestion made her nauseated. "We might want to suggest that the police broaden their search to professionals working in the area he was found, then. Maybe canvass some of the nearby office buildings. I'm sure they've already asked around at the nearby bars, but maybe if they say they are looking for a... businessman rather than a homeless guy, they would have better luck."

"I'll pass that along."

Kenzie nodded, relieved. "Sounds good. I think I'll lock up, then. You're heading out soon too?"

"I am. And Kenzie," he stopped her as she was ducking back out the door. Kenzie paused and looked back. "That was a good catch. Good thinking."

"Actually... I can't take the credit on that one," Kenzie reminded him. "Zachary saw his picture in the news and said he didn't think the man was actually homeless. Going by his haircut."

"Your Zachary has got quite the eye."

Wiltshire hesitated, but Kenzie could tell he wanted to say something else to her. She lifted her brows, waiting.

"How is he doing? How are... the two of you?"

Kenzie's cheeks burned. They didn't talk much about their personal lives while at the office. Wiltshire had known when she and Zachary had broken up. It had been impossible for her to hide her emotions. He had seen reports on Zachary's kidnapping in the news before that. And he knew, of course, that they were now back together.

"We're good. Uh... closer than ever, actually." Wiltshire had only ever seen the two of them together once, and Kenzie had been furious with Zachary at the time, so she probably hadn't made a great impression on Wiltshire about the strength of their relationship. Kenzie pressed her hand against her warm cheeks. "As far as how he's doing... he suffers a lot from depression, and I think... he's on a downhill right now."

"I'm sorry to hear it. Does he see someone? Is he on antidepressants?"

"Yes to both. A number of medications. We have a therapy session tomorrow afternoon. That's why I need to take off early tomorrow."

"Right. I had just assumed..." He trailed off and didn't complete the thought. "Well, hopefully, his doctor will be able to get him straightened out."

"I don't know. He has a lot of trouble before Christmas. I know that this is only October, but I can see he's already headed that way."

"Seasonal Affective Disorder?"

"No. Trauma. Once he gets past Christmas, he's a lot better. But as we approach it... it's not easy. I have to keep a close eye on him."

At least this year, they were really living in the same house, so it would be easier to keep track of Zachary and not worry that he might overdose on all his meds some night when he was in his apartment alone.

"I see. Well... do let me know if you need anything. I will help any way I can."

"Thanks. I'll see you tomorrow."

Wiltshire nodded and took off his glasses to rub the bridge of his nose. "See you then."

21

———————

K enzie was awakened by the ringing of her phone. Immediately alarmed and disoriented, she grabbed for it on her side table, knocking over a water glass and who knew what else from the surface. At least the water glass was empty. She continued to feel for the phone, then saw the glow of the screen on the floor and picked it up. She tried to keep her voice down so that she wouldn't wake Zachary up and swiped the screen to answer.

"Hello?"

"Good morning, Mackenzie," a pleasant, cultured voice replied.

Kenzie slumped back into her pillows. She squinted at the bedside clock, trying to get a good view of the time. "Mother... it's six o'clock in the morning."

"Yes, dear. I wanted to catch you before work."

"Well, you did."

There was a beat in which Lisa analyzed her voice. "Did I wake you up?"

"Yes."

"Oh. I assumed that you would have to be up to get to work in time."

"No. I'm not usually up by six. Is there something wrong, Mom? Is everything okay?"

"Yes, I'm well. Everything is fine."

"And Dad? He didn't have a heart attack or something?"

"No..." Lisa's voice was uncertain. "Has he been having heart trouble?"

"Not that I know of. But I can't figure out why else you would be calling me first thing in the morning. I have a phone with me all day. You can reach me any time. Why did you need to reach me so early?"

She realized that her voice was raised and looked over at the other side of the bed to make sure she hadn't disturbed Zachary. His space was empty. He was up before six. That wasn't unusual for him. She rarely beat him out of bed.

"It isn't because it's an emergency," Lisa explained. "Just because I wanted to be sure to get ahold of you. And I don't like to talk to you when you're at work. You're doing an important job and I don't know how your boss would feel about you taking personal calls while you were on the job."

"He knows I have a life. You can call me at work if you need to. If you don't want to get me at work, then call in the evening when I'm usually home. I'm usually out of there by five or six."

"Yes, but I have my events. Dinner onward, I am usually out. And when I get home, I want to get straight to bed because—"

"Because you're up so early. But couldn't you take a break from one of your events or call me some night when you are free?" Kenzie shook her head. She switched her phone to her other hand and rubbed her eyes. "It doesn't matter. I'm awake now and I won't be going back to sleep. So what did you want to talk to me about?"

"It would be nice just to visit with you sometime, without an agenda."

"Yes, it would," Kenzie agreed pointedly.

There was silence from her mother for a few seconds. Then Lisa went on as if the barb hadn't reached home. "There is a fundraiser in Burlington that I was wondering if you would like to attend with me. Of course, you could bring Zachary along, if you like."

She had asked to meet Zachary more than once. But Kenzie didn't think putting him into an emotionally stressful situation was the best idea.

"We're really not into fundraisers." Kenzie looked toward the living room where Zachary would be working, as if she could see him through the walls. "And he's not in the best of health right now. I don't think he would want to go."

"I would really like it if you could be there. It's only one night. Maybe he could stay home and you could just go with me. It would be really nice to see you again."

"I don't know if I'll be free. Or if I want to go to Burlington. Why do you want me to go?"

She knew that her mother usually found another escort to go with her, Kenzie's father or a widowed man or one of her society ladies. She had given up on taking Kenzie to all the premier events when she had gone into medical school. Kenzie had been justifiably too busy for a lot of social engagements.

"It's a kidney research fundraiser," Lisa explained, her voice taking on a pained tone. "It would be really nice if you could put in an appearance."

Kenzie took a deep breath and let it out, trying not to let the guilt in. If she caved in to her mother one time, it would be that much harder to maintain boundaries later. Lisa would be calling her for everything.

But she didn't want to forget Amanda or to pretend that her death didn't matter.

Kenzie's sister had died from complications of her last kidney transplant. Many of the fundraisers and events that Lisa went to were centered on kidney research, supporting survivors, making changes to regulations to make it easier and cheaper to get a transplant, or other kidney-adjacent issues. When she had been alive, Amanda had gone with Lisa to a lot of those events. When her health would allow it. She had been Lisa's very own poster child for any kidney disease or transplant issues.

Kenzie just wasn't the same. She had been an observer, not a victim of kidney failure. She had done all that she could to help Amanda but, in the end, there was nothing any of them could do to keep her alive. Kenzie had put everything she could into keeping Amanda alive, including one of her own kidneys. That had given her little sister a few more years of life without being tied to a machine. But eventually, Kenzie's transplanted kidney had failed too, and they'd been forced to consider other options.

It was after Amanda's death that Kenzie had decided to go into medicine. It had never been with the goal of doing kidney research or designing a new artificial kidney, or any of those things that Lisa had thought Kenzie should pursue. But Amanda was always there, a shadow in the back of Kenzie's mind, reminding her that no one was immortal.

"I really don't want to go to another one of those things," Kenzie told Lisa, aware of the whine that was entering her voice. "But why don't you email me the details and I'll see whether I can be there or not."

"It's on the twenty-fourth," Lisa said promptly. "Burlington. I'll send you the address. It's a masquerade. Because of Halloween, you know. Unmasking kidney disease and all that. It is a very big deal. A lot of the elite will be there. The governor and other government officials, all of the heads of the different foundations, families representing those who have been lost, and so on."

And current sufferers. White-faced waifs on display to make everyone feel bad if they didn't pull out their pocketbooks and give until it hurt. Or e-transfer donations on their phones.

"I'll check my calendar later, when I'm up. But I think I might have something else going on that night."

"You could make time if you wanted to," Lisa reproached.

They both knew it was true.

But Kenzie's way of dealing with Amanda's loss had always been very different from her mother's.

22

Kenzie wandered out to the living room, yawning, rubbing her eyes, and generally feeling like a zombie. Zachary looked up from his computer and assessed.

"Is everything okay? I heard you talking. Sounded like you were on the phone."

"Yeah, I was." Kenzie covered a big yawn. She looked down at the phone still in her hand. Still too early for her to be up, but if she tried to sleep longer, she would be even more tired and wouldn't be able to get ready in time for work. Best to get some caffeine into her system, have a nice shower, and get moving. The more she moved around, the better she would feel. "It isn't even light out."

"Sun is coming up soon. Is everything okay?"

"Yeah."

"Work call?"

"No. My mother. But it's okay. No one is dying."

"Oh. Okay."

"I'm glad she didn't wake you up."

Zachary smiled slightly. They both knew what he was thinking. Lisa would have to call pretty early to wake Zachary. Some nights he didn't sleep at all. He went to bed and cuddled with Kenzie until she was asleep or close to it, and then he would get back up without disturbing her and get

87

back to work. Or maybe he would watch a late-night movie to relax. But she would know when she woke up at one or two in the morning and reached for him and found an empty bed, that he was having a sleepless night.

"Do you want me to make you coffee?" Zachary asked. "Are you going to shower?"

"I need coffee before shower today, or I'll fall asleep in there."

Zachary nodded and moved to stand up, but Kenzie motioned him down again. "No, no. I'll get it. You stay put. We'll have breakfast together after I get out."

Kenzie was still feeling irritable and out of sorts when she arrived at the kitchen table. Zachary had laid out her usual breakfast, but she wasn't feeling like marmalade with toast. She wanted something more decadent. Comfort food. But her stomach was queasy and definitely did not want anything sweet or rich. She could feel for Zachary, trying to eat something every morning when he was nauseated due to his meds. She sat down and looked at the buttered toast, thoroughly disgruntled.

"So, what did your mom want?" Zachary asked. "If it's okay and you don't mind me asking."

"I don't really want to talk about it. Another one of her fundraising events. She's always trying to get me to go to them with her."

"Maybe you should..." Zachary started hesitantly. He toyed with the wrapper on his granola bar, not yet opening it. Maybe he was hoping she wouldn't notice and he could get away with not having any breakfast. She really wanted to help him keep his weight up. He'd looked so gaunt and ill the previous year, after the depression and not sleeping for days. Not to mention hunting down a vigilante killer who had turned on him. She was hoping things would be better for him this year, but if he was already going downhill in October, what kind of shape was he going to be in by Christmas?

It might be one of those times when he had to check into the hospital to get through it. She needed to be prepared for the possibility. And not as a last resort.

"I'm not going," Kenzie said firmly. "I have no interest in going to a fundraiser on my mother's arm. I did enough of that when I was younger. It brings back too many memories—*you* should get that."

He nodded, biting his lip.

She had only recently told him about Amanda. Until then, she had professed to be an only child. But the past came knocking at her door too many times and she had needed to talk to someone about what she was going through. That was what being a couple was all about, according to Dr. Boyle. A safe place where they could talk about their feelings and support each other.

"My mother thinks I should go to honor Amanda and show that I care about what happened to her. But it's just too painful. Like if you went to fundraising for... a program to help rehabilitate abusive parents. It's a good cause, yeah. And it would have been great if someone had been able to get your parents straightened out before everything that happened to you. But would you go to something like that?"

Zachary shook his head, his eyes dark pools of pain. Kenzie felt guilty making him feel that way, but she had to express to him how abhorrent the idea of having to go to such an event was.

"Do you want something else on your toast?" Zachary asked, looking down at the untouched triangles of buttered toast. Kenzie picked one up and nibbled on the corner.

"I don't know what I want. I just feel really... unsettled today. I really don't want anything."

Zachary got up from the table without a word. He hadn't touched his granola bar either. Maybe he figured if she could skip breakfast because of how anxious she felt, then he could too. He went silently to the cupboards, grabbing a few random items and eventually putting them into an insulated lunch bag she had bought for when he went on long surveillance gigs.

He handed it to her. Kenzie opened the lunch bag and looked inside. Zachary had given her an assortment of the snack foods she kept on hand mostly for him, trying to tempt him into eating healthy snacks during the day to keep his weight up and get the vitamins he needed. An applesauce cup. A yogurt drink. A box of raisins and a package of nuts. A cheese string. Kenzie chuckled at the odd assortment and looked at him.

"If you can't eat now, you'll get hungry later in the day," Zachary pointed out. "I don't know what you have in the vending machine at work, but it didn't look too appetizing last time I was down there. This way... when you start feeling like you can eat something... you can see what you feel like. Just grab something to eat at your desk when you're ready."

Kenzie smiled. "Thanks. That's really sweet. I'll need a spoon too."

"Oh, right." He opened the drawer beside the fridge and selected a spoon for her. "Sorry."

"Don't apologize. It was a great idea. And there are probably plastic spoons at the coffee station at work."

"No point in clogging up the landfills."

Kenzie rolled down the top of her lunch bag. "Do you want my toast?"

Zachary glanced at it and shook his head. There weren't very many foods he could manage first thing in the morning. Later in the day, he had an iron stomach. He just didn't eat enough. But first thing in the morning, even a strong smell could send him racing for the bathroom.

Kenzie looked at the time on her phone, then swiped over to review her task list and calendar.

"Oh. Don't forget about couples therapy today."

Zachary sighed and nodded. "I'll be there."

It had been a busy night and there was a lot for Kenzie to process on intake in the morning. She made sure that everything was accounted for and all the appropriate forms had been filled out, feeling clumsy and forgetful as she went from one room to another, making sure that everything was in order for Dr. Wiltshire's arrival. It wasn't like she was *that* short on sleep. But the combination of the early hour plus a request from her mother and then not eating was enough to put her into a fog. She kept getting things wrong, then criticizing herself for making such stupid mistakes, which made her feel all that much worse about herself and her abilities. Did she really think that she could be a medical examiner herself one day? Running her own office? When she couldn't even keep up with her job handling mostly administrative work? What if she'd been a surgeon trying to operate in that state? She'd end up cutting an artery or leaving a sponge inside of someone for sure.

She looked at the time and wondered where Dr. Wiltshire was. He didn't have a set time when he was always there, but it wasn't usually so late.

Kenzie could hear the phone ringing out at her desk and hurried to answer it, banging her shin against a desk drawer she had left open.

She muttered a few curses under her breath and reached for the phone, but the ringing stopped and the lights and display went back off again. She'd missed it.

Kenzie closed the drawer and sat down. It was bound to start ringing again. She brought her digital notepad up on her computer screen and looked at the phone, waiting for it to ring again. It didn't. Kenzie went back to her inbox and started processing mail, printing off reports and filing things in the electronic system. There were a few emails to forward to Dr. Wiltshire for his response, stuff that Kenzie wasn't experienced or senior enough to deal with herself. And that she certainly wasn't qualified to handle them on such a harried day.

Her stomach started to rumble. Kenzie was glad for the snacks that Zachary had packed for her. She dipped into the bag and decided to start with the raisins. If her stomach didn't like them, they were small but would still give her a concentrated sugar boost. They helped to quell her growly stomach, and Kenzie went to the coffee station for another cup. She told herself that she was short on sleep, so the extra caffeine would help her to get through the day without any significant foul-ups.

She looked at the time again as she walked back to her desk and nearly collided with Dr. Wiltshire, moving quickly toward her. Kenzie splashed the coffee but managed to stop in time to avoid drenching both of them with scalding coffee.

"Whoa. Sorry, I didn't see you," she apologized. "Everything okay? I was expecting you earlier."

Dr. Wiltshire grunted. "Got an early call. Didn't you get the message?"

Kenzie looked at her phone but didn't have any voicemails or texts from him. "Uh... no."

"On the other phone. I wanted the Cartwright file on my desk. The family is getting anxious and making phone calls to people who can make our lives very uncomfortable."

"Oh. Sorry. I'll get it for you. And there were some additional test results in the email this morning. I'll get it all assembled."

"Yeah. Great. Next time pick up your messages."

"Yes, sir."

He continued on to his office at a brisk pace. Kenzie moved more slowly to her own desk. She didn't want to spill any more of the hot coffee or risk making any further mistakes by being in too much of a hurry and forgetting or misfiling something. If Dr. Wiltshire was getting harassed by higher-ups, Kenzie couldn't afford to make any mistakes. He would want everything possible in front of him on his desk so that he could come up with required details in an instant. No matter how hard Wiltshire pushed, she needed to take her time and get everything assembled properly.

Eventually, she was confident that she had caught all the required reports and materials, and she took the file in to Dr. Wiltshire. He looked at the folder impatiently. "Are your memos in there too?"

"My memos?"

"What you were working on yesterday. The previous deaths, your hypotheses..."

"Uh..." Kenzie swallowed, hating to look stupid in front of her boss. "No. Sorry, I didn't know you would want them, so I haven't written everything up. I just have rough notes..."

"Well, give me what you've got then."

"Okay. I'll just be a minute."

Kenzie hurried back to her desk. There was no time to rewrite or type anything. Her notes and diagrams were a mess, never intended for anyone's eyes but her own. She knew that she should be flattered that Wiltshire had asked for them. She hadn't expected her half-baked ideas to be of any interest to him. Especially if he was getting pressure from higher up the food chain.

As long as he wasn't looking for someone else to blame. "My assistant is holding things up on a wild goose chase about a parasite or serial killer. Your guess is as good as mine as to which..."

But he wouldn't do that. He'd always been professional with her, honest and upfront, and he never dressed her down even when she probably deserved it. He treated her like she was already the assistant medical examiner that she wanted to be.

23

Kenzie ended up having to take a late lunch, the morning too hectic for her to leave her desk for long, and she did have to use the evil vending machine that Zachary had referred to, choosing a sad-looking sandwich that she thought might be turkey, and a small carton of milk. Neither was particularly appetizing, but she was famished despite her stock of snacks and had to get back to her desk quickly. There had been an unusual number of request forms to see to that morning.

The phone was ringing when Kenzie got back to her desk and she barked her shins for a second time, even though this time the drawer wasn't open. She saw before she picked it up that it was an internal call from Dr. Wiltshire.

"Hello?"

"Kenzie, could you join me on a call?"

Kenzie froze, not sure what to do. "Uh... you want me to three-way someone for you, or...?"

"Come into my office. We'll take the call on the speakerphone."

"Okay. I'll be right there. I just have to get someone to watch the desk."

There were a few people that Kenzie could call upon when she couldn't be at her desk. She didn't like to unless she was assisting in an autopsy. Everyone else had enough work to do without taking her responsibilities too. But she couldn't just leave her station unmanned while she joined Dr. Wiltshire on whatever the call was. She called on Julie, a college student who bounced between departments as she was needed, to see if she could leave her duties in the forensic accounting department to help out.

"Thank you!" Julie breathed. "I needed a break from filing. You wouldn't believe the amount of paper this department produces. Paperless office? Remember that concept? Somebody got it backward. We aren't going to be paper-free until we're dead."

"Uh, have you seen my department?" Kenzie teased. "I'm sorry, but being dead just means more paperwork. Only the stiff is lucky enough not to have to fill it out himself."

Julie giggled. "I'll be right down."

"Thanks. I appreciate it."

It was closer to fifteen minutes before Julie showed up at Kenzie's desk. During that time, Kenzie was on pins and needles, worried that Dr. Wiltshire was going to call her again or to show up in person to find out why she hadn't yet made it to his office for what was obviously a very important call.

As long as that wasn't code for him firing her. But she didn't think she had done anything to warrant firing or even a reprimand. She had just missed a voicemail message. And she normally picked up voicemail several times a day. It was more efficient than stopping what she was doing every time she was notified that she had a message.

She hurried to Wiltshire's office, stomach full of butterflies, a pen and notepad in hand to be able to take down notes as required.

"Ah, there you are." Dr. Wiltshire looked up from his work and pushed his glasses up his nose. He looked at his watch. "That call should be coming through any time. Nothing to worry about," he assured her with a grimace. "Just the governor's office checking up on the investigation." He rolled his eyes. "The governor's. Like he has any say over how I run my morgue. Why would anyone go to him to move a medical examiner along?"

Kenzie blinked, surprised. "Yeah. That's kind of weird."

"People will use whatever kind of political pressure they can reach. If they have a friend in the governor's office..." Wiltshire waved his hand like he was performing a magic spell. "You call the governor's office."

"I guess so." Kenzie was thinking of her father. A lobbyist often stationed at the statehouse, Walter Kirsch spent all day pressing the flesh and putting political pressure in the right places. Using personal relationships to get what he wanted was his bread and butter, and he was very good at it.

She sat down in the guest chair in front of his desk and put her notepad down on the desk. Luckily, Wiltshire kept a pretty tidy desk—which Kenzie helped to keep clean—so they were not crowded. Otherwise, she would have had to balance her notebook on her lap.

Dr. Wiltshire kept working on something on his computer while they waited. Kenzie looked around the room and looked at her phone a few times to try to appear occupied. Eventually, the phone began to ring. Dr. Wiltshire checked the screen, then answered it on speakerphone.

"Dr. Wiltshire, Medical Examiner."

"Doctor," a resonant voice boomed from the speaker. "Commissioner Toby Fletcher here. I'm glad I was able to get you. I hope I'm not taking you away from anything important?"

"Well, if your intention is to move the Cartwright investigation forward, then it might be best not to interrupt the process."

The man on the other end of the line chuckled. "I understand you've already completed the autopsy, so I'm not sure what else you would have to do. The body should be able to be released at this point, shouldn't it?"

"Just because we have done a postmortem, that doesn't mean that our investigation is complete or that we can release the body. There may still be some other tests that need to be done before we can make a determination. It isn't like you see on TV, you know, where I have a wall of computers that spit out the answer to every question I might have or test I need to perform. Things take time, and as our investigation proceeds, the data we find may require additional tests that weren't considered necessary in the beginning."

"Sounds like a lot of hot air to me. When will the body be released?"

"I have my assistant, Dr. Kenzie Kirsch, with me, and we can go over some of the preliminary investigations we have done. I think you will see that we have been actively pursuing the case and have several viable avenues of investigation we need to follow before making a determination."

"Who?"

Kenzie would have sunk down into the floor if she could have. She was a nobody. Of course, this politician from the Capitol didn't have any idea who she was. And he didn't care, either. The buck stopped at Dr. Wiltshire. He was the authority in the case; the responsibility all landed on him.

"Dr. Mackenzie Kirsch," Wiltshire repeated slowly and clearly.

"Kirsch. Any relation to Walter Kirsch?" Fletcher inquired.

Dr. Wiltshire looked at Kenzie, waiting for her answer. Kenzie's stomach muscles tightened and she found her breathing constricted. Her mouth was dry, but she hadn't brought a bottle of water in with her. She licked her lips, feeling like the silence was drawing out much too long. Fletcher would think she was an idiot.

"Walter is my father," she confirmed finally.

"Your father?" Fletcher laughed and swore jovially. "I probably bounced you on my knee when you were a little girl. Walter and I go way back. And how is Lisa these days? The two of them seem to get along pretty well for a divorced couple. Better than I get on with my ex-wives!"

"Yes, Lisa is fine. She's planning to be over your way for some masquerade fundraiser later this month."

"No kidding? I'll have to make sure I go to that one. So, Walter's little girl made it to the Medical Examiner's Office. Good for you! Do you have any other siblings? I remember Lisa and Walter lost one years ago."

"That was Amanda. Yes. So it's just me now."

"Ah, that's too bad. But at least you get all of mom and dad's attention, right?"

Kenzie rolled her eyes and didn't have an answer to this. She would much rather have had to split her time with a sibling. She would rather Amanda was still alive and demanding much of her parents' attention. She had never been jealous of the time Walter and Lisa had spent with Amanda.

"Can we focus on this case?" Wiltshire suggested, rescuing Kenzie. "As I'm sure you know, we're quite busy here, so we should get to the matter at hand."

"Of course," Fletcher agreed. "So what's going on with this Cartwright fellow? He was old. He was in a nursing home. You basically just certify that it was natural causes, right?"

"I'm sure it was," Wiltshire assured him. "But natural causes is the *manner* of death. And we also need to determine the *cause* of death. What it was that actually killed him."

"He was old. It was old age. His heart gave out. It wasn't exactly unexpected, was it?"

"Are you a doctor now?" Wiltshire challenged.

"You know I'm not saying that," Fletcher protested. "I'm just saying, there's no real mystery about it, is there? Nursing home death, it should be pretty quick to certify."

"In most cases, it is," Wiltshire agreed. "But there is not a clear cause of death in this case, and we're investigating it further. Sometimes when you open someone up... you find something unexpected. And you have to deal with that before you can move forward. Decide whether it is relevant, whether you have all the information you need about the circumstances leading up to death, and all that sort of thing. There are several complications in this case that have forced us to take a little longer with it than we normally would. That's just the nature of the job."

"Unexpected? Like what?"

Dr. Wiltshire sighed. He leaned forward, toward the phone. "You're not a medical professional, so I really don't know if it is helpful to discuss all of the details..."

But he'd had a pretty good idea from the start that Fletcher or whoever called from the governor's office was going to want details. That was why he had asked for Kenzie's notes and for her presence on the call.

"I have to have something to report to the governor."

"As you probably were told, Mr. Cartwright had a scalp laceration where he had fallen and hit his head. It was minor and didn't appear to have anything to do with his death. But we didn't find anything on the gross examination of the body that would indicate cause of death, and when we proceeded with the postmortem, his heart and lungs appeared to be in pretty good condition. The nursing home had reported that he had been in good health and I agree that appears to be the case."

"So maybe it *was* the conk on the head."

"That was our thinking as well. But when we examined the wound, there was no indication that it was serious. We did open up his skull to see if there was a bleed or swelling of the brain that might have resulted in his death. Closed head injuries don't have outward indications."

"And...?"

"That's where the unexpected part comes in. We did not find any sign of a bleed, concussion, or stroke. We had slides prepared of the brain tissue as a routine measure, and that's where we did find something surprising. Mr. Cartwright had extensive protein deposits in his brain tissue that would be expected to cause him problems."

"Protein deposits. What does that mean? What kind of problems?"

"He had amyloid plaques, which are a key indicator of Alzheimer's Disease."

"Ah. Well, like I said, he was old."

Kenzie wished he wouldn't keep saying that. Eighty-seven was elderly, that was true, but if Fletcher was one of Walter's contemporaries, then he wasn't that much younger than Cartwright himself. He was likely in his seventies.

"He was getting on in years," Wiltshire agreed. "And Alzheimer's Disease would not be unusual. Except that he didn't have dementia symptoms. He was supervised, but he was in the independent living section of the nursing home. He was able to look after himself and only had minimal support from the staff."

"They must not have noticed."

"That's one reason I had Kenzie out to the nursing home yesterday. To see if there was any possibility that the nursing home had missed symptoms or been negligent in their care of Mr. Cartwright. Maybe Kenzie could tell you a little bit about what she found there."

He nodded for Kenzie to step in. Kenzie swallowed and nodded back and tried to gather her thoughts.

"The unit he was in is not equipped to handle someone with serious needs like advanced dementia. If his care was too difficult, then they would have transferred him to one of the other units, based on his symptoms and the kind of care that he needed." Kenzie cleared her throat. "He did have some new symptoms cropping up in the week before he died. Issues with forgetting or disorientation. He had at least a couple of falls. He wasn't eating. But all of that could just have been the temporary effects of a virus, too. They were starting to run some tests, but didn't think it was serious enough to worry about. They figured it would just run its course and he would be fine again."

"Viruses can be pretty dangerous to the elderly."

"They can. But he didn't have a lot of viral symptoms like you would expect. No vomiting or difficulty breathing. No rash. Just those very vague symptoms that people sometimes get before the actual virus symptoms show up."

"But say it was the flu or something like that. His body is fighting the virus and he's just having bothersome symptoms. Maybe he doesn't even realize he's feeling sick because it's causing tiredness and confusion. Then it really hits in the night. He spends a few hours throwing up, but doesn't think he needs any help from the staff. Doesn't realize that he's gotten dehydrated, and..."

Kenzie looked at Dr. Wiltshire.

"Something like that is certainly possible," Dr. Wiltshire agreed. "But it still doesn't explain the signs of Alzheimer's Disease in his brain. With everything that we know, he should have had advanced dementia symptoms. The question becomes, did he not have symptoms? Did he have them and they weren't recognized? Is there something other than Alzheimer's Disease that caused these plaques?"

"But if it's the flu that killed him, then you don't need to worry about the plaques," Fletcher said reasonably. "You just focus on what *did* kill him. Any other... anomalies... well, they don't really matter, do they?"

"We haven't established that he had a stomach bug. We've sent in swabs for virology. He didn't have vomit on his clothing. There wasn't anything in his stomach, but the staff said he hadn't been eating. He didn't have an inflamed throat."

"It could be a virus," Fletcher said petulantly.

"Yes, it could. But a virus doesn't cause amyloid plaques."

Kenzie made a couple of notes on her notepad to follow up on. Fletcher was pushy, but hopefully, he was starting to get a better picture of what they were doing. And as Dr. Wiltshire had said, the governor's office didn't really have any say in how quickly he completed an autopsy. They could put on all the pressure they liked, that wasn't going to move anything forward.

"So what else causes amyloid plaques?" Fletcher asked.

"We'll do some more research into that. But it is a hallmark of Alzheimer's Disease. I have heard of amyloid plaques sometimes showing up with Creutzfeldt-Jakob Disease."

"Mad cow?" Fletcher demanded. "Are you telling me that Cartwright might have had mad cow disease?" He swore.

"No," Dr. Wiltshire hurried to head Fletcher off before he could drop the phone and go tell everyone he knew that Cartwright had died of mad cow disease. "There are several kinds of Creutzfeldt-Jakob Disease. It can be inherited, sporadic, or it can be transmitted by eating contaminated meat.

But we don't know anything about whether Mr. Cartwright had any form of CJD. So don't go spreading that around."

"Can't you test for it? You are going to test for it, aren't you?"

"We'll test," Dr. Wiltshire assured him quickly. "Of course. And if he had CJD, that doesn't mean that there is any problem with our food chain. Remember that it can lie dormant for years, even decades. Who knows when he might have been exposed if, in fact, he was? There are other prion diseases as well. Some of them are very rare and I would have to look up the symptoms to even know what to look for."

"If he had mad cow, what would that look like?" Fletcher demanded. "I mean, I know it's not like rabies, he's not running around trying to bite people or afraid of water. But what would his symptoms be?"

"Dementia," Dr. Wiltshire admitted. "Very much like Alzheimer's Disease. The two can be easily mistaken for each other without testing. CJD is generally faster than Alzheimer's Disease. It can take someone within a year of onset of symptoms."

"So it could be that."

"He wasn't showing any symptoms until just before his death," Wiltshire reminded him. "CJD is fast, but not that fast."

"Variant CJD is even faster," Kenzie said thoughtfully, careful not to refer to it as mad cow disease. Even though variant CJD was, in fact, the disease dubbed mad cow. "But still. Not a week. Sometimes as fast as six to eight weeks."

Dr. Wiltshire nodded, but his expression was disapproving. He didn't want Kenzie getting Fletcher wound up about the possibility of vCJD in the food chain. Kenzie looked down at her notebook, writing a few more details. She'd never heard of a case of vCJD that had taken someone that fast. But it was something to consider.

"We need to be thinking about how this is going to play out in the media," Fletcher said. "If this is a case of mad cow disease—"

"It isn't. If we find it is CJD, we can talk about the impact then, but right now, nobody is saying that it is Creutzfeldt-Jakob, and we are not going to start talking about it to the public. We are just investigating the death of a man who may have died of old age, a viral or bacterial infection, or Alzheimer's Disease. All routine illnesses that everyone is familiar with. No one in my office is talking about CJD or releasing anything to the public. When we know what killed him, then we'll issue a report. Until then, no one talks about it."

"I'll need to take this to the governor," Fletcher said, still not calming down. He was acting as if he were in crisis mode already, trying to deal with an epidemic or another threat to public safety before anyone had any idea what they were dealing with.

The man needed to cut down on the caffeine.

24

After they were finally able to end the call with Fletcher, hopefully having deterred him going off like a cannon to the governor and telling him that there was an outbreak of mad cow disease, Kenzie stayed with Dr. Wiltshire for another half hour or more, going over the various points for each of them to follow up on while they tried to sort out the case. More swabs and samples to be taken and sent off for testing for bacterial, viral, or prion diseases. Research to get started on. Dr. Wiltshire had a few doctors to follow up with whose specialty areas would give them a better feel for what they might be looking at than Dr. Wiltshire or Kenzie had.

And there were other cases that they couldn't let drop off the radar either. The John Doe had not yet been identified. They would wait for a while, hoping to release him to his family rather than the city for a pauper's burial. And there was the new case that Dr. Wiltshire had been called out to that morning. Kenzie had done the intake forms, and they would need to get to the postmortem as soon as they could to keep bodies moving through the system. They couldn't let one case block everything up.

Kenzie left Dr. Wiltshire's office, rubbing her forehead and temples. She wasn't sure whether the headache that was starting was from tension, or lack of sleep, or lack of food. Maybe a combination of all three. It had been a long, intense day. She hadn't expected to be pulled into Wiltshire's office for so long. Poor Julie had been pressed into service for much longer than they had expected and was probably bored silly. And Kenzie had a lot of jobs to do that she would have to let slide until the next day. There was no way that she was staying any later with the headache that was starting to settle in.

"Sorry to be so long," Kenzie apologized. "I thought it would only be a few minutes." She looked at the time again, even though she had already done so at the end of the conversation with Dr. Wiltshire. "I'm so sorry. I should have told you to just go home if it got to be past closing time. You really didn't need to stay."

"It's okay," Julie looked up from the conversation or game she was involved in on her phone and gave Kenzie a warm smile. "Really. I didn't have anywhere else I needed to be. And I can claim overtime. Pay off my school bills faster."

"Then I did you a favor," Kenzie teased. But she knew it wasn't true, and she shouldn't have left Julie there to her own devices for so long. "Did everything go okay? Any problems?"

She had only been down the hall; Julie could have fetched her if something had really blown up while they were busy.

"No." Julie pushed herself back from the desk, sighing and stretching. "The only one was your boyfriend."

"My boyfriend? Zachary?" Kenzie's mind spun into high gear, forgetting about her headache and fatigue. "What happened? Is everything okay?"

"Yeah. Sorry, I didn't mean to make you think that anything had happened to him." Julie held her hands up in a calming gesture. "No, just that he called." She grimaced. "A few times."

Kenzie swore under her breath. She moved in beside Julie to get out her purse and lunch bag and to gather up the rest of her papers to put securely away for the next day. "Did he say what was wrong?"

Julie said he was fine, so he hadn't done something stupid like overdose on his meds or slit his wrists. But he knew better than to call her multiple times. He could call her once, and if she didn't answer, just leave a message and wait for her to call him back. Sooner or later, she would. He knew that her job was important and that sometimes it had to come before their relationship. Dinners and dates could be put off. Death and high-powered politicians could not.

"He said that the two of you had an appointment. He wanted to know if you were on your way." Julie shrugged, looking apologetic. "He wanted me to interrupt you, but I knew you and Dr. Wiltshire were on a conference call. He called back a few times. He wasn't screaming or rude or anything... but I could tell... he was pretty ticked off. Sorry," she said again.

"No, no, you did the right thing." It wouldn't have been good for Julie to interrupt the conference call. Not unless Zachary were in the hospital or there were some other dire news.

But she knew what she had missed.

Their couples therapy. The appointment she had reminded him of just that morning.

25

K enzie would have kicked herself all the way home if her feet weren't already occupied with the pedals of the little red convertible. She had hurried past the security guard without their usual friendly conversation, focused solely on getting home and dealing with Zachary.

She couldn't believe she had missed the appointment. It was on her calendar. She knew about it. Dr. Wiltshire knew about it. She had reminded Zachary and she had always been there for him any time before then that he needed her. Other than when they were broken up. He had been so distant and remote then, angry at her for a conversation she'd had with Pat and Lorne without his knowledge. His anger over her talking behind his back had made him furious and had set their relationship back so far she had been afraid that it was unsalvageable.

And now she had screwed up again.

But that was the way relationships were. Sometimes, one person or the other fell short of expectations. No one was perfect. The important thing for them was to keep talking. She would tell him how sorry she was. Explain how Dr. Wiltshire had called her into the phone call without prior warning. He knew her job was important to her. He wouldn't hold that against her.

That was what she kept telling herself all the way home.

Kenzie was relieved to see lights on when she reached the house. At least he hadn't abandoned her and returned to his own apartment in his anger. There was still a chance for her to apologize and explain.

She entered from the garage and took a quick look around the kitchen. Had he eaten? Had he been drinking?

But the kitchen was clean, looking pretty much how she had left it that morning, as if he hadn't even been in there. If he had eaten, he had remembered to put all his dirty dishes into the dishwasher, which would be rare. Normally even if he remembered, he would still neglect one bowl or mug, either thinking he would use it again later or just getting distracted by something else.

"Zachary?" she called, not just wanting him to know she was home, which he had probably figured out when the garage door opener had ground into action, but because she wanted him to know that her first thought was of him and connecting with him.

There was no answer. Kenzie went from the kitchen into the living room, where he was sitting in front of his computer with headphones on. Kenzie glanced at the screen to see what he was doing. She didn't want to walk in on some conference session with a client. The moving image on the screen appeared to be a surveillance video. Maybe one he had taken, or maybe one taken from a camera at a business or someone's doorbell camera. Cameras were so omnipresent in their lives.

Kenzie took a few steps to the side, trying to get into Zachary's peripheral vision so that she wouldn't startle him. His eyes flicked to the side and he didn't jump. He pressed a key on the computer and lowered the headphones.

"Hi."

"Zachary, I'm so sorry I missed our session. I was tied up in a meeting with Dr. Wiltshire. I couldn't even call. We had a big phone call with the governor's office."

"Okay." He put the headphones back on.

"Zachary!" Kenzie touched his arm to regain his attention. He glanced at her again, then continued to watch the video. "Zachary. Come on." She tapped him several times. Zachary took a breath and lowered his headphones again.

"Yes?"

"We should talk. Don't just block me out."

"You were busy. I heard you. Now I have work to do." He indicated the computer screen.

"I know you're angry. You're probably hurt. Pretty upset with me."

He blinked and said nothing.

"Did you go ahead and have a single session with Dr. B?"

"Yes. Didn't want to waste the money. I have enough crap to deal with that there was plenty to cover all by myself."

"Did you talk about me?"

Zachary pointed to his computer screen again. "I should work on this."

"Did you at least tell *her* your feelings about me missing?" Maybe if he'd had a chance to vent already and to work through his emotions with Dr. Boyle, he was okay and didn't need to talk it through with her. If it were already settled without her apology and explanation, then insisting on going over it again could be more harmful to their relationship than helpful. If he'd already gone through it with an impartial third party, maybe that was for the best.

"I told her you were in a meeting. That's what the intern said."

"Yes. I was. I just... I don't want you to think that our couples therapy isn't important to me. It is, okay? This was just a one-time thing. I'll go in tomorrow and I'll talk to Dr. Wiltshire about it and explain that I can't stay if we have something scheduled. I can't go into a meeting right before an appointment."

"Sounds good." He looked at Kenzie, his aspect totally flat. He held the headphones ready, eyes drifting back to his computer screen. "Did you need anything else?"

"Have you eaten?"

"I'm not hungry." He put the headphones back on, blocking out any further discussion or argument. He pressed play on the video on his screen and watched it intently.

"I'll order something in. I don't have the energy to make anything today," Kenzie said. Maybe the headphones blocked her out completely, but she suspected they did not.

Kenzie went back to the kitchen to get herself a drink and decide what kind of takeout to order.

2 6

Kenzie didn't know how long Zachary was going to give her the silent treatment. She couldn't complain, since she was the one who had wronged him, and he did answer her when she spoke to him. Or at least, when she made him take off his headphones so that he could no longer pretend not to be able to hear her. She couldn't complain about him not sharing his feelings with her. He gave every indication that he had forgiven her and it was no big deal.

Except that she knew it was a big deal for him.

After being abandoned by his parents and kicked to the curb by his ex-wife, he didn't need any more rejection. He didn't need anyone telling him that he wasn't important, through their words or actions.

He wouldn't tell her how much it hurt. Maybe he would bottle it up, or maybe he had already talked to Dr. Boyle about it, in which case he had already been reminded how damaging it was for him to just stuff his emotions. He knew that for him and Kenzie to have a good relationship, they needed to talk about things.

But he wasn't going to talk. He would stay remote and resist any of her efforts to get in.

When the pizza arrived, Kenzie put a slice on a plate for Zachary and took it to him. She put it on the side table within his reach. Zachary glanced at it and took his headphones off again. "I'm not hungry."

"I know you said that, but you still need to eat. Even if you're upset."

He put the headphones back over his ears and continued watching his videos. He didn't touch the pizza. Kenzie sat down on the couch close by with a couple of slices for herself. "Did I tell you that we think you're right about the John Doe not being a homeless guy?" Kenzie asked, as if Zachary weren't wearing his headphones and doing his best to block her out for the evening. "I had a look at his clothes, and you're right. Trendy brands. Nothing with stains or ground-in dirt, just the oil and dirt from where he was found in the alley."

He didn't say anything.

"And his teeth. They were in very good shape. You don't see homeless guys with that kind of work. Not usually, anyway. Even if he was only recently homeless, you would still expect to see some gum disease. Signs that he hadn't been taking care of himself."

He still didn't look at her or give any sign he was listening.

"I could use another set of eyes on these nursing home deaths..."

Zachary's eyes darted to her for an instant and then were carefully turned away again as if it had never happened.

Kenzie sighed. She picked up the TV remote to find something to watch and ate her pizza in silence.

27

The rest of the evening was pretty much like that. Zachary going through video after video of surveillance. Or maybe watching the same one over and over again, Kenzie really couldn't be sure. She watched a little TV, but she was tired and ready to hit the hay. She put away the leftover pizza. At least Zachary would eat cold pizza for lunch if he remembered it was there or saw it when he opened the fridge.

She paused in the living room, looking at him. "I'm heading to bed. You going to come in?"

He turned his head slightly toward her, but he didn't meet her eyes. "I'll be in in a while."

"Okay." Kenzie hesitated for a moment. She had so many things to say to him. She wanted their relationship to be a good one and not be thrown off the rails whenever she made a mistake. Zachary got to make mistakes, to be impulsive and distracted, so why couldn't Kenzie forget something and make a mistake now and then?

She didn't want to go to bed alone. She didn't want to go to sleep with him angry at her. But he needed time to work things out for himself. She couldn't force him to see things her way.

Kenzie was quite sure the next morning that Zachary had not gone to bed any time during the night. His side of the bed was far too neat to have been slept in, even if he'd pulled the sheets straight upon rising.

She got up and found him in the kitchen, looking at his phone while he waited for the coffee to brew.

"Hey. How are you?" She forced herself to act as if everything were perfectly normal between them, walking up to him for a morning hug and kiss as usual.

Zachary remained stiff, but he gave her a squeeze and a peck on the cheek in return. "Fine."

"Did you get any sleep?" She studied his face. He hadn't shaved, which helped to hide the hollowness of his cheeks from her. But she could still see bags under his eyes. Of course, he almost always had bags under his eyes; it didn't mean that he had worked all night. His eyes were not bloodshot. So maybe he had stretched out on the couch once she was in bed.

"A bit."

"Good. You know you have to take care of your body for good physical and mental health."

"So they tell me."

She gave him another hug and a quick smooch on the lips, trying to draw him out. But he remained remote.

"I'm going to have a shower. Then we can have breakfast together."

"I'm eating now." He indicated a granola bar wrapper on the counter.

"That's good... then you can sit with me while I eat. You don't have to go out anywhere this early, do you?"

Zachary looked down at his phone to check the time and tried to come up with a lie about why he had to go out so he could avoid having breakfast with her.

"See you in a few minutes, then," Kenzie said breezily.

Breakfast was awkward, but Zachary did sit with Kenzie and made agreeable noises about having some pizza for lunch if he was at home when the hour rolled around. He had things to do that would take him away from the house. Unspecified things. She couldn't tell whether he was keeping client confidentiality or blocking her out.

She would allow him the rest of the workday to sulk, but she expected to see a change when she got home again. She wasn't going to put up with him sulking around for another evening. It would be time to either talk about things or move on. The choice was his. But she wasn't going to walk around on eggshells for weeks this time.

She gave him another hug and kiss in farewell and headed into work.

There was plenty to catch up on from the day before, and Kenzie also wanted to get some research done. She needed to make sure she understood everything she could about amyloid plaques. Anything that the scientific world knew about how they were formed, how they caused damage to the brain and loss of function, and what they might indicate other than Alzheimer's Disease or CJD. They couldn't be the first ones who had run into that situation.

But first, there were new intakes to be done, email to process, reports to be printed, Dr. Wiltshire's desk to tidy, and taking care of anything else that had happened during the night. In a bigger city, they might have a fully functioning night shift as well as the day shift but, as it was, they operated with only a skeleton staff to keep an eye on things at night. The staff being one person, usually rotating in from other departments. And that meant that sometimes things didn't get done the way Dr. Wiltshire liked.

Eventually, Kenzie felt like she could take a few minutes to start on her education about amyloid plaques and differential diagnoses for Alzheimer's Disease. Unfortunately, it was noon. And who knew what the afternoon would bring. She already had a list of things that she would need to take care of. So, it was another sandwich from the lone vending machine, eating over her computer while reading through medical studies and articles.

There were several theories about amyloid plaques. Everything from their being another prion disease like CJD, to being produced in response to attack by a virus or bacterial infection. It wasn't necessarily as Kenzie had imagined, just a metabolic error or something that built up as people aged. While it was the most common cause of dementia, they didn't affect everyone, like wrinkles or muscle degeneration.

One takeaway from her study was that tau tangles correlated better with how advanced the dementia was than amyloid plaques. But Cartwright's slides had shown extensive tangles, which suggested he should have had advanced dementia.

Another study suggested that amyloid plaques were not a problem until they started to appear in the synapses between neurons. Plaques inside the neurons apparently did not cause the communications problems that a build-up between the neurons did. All of that made sense to Kenzie. If the impulses between cells were obstructed by protein deposits, the cells could not pass messages along.

But once again, Cartwright's results defied the study. He had extensive plaques in the synapses. By every measurement and predictor Kenzie could find, he should have been disabled by the amount of damage in his brain. It would not be surprising for someone to die from such extensive damage. What was surprising was that he had not experienced any symptoms until a few days before his death.

Kenzie took notes and tried to come up with a hypothesis that made sense. Several of their theories so far had been disproved by the laboratory tests. She couldn't predict when they would get the bacterial and virology swab screens back to give them a better idea of whether they were looking for an infectious agent.

Dr. Wiltshire was at her desk just before Kenzie could finish her sandwich and clear away the work she was doing. "Oh, sorry, didn't realize you were on your lunch break."

"No, it's okay. I didn't really take a break. But I thought I'd better have something to eat." She wondered whether Zachary had or would actually have a slice of pizza as she had suggested. He hadn't called or texted her all morning. That wasn't particularly unusual, especially if he were engaged with a case, but she had hoped that she would hear something from him, just so she could stop being so anxious about whether he were okay.

"Good thinking." Dr. Wiltshire's eyes lingered on the few bites of her sandwich that were left. She hadn't seen him go to the vending machine or out for lunch. Had he brought his own lunch in, or was he, like Zachary, inclined to just work straight through the day without a thought of something to eat? She didn't know how Zachary could do it.

"I thought you would want to know that our John Doe has been identified," Dr. Wiltshire offered, his eyes returning to Kenzie's face. "Thanks to your insight on the fact that he might not actually be homeless and we should broaden our search to businesses in the area, not just services for the indigent."

"Oh, that's good news! Who is he?"

"He was a businessman living near the site where he was found. He lived alone, so he hadn't been reported missing. The police are contacting his next of kin, so we may get transportation instructions today or tomorrow."

"They didn't want anything else for their investigation?"

"Who, the police?" Dr. Wiltshire shook his head. "No, why?"

"I just thought that since he was killed by alcohol overdose and was found in a back alley... it's a little more suspicious if he wasn't actually a homeless man. If he was an alcoholic on the streets, it's not hard to believe. But a businessman going home from work at the end of the day..." She shook her head. "I would think they would want to investigate that a little more."

"And they probably are. But they haven't asked for anything else from our end. We've already collected all the evidence and established cause of death. Manner of death is accidental, unless I get other information."

"Yeah." Kenzie scratched the back of her head, thinking about it. Alcohol toxicity was almost always accidental. Unless they had some kind of evidence showing that the alcohol had been forced down his throat, which they did not. His teeth had not been broken, as they might have been if a bottle were forced into his mouth. There were no bruises or defensive injuries to indicate that he had fought off an attack. "I guess so. I'm just surprised that it was someone white-collar."

"The rich can still be closet alcoholics and can overdose if they consume too much too fast."

"Yeah. But he wouldn't be drinking at work, would he? They would catch on if he was drinking that much on the job."

"Maybe he went out for drinks with the boys after work. Hit a bar or two. Everyone heads for home, only he doesn't make it. Maybe he continued drinking after they went home."

"But then wouldn't they wonder what had happened to him if he didn't show up at the office the next day?"

"We don't know that they didn't. They may have called him to see if he was okay, but not reported it to the police or to the boss at work because they didn't want to get him in trouble. They might say that he was sick, or that they don't know what happened to him, to cover for him."

Kenzie nodded. "Yeah. I guess that makes sense."

It wouldn't be the same with her friends. If one of them thought that she had drunk too much the night before and she had dropped out of sight, they would undoubtedly do more than just call her and cover for her. But it was different for women. They were more vulnerable. Her friends wouldn't even have left her at a bar or let her walk home by herself if they thought she might have had a bit much to drink. But with men, it was different. They wanted to show their crew how invulnerable they were. How they could drink massive quantities without being affected. Walk alone at night as if it were nothing.

She remembered how Zachary had been jumped after leaving a bar when on an investigation. He had been badly beaten by a gang of skinheads. Men were not invulnerable, even if they thought they were. Zachary and John Doe could both attest to that.

"What was his name?"

Dr. Wiltshire looked down at his hand, where he held a sticky note. "Jeremy Salk. We can update our records."

Kenzie nodded and typed it into her notepad. "I'll do that."

D r. Wiltshire looked down at Kenzie's notes. "You've been working on the plaques?"

Kenzie nodded. "There was a lot to do today, so I haven't spent a lot of time yet. But it's interesting stuff. We never really covered the theories in school, just that Alzheimer's Disease was caused by these amyloid plaques, and if you saw amyloid plaques, it was Alzheimer's Disease."

"But things are rarely that simple in medicine."

"No, I guess not. There is the whole question of why people get these plaques. I thought that it was just a function of aging. Some processes in the body slowed down, and these plaques started to accumulate. But that's not necessarily the case."

He nodded. He glanced around him. There was nowhere to sit down around Kenzie's desk. People stood there to make inquiries or fill out forms, and then they left. They didn't stay to chat.

"Let's grab the boardroom," Dr. Wiltshire suggested. "You can still see if someone comes in."

Kenzie nodded and picked up her notes. She would hear if her phone rang. No need to call Julie in this time.

They sat at the table and Dr. Wiltshire got comfortable. "So, what can you tell me?"

"I don't know how much of the theory you know..."

"Pretend I know nothing. I'm a layman. You're explaining it to Zachary."

"Okay." That helped Kenzie to relax and feel less anxious about it. She didn't want to be lecturing her boss, either assuming he was ignorant or that he knew something he didn't. The permission to treat him like a layperson meant that she didn't have to worry about offending him.

"One of the most compelling theories is that amyloid plaques are actually a defense mechanism. Like fever. We see it as a symptom, something that must be treated to make the person well again. But when we artificially lower a fever, we are not letting the body use its own defenses. We should let it run its course, unless it is too high and endangers them."

"Right. So amyloid plaques could be a defense against what?"

"There are several bacteria implicated and possible viral involvement as well. For example, we know that people suffering from dental infections are at a much higher risk for Alzheimer's disease. There is a significant risk of bacteria making its way from the teeth to the brain and causing real damage. A brain infection puts the person's life at risk."

"So the plaques may be a way to prevent bacteria from entering the brain, or they might interfere with the bacterial growth or be a sort of scar tissue caused by bacterial damage."

Kenzie gave a nod. "We don't know why or how, but we know that people who have amyloid plaques are able to fight infections for longer. They are somehow protective and slow down the disease process."

Wiltshire nodded. "What bacteria appear to be involved?"

Kenzie gave him the specifics. She paused. "Also, there is the possibility that they protect against some viruses as well. In particular, herpesviruses."

He considered. "Which herpesviruses?"

"Human Herpesvirus 1, 6A, and 7. That we know of."

Dr. Wiltshire shook his head. "Which, all together, are endemic to what percentage of the population? Ninety percent?"

"I haven't been able to come up with a number for all three together. But yes... it is endemic. But not in *brain tissue*. Usually, our immune systems are effective in keeping herpesviruses out of the Central Nervous System. The percentage of the population with herpesvirus in the *brain* is much lower."

"So if the plaques were caused by a virus, the serology is not going to tell us what we need to know. We don't need to know what viruses were in the blood; we need to run PCR on the brain tissue and CNS fluid."

Kenzie nodded. "But this is all theory, and we could still be looking at two separate issues—what caused the plaques, which may be benign, and what caused his death. He could still have died from a virus or bacterial infection, and the plaques have nothing to do with it." Kenzie had her doubts about that, but it was a possibility. The literature confirmed that some people with amyloid plaques did not seem to have any AD symptoms.

"Of course," Dr. Wiltshire agreed. "We'll pursue both avenues and, hopefully... come to a conclusion in the end."

29

Despite how busy Kenzie was, she watched the clock, and when five o'clock rolled around, she put away her active projects and began the night shut-down procedure. Before the clock struck six, she was pulling into the garage and went into the house.

"You home?" she called out as she walked in the door.

She could hear Zachary moving around in the living room. He poked his head into the kitchen, looking at her and rubbing the bridge of his nose. He looked tired and drawn. He had probably not crashed on the couch during the day like he should have.

"Yeah, I'm here. You're home early."

"Well, I'm home on time. For once. After how crazy it has been this week, I decided I'm not spending any longer at the office today. Unless there's an emergency, I'll put in my time tomorrow and take the weekend off." Considering the fact that she frequently put in at least one weekend shift, that was significant. She hoped it signaled to Zachary that he was an important part of her life too. That she was willing to make the time for him.

"Sounds nice," he said noncommittally. No inflection. No suggestion of something they should do together, since they would have the time. She hadn't asked whether he had any surveillance he would need to be away for or if he wanted to drive out to see one of his siblings.

"Did you have any plans?" she asked tentatively.

"I don't know. I'll need to look at my calendar." He didn't pull out his phone to look and she knew he was just putting her off.

"We could do something nice. Go out to Old Joe's. A movie. Something we haven't done for a while."

He nodded.

Kenzie sighed. "What do you want for supper?"

"Nothing. Whatever you like is fine."

"I'm not sure I'm even going to make anything." Kenzie kicked off her shoes and hung up her jacket on the hook on the mudroom wall.

"You don't have to. Do you want me to order in?"

"Not if you're not eating."

Even though Zachary was giving her something of a cold shoulder, she could see his consternation over this statement. He knew that she got concerned when he didn't eat, so it was something he could fall back on if he were angry and wanted to let her know it in a passive-aggressive way. He hadn't exactly said that he wouldn't eat supper, but he had implied it. On the other hand, he would be very upset if Kenzie didn't eat because of him. Ordering in was one way that he nurtured her and showed that he could be a partner in their relationship, but if she didn't accept his offering and intentionally went hungry because of him, he would obsess over it for days.

Kenzie went to the bedroom to put down her bag and change into something comfortable. It might still be early in the evening, but she was going to pamper herself with a nice cozy set of jammies.

When she finished and left the bedroom, Zachary was standing there in the hallway, looking as though she had caught him red-handed at something. He looked back the way he had come, then ahead to the bathroom, and didn't know what to say. He had clearly wanted to continue their conversation but didn't know whether to follow her or give her some space.

Kenzie raised her brows. "Yes?"

He just motioned to the bathroom and hurried past her. He shut the bathroom door and turned on the tap. Kenzie waited for a moment, then went back out to the living room. Zachary had learned a lot of different coping mechanisms in foster care, not all of them functional. She turned on the TV while she waited for him to sort himself out and decide to talk to her. He could keep pretending that he wasn't upset with her, tiptoe around and act like everything was normal, and be increasingly anxious because of it. Or he could just get it off his chest and they might be able to enjoy the upcoming weekend.

30

Unfortunately, it was doomed to be a tense and awkward evening of avoiding speaking to each other unless absolutely necessary and pretending that everything was fine when they did speak. Kenzie eventually broke down and heated up the leftover pizza, which they both had some of.

"How was your day?" Kenzie asked as she nibbled at her slice. "Work good?"

"Yeah. How about you? Make any progress on that case? The... nursing home case?"

"Not really. We're waiting for a bunch of testing back. I did some research for it today, but I'm not sure how it will turn out. We may be seeing a problem where there really isn't one."

Zachary nodded. He lifted his slice and smelled it, but didn't eat. She waited for more questions, but there didn't appear to be any forthcoming.

"We identified that John Doe. You were right; he wasn't homeless. He was just... in the wrong place at the wrong time. With the state of his body and clothes, the police assumed that he was homeless and that's what they told us. They happened to be wrong, and we were operating under a false bias."

He nodded again and looked away from her, into the living room where he had a line of sight to the front window. He always sat in the same kitchen chair. In the beginning, she thought it was just habit. Zachary had a definite preference for sameness and rituals. But she had started to see that maybe it wasn't just habit, but the need to be able to see as much of his surroundings as possible. To know if a stranger were lurking around the house, a car parked on the street that shouldn't be there, any sign of emergency vehicles or other possible dangers. The kitchen only had a small window and a door into the mudroom and garage. The window faced a neighbor's house. While it helped to brighten the room during the day, it wasn't much of a view. Only the big living room window afforded him a good view of the street.

"We were both pretty impressed that you could guess that he wasn't homeless just from his hair," Kenzie offered.

"Not just his hair. The way he was groomed. His skin. A lot of little things."

"I guess that's what makes you such a great private investigator. Being able to see all of those little things and draw conclusions from them."

Zachary shrugged off the compliment. He took his first bite of the pizza. Kenzie was nearly finished eating her first slice.

"Nothing interesting for you today?" she prodded. "Talk to Heather or anyone?"

"Talked to Heather," he admitted. He had introduced his big sister to PI work, and she quite enjoyed the work she was able to do for him from her computer and phone. She didn't do fieldwork like surveillance or accident reconstruction, or going to people's houses or places of business to talk to them. The home-based work was enough for her.

"How is she?"

"Good."

"It was really a good idea to get her involved with your work. You needed someone to help out with those jobs to free up your time. And it's been really good for Heather and her self-esteem."

"Uh-huh."

Kenzie ate her second slice of pizza without any further attempt at conversation and put her plate in the dishwasher. She walked away from the kitchen without excusing herself or saying another word to Zachary. A few minutes later, she could hear him putting his plate into the dishwasher as well. There wasn't really enough in the dishwasher to run it, but she heard him start it anyway. Hopefully, he had remembered to put detergent in the dispenser.

Kenzie shut herself in the bedroom and worked from her laptop and her tablet on the bed, catching up on some correspondence with friends, paying bills, and writing dutiful emails to her parents. She downloaded a book and read for a while, but couldn't focus on the story, her mind on Zachary and work. The puzzle of what had killed Willis Cartwright festered. Would they end up just writing it off as natural causes? Age? It wasn't a great solution, but she wondered if they would be left with any other option.

She started to think, after a while, that she should call Dr. Boyle. Of course, she should call during the day when Dr. B would be at her office. But she would probably have appointments booked most of the day, and Kenzie would have a hard time finding private time during her own work-day. She didn't want to be discussing ultra-personal matters while sitting at her public-facing desk. For most of the day, she was alone, but she could be approached by the police or a member of the public for a request at any time. That meant that she had to be careful what she said and did there.

Dr. B had told Zachary and Kenzie to call her at home if they needed to. Kenzie didn't like to do that unless it were an emergency. But she was worried about Zachary. Not about his immediate safety, but she did worry that if she let him go downhill now, in October, then there wouldn't be anything she or anyone else could do when he hit the really black time in the week or two before Christmas. Maybe there wasn't anything any of them could do anyway, but she had hoped that if she kept track of his moods and was there to give advice and help him along, that he would do better this time. They could have a quiet December and give Zachary plenty of time and control over his own surroundings, and with her help, he could get through it more easily.

Maybe that was naive of her. She'd seen him the previous Christmas and really understood for the first time that it wasn't just December blues, but a real crisis point.

The other question, besides whether Dr. B would want to get a call from Kenzie during the evening when it wasn't an emergency, was how Zachary would feel about her calling Dr. B.

Kenzie had made mistakes in that area before, talking to outside parties instead of directly to Zachary. But he wasn't talking to her. Any time she asked him how he was, she got a one-word answer. She'd tried to engage him in various other conversational topics, but had failed.

Eventually, Kenzie gave in. She would call. She would see what Dr. Boyle thought. And if necessary, she would go back to Zachary to ask for his permission. Dr. Boyle was Kenzie's therapist too, after all. Maybe just for the couples stuff, but they did have a professional relationship.

The phone rang a few times and then was answered by Dr. Boyle's quiet, cultured voice. "Hello?"

"Dr. Boyle. Hi, it's Kenzie Kirsch. I don't like to disturb you at home. Are you busy? Is there a time I could talk to you tomorrow?"

"I have a few minutes now. What can I help you with?"

Kenzie took a couple of deep breaths, trying to prepare herself. "Well... I guess you know I missed couples therapy this week."

"I did notice," Dr. Boyle said dryly.

Kenzie gave a weak laugh. "Yeah. I guess you probably did. How was Zachary? Was he okay?"

"You should ask him that."

"I did. He says everything is fine. He says he understands that sometimes I have to work late unexpectedly and that I was called into a meeting with my boss and couldn't call him to let him know what was going on. But... I know he's still upset. He won't talk to me about it. I'm not sure what to do. I don't want to just let it go until he's ready to talk about it. That's what I did the last time, and it was weeks before he was ready..."

"I would suggest that you continue to let him know that you will talk to him about it, that you're prepared to hear his feelings. But know that he isn't necessarily going to be open to sharing those feelings right now. It was a bit of a shock for him when you didn't show up."

"And in the meantime, when he won't talk to me? Do I pretend that everything is fine? Act like it's all normal? Because things are pretty tense around here. I don't know how to deal with him. He's blocking me out."

"He might need a bit more time. It was just yesterday."

Kenzie let out her breath. Was it even possible that it had only been a day ago? It seemed like ages already. Every minute that she sat with Zachary, or separate from him, it felt like there was a war going on between them. A silent war, but a war nonetheless. And she didn't know how to win it. Or if she needed to win it. She wanted things to go back to normal. Like the blissful night when she had invited Zachary back, and they had lain in each other's arms for hours. It had seemed like everything had been healed between them and nothing else could ever open that rift again. And now she'd done it. It was as easy as forgetting an appointment she'd promised to attend with him.

"There isn't anything I could do to help him get through it faster? I'm worried about him. About his depression. It's already getting worse and Christmas is more than two months away. What if I can't reach him before that?"

"That's two months away," Dr. Boyle assured her. "A lot can happen in that length of time. If you've apologized for what happened and he's accepted it, I think you just need to wait patiently. He has a lot of emotions to work through."

And it would take longer than a day. Kenzie knew how he was still stuck on forgiving his mother for abandoning him and his siblings to the foster care system. She had demanded that they be taken away because she didn't want to deal with them anymore. That was a decades-old hurt.

And he was still dealing with his feelings for Bridget when she had kicked him out of the house and divorced him. That one festered not just because of Zachary's feelings, but because of the things that Bridget had done since, using him, being verbally and emotionally abusive, if not physically abusive. Kenzie had seen Bridget slap Zachary once, and she was pretty sure that wasn't the only time it had happened. The recent revelations about Bridget's unborn twins and her own challenges had not helped Zachary to put the past behind him.

So why did she think that he should be able to recover in a day after they'd had a major disconnect? Especially when his feelings with her were bound to be wrapped up with his feelings toward his mother and Bridget?

"How do I wait? I want things to go back to normal. Not to feel like I have to tiptoe around here and avoid doing anything that will make him feel worse? I keep trying to talk—just about normal stuff, not the relationship and my screw-up—and he just won't engage."

"Do you want me to talk to him?"

Kenzie considered. She wasn't sure whether that would be helpful or harmful. She'd talked herself into calling Dr. Boyle, telling herself it was the right thing to do, but was talking to Dr. B or asking her to intervene a betrayal of their relationship? Kenzie didn't want to do that again.

"No. I don't think I should put this on you. I think that if he feels like I went to you and asked you to straighten him out..." Kenzie shook her head to herself. "That's just going to make things worse. It's going to break our trust again."

"Okay. Then all I can say is that you're doing the right thing, letting him know it's okay to share his feelings and then trying to live a normal life while you wait for him to process it. It isn't going to be a smooth, easy path. There might be a few blow-ups along the way. But you're going to need to give him time. More time than you think it should take."

"All right." Kenzie sighed. "That's what I'll do, then. At least... at least I know what he's upset about this time. Before, when I didn't know why he had suddenly withdrawn... all I could think was that something had happened and he didn't care anymore. He didn't want me around and just didn't know how to say it. When Lorne told me... it was a relief to at least know what it was we were fighting about."

"Good luck. You have his schedule, so you know when his next therapy session is. Expect some fireworks that day. And then the next week we'll have another couples session. And hopefully, Zachary will be okay with that, and you will be able to be there. Make an effort to be around when you say you will, to keep all appointments, even if they seem like small, unimportant things. He can get through this. If you both work at it."

"I will. Thanks."

31

After hanging up with Dr. B, Kenzie just lay in bed for a while, sometimes with her eyes closed and sometimes staring up at the ceiling. She tried to put herself into Zachary's place. To imagine what was going on inside his head and how it was affecting him. Eventually, she forced herself to roll out of bed, put her devices away, and go out to the living room to talk to him one more time.

Zachary's head twitched toward her for an instant when she entered the room, so she knew that despite the fact he pretended to be occupied with his computer, he wasn't so hyperfocused on his work that he didn't see her.

"Hi," Kenzie said and sat down on the couch. Near where he was seated at his computer, but not too close. His eyes went to her, then to the empty space between them. He turned back to his laptop.

"Zachary."

"Uh-huh?" He deliberately made his voice sound far away.

"I called Dr. Boyle. I wanted to make sure you knew. So you don't think I'm talking to people behind your back."

His eyes turned to her, dark and intense. Already looking hurt and betrayed. "What?"

"I wanted to know her thoughts on what I can do. I know I screwed up. I just wanted to know if there was anything she thought I should be doing to... let you know that I'm sorry and that I care about how you feel. To let you know that you can talk to me about it. When you're ready."

He looked away again, tapping a key on his computer as if he were still engaged with what was on his screen.

"Great. You didn't need to do that. What did she say?"

"Just to carry on. Give you time to process. However much you need."

Zachary nodded.

"And I'm doing that. I didn't come out here to push you to talk or to feel differently than you do. Just to let you know that I'm working on myself. And that I talked to Dr. B. I'm not trying to hide anything or to push you."

There was a long period of silence. It might have only been a few seconds, but it felt like forever. After a long time, Zachary nodded and said, "Okay."

Kenzie didn't know how long it would take before things were normal again between them, but she felt like at least they had made a step. She had made sure that he wasn't going to be taken by surprise by her call to Dr. Boyle and that he knew she was just going to continue to be patient and wait. As much as she was able to do that. What she would really like to do some days was just to smack him and tell him to grow up and get over it. But the fact was, he really *was* still that ten-year-old he'd been when his mother had abandoned him. And he was still the damaged kid he had been in foster care when his behavior had been too much for the Petersons to handle and he had spent much of his time in institutional care. And he was still the man he'd been with Bridget, beginning their life together, happy as two lovebirds should be, and then devastated when her love for him had soured and she had kicked him out. He was still all those people and stuck in all those relationships.

But in an improvement over the night before, he agreed to go to bed with her. His body was too stiff and his movements conscious and forced, but he was at least trying to go through the motions, just as Kenzie was.

After the restless night before and a couple of very long workdays, Kenzie couldn't stay awake even if she was worried about their relationship. After a few minutes, her body relaxed and she drifted off to dreamland.

But it wasn't to be the peaceful, regenerating sleep that she hoped for. She was jolted out of sleep by Zachary a few hours later. Not having nightmares, but shaking her shoulder gently. Kenzie tried to open her eyes, rubbing one with her fist.

"What? What's wrong? Did you have a dream?" Kenzie croaked.

"Your phone."

"What?" Kenzie forced herself to sit up and look for it. It flashed and vibrated on the bedside table. "Oh... dang!"

Her phone was set to Do Not Disturb after ten, and the only people who were allowed through were Zachary and Dr. Wiltshire. And her parents, of course. Kenzie couldn't shake off the memory of late-night and early-morning calls when Amanda had been alive. Gut-wrenching calls when no one knew if Amanda was going to make it through the night. Kenzie wouldn't leave her mother to her own devices if Walter had a heart attack, or vice versa. She would be there when her parents needed her, no matter what their relationship was like.

Kenzie fumbled her phone and scooped it up. She squinted at the bright screen. Not one of her parents. Dr. Wiltshire. Kenzie swiped and put it up to her ear. "Hello? Dr. Wiltshire?"

"Sorry to call you in the middle of the night, Kenzie."

"No. It's okay. What is it?"

"There has been another death at Champlain House. I'm going to attend this time. Do you want to come along?"

"Oh. Yes." Kenzie pulled off the blankets. "Are you going right now?"

"I'll be on my way shortly. You don't have to come if you don't want to. But you've been very involved in the Cartwright case and I thought you might..."

"Yes, definitely." Kenzie slid out of bed and went to her closet, squinting into it by the light of her phone to pick out a shirt and pants for the visit to the nursing home. "I will be there as soon as I can be. Do you know what we are looking at yet?"

"No, not yet. They did not sound concerned. They don't, I think, view it as suspicious."

"Okay. I'll see you there."

Kenzie hung up the phone and started to dress.

"Where are you going?" Zachary asked.

"Champlain House. It's just down by the river. Not far."

"I can drive you."

"And then you'd have to just sit in the car in the dark and cold waiting for me. You don't need to do that. Just go back to sleep."

"You know *that's* not going to happen," he said with a hint of a laugh. "And I'm not exactly a stranger to sitting in a dark, cold car. If I take you, then I'll know that you're safe and not worry about you."

"I can drive myself. I'm awake. You may as well get what rest you can."

She could feel him watching her in the dark. "If you tell me not to go, I won't. But if you don't mind... let me drive you."

Kenzie was irritated and pleased in equal measures. He wasn't acting remote and angry. And he wasn't acting needy. He communicated his feelings, gave Kenzie a choice, and then waited. Just like they'd been taught in couple's therapy.

"You'd really rather sit in the car than stay here?"

"Yes."

"And you know that afterward, we'll have to come back here so I can get my car for work? I don't want you to have to pick me up at the end of the day too. That's a lot of extra driving around when I'm just going in to... observe."

"I know. I'd rather go."

Kenzie sighed. "Okay, then. I suppose I should be grateful to have you along and give me time to wake up." She knew that Zachary didn't need time to wake up. Even in the middle of the night, his usual state of affairs was hypervigilant, not drowsy. He had woken up to the vibration of her phone, hadn't he? While she was yawning and rubbing her eyes, he sat on the bed like he had just come in to watch her sleep rather than needing any sleep himself.

He sprang up off the bed and was fully dressed before Kenzie, despite her head start. He slid out of the room as silently as a ghost, not waiting for her. Kenzie finished dressing, went to the bathroom, gathered her bag and her phone, and made her way out to the living room.

"If you can wait thirty seconds, I've got coffee on," Zachary told her, looking at the time on his phone.

Kenzie didn't want to wait, but thirty seconds for coffee beat going out immediately with nothing to fortify herself. She breathed out, trying to catch her breath and slow her heart, which was thumping rapidly with excitement. "Okay. Thanks. That was thoughtful."

"Dr. Wiltshire can take you for donuts in the morning."

Kenzie chuckled. He probably would, at that. They wouldn't be taking time to go back home and follow their usual morning routines. Another reason it was probably a good idea to go with Zachary. Then he wouldn't feel like he had been abandoned by her the whole day.

"I'll get the car warmed up." Zachary pulled on a jacket, turned off the burglar alarm, and went out the front door to his car parked at the curb in front of the house. His breath was frosty in the air, reminding Kenzie that she'd better get her coat as well. She put on her jacket and shoes while she waited for the coffee machine to finish filling the large carafe, then used it to fill the two travel mugs waiting on the counter. Try to get Zachary to make a simple lunch while he was distracted by something else, and he would forget a major component. But when he was focused on a mission like getting Kenzie safely to the nursing home, it was a totally different story. He was as prepared as a boy scout. Or a drill sergeant.

Kenzie grabbed the two mugs and her bag, re-armed the burglar alarm, and left the house.

3 2

Zachary drove up to where the official Medical Examiner's van was parked to drop Kenzie off at the correct doors. The night was quiet and still. It wasn't like crime scenes that Kenzie had seen on TV. Not bustling with action, police walking in and out, crime scene techs dusting every surface for fingerprints or scouring the property for other evidence. No bystanders or media calling out questions, wanting to know what had happened.

Instead, it was quiet and peaceful. Like the hospital room of someone who was gravely ill or a funeral home. Everyone spoke in hushed voices, moved slowly, and showed deference and respect. When Kenzie entered through the side door, she was met by a security guard who clearly knew who she was and escorted her to the room where the body and Dr. Wiltshire awaited her.

Dr. Wiltshire talked to one of the nursing staff in a low voice, both of them nodding and looking grave, but not worried. Dr. Wiltshire nodded to Kenzie as she entered the room. There were no police there, no one saying that she needed to put on booties and coveralls to avoid contaminating the scene.

"This is my assistant," Dr. Wiltshire introduced her. "Dr. Kenzie Kirsch. Kenzie, Nurse Sheila Cook. We have here," Dr. Wiltshire indicated the bed, "Mr. Stanley Sexton, age seventy-two. Nurse Cook...?"

"He pressed his call button," Nurse Cook explained. "When Jason—Munro—came to see what he needed, Mr. Sexton was unable to speak. He made some noises, but it wasn't clear whether he was coherent and unable to speak or whether he was unaware of his surroundings and making random noises or the kinds of sounds someone makes when they are asleep. Jason attempted to communicate with him, and when he was unable to get a coherent response, he returned to the nursing station to get someone else to help. By the time he and I got back to the room, Mr. Sexton had passed."

Kenzie looked at Dr. Wiltshire to see if there were anything else. It sounded pretty straightforward. Maybe a stroke. They would know better when they examined him. She and Dr. Wiltshire approached the bed together. Kenzie didn't touch anything, looking the bed and nearby surfaces over for anything that didn't sit right. It all looked straightforward. No blood or other fluids. No strange smells. No indication that Mr. Sexton had been trying to get out of the bed. The call button was within reach.

Kenzie heard the click of claws on the hallway floor and turned to see Lola coming in. She approached Kenzie and nuzzled her hand. Kenzie petted her for a minute. "This is Lola," she told Dr. Wiltshire. "I met her last time I was over."

"Hello, Lola," Dr. Wiltshire said solemnly before continuing with the investigation. He put his fingers over Mr. Sexton's pulse and waited for a moment. He checked the man's pupils for reactivity to light. Kenzie certainly couldn't see any signs of life. "Dr. Kirsch, would you verify lack of pulse?" Dr. Wiltshire said formally.

Kenzie moved in to obey, wondering why he would want her to verify his findings. When she touched Mr. Sexton's arm, she was surprised and almost jerked her hand back away. His skin was cool to the touch, waxen under her fingertips. She looked at Dr. Wiltshire. Sexton had been dead for longer than the half hour it had taken them to get to the scene.

"Better do a liver temp," Kenzie said in a near-whisper.

He nodded his agreement.

Kenzie looked around the small room again. If the staff had lied or misled them about one thing, chances were, there were other things. And it was probably their only chance to spot anything out of place or any evidence that needed to be preserved.

Lola whined. Looking at how Sexton was positioned on the bed and the sheets pressed down on one side, Kenzie turned to look at Nurse Cook. "Was the dog in here with him?"

"Well..." Cook looked awkwardly from Kenzie to Dr. Wiltshire and back again. "Yes, Lola was in here earlier."

"Sleeping on the bed with him?"

She nodded. "I didn't see any harm in it. Mr. Sexton had been agitated earlier, and Lola helped to settle him down so that he could go to sleep. She's very good with the residents."

Dr. Wiltshire raised his eyebrows at Kenzie and nodded, a signal that she had done well. Kenzie scratched Lola's ears. She examined the dog covertly for any sign of illness. Her eyes and conjunctivas were clear. Her nose, when she shoved her snout into Kenzie's hand for more love, was wet and cool. Kenzie didn't smell anything foul. Lola wasn't limping or favoring any part of her body that Kenzie could see. Her fur was well-brushed and shone. Nothing that Kenzie could see that would give her any reason to believe that Lola was sick with any illness that she might have passed on to the residents at Champlain House. Of course, she could be a carrier of numerous pathogens without ever showing any symptoms.

"What time was it when Mr. Sexton hit the call button?" she asked Cook.

"I'm not sure. Not long ago."

Kenzie waited for further explanation. Nothing was forthcoming. She looked at Dr. Wiltshire, then back at Nurse Cook. "Don't you have a system that registers what time a call button is pushed?"

"Uh, we do," Cook admitted. She waited for more questions, then looked uncomfortable. "I suppose I can check, if you really need me to."

"That would be most helpful," Dr. Wiltshire agreed.

Nurse Cook didn't move to do so.

"If you could do that now," Dr. Wiltshire suggested.

"Well... I suppose." She eventually gave a shrug and left the room.

Dr. Wiltshire looked at Kenzie. "The timelines may be a lot broader than they would like us to think. Things don't move quickly in a place like this. Even at a hospital, it may be an hour before someone answers a call, if it is a busy time or the patient had been bothering them with trivial things."

"And he was 'agitated' earlier. They might have waited, hoping he'd go back to sleep on his own, rather than having to deal with him."

"Would you mind making note of the ambient temperature...?"

Kenzie went to Dr. Wiltshire's medical bag and found the electronic thermometer. She turned it on and waited. The room was warm, as she had previously noted. Mr. Sexton's body temperature would not fall very quickly in that environment. She opened her notebook and wrote down the date and place, Stanley Sexton's name, the ambient temperature, and a couple of other notes they would want to include when they did up their site report.

Kenzie looked at the doorway. She had expected Nurse Cook to be back with the information about the time that Sexton had pushed the call button. But so far, there was no sign of her. Had she been unable to find the information? Trying to cover it up? Maybe she had just been sidetracked by another patient or a task that only she could take care of. Dr. Wiltshire pulled off Mr. Sexton's bedding to examine him in situ. Kenzie looked him over, but nothing jumped out at her as being wrong. He was dressed in light pajamas and had been covered by a sheet and a single thin blanket. Kenzie would have been too warm to sleep there with even just the blanket.

There were no significant marks or bruises on Sexton's face or neck. Dr. Wiltshire pulled up his shirt to inspect his torso, then let it fall back into place. Kenzie moved closer. She indicated the mark on Sexton's arm.

"He's had an IV recently."

Wiltshire nodded his agreement. There was an IV pole nearby, though no bags hung on it.

"If there is any possibility that this is an angel of death," Kenzie murmured, looking toward the door to make sure that Nurse Cook didn't walk in on the conversation unexpectedly, "then we should take the opportunity to check for insulin tonight. Before it's had a chance to break down."

"Yes. Good thinking. And screen for any other popular drugs used in mercy killings."

Kenzie nodded. "Yeah." She thought about one of Zachary's previous cases. They had thought at first that it might be an assisted death or mercy killing, but it had turned out that just the opposite was true. The perpetrator had wanted the victim to experience as much pain as possible before her death. People's motives could be very complex.

Nurse Cook returned to the room with a young man, also a nurse. Kenzie took a couple of steps toward him to confirm that he was, in fact, Jason Munro, the one who had discovered Sexton in distress and had gone for help. He looked extremely uncomfortable. He glanced back at the door as if measuring whether he had the time to run for it. But how far would he get if he ran? Champlain House undoubtedly had his address and would have cops there waiting for him to explain himself. He shifted his feet back and forth and looked at Nurse Cook but didn't meet her eyes.

Nurse Cook's face was stiff, her lips pressed together in a long, thin, downward curving line and her eyes hard and unwavering.

"This is Nurse Jason," she said unnecessarily. "He would like to revise his story." She turned her stony eyes on him and waited.

Jason gulped. He was still eyeing the door and trying to decide how to get out of the fix he was in.

Dr. Wiltshire tried to meet Jason's eyes, giving him an encouraging smile. "Jason? I'm glad you were so quick to come forward so that we can find out the truth of the situation here. It's essential that we get the real story about what happened tonight, even if you are embarrassed about it or think that we will be upset. I assure you that it will be nothing compared to what would happen if you continue to obfuscate the truth."

Jason gave a mute nod.

"Did Mr. Sexton press the call button tonight?" Dr. Wiltshire prompted, hoping to get the ball rolling.

Jason shook his head. "No. That isn't the way it happened."

"Ah. Why don't you tell me, then, how it did happen?"

"He didn't press the call button. It was Lola. She was barking."

"And you came in here to see what the matter was or to take her away or quiet her down?"

"Not at first." He swallowed and looked at Nurse Cook.

"I see. To begin with, you let it go, hoping that she would quiet down on her own."

"Yeah. I mean, yes, sir. Sometimes she barks. She sees a squirrel outside, or she wants to play. Or, I don't know, she just likes to hear the sound of her own voice."

"It's not the first night that you've heard her bark."

"No. Sir."

"How long did you wait before going to see what she was barking about?"

Jason's eyes rolled up toward the ceiling, thinking about it.

"Tell them the truth," Nurse Cook warned.

Jason shrugged with one shoulder. "I don't really know. That's the truth.

I was trying to ignore her. I didn't look at the time; I just tried to block her out."

"Wasn't her barking bothering anyone else?"

"No. No one had woken up. The other staff... they're used to hearing her bark now and then. And she wasn't barking constantly. Just one or two barks every now and then."

"Go on."

"When I went in and looked to see what she was barking about, that's when I found Mr. Sexton dead." He stared at a spot on the rug in front of him.

"He was already dead when you went in there," Dr. Wiltshire stated.

"Yes."

"He wasn't incoherent, trying to communicate something to you."

"No. Well—no."

Kenzie pursed her lips, wondering what else he was trying to hide. They didn't yet have the full story. He was still trying to hold something back. Dr. Wiltshire recognized this as well.

"He was dead," he said slowly. He raised his brows at Nurse Cook. "He has been dead for some time."

She rubbed her head, tense fingers showing that she was just barely keeping herself in check. If they weren't there, she suspected Cook would have flown at the young man, berating him at least, if not giving him a few sharp thwacks with a ruler or whatever else she might have handy.

"How long?"

"We will have to determine that. It would be good if we had a witness who could narrow the time frame."

"I don't know," Jason admitted. "I hadn't been in there all night."

"Not at all?" Kenzie asked in surprise. She was sure that protocol must suggest checking in on each patient at least a couple of times a night. Then again, they were in the independent care unit. Maybe the residents were allowed to just sleep all night without any observation.

"I checked in on him after he went down to sleep," Jason said. "He'd been shouting at everyone, angry about something that didn't make any sense. Kept saying that he was right and trying to sell us bears. Don't ask me. He was... delusional. I don't know if he was seeing things or just having trouble finding the right words. Sometimes, dementia patients, they mislabel things, and if you can't figure out what they meant to say, they just get more upset because you can't understand them."

"Did Mr. Sexton have dementia?" Dr. Wiltshire beat Kenzie to the question.

Jason said "yes" at the same time as Nurse Cook said "no." Everybody stood there, looking at each other. Nurse Cook gave Jason a warning look and spoke.

"Mr. Sexton was not diagnosed with dementia. But he had shown some behavioral changes over the last couple of weeks. That is not uncommon. I don't know if he would have eventually been diagnosed with dementia or not. And clearly, we will never know now."

"So..." Dr. Wiltshire addressed his words to Jason. "Where did this story about Mr. Sexton trying to say something but being incoherent come from? Was that pure invention?"

"No," Jason said defensively. "That really happened. I said I checked in on him. He was quiet and Lola was on the bed with him. But he wasn't asleep. His eyes were open and he was making noises. Like... animal noises. Not words."

"Was he moving around? Restless?"

"No. Just laying there, rigid, his hands kind of, up here." Jason demonstrated a posture with both hands raised to chest level, fingers forming stiff claws.

"And did you ask for help?"

"No." Jason was looking at the floor again, avoiding Nurse Cook's wrath. "I just let him be. Figured... at least he was being quiet, and I didn't want to have to deal with more swearing and paranoid crap."

"You should have talked to another nurse if you weren't sure what to do," Nurse Cook said. "You should have called the doctor to find out whether to call for an ambulance or if there was some medication he needed. You don't just leave a distressed patient alone in his bed."

And even though he had known that Lola was in with Sexton, a patient in a clearly altered state of consciousness, he had still not looked in on him when Lola began to bark.

33

K enzie had been so caught up in the on-site visit with Dr. Wiltshire that she had completely forgotten Zachary was outside in the car waiting for her. She felt guilty about it, but he had been the one to insist upon the arrangements. And it had been nice to have someone drive her over while she woke up and not to have to worry about being out by herself when it was dark out. It wasn't like Zachary was the big tough gun-toting private eye they liked to portray on TV. He had a lot of issues and imperfections, and in a situation where they faced mortal danger, she wasn't sure she would rate his skills over hers. It was just nice not to have to drive and walk through the dark parking lot alone, feeling exposed and vulnerable.

As she walked behind Dr. Wiltshire and Carlos transporting the body on a gurney to the van, Kenzie tapped the icon with Zachary's face in her phone app.

He answered almost immediately. "Hey. How's it going?"

"Good. We're just getting ready to transport, so I'll be out in a minute."

"Great. I'll drive up."

She heard his engine start through the phone and saw his headlights come on across the parking lot. She walked around the van. "That's Zachary. He's going to take me home, then I'll grab my car and come in."

Dr. Wiltshire pushed up his glasses. "If you like, you can take a break. Have a nap. Come in a little late."

"No. I'd like to help with the initial prep. I don't usually get to be involved in all stages."

"All right. You should have told me you were going to have Zachary bring you in. You could drive back to the office with me, and I could drop you at home after work."

"No, it's okay. It was his idea; he wanted to come with me, even though it meant him sitting in the car and extra gas." Kenzie shrugged. "Just being a gentleman, I guess."

"He is a fine fellow." Wiltshire slapped Carlos on the back, indicating that they were done, and he walked around to the passenger door.

Kenzie walked over to Zachary's car and got in. It was cold outside, but there was a toasty pocket of air inside the vehicle, already heated to just the right temperature. Kenzie leaned over to kiss Zachary on the cheek. She buckled herself in and settled down into the seat and her coat, enjoying the warmth.

"Were you bored to death?"

"If I was, at least the Medical Examiner would be close by," he joked.

Kenzie smiled, happy to see him making a joke, even if it was just a minor one. It was much more natural than the tense silence between them for the last couple of days. "Yes, and I could always assist."

"You wouldn't be allowed to, would you?" he asked. "If you knew the deceased, you would have to... recuse yourself or whatever."

"I don't think there's any policy that says I would have to. It's not like a policeman investigating someone he knows. It would probably be best practice, but not a requirement."

"Well then, I feel much better knowing that."

He pulled out of the nursing home parking lot and drove back toward the house in silence.

Kenzie watched the road in front of them, but what she was thinking of in the darkness wasn't just the trip home, nor Sexton's postmortem. It was her fear that someday it *would* be Zachary on a slab. And, of course, she would not be involved with his postmortem. No matter how many autopsy photos she and Zachary had looked at together over some meal, there was no way she would be able to handle his like it was just routine.

One of her worries before they had been living together was that one day, she would return to his apartment to discover his suicide. Every time she went back, she had a little twinge of pain and tightness across her chest as she held her breath and opened the door. Especially on those blacker days. There had been one time...

"Kenzie?"

Kenzie looked over at Zachary, suddenly aware that he had said something, but she had been too lost in her own dark thoughts to hear him. She had to stop doing that. She was a happy, upbeat person. She didn't want to change into someone who was always worrying and having morbid thoughts.

"Sorry? I guess I was thinking about the case."

"I shouldn't interrupt you. I was just wondering if you wanted to get something to eat. When we get home, or a drive-through or coffee shop on the way?"

"No. I'm not hungry yet. I'll get something at the office. Like you say, Dr. Wiltshire will probably bring in some donuts or pastries. Bad for me, but..."

"When you get up that early, you burn off extra calories. So really, you need them," he offered.

Kenzie nodded. "Yeah. Exactly." She smiled

He didn't say anything for a few beats. His expression was still serious, his jokes delivered deadpan. He glanced over at her, saw her watching him.

"Are you okay?" he asked.

"Yeah, fine. Why?"

"Nothing. Just wondered if you were okay."

"Sure." She didn't tell him the direction of her morbid thoughts. Dwelling on his potential suicide was not the way to help keep him from sliding farther into depression. Let him think that she had just been occupied with thoughts of the new case.

"How was he? Or she?" Zachary asked, with a jerk of his head back the way they had come. "Your... new client."

"Well, pretty dead. Certainly not feeling any pain."

"I just mean... you didn't say what kind of death it was. It wasn't anything violent? Something that upset you?"

"No. Nursing homes see a lot of deaths. It's only natural. This one was in the independent living unit, so he wasn't wasting away sick with something. And nothing violent. Just died in his own bed."

"Natural causes?"

"That will be for Dr. Wiltshire to determine."

"But, I mean, it *looked* like natural causes?"

"Yes. And I'm sure it was. But we'll need to check out all the possibilities, just like with any other unattended death."

Zachary nodded, not turning back to her as he drove. In a few more minutes, he was pulling into the parking space in front of Kenzie's house. They both got out of the car.

"Do you need anything from the house?" Zachary inquired.

"No, I have everything I need for the day. Just got to grab my baby." Kenzie indicated the garage.

"Okay." Zachary stood there as if uncertain what to say or do next. Kenzie covered the few feet between them and gave him a hug.

"Thanks for looking after me. I'll be fine the rest of the day. Just the usual stuff at the office. So you don't worry about it."

"Nothing to worry about," Zachary agreed with a shrug. As if he were the calmest, coolest guy ever. But of course he would find something to worry about. He always did.

Kenzie used her key fob to open the big garage door. She hopped into her car and smiled as the engine roared into life. It made her feel warm all over. She really did love that little car. It wasn't very often anymore that she thought about Lance Reacher, the private investigator she had known before Zachary. He had suggested that Kenzie really needed something flashier than the boring little compact she had driven then. Who cared about maintenance costs? Gas mileage? Foreign parts? Those were not the things she was thinking about when she got behind the wheel. What she was thinking of was how she loved the power of the car, the silky red paint job, and, in the summer, driving with the top down. She would pay what she had to. She had a trust fund if her salary at the medical examiner's office didn't support it.

She backed the car out. Zachary was still standing on the sidewalk, watching for her departure. Kenzie waved at Zachary as she left him behind.

On her way there, Kenzie's phone buzzed in her bag, but she ignored it. There weren't likely to be any emergencies in the few minutes it would take her to get to work. If it were Dr. Wiltshire, he could wait until she arrived. If Zachary had some last-minute concern, she could call or text him to reassure him once she was at her destination. For a few minutes, she was just going to relax.

Kenzie turned the radio up to drown out any additional buzzes from her phone.

When she arrived at the office and pulled into her reserved parking space, she pulled her bag into her lap and dug the phone out. She looked at the screen, expecting to see Dr. Wiltshire's number or Zachary's. Instead, there was a long list of missed calls, some of them Zachary's and some of them her security company or a blocked number. Kenzie knew immediately what had happened.

She swore under her breath.

She couldn't very well call the blocked number back. She tried Zachary first to try to calm him down.

There was no answer on his phone.

Kenzie hung up when it rolled over to voicemail. She dialed her security company and identified herself.

"Ah, Miss Kirsch," the male phone operator greeted after getting her passphrase and other confirmations of her identity. "Thank you for calling back. We've had a call out to your home. Everything is fine. The police and our representative are on the scene, and as far as we can tell, nothing has been harmed or stolen. But there is a male subject who claims that he lives there, and..."

"Yes. Yes, Zachary lives there. He's not a burglar. I armed the system when we left early this morning, and he must have forgotten to disarm it when he got back."

"That can happen," the man admitted. "Everybody has false alarms sometimes. There is a warning period after the system has been triggered to allow you to turn off the alarm before the police are alerted. Does your friend have the code to arm and disarm the system?"

"Yes. I haven't been able to talk to him yet. I don't know whether he panicked and forgot the code or if he just didn't notice that he'd triggered it in the first place. I'm really sorry about this."

"I'm very glad that nothing was stolen or damaged. Your system has been silenced and reset. We will have our representative confirm to the police on the scene that your friend is authorized to be there and can be left in the home...?"

"Yes, please. I'm really sorry. It won't happen again."

Although chances were, it would happen again. Kenzie had set off the alarm more than once herself; Zachary was bound to trigger it again too.

"Listen, can I add Zachary as someone authorized to talk to you to have the system reset? If anything goes wrong and he's around instead of me, he should be able to deal with it."

"We can do that, of course," he agreed politely. "I will need his full name and particulars, and we will need to set up a passphrase for him. It shouldn't take more than a few minutes."

There was a beep in her ear. Kenzie pulled the phone away from her ear to peer at the screen. There was a call incoming from Zachary.

"I'll have to call you back with that information. I need to take another call now." She hung up on the man without waiting for an answer, taking Zachary's call. "Zachary. I'm sorry. Are you okay?"

"Yes. I'm fine." He was terse, his voice clipped but toneless. Definitely upset.

"The security company will be calling to give the police the all-clear and then you can go back inside the house."

"They already have. Which is why I'm no longer in handcuffs."

The phone operator must have sent out a text or some other remote notification to his man on the scene while still on the phone with Kenzie.

"They put you in handcuffs? Zachary, I'm sorry. I never thought they would do that. I didn't even think to remind you about the alarm when we got home."

"I should have remembered. Or at least noticed that it was beeping," Zachary said with disgust. "I didn't have a clue there was a problem until the alarm started whooping full-force. If anyone in the neighborhood wasn't yet awake at six..."

"These things happen," she said, echoing what the security guy had said to her. "I've set it off before too. I'm going to get you added as a person authorized to give them the all-clear and have the system reset, okay? So that if it happens again, they'll talk to you instead of just having the police arrest you."

"That would be nice," he acknowledged, voice still tight.

"I should have thought to do it before. I don't know why I didn't."

In fact, she had thought about it, but had disregarded the need. She hadn't anticipated that Zachary would set it off when she wasn't around or that the police would react the way they had even after Zachary explained that he lived there. It was one more thing that she had thought would be better if she could just keep it under her own control.

"I am sorry," she repeated to Zachary.

"Not your fault. Well, you'll be wanting to get to work now, so I'll leave you to it..."

"You're okay?"

"I'm fine."

"Okay. We'll talk later. Have a good day..."

34

Kenzie had made notes of the things that needed to be followed up on immediately with Sexton's postmortem, calculating the rate at which he would have lost heat in the ambient temperature of the room in the nursing home and drawing blood to check for insulin. She browsed through a number of internet articles on angel of death killings and wrote down a few medications favored by nurses and doctors who killed. If Jason or one of the other nurses had had something to do with Mr. Sexton's death other than ignoring his medical needs, she wanted to know right away. They did not want to be guessing about it months later or exhuming his body to look for something else.

They proceeded to the gross examination of the body, looking for any other bruises, puncture wounds, or anything else indicating what the conditions had been like at Champlain House. Like Cartwright's body, the gross examination was unremarkable. He had a few minor bruises like everyone got—especially people who were over eighty and tended to bruise more easily as a result.

"Hypotheses?" Wiltshire asked as he began the Y incision.

"Nurse Jason's description sounds like a stroke or a seizure. So I'm inclined to think something neurological. Of course... it could be whatever it was that Cartwright died of. They were both in the same unit, dying within days of each other, both with similar early symptoms of dementia before their deaths."

"Right," Wiltshire agreed with a nod. "Anything else?"

"Angel of death killing. Or some drug self-administered. I still find it interesting that the dog was in each of the men's rooms at the time of their death or shortly thereafter. Why? Did they call her? Did she sense something? Did something she did trigger their deaths? I haven't had any luck identifying a parasite or other condition that might have come from the dog."

"What could a dog have that would give them neurological symptoms and such a quick death?"

"I don't know... rabies? But the dog wasn't acting like it has rabies. They are supposed to be violent and aggressive."

"There have been cases where the animal has not shown signs of aggression, but has been unusually friendly. It really doesn't matter which, as long as their saliva transfers the virus from one host to the next."

"Do you think these men had rabies?"

"I doubt it. But they were showing signs of dementia, maybe delusion. The nursing staff noticed that Mr. Cartwright wasn't eating or drinking and had an IV for Mr. Sexton. Problems with drinking and swallowing are red flags for rabies."

Kenzie remembered petting and scratching the dog and letting it lick her hand. She tried to remember whether she had washed right away. Whether she had any cuts on her hands that would have allowed a virus to get into her bloodstream. She shuddered at the thought. But Wiltshire had said no, he didn't think the men had died from rabies.

Kenzie watched as Wiltshire proceeded to examine and weigh each organ. If he saw anything unusual or educational, he would point it out to Kenzie, having her examine it and asking questions to help direct her to the right answers.

The heart and lung tissue were not quite as healthy-looking as Mr. Cartwright's had been, but they still looked pretty good. They didn't find anything to show that a clot had traveled to the heart or lungs. The big vessels feeding into Sexton's heart were partially occluded with fatty deposits, but they didn't find anything to show that one of these had been the cause of his death.

In due time, Dr. Wiltshire moved from the torso to the brain. He gave Kenzie a brief nod. Now they would see whether there were any other similarities in pathology between the two latest nursing home patients.

Kenzie drew closer to watch the careful removal of the top portion of Sexton's skull to expose the brain. She and Dr. Wiltshire both bent close to examine the surface of the brain for signs of intracranial bleeding or any other obvious signs.

"This one was in his bed," Wiltshire said aloud, "so no fall or bump on the head to confuse the issue."

Kenzie nodded her agreement. Both of them moved around the table, making what observations they could.

"Some age-related shrinkage," Kenzie observed.

"Yes. But not drastic changes like you might see with Alzheimer's Disease."

Kenzie nodded. She was eager to get some samples of the brain tissue to see if it showed the same amyloid plaques as Cartwright's did. But she didn't say so. She let Dr. Wiltshire continue to direct the postmortem, going through it one step at a time, unhurried, careful not to miss anything or to jump to any conclusions.

Finally, he nodded to Kenzie. "Okay. Let's get some slides, swabs, blood and CNS samples, anything that might help point us to an answer. If this is some brain disease that we have not yet recognized, we need to get it pinned down. Is it something known or unknown? Or are we chasing after something that is not there?"

He and Kenzie worked together to gather all the samples that they could conceivably need to run.

"Can I...?" Kenzie started, indicating the microscope.

Dr. Wiltshire nodded. "Of course. Please."

Kenzie hurried over to the bench to prepare the slides and secure them to the stage of the microscope. She took a deep breath and looked through the eyepiece. It took a few moments to focus on the cells. Kenzie let out her breath in a whoosh.

"It's almost identical. Extensive amyloid plaques and tangles."

Dr. Wiltshire approached and Kenzie moved to the side to allow him to look through the eyepiece to study the sample.

"Identical," he repeated. "What are we missing here? This is not the dementia unit. These are not Alzheimer's patients. These men did not come from the same background or experience. Why would they both have plaques with no noticeable Alzheimer's Disease until a few days before death?"

"It could be a coincidence."

She could tell Dr. Wiltshire did not like the idea. "Granted. But we need to look for other explanations first."

"Something in their environment? Or it's some genetic thing and they are actually related?"

"Could be old Vermont families. Intermarriages over generations. There are genes known to be associated with Alzheimer's Disease, but none of them are great predictors. Environmental... sounds more likely. But what in the environment could have caused this pathology? There are possible links to DDT and other toxins, but this is not an area with high levels of pollutants in the air."

"And that's Alzheimer's Disease, not non-Alzheimer's amyloid plaques."

He squinted at her. "Is that what we're calling it?"

"Tentatively." Kenzie shrugged, embarrassed. She wasn't trying to name a new disease or condition, just to label the signs that they were trying to understand. It wasn't like she was writing a paper on it. Thought it might be a good idea to, once they had a better handle on what they were seeing.

"Ideas? What could be in the environment to cause the development of these plaques?"

"Do you think that they developed rapidly or slowly?" Kenzie ventured. It was something that she had been puzzling over. These were old men. The plaques could have been developing for years. Or they might have developed very quickly, like the symptoms the men had experienced before death. Was the rapid development of dementia symptoms followed by death symptomatic of how quickly the amyloid plaques were growing?

"Difficult to form any hypothesis on the limited information that we have," Dr. Wiltshire mused. "Are these the only two patients with these signs? It seems unlikely that we would find the only two men and that they would die so close together in time and space. How many of the physician-attended deaths during the last few weeks have had similar pathology? How many deaths that we may have put down to accident or natural causes and never knew they had amyloid plaques because we didn't examine the brain?

If it is slowly-developing, then why did these two men die within a week of each other? Coincidence?"

"Maybe. But I think it must be rapidly developing. And if it is…" Kenzie didn't like the conclusion this led her to. "Then everyone in that nursing home is potentially at risk. Whatever toxin or pathogen they were exposed to, everyone else in that building could also have been exposed to."

35

The very early morning made it a much longer day than Kenzie had anticipated. She was definitely lagging by the afternoon. Returning from a meeting in another part of the building, Dr. Wiltshire saw Kenzie yawning as he walked past. She smothered the yawn the best she could.

"About time for another coffee," she confessed.

"Or about time to go home. Get Julie to cover the desk for the rest of the afternoon. We can afford for you to go home. Have a nap and then enjoy the evening instead of turning into a zombie. I'm sure Zachary will be much happier if you aren't spending your entire evening trying not to fall asleep."

"I have things I should be working on."

"One of the benefits of working in the morgue is that you don't have to worry about your patients taking a turn for the worse when you are gone. You're better off catching up tomorrow when you are fresh than making mistakes because you are too tired today. You've put in your hours. So go home."

Kenzie tried not to yawn again. Just thinking about being tired was making her exhausted. And she still needed to drive home. It wasn't a long way, but she didn't want to be falling asleep at the wheel.

She sighed. "All right," she agreed. "When you're right, you're right."

She and Zachary had a more normal evening together, after Kenzie had taken a couple of hours to catch up on her sleep. She thought about Zachary doing night surveillance and how he often functioned on only a couple of hours of sleep on a regular basis. She didn't know how he did it. Kenzie had always needed her sleep to function properly. Even in medical school, she hadn't been able to pull all-nighters to study. And residency had been brutal.

Once up and bright-eyed once more, Kenzie was happy to find that she and Zachary were able to talk casually without the same level of tension that had underlaid their conversations since she had missed the couples session. There was still emotion there. She could feel it and she thought a couple of times that Zachary was close to bringing it up, but then he would look away from her again and not say anything, pretending all was normal.

They went to bed in good time even though Kenzie wasn't sure she would be able to get to sleep after her afternoon nap. She was yawning again, and if she didn't want to get thrown off her usual sleep schedule, it was important to stick to her usual bedtime and rising times.

And as it turned out, falling asleep again did not end up being a problem.

Morning was a different story. Kenzie awoke early and tossed and turned restlessly, trying to get back to sleep, unwilling to get up again so early. But her body had decided that she'd had enough sleep. Or maybe it had decided it liked getting up early the day before. She wasn't able to sleep as late as usual.

Lisa would have been shocked to see her out of bed so early in the morning. Zachary seemed slightly surprised and she saw his eyes slide to the clock to verify that she was up early, rather than his having lost track of time.

"You ready to be up already?" he asked. "Or are you sick?"

"No, I'm fine. Just couldn't sleep any more. I'll hit the shower and then we can have an early breakfast?" Kenzie's stomach was already growling. It didn't realize that she was still supposed to be asleep.

"Uh... sure." Zachary wasn't excited about breakfast, but he never was. They both enjoyed the morning ritual, seeing each other and spending a little time together before Kenzie left for the Medical Examiner's Office. But morning and food didn't go together in Zachary's world.

"You don't have to eat yet—though you probably should so that you don't forget—but I'm already hungry."

"Sure. Of course. I'll get everything ready."

When Kenzie was out of the shower and dressed, and walked into the kitchen, she saw that it was one of Zachary's distracted days. That was probably her own fault, throwing him off their usual schedule.

The coffee machine had been run. Luckily, he had remembered to put a mug under the spout, but it still sat on the counter when normally Zachary put it on the table. There was toast sitting in the toaster instead of buttered and on the table. Nothing else was ready. Kenzie busied herself with buttering her toast and putting everything on the table. Then she went back to Zachary's computer station in the living room.

"Ready to take a break?"

"Uh, yeah..." Zachary looked up from what he was reading. At least she didn't have to shake him to physically pull him from his focused state. Zachary sat back and rubbed his fingers over his eyes. "There's a story in here. I think it's to do with your case yesterday."

Kenzie looked at his computer screen. It was a news site, and the story he indicated included a large picture of Lola, with the headline "Comforting the Dying" and a caption below the picture with something about a hero dog.

Kenzie swore. "I can't believe it! Who called the media? It must have been someone at Champlain House. Can I see?"

She could have searched it up on her own phone or computer, of course, but with it being right there on Zachary's screen, she didn't even consider that. Zachary scrolled down and moved to the side so that she could read it and take over the trackpad. Kenzie read quickly through the article. It was mostly fluff, of course, but it had clearly been one of the nurses who had called the news outlet. A nurse Camille Jackson was quoted extensively, though there were brief comments from other staff as well.

"I can't believe she called the news," Kenzie muttered again. She pulled out her phone and dialed Dr. Wiltshire. She waited impatiently, and he answered after three rings.

"Kenzie. How are you doing this morning?" His voice was cautious, probably wondering if she were calling in sick or saying that she couldn't be there for some other reason related to her early morning the day before.

"I'm fine. I'll be in today," she told him to immediately assuage any concerns he had about her not being available. "I don't know if you've had a chance to see it yet, but there is a news story on the Sexton death."

"What? What does it say?"

"It's a story about the dog. How she senses who is going to die and spends extra time with them to comfort them."

Wiltshire swore. "Why didn't anyone say anything like that yesterday when we were there?"

"I don't know. I asked when I was there about Cartwright. Apparently, she was with Cartwright when they found him. I asked Nurse Ellie if Lola had spent more time with other residents who were sick or dying. She said no. Which is completely contradicted by this article. It makes a big thing of her knowing who needs her and spending time with them."

"We're going to need to go back to the possibility that the dog has something to do with their deaths. You checked for parasites?"

"I ran through some slides myself and sent others to the lab. Haven't heard anything back yet, but I couldn't see anything of concern. What about something else... what if she laid on them and hampered their breathing? Or smothered them somehow?"

"It sounds from Nurse Jason's story that Sexton was in trouble before the dog went in there. They said that he'd been showing signs of dementia or behavioral changes for a couple of weeks. He was angry, paranoid, and delusional the evening before his death. When Jason checked in on him, he was already in some kind of seizure or altered state. I don't think the dog laid on them or blocked their breathing."

"Can we get in there and get swabs from the dog? Do you think they would let us? Or get a vet to get what we need, including blood and stool samples?"

"They may object. I'll give the boys upstairs a call and see if they can get a subpoena. I think that with an article saying that the dog has been with multiple patients who have died, we would look negligent if we didn't."

"Yeah. And we're going to need to re-interview Nurse Ellie. And Jason. And whoever else over there will confirm or refute these allegations."

"Leave that to the police. They are the ones trained in interrogation. It's our job to point them in the right direction, not to do the questioning ourselves. And I think we need to know this dog's history. Where she came from, what her background is. I doubt if she's been there since she was a puppy or they would have said so. Probably some rescue!"

Kenzie could practically hear Dr. Wiltshire rolling his eyes. "Yes. Knowing something about where she came from might help us to track down any pathogens."

She and Dr. Wiltshire exchanged a few more remarks, and then Kenzie hung up. They could—and would—continue the conversation later when she arrived at the office.

"Not good news, I guess," Zachary commented.

"No. Well, even though I say that, it could still be helpful. Having the information that was 'leaked' in this article might just help us to figure out cause of death in a couple of cases."

He watched her eat, not yet tackling his own breakfast. "Are you going into work today?"

"Yes. Why?"

"It's Saturday. Didn't know whether you were on or not."

"Oh, yeah." The day of the week had completely gotten away from Kenzie. She wasn't scheduled to be on, but she had just finished telling Dr. Wiltshire that she would be in, and she didn't feel like calling him back to say she'd gotten her days mixed up. So it looked like she was going in. "Just for a while. Maybe not the whole day."

3 6

Kenzie didn't look at the ringing phone before picking it up. She was intent on what she was reading on the screen and, while she would stop reading once she was actually on the phone, she wouldn't break her focus until she absolutely had to.

"Medical Examiner's Office. Kenzie speaking," she rattled off, reading the next couple of lines on the screen.

"Mackenzie. You sound a million miles away."

Kenzie's attention snapped to the call immediately. Even though she knew the voice, she still looked at the LCD screen to confirm the number that was calling her. Walter Kirsch.

"Hi, Dad. I wasn't expecting to hear from you. Everything okay?"

"Of course. Right as rain. How are you doing?"

"Pretty good." Kenzie leaned back in her chair, closing her eyes, and thought about what to tell him. it had been a few weeks since they had talked. He was always interested in little tidbits of her life, but his attention didn't last long. And he almost always wanted something from her when he called her instead of waiting for her to call him. "Job is good. Zachary and I are..." she faltered, then recovered. He didn't actually want to know the details. It didn't matter whether she told him the whole truth or not. "Zachary and I are good. I heard from Mother the other day."

"Oh, did you? Glad you're keeping in touch." There was a pause as he considered his approach to her. "I can't believe it's already so late in the year. Seems like just a couple of weeks ago, we were heading into spring. Now it's long gone."

"Yes. Fall now and getting colder." Weather? They were going to discuss the weather? "Before you know it, it will be Christmas." Her heart gave an extra little thump. She wanted it to be Christmas already, to know that Zachary was past his worst days, but she dreaded the fact that she had to get through all of the days before Christmas as Zachary sank deeper and deeper into himself.

"Christmas was always one of my favorite times of the year," Walter boomed cheerfully. "You remember what the house would look like? All of the decorating Lisa did? It would look so good... I was afraid to touch anything. Like just stepping into the house might break some fairy spell. It was so stunning."

"*Was?*" Kenzie was surprised to hear him use the past tense. "Doesn't she still decorate?"

"Not like that, no. Maybe a wreath and a tree, but... just sedate and understated. Nothing like what she did when you girls were young."

It hurt Kenzie to think that her mother, who was always so excited about Christmas, had left that tradition behind. Kenzie remembered those magical fairyland decorations. It was like stepping into a dream or a scene in a movie. Otherworldly. But the little girls were gone. Amanda had passed away years ago, and Kenzie wasn't sure when the last time was that she had gone home for Christmas. It never appealed to her. With her parents divorced and Amanda gone, it didn't feel like she had a family anymore. It was just a house. Lisa always invited her, but Kenzie still found a reason not to go. She didn't even realize that Lisa had given up on decorating without them both there.

"That's too bad. I didn't know that. Is she... okay? Does she get sad at Christmas?"

"Of course. She's a mother. She can't get through Christmas without thinking about her family and the way things used to be. It's not your fault, Mackenzie. You're a grown woman with your own life and starting your own family. We fully expected you to. That's the way things work. Maybe one day you'll have children, and you can visit Grandma for Christmas, and she'll make the house just like she used to for you girls."

"I don't know." Kenzie didn't really see herself as the motherly type, even though she had loved and doted on and helped to raise Amanda, who had been several years younger than Kenzie. And maybe that was it. Perhaps she was afraid of getting that attached to another person and then having them die. Having them disappear from her life forever, with no hope of reunion.

She knew Zachary would like children. He confessed that he had always been more baby hungry than Bridget, who was now pregnant and expecting twins. He loved his younger siblings. Being one of the older children, he had helped to raise them. He had more parenting experience than Kenzie, and she knew he would love to have a big family of his own. But she had a career, one she didn't want to give up to have babies.

"I should probably get off the phone," she told Walter. "Things are pretty busy here today and I have a lot to do if I'm going to get home in good time tonight."

"What's got you so busy?"

"People are dying to see us," Kenzie quipped.

Walter chuckled, even though it was a line she had probably used on him a dozen times. Had they actually talked a dozen times since she had started there?

"I guess they are," Walter agreed. "Don't tell me you've had a crime spree there. Some serial killer? I understand that boyfriend of yours might be helpful there."

Kenzie had never talked to him about the serial killer case that Zachary had solved. Or about the effect it had had on his life. While it had been essential to get the man off the street and protect the community he had been preying on, the negative impact on Zachary had been significant. A year later, it was still affecting him and the relationship between him and Kenzie. The way that Walter talked about it, in a laughing, teasing manner, didn't match up with the way it had impacted Zachary's and Kenzie's lives.

"Yeah. That was a really bad thing, Dad. Not something we joke about."

He didn't say anything for a moment, taken aback by her serious tone.

"Oh. Of course it was. I didn't mean to offend you. So what's going on? Do you have more going on than usual right now? Stacking them like cordwood in the refrigerator?"

Kenzie nearly hung up on him. She didn't need the images his words brought back to mind. Even years later, she was still affected by what she had seen in the pictures taken during Amanda's overseas surgery. Images she could never wipe from her mind. She didn't usually think about them or connect them with the work they did in the morgue. They were two different worlds.

"We have had a few new bodies in. More than usual." She hoped that her clipped tone would dissuade him from asking any further details. "We have a couple of... very puzzling deaths to deal with."

"I haven't heard anything in the news. Nothing... violent, I hope?"

"No. Just strange. We need some more data before we can make a call. And speaking of which, it looks like I just got some samples back," Kenzie lied. "I have to go now. Take care, Dad. And say hi to Mother if you see her before I do."

She kept talking right over his protests and pressed down the hang-up switch, holding it there for a few minutes to ensure that the call was dropped before releasing it and putting the phone receiver down.

"Just got a call from the police," Dr. Wiltshire announced as he walked toward Kenzie's desk at a quick clip. "We've got another body I need to check out. Violent death, from the sounds of it. You've got quite a bit on the go here...?" He looked over the piles of papers and files on her desk.

Kenzie looked around at them, sighing. "Yeah. I'd like to say that this can all wait and come along with you, but I think I'd better keep trudging away here. Do you need me?"

"I'll be fine with Carlos to help transport the body. I'll send you pictures," he said in a teasing voice.

"Oh, will you? Please?" Kenzie laughed. "What happened? Do you know?"

"I don't. Not yet. Dead body in a motel room, but it doesn't sound like it was just a heart attack. Police wouldn't want to light a fire under me for that. It would be 'whenever you can' for a routine death like that. Not 'grab your bag, Doc, and get your butt over here. You'd better see this.'"

Kenzie nodded. "Sounds serious. I hope it isn't too bad."

"Well, that's the thing about our patients... they aren't going to complain about how we treat them. They're past caring about how they look. There isn't much that would shock me anymore."

"I guess not. Well, good luck."

At least if it was a violent death, it wouldn't be so hard to figure out the cause.

Dr. Wiltshire gave a nod and headed out.

There was no one from the public around, so after he had left, Kenzie pulled out her mobile radio unit and turned it on to listen to the chatter back and forth between the police and the medical examiner and anyone else being dispatched to the crime scene. Although they didn't say much over the radios, it sounded like Dr. Wiltshire was right and it was a violent death.

While she worked through her emails and reviewing reports as they came in, she kept an ear on the radio and what was happening. She heard Dr. Wiltshire arrive at the scene and begin issuing instructions. "I don't want anyone in there who doesn't have to be," he snapped. "And no one walks in without full gear. There is biological matter all over this place. Techs are on their way?"

Kenzie had heard this confirmed just a few seconds earlier on the radio and had no doubt that Dr. Wiltshire had heard it too.

"They'll be here soon, Doc," the dispatcher acknowledged. "Are you able to confirm death without damaging any evidence?"

Dr. Wiltshire grunted. "Looks like half a dozen people have already been traipsing through the blood. One more isn't going to make much of a difference."

Kenzie felt sorry for him. He hated it when people didn't follow proper protocols. Even though he wasn't a detective and didn't "own" the scene, he was still pretty possessive about any location where there were bodies. He was a stickler about every piece of biological matter getting back to the Medical Examiner's Office for processing. It sounded like that was going to be a challenge.

But of course, the motel manager or maid who had discovered the body would have walked in without realizing they were trampling through evidence. When they called the police, the officers who initially arrived at the scene would also have to walk through to confirm the victim's death. That was at least three people in and out. Hopefully, the officers would secure the scene and not let anyone else in until a representative from the Medical Examiner's Office had arrived. Still, if they were a bit green or not as well-trained as they should be, they might let other law enforcement officers in to look things over. It could end up being a three-ring circus, with half a dozen different shoe prints to be eliminated as well as Dr. Wiltshire's own.

There was a lot of routine calling back and forth to confirm orders and arrival times. Kenzie heard Dr. Wiltshire come back on over the radio. "Confirmed death of the subject. As if anyone needed me to confirm that someone with his head beaten in so severely is actually dead."

Kenzie heard one of the detectives in the background before Dr. Wiltshire released the button on his radio. "Is that cause of death?"

"You need a doctor to tell you that?" Dr. Wiltshire growled back.

Dr. Wiltshire would have to let Kenzie know the details of what had gone on at the crime scene, but she could fill most of it in herself. She set up several bins in the autopsy room for the various bags and samples to be collected when Carlos and Dr. Wiltshire returned. It would be less stressful for them if everything were ready upon their return.

She tried not to imagine what the inside of the motel room might look like. Or what the subject would look like when his remains were brought to the morgue. She could maintain her medical detachment. Pretend to herself that it was no more than a picture or a movie prop. Or one of the models or cadavers she had dealt with when she was in medical school. People who had died in their sleep. People who had wanted their bodies to be used for education when they were gone.

Those bodies were a lot easier to deal with than an eight-year-old who had fallen into the rain-swollen river or a teenage dope addict. Or so many more of the tragic things that they saw from one day to another. The nursing home deaths were, by comparison, clean and peaceful, and any lingering questions could be brushed away gently in the end. There was no one responsible for their deaths. No one she needed to help the police to catch so that the streets would be safe again.

3 8

K enzie had been right to prepare herself for her first view of the dead body. Dr. Wiltshire and Carlos brought the anonymous-looking body bag in through the delivery doors and took it straight to the morgue.

"I'm going to need bins and labels," Dr. Wiltshire advised. "And a ton of swabs and tubes. I'm going to want to get started right away—"

"Already done," Kenzie advised him briskly. "Let me know if you need something you don't see."

"Thanks, Kenzie. That's great."

"I'm free to help if you need some assistance."

Dr. Wiltshire looked at Carlos. Although he was technically available to help out, he preferred to stick to transportation and helping to move bodies when they needed another hand. He could hand Dr. Wiltshire equipment, bag evidence, and put things into the right bins for the right labs, he was already looking pretty green and Kenzie doubted if he would last.

"Yes, that would be helpful. Carlos, you can help me with the transfer to the table, and then go have a coffee."

Carlos helped Dr. Wiltshire to heft the body in its bag from the gurney to the slab, then gave a nod. "Call me if you need me. I'll be close by."

But not too close, Kenzie knew. He wasn't a full-time employee and would clock in and out as needed. It wasn't like they had enough bodies rolling in to keep him occupied with transporting them full time. Like Julie, he had contracts with several other departments as well.

Dr. Wiltshire, eager though he was to get started, waited until Carlos was out of the room before beginning to unzip the body bag. Though undoubtedly Carlos must have helped him to get the body into it in the first place.

"You heard enough to be forewarned?" Dr. Wiltshire asked, his eyes on the task at hand and not on Kenzie.

"It sounds like he took quite a beating to the face. And there was a lot of spatter."

"Yes," Dr. Wiltshire confirmed.

Kenzie waited while he opened up the outer bag and then the inner one. She had prepared herself the best she could, thinking about her job as an observer and investigator. Steeling her stomach. Putting on her "clinical" hat to observe the body dispassionately. It was going to be difficult. He would look bad. But it wasn't a family member or a friend. It was a stranger. And whatever had happened to him, he was past feeling now.

Not that she would have been able to recognize if it were a family member. The damage done to the face had wiped out any hope of making an identification by either facial recognition or dental records. They would have to employ another method. Kenzie looked down at the hands. She could start on fingerprints once Dr. Wiltshire had swabbed down the hands.

But when she looked at them, it became apparent that wasn't going to help them either. The man had been tortured before he was killed. Burns that had destroyed any fingerprints as well.

"How was he checked into the motel?" Kenzie asked. "Did he have any ID on him?"

"Police will be following up on that end of it. But... no, I gather any wallet or electronics that he had on him were stolen. It doesn't look like robbery gone wrong, but... who am I to say? The police will get back to us on anything they think might help to identify him."

"It's going to be hard. Maybe just checking his general description against missing person reports."

"That's a start. Maybe they could hire your Zachary to find out his identity."

"Yeah, I don't think that's going to happen."

Zachary had a good relationship with Campbell, and, of course, with

Mario Bowman, but many of the other law enforcement officers were not on nearly as cordial terms with him. Zachary was careful to communicate to the police whenever he was involved in a case that they had been or were investigating. He always passed on information he found if it were pertinent to the investigation. But still, many cops just didn't like PI's around out of general principles, and it didn't matter how careful he was not to get in their way.

Dr. Wiltshire began by removing the clothing still on the body. Kenzie helped in silence, removing or cutting away each article of clothing and inspecting them for what trace evidence might need to be processed. Hair, fiber, bloodstains or other biological materials. They laid each item out individually, assigned them evidence numbers, and read the inventory aloud for the autopsy transcription.

The victim was male, white, with dark hair and brown eyes, and was of medium height and build. He had a sizable port-wine birthmark on the outer side of one thigh. Wiltshire took all his measurements and carefully logged them.

"What would be your age estimate?" he drilled Kenzie.

She looked over the body. Good muscle mass. A bit of a belly, but not enough that it would be noticed when he was dressed. No age spots or wrinkles in the neck or places an older man was likely to get wrinkles—all in all, relatively young.

"Maybe thirty," she said, "I don't think as old as thirty-five."

He nodded. They would do other tests to try to determine age, but the visual inspection was important. They inspected the body thoroughly for any trace, then carefully washed the body.

"Body is unremarkable," Dr. Wiltshire said. "I don't see any injuries or signs of disease on the torso or extremities. Everything seems to be confined to the face and hands."

Kenzie frowned, thinking about that. Wiltshire raised an eyebrow. "You have a thought?"

"He wasn't beaten up?" She touched his ribcage, looking for any peri-mortem bruising or sign of broken ribs. "It seems to me that if you're going to burn someone's fingers and beat their face in with a baseball bat—or whatever he was beaten with— that there would probably be a struggle. He must have been restrained either manually or mechanically. There are no defensive wounds, no sign that he took any blows to the body to subdue him."

Wiltshire nodded. "True. He must have been restrained."

They both examined his wrists, ignoring the burned flesh of his hands. Kenzie shook her head. "Some faint bruising, but I don't think there are ligature marks. Maybe it will darken in a few hours and we'll be able to see how he was held down."

"We'll do a tox screen too. He might have been given something to sedate him."

"And *then* torture him? Wouldn't you get your information from him before sedating him instead of trying to rouse him enough to get a coherent answer after?" Kenzie shook her head, trying to sort it out. "And if they sedated or restrained him, then why destroy his face like that? That's rage. Don't you think?"

"Maybe, maybe not. You may be jumping to conclusions too quickly."

"You have another theory?"

"I do," he agreed, but didn't tell her what it was.

Kenzie sighed and they continued.

"Let's get x-rays," Dr. Wiltshire said. "I want to see the damage to the skull and to confirm that there are no other broken bones before we start on the head."

39

Kenzie looked at the clock on the wall. She knew it was going to be late. Dr. Wiltshire hadn't headed out to pick the body up until the afternoon, and they had been processing it for a couple of hours.

He saw her look at the clock and glanced at the face himself. "Why don't you head home? I can finish up here."

"I should stay until it's done. And help you to move him to cold storage."

Wiltshire shrugged. "You need to take time for yourself and your family when you can get it. I've been handling dead bodies for years; this one won't be hard to wrangle. Go home. Get a good rest. Take Sunday off. We'll send out samples for processing Monday morning."

"You're sure?"

"I'm sure, Kenzie. I won't be here much longer. We can't send samples out for testing until Monday. You're not going to miss anything earth-shattering."

"Well... okay. Are you hungry? Do you want me to grab you something from the machine?"

"No. I'll hit a restaurant after I'm done. Those sandwiches are atrocious. Somebody should be autopsying *them* to see what they died of."

Kenzie grinned. "They are pretty bad," she agreed.

"Get on your way. I'll see you Monday morning."

"Shoot me an email if you have anything particular you want to be done when I get here."

"I will."

Kenzie cleared away her files and got ready to go. She would pick up food on the away home so she didn't have to make anything. But then she remembered that Zachary hadn't eaten what she bought the last time she had done that. She hadn't checked with him first, which was the sensible thing to do. She didn't like to call him when she was late getting home, because it just emphasized the fact that she was away from him rather than being home. If she just went straight home without talking to him, then his first contact with her was when she was home, which was what they both wanted. It just felt kinder for some reason. No extra anxiety as he waited, wondering if something had happened to her on the way.

But that wouldn't solve the supper problem. Kenzie picked up her phone and hit the icon with Zachary's picture on it as she walked to her car.

"Kenzie."

"Hi. I know I'm late. I'm on my way now. I was going to stop to pick up some takeout on the way home. What do you feel like?"

"Uh... whatever you want to get is fine."

"But what do you feel like? Chinese? Burgers?"

"Either one."

"Pizza?"

"Sure."

"You're not being helpful. So you're going to eat whatever I bring home?"

He didn't answer at first, then finally agreed. "Yeah. A bit."

"You need to eat more than a bit. You should talk to your doctor about your lack of appetite. Maybe there's something else he can—"

"I've already tried everything else, Kenz."

She knew that he had been through a lot of different protocols, from the time that he'd been just ten years old. He probably had tried pretty much everything on the market. And switching meds was not just a simple change from taking pill A each day to taking pill B. Many of the drugs, he would have to wean off. Get a baseline. Maybe have to have hospital supervision because of the danger of suicide. Then start on the new medication. Wait for weeks for it to reach full efficacy. Then determine whether the benefits outweighed the adverse side effects. Adjust, wait, adjust again, wait some more. It could take months to get him stabilized again. If they could.

"Yeah, I know," she sighed. "Well, I'll grab something, then, and I'll be home soon."

"Do you want me to order in, so you don't have to stop somewhere? You can just come straight home."

"Faster if I stop for something. And then we don't have to pay delivery fees. Unless... you need me home sooner. It should only take ten minutes."

"I'm fine. Ten minutes isn't going to make any difference."

"Okay. See you soon, then."

Kenzie felt like Chinese, and Zachary usually ate a good amount of that, so she picked up their favorite dishes. That took more than ten minutes like getting a burger or pizza would, but she thought the benefits were worth it. She texted Zachary while she was waiting so that he wouldn't be worried.

They had a nice meal. Things seemed to be mostly back to normal, though there were a few times when the conversation became stilted and she wondered whether it was because he was distracted or that he was thinking about her failure to show up for their couples therapy and whether he could trust her. Which wasn't really fair, since there were plenty of times when he had forgotten about things she had asked him to do. And she had always forgiven him. Eventually.

Zachary put on an old movie, but Kenzie had a feeling that neither of them was paying close attention to it. Zachary had his computer in his lap, and it looked like work, rather than checking his personal email or social networks, which was what Kenzie was doing on her phone. She just needed to make sure she hadn't missed anything, and then she would turn her phone screen off and put it away so she could focus on the movie and Zachary. He was busy anyway.

Skimming through her unread email messages, Kenzie saw that there was one from her father. She clicked it and checked the time. It had been sent after she had talked to him. Probably this was the hit, the real reason he had called her. She read through the message and snorted.

Zachary looked at her, eyebrows up, mouth quirked into a half-smile. "What was that?"

"Is everybody in Vermont going to this masquerade ball?"

He looked blank. "Uh... my guess would be no. What masquerade ball?"

"There's a fundraiser thing. I guess all the bigwigs are going to be at it. The one my mom called to ask about?"

"Oh yeah. You're not going to go?"

"Not if I can help it. I don't like these things. They're just a lot of posturing and hot air. I'd rather write a check than to have to shake everyone's hands and listen to them prattling on about their concerns."

"And who else?"

"What?"

"You said everyone in Vermont. So I assume there's at least one other person you know who is going and wants you to go too."

"Yeah. My dad."

"Also because it is for kidney research?"

Kenzie considered that. Her dad was, of course, interested in raising money for kidney research. But he was more interested in changing the political landscape, making changes to transplant legislation, and making high-power political contacts. If he wanted her to be at the ball, he wanted to show her off or make introductions for some reason.

"He doesn't say," she told Zachary.

"Maybe he's just going to support your mom."

"I don't think so. They are still good friends, but he doesn't do things just to support other people. Not since Amanda died, anyway."

Zachary slowly closed the lid of his laptop. "Things changed after that?"

"I don't know if things changed, or if the way I saw him did. Or maybe he was so shattered when she died that he decided he wasn't getting emotionally involved again. But after that... he was a lot more distant. It's not surprising that he was more distant from me, because of the difference in our foundational beliefs... he and I had a falling out. But I've seen it with others too. He doesn't get together with my mom like he used to, and when he does, it's more like a chore. He's not... open to her like he used to be. Even when they first got divorced, it wasn't because they fought or didn't love each other anymore. They were just on different trajectories. Interested in pursuing different things. At least, that's what they told me. But maybe it was all a bunch of crap."

"And it must have affected you pretty deeply."

"Their divorce?" Kenzie didn't offer that she hadn't even known about it when they got a divorce. They were already leading very separate lives. All that had been left was the division of their property.

"No, I mean when your sister died. It must have been pretty horrible for you."

"It was." Kenzie snuggled into Zachary's side and he put his arm around her. "It totally changed my life. Her dying and... everything that happened around that. That's when I decided I was going back to school. To go into medicine."

He nodded as if it were perfectly normal for her to decide to become a doctor after losing her sister to kidney disease. But he didn't know all the details. And there was the fact that she had gone in with a focus on death and forensic investigation rather than living patients. That wasn't normal. Plenty of people went into medicine to save the people who represented the loved ones they had lost. Not so many went into it to track down killers, whether human or pathogen.

40

onday morning, Kenzie went through all the work that Dr.
Wiltshire had done on the body from the motel, noting the
samples he had taken, the tests he wanted to be performed,
and any other questions or concerns that he wanted to follow up on. She
played back the recording of the postmortem, jumping to the point when
she had left, and then listening to the items he had dictated, and not the
silence in between. It wasn't quite the same as finishing the autopsy with
him, but it was pretty close.

She applied labels and sent the various packages out to the labs where
they would be processed. While it would have been nice to be a part of one
of the big cities where they could do a lot more of the processing in-house,
that wouldn't have afforded her the same opportunities as working for Dr.
Wiltshire, where she could learn at his feet and get hands-on experience. As
a tech or receptionist for a big medical examiner's office, she wouldn't have
been able to do those things.

Dr. Wiltshire was later than usual getting into the office. Which might
have had something to do with the fact that he was still catching up on
sleep. Or he might have had an early meeting he hadn't mentioned to her.

She was well into her desk work when Dr. Wiltshire arrived. He nodded
and greeted her cordially, as usual. "Feeling better today?"

"Bright-eyed and bushy-tailed," Kenzie told him. "It was good to just take yesterday off."

"Glad to hear it. You needed a break. And you've started in on our new guest?"

Kenzie nodded and summarized what had been sent out and the status of his dictation.

"I was thinking about how we're going to identify him," she confessed. "No face or teeth. No fingerprints. No tattoos, though he does have a large birthmark that might help. We can't just rely on missing person reports. We don't even know where he is from. He was checked into a motel; he could be from another city or state, even another country. And unless someone is looking for him *here*, we don't have a lot of leads on identifying him."

"The police are doing what they can. We've ordered DNA and we can hope that it triggers a match in the offender database."

"I was reading about this forensic artist out in Montana..."

"Given the state of his skull, I'm not sure we could ever reconstruct a face for our latest John Doe."

"She doesn't use bone structure. She uses DNA."

Dr. Wiltshire had been looking toward his office. He turned back to look at Kenzie, frowning. "She uses DNA to do what?"

"To do forensic DNA phenotyping. Using the genes to construct a picture of the victim. They do it for unknown suspects too. In this case, we'll at least be able to tell her hair and skin tone without her going from the DNA."

"That can't be very accurate."

"She does some great work. I've been looking at their website. Hang on, let me show you some of the pictures." Kenzie quickly typed the URL for EvPro into her browser and brought the site up again. "Look at this... here are some examples of the pictures she generated and the actual subject."

There were various samples, ranging from the criminals they had caught to the victims they had identified and blind tests for demonstration purposes. Dr. Wiltshire lowered his glasses and looked at the screen as she showed him the comparisons.

"Obviously, they are only going to put the best matches on their website, but these *are* remarkable."

"Some of them, she generated several pictures, you can see the others if you click..." Kenzie demonstrated, fanning out a stack of pictures on the screen so that Dr. Wiltshire could see the portfolio of faces that the artist had created, with varying ages, weights, and hair or facial hair styles.

"Amazing. I had no idea that our DNA science was to the point that we could do this."

"The website says that they are the only company that has established protocols for epigenetic data as well as genetic data. So they can more accurately predict age, diet, and other background factors that help to produce a better representation."

"That can't be established science."

"Not established, no. Cutting edge. Experimental, maybe. But they seem to be able to produce a really good product." Kenzie raised her eyebrows in a question. "What do you think?"

"There is probably a pretty hefty sticker price."

"Well, there is, but it's not that much more than we would pay for other tests. And if it will allow us to identify a subject that we wouldn't otherwise be able to..."

"It would have to go up the chain for approval. Why don't you find out what you can? Talk to this artist. Find out what the options are, how long it would take, what their match rate is like. Something that we can present to the detectives in charge of the case to show that it's a reasonable expense. Then if they want to pursue it with their sergeant..."

Kenzie nodded. It would take time to work its way up the chain of command to either get a yes or a no. It would be best to get started on it right away before the case went cold. "Sure. I'll find out more. They'll have brochures and presentations too, I'm sure."

"New technology is always a hard sell. Don't be disappointed if you don't get it in this case. We'll probably have to present it as a possibility on several different cases before they decide it's well enough established that they'll risk it."

Kenzie nodded. While she wanted to see if forensic DNA phenotyping would work, and this was a perfect case to try it out on, she would have to be patient. Sometimes it seemed like the cops she worked with were back in the dark ages as far as the technology was concerned.

Dr. Wiltshire went on to his office to start on his day's work, and Kenzie clicked through screens to find the contact information for EvPro. There wasn't anything about their artist on the website, so she would have to go through the main switchboard. Kenzie called the company and explained to the young woman who answered the phone what she was looking for.

"That would be Micah Miller," the receptionist told her politely. "I'll put you through. If she doesn't answer, please leave a message. She doesn't like to be interrupted, but she will return calls."

Kenzie waited while the phone rang through. Maybe she wasn't going to get to talk to the artist after all. Until she wasn't busy, whenever that was.

The phone rang several times and there was a click. Preparing a message in her head, Kenzie was surprised to hear a live voice rather than a voicemail greeting.

"Micah here."

"Oh. Micah. Hi. I asked the receptionist who does the forensic DNA phenotyping in your company, and she put me through to you."

"Yes," Micah agreed briskly. "That's me. Are you familiar with what forensic DNA phenotyping is?"

"I'm a doctor, and I read through the information on your website. So I get the basics."

"Great. What's your name and email address?"

"Uh..." Kenzie was surprised at the request. She faltered for a moment before giving Micah Miller the details.

"I'll send you an intake package," Micah promised. "What evidence do you have? Blood?"

"Whatever you need. I work with the medical examiner's office."

"Fresh body? Not a cold case?"

"Yes."

"Okay. That sounds good. I'll need as much background on the subject as you can give me. Even stuff that seems irrelevant. Every little bit can help me to generate a better picture for you."

"I will. It's just... I don't know yet whether we'll have the approval to use you. I wanted to ask some questions about the cost, time turnaround, match rate, things like that. So I can present a case."

Micah let out an impatient breath. "You'll find all of that in the intake package."

"Okay... can I ask if you're the artist, the person who actually does the pictures?"

"The computer generates an initial composite, which I then alter based on different possibilities for hairstyles, dress, that kind of thing.

And then I render them with colored pencils so that they look more lifelike."

"Are you the only one in the company who does it?"

She could hear Micah typing in the background and wondered if she had already lost interest in the conversation and was moving on with something else while she tried to get Kenzie off the phone.

"Why do you want to know?" Micah asked.

"Well... just curiosity. I was looking at the pictures on the company's website, and I wondered whether you do all of them or whether you have a pool of artists."

More keyboard tapping. Kenzie closed her eyes and rubbed the back of her neck, waiting for Micah's response.

"The reason my name and information are no longer on the website is that I have been targeted in the past," Micah said. "I don't want to be the bulls-eye for everyone my pictures helped to put behind bars."

"Oh. I never even thought of that."

"I see your name on the medical register in Vermont and listed as a staff member at the Medical Examiner's Office."

She'd looked that up pretty quickly. "Yeah. I'm not a stalker, I promise," Kenzie laughed.

"That's exactly what you would say if you were."

"But you can see from my credentials that I am not."

"I can see that you've assumed the identity of someone at the Medical Examiner's Office, anyway. I'll call you back."

Kenzie looked down at her phone and saw that Micah had disconnected. She shook her head at Micah's abrupt manner and looked at her screen to determine her next task for the day. A few seconds later, the main line started ringing. Kenzie looked at it, but it wasn't the caller ID for EvPro in Montana.

"Medical Examiner's Office, Kenzie speaking."

"Yes, I'd like to speak to Dr. Wiltshire."

Kenzie raised her brows at the familiar voice. "Hello, Micah."

"Hi. So I guess you are who you say you are."

"I am," Kenzie agreed. "Do you still want to speak to Dr. Wiltshire?"

"I don't think there's any need to bother him."

"What number are you calling me from?" Kenzie asked curiously. "That's not even a Montana area code, is it?"

"With cell phone plans now, you don't need to live in the area that your phone number is in. I got an out-of-state number to make it more difficult for people to identify me. For cases like this when someone is asking too many questions."

She really was paranoid.

"I'm sorry for asking too many questions. I was just very interested in what it is that you do. All those pictures on the website... if all of them are yours, you have certainly been involved in a lot of cases, and your phenotypes are very lifelike. I can see how helpful they would be in narrowing down suspects and identifying victims."

"Thanks. I'm sorry for being so suspicious, but... they broke into my house, attacked me, kidnapped me, put me in the hospital. I can never let my guard down."

Kenzie blew out her breath in a whistle. She knew a little bit about what kind of effect an experience like that could have on a person. Zachary had not been the same person since his kidnapping. He tried, but he wasn't the same. Someone could argue that he should have been tougher because of the traumas he'd been through as a juvenile and not have been so affected by it. But it had brought to light a lot of bad stuff he'd previously been able to bury.

"I'm sorry you've had to go through all of that."

"Thanks. I am the only artist with the company. All the phenotyping that you see for the past three-plus years is mine. I'm a forensic scientist as well. One of the lucky few who can combine both art and science in my job."

"You do an amazing job of it. I'm very impressed."

"Tell me about your case," Micah suggested, sounding more relaxed and willing to talk with her.

"We have a victim who needs to be identified. Checked into a motel using a pseudonym, no ID or credit card. Severe injuries to the face, so we can't identify him by facial recognition or dental match. Tortured before he was killed, no recoverable fingerprints."

"A good case for phenotyping. You can give me a lot of the features; I only have to do the facial structure."

"I guess so, yeah."

"You can tell me hairstyle and color, age, height and weight, skin tone, how he dressed. Normally I don't have those details and have to get them from the genome or epigenome, or to hypothesize based on where the body was found, cultural background, that kind of thing."

"Right. We do know all of that already."

"In fact, you might be able to get an ID even though you don't have his face. Once a missing person report shows up."

"I figure from the fact that he was staying in a motel that he might be from out of town or even farther afield. So we might not ever see a missing person report, even if one is filed."

"Well... I've sent you the introduction and intake file, so have a look through there, show it to your guys, and if you get approval to go ahead, fill it all out and send me some blood."

"I'll do that. Thanks for your time, Dr. Miller."

"Micah. You're welcome. Look forward to working with you if the expense is approved."

Again, Micah hung up without an actual goodbye. Kenzie shook her head, bemused, and checked her email inbox for the package.

41

T hings were pretty quiet the rest of the week. Kenzie caught back up on her pending projects, and nothing untoward happened at work or at home. It was Zachary's week for individual therapy, so she didn't have to be there. She felt like she was on top of everything.

"Did you put a rush on the virology for Mr. Cartwright?"

Kenzie looked up from her work. Dr. Wiltshire stood in front of her desk, looking down at his tablet, puzzled.

"No..." Kenzie frowned, shaking her head. "Did you want me to? I didn't think there was any need to expedite it... I know they're pushing you to make a finding, but I didn't know you wanted it rushed."

"No, I didn't. I'm just surprised to see results back already. The lab is always backed up. Someone must have put a flag on it for some reason, because I never see results back this quickly unless it's a high-profile case with a rush on it and feds standing around with their hands out."

Kenzie chuckled at the mental picture. "So was there anything interesting? Is it all of the virology, or only the blood?"

"I don't even see the bloodwork. Just the later test for the brain tissue."

Kenzie straightened, bracing herself for whatever the tests showed. Helpful or another dead end? She laced her fingers together, waiting. "Well...?"

Dr. Wiltshire grinned. He was clearly enjoying drawing it out, making Kenzie wait for the punch line.

"Well, let's see here..." He tapped his screen. "I'm always all thumbs operating this thing..."

Which Kenzie knew wasn't true. He needed a hand getting something straightened out every now and then, but he was actually pretty good at it most of the time. He was just teasing her.

"Why don't you give it to me?" she suggested, putting her hand out. "I'm sure I could figure it out."

He laughed. His eyes started scanning back and forth and he read through the results of the report he had opened. Kenzie was quiet, waiting.

"Remarkably clean, considering his age and the fact that he's dead. The blood-brain barrier did what it was supposed to, keeping invaders out of the brain."

"So, nothing?"

"There was one virus in the brain tissue. An active infection, from what they could tell."

"Great!" Kenzie felt like punching the air in celebration. "Maybe that's our answer. Was it one of the herpesviruses?"

"Yes and no."

"How is it yes and no? Either it's a herpesvirus or it's another virus family."

"It is a herpesvirus. But not one of the ones that you suggested. Human Herpesvirus 4."

"HHV-4," Kenzie said slowly. She tried to remember if she had read anything in the studies she had looked at about HHV-4 having anything to do with amyloid plaque production. But she didn't remember seeing it in any of the medical journals. So had they made a new discovery, or were they on the wrong track? "That's Epstein Barr Virus, isn't it? The one that causes mono?"

Dr. Wiltshire, still looking at the report, nodded. "Apparently, that isn't the full story, though."

"Was there another pathogen?" Sometimes it took several viruses together to take down a person's immune system. And that's how viruses mutated, one virus borrowing a sequence from another virus present in the same host. Recombining to form something that hadn't been seen before, something that no one had an immunity to.

"No, not that they have mentioned, but they asked me to call them after reviewing the report to discuss further details."

"If there were further details to be discussed, then why didn't they put them into the report?"

"That, Dr. Kirsch, is an excellent question."

4 2

O f course, it figured that the lab tech that had done the virology was not available to talk to them. Dr. Wiltshire and Kenzie both tried several methods to get ahold of him, but neither of them was having any success. The receptionist wouldn't explain why he wasn't available, and Kenzie wondered if he had left on vacation or called in sick since writing his report.

"We'll just have to wait," Dr. Wiltshire said. "We weren't expecting to have these results today anyway, so if we have to wait a day or two to find out what he wanted to discuss, then we're no further behind."

"I know, but it must have been something important if he wanted you to call him back."

"Can't be helped. If it was important, maybe he'll have left a message for one of his coworkers to call us. Until then, we'll just have to do a bit of our own research and hypothesize about whether this had anything to do with Mr. Cartwright's amyloid plaques or his death. Or both."

"It must have something to do with it. If he had an active infection when he died."

"That's a leap in logic. If you have the flu and I shoot you through the heart, it isn't the flu that killed you."

"Well, no, but in this case, when we can't find anything else..."

"You're assuming a connection that we can't just assume. It might have something to do with the cause of death, but it might not."

"Okay. I'll do a bit more research. But I've got other files to work on too."

Kenzie's phone chimed once, and she checked the screen for the notification. An email from Zachary. He didn't often email or text her during the day, so she opened her phone to have a quick read and make sure nothing was wrong.

The subject line 'you were right' didn't tell her anything other than that he had finally noticed the obvious. She opened the email.

Everyone and his dog is going to the masquerade ball

There was a snippet from a news article with a picture of Lola the dog. Kenzie tapped the link. The news article appeared in her browser.

It was a puff piece about how the hero dog, Lola, had been invited to attend the premier social event of the fall, along with the likes of... there was a list of minor local celebs who had RSVP'd that they would be in attendance.

It went on to describe the various charities that funds were being raised for, the prevalence of kidney disease and prominent people who had died from it, and so on. Kenzie closed the news article.

Her email back to Zachary was short.

Oh, brother

Kenzie's desk phone rang. She looked over at it to see that Dr. Wiltshire was calling and picked it up immediately.

"Hello?"

"Kenzie, can you join me in the boardroom? They've finally got their ducks in a row at the lab, and it isn't the tech who will be talking to us; it is the Executive Director. And some of his staff."

"What's going on?"

"I don't know yet. But I think we're about to find out."

"I'll see you in a minute."

The boardroom was closer to her desk than to his, so she beat him there. They both put down their notepads and pens. Dr. Wiltshire had a printed copy of the lab's report. He checked his notes and, putting the phone on the table into speaker mode, dialed the lab and gave his name. In a few minutes, they could hear the background hum of voices as they were transferred into a meeting room at the lab.

Dr. Wiltshire introduced himself formally and added Kenzie's name. Then the Executive Director, a Pascal Savage, gave his name and position and the names of a few of the techs or assistants who were there to back him up.

"Dr. Wiltshire, we'd like to know a little more about the patient whose samples you sent us," Savage explained. "These results were very unusual, and we need to track the source of the infection if we can."

"I know we don't usually look for HHV-4 in the brain," Dr. Wiltshire agreed. "What exactly are you looking for? This was an old man; maybe his immune system was compromised. I think that while we don't expect to see it crossing the blood-brain barrier, it's not unheard of."

It was like they were both feeling each other out, trying to figure out how much the other already knew. Both trying to keep their own information private.

"This wasn't a normal HHV-4 virus," Savage said reluctantly.

"What does that mean?"

"It was a variant we haven't seen before."

43

D r. Wiltshire leaned forward, putting his elbows on the table.
"A variant?"
"We have been analyzing it. It isn't like any version of HHV-4 we've seen before. We're concerned that if this infection is in the wild, and you're seeing people die from it, we could end up with an epidemic on our hands. No one will be immune to it. We don't know what its spread might be since this is the first time that we've seen it. This victim, you say he was an elderly man? What kind of a situation was he living in? Was he a farmer or a veterinarian?"

"A farmer. No. He's living in a nursing home. He's been there for several years, right Kenzie? He wasn't a new resident."

"No. He'd been there for a few years. As far as I know, he didn't go out anywhere. We can ask the nursing home whether he went anywhere or had any visitors that he might have caught this virus from."

"Could it have been dormant?" Dr. Wiltshire suggested. "Something that he picked up years ago before he moved to the nursing home?"

"I think if this was an old virus, we would have seen it before," Savage countered. "We've been looking through databases and other media, and we can't find any suggestion of it having been seen before."

"Maybe *really* old?" Kenzie suggested, "from when he was a kid or a young man? We don't know what exposures he might have had that far back. There wouldn't be any records showing you the genome of this virus. Some herpesviruses go into dormancy and then pop up again years later when the patient is stressed or there is some other activating trigger. Maybe triggered by the presence of another herpesvirus. Did you find anything in the serum sample we sent previously?"

"Was there a serum sample for this patient?" Savage addressed his own people, but no one seemed to have an answer.

"We sent it earlier," Kenzie explained. "Before the brain tissue. But it has the same patient number on it."

There was some back and forth among the lab folk before Savage broke in again. "It looks like it hasn't been processed yet if we did receive it."

"I can send another sample if you think it got lost."

"I'll have someone get back to you to either let you know that we've got it or that we need you to send a second sample. Blood is more backed up than brains at the moment."

"What?" Kenzie asked blankly. Then she realized he meant that it was taking longer for the lab to process blood samples, probably because they received a lot more of them. That was why the brain had been processed first. "Oh, I got it. Sorry."

"Nothing to apologize for," Savage said. "I'm sorry we don't have the serum results on hand yet. That would have been helpful."

"We had another patient with similar symptoms to this one," Dr. Wiltshire told Savage and his people. "From the same nursing home unit. They died a couple of days apart."

"You need to send me his samples as well. To be processed as soon as possible." Savage swore. "If this is highly contagious... you know how endemic herpesviruses are..."

Dr. Wiltshire looked at Kenzie.

"His brain samples have already been sent in," Kenzie confirmed. "I'll send you the patient number."

"That would be helpful. We'll get right on it."

"There have been other deaths at that nursing home recently. But there always are. It's a nursing home. That said, it was the independent living unit, so we didn't expect to see as many deaths there."

"How many deaths?"

"We had a few through here—more than I had thought. But even more were just handled by the nursing home as doctor-attended deaths and didn't come through our office. I'm not even sure where to start."

"With the samples we have," Dr. Wiltshire said with a shrug. "We'll need to assemble any samples from nursing home patients in the last... let's start with three months. We can send the tissue samples in for testing. Do you want blood samples too?" Dr. Wiltshire directed this question to the speakerphone.

"Yes. I think it's important to see how many people were infected and what percentage of those had the virus in their brains. Does this virus migrate to the brain? Do we only see it when it reaches a certain level in the body? Only in the immunosuppressed? We need to start gathering data."

Kenzie jotted a few notes down on her pad of paper, thinking through everything that had been said during the phone conversation.

"Dr. Savage... you're obviously very concerned that this could spread. Is it just because it is a variant you haven't seen before and you don't know how infectious the new variant is? Because it may be associated with our patient's death?"

The background noises on the speakerphone ceased as if everyone in the room at the lab had gone still. No more shuffling papers or whispered conversations. Kenzie looked at Dr. Wiltshire, and they both waited for Dr. Savage's answer.

"I am most concerned," Savage said slowly, "because it would appear that this virus was engineered in a laboratory."

44

Kenzie and Dr. Wiltshire looked at each other.

"What makes you think it was engineered in a lab?" Dr. Wiltshire asked. "Or rather, how can you tell it was engineered in a lab?"

"This is highly confidential," Savage warned. "Is there anyone else within earshot? I need your promise that this will not be written down or communicated to anyone else."

"We are alone," Wiltshire said, with a glance at the open boardroom door. Kenzie got up and shut it. "And of course, you have my word that I will not communicate any confidential information outside of this office."

There was silence as Savage apparently considered this wording. Then he spoke. "There is a protein sequence in the RNA of this virus that constitutes... a signature, if you will. In the same way as you can recognize an artist by his brushstrokes or a computer programmer by specific subroutines that he reuses from one program to the next, we can tell that these proteins were edited in a lab. They are a different sequence than you would find in any virus in nature."

"Can you trace them back to a specific lab or scientist, then?" Dr. Wiltshire asked.

"We're working on that. Experimental material does get transferred from one lab or project to another, so there's a bit of detective work to do...

189

lab A passed it on to lab B and C for subsequent studies, lab B passed it on to E, and C to F... It's going to take some time, especially if the transfer wasn't well-documented or a sample was mislabeled or mixed up. If, for instance, they were supposed to send out a non-engineered virus and sent out the engineered one instead."

Kenzie reached to write something down on her notepad. Dr. Wiltshire caught her eye and shook his head. Savage had asked them not to write down anything about the virus being engineered.

"The next question is how did our patient contract the virus?" Dr. Wiltshire said. "Did he take part in an experimental program? Or is it in the wild? Has it mutated from the form that the lab developed?"

"All good questions," Savage agreed. "We are concerned that it may be in the wild. Were you aware of your patient taking part in any medical testing?"

"Not that we know of. It wouldn't be normal course to be testing a virus on seniors unless they are targeting a disease that would normally only be found in seniors."

"Like Alzheimer's Disease?" Kenzie asked him softly, her face turned away from the phone so they wouldn't pick up her question. Dr. Wiltshire's eyes widened as he considered the possibility.

"What makes you think it is in the wild?" Kenzie asked. "Do you have anything to back it up? Have you seen it somewhere else?"

"We are working on identifying the origins of this virus. The sequencing suggests that the HHV-4 has recombined with at least one other virus to form a new variant. Of course, it is possible that it was recombined in a laboratory setting, but usually, a lab wants to maintain more control than recombining two viruses would allow. They splice specific gene sequences rather than the larger chunks that we are seeing. What happens when two viruses recombine is too unpredictable."

"So it has mutated, and now you don't know what properties it has."

"Yes," Savage agreed, his voice suddenly lower and gravelly like he'd been up all night talking. As he probably had. "Your case confirms that it is contagious. How contagious it is, we don't yet know. Epstein Barr is usually transmitted through saliva. That's why mono is called the kissing disease. Did it contribute to the death of your patient? If it did..."

"There may be an outbreak at the nursing home and they don't even know it yet. And it could be fatal."

"We have no idea how many people may have it already. A nursing home is a perfect environment to spread an infectious agent. Lots of vulnerable people close together on a daily basis. Outside visitors, doctors, nurses, cleaning staff, volunteers, lots of ways for viruses to get into—and out of—the nursing home. Kids with runny noses visiting grandma..." Savage made a noise of disgust. "You couldn't engineer a much better environment for spreading a novel virus."

45

K enzie's head was whirling after they hung up the phone. She and Dr. Wiltshire just sat there for a while, saying nothing, considering everything they had heard. Dr. Wiltshire wrote a number of notes on his pad of paper. Kenzie didn't interrupt him, not wanting to break his concentration. Eventually, he put his pen down and looked at her.

"I don't know what to think," Kenzie said. "This is incredible."

"We have a list of things to do, including sending them Mr. Sexton's ID number so that they can test his samples next, and pulling samples for any other cases from the nursing home that we have handled in the last three months. That is going to take a while. I have some other calls and research I would like to do while you get started on that."

"What about talking to the nursing home?"

Dr. Wiltshire's lips pressed together tightly as he considered this. "We don't want to start a panic. But we have to be responsible and prevent harm wherever possible. It's too early to recommend a quarantine. Not until we have more data. For all we know, Mr. Cartwright did take part in a medical experiment and it is not contagious at all. One dead man with this novel HHV-4 does not constitute an outbreak."

"But that's not what the lab thinks."

"And since they are the ones who discovered it and have the expertise, it falls on them to inform the Vermont Center for Disease Control and to make recommendations on quarantines or other measures to be taken."

Kenzie scribbled on her notepad. Not words, just shapes and scribbles, trying to get her mind around all of the issues. "What if we told the nursing home that there is a particularly virulent strain of the flu around and that might be what killed Cartwright and Sexton?"

"That's not exactly honest. It would be a breach of ethics."

"But so would *not* telling them."

"We might be able to get away with slightly different wording... a virus that we are trying to identify. Something that they should take extra measures to avoid transmission from one patient to another. Hand-washing, staff wearing masks, and so on."

"And you don't think that will cause panic or spread to the news media?"

Dr. Wiltshire shook his head, not liking the question. They were in trouble either way. They couldn't ignore the potential for an outbreak, but they didn't want to cause unnecessary panic. No matter how careful they were in their wording of a warning to the nursing home, the staff there could overreact or underreact.

"We need more data," Dr. Wiltshire said finally. "We don't know what we're looking at or what the danger is until we have more. We can't make an informed decision without the facts. Then we can make a careful, informed decision. If the lab hasn't already issued a warning. And they may do that once they know enough. It really is their responsibility. Or that of the lab that released the virus. It isn't the place of the Medical Examiner's Office to give warnings about contagions."

Kenzie nodded slowly. "Okay. But if it turns out there is an outbreak of this new, engineered virus... we can't ignore it."

"We won't."

Kenzie stood up and picked up her notepad. "There's one thing that the lab didn't say, and we didn't ask."

Dr. Wiltshire nodded his agreement. "*Why* was this virus created? Was it part of a study to prevent disease or part of a bioterrorism program?"

Kenzie walked back to her desk, a knot in her stomach. She knew why they hadn't asked the question.

At the end of the day, there was nothing to do but wait. Kenzie had sent the information and samples that Savage and his team needed to the lab. Dr. Wiltshire was making his phone calls and doing research, but she didn't know who he was consulting with or exactly what he wanted to know about the virus.

So it was a waiting game. Wait for the lab to process all the samples and then get back to them about whether they were positive for the virus as well. Sit through the weekend wondering whether more people would end up dead because of the length of time the testing process would take.

Kenzie felt like a zombie throughout supper, her brain in a completely different place from her body. She tried to talk with Zachary as if everything were normal. She couldn't tell him that they might have an outbreak of a genetically engineered virus. She had been told not to tell anyone about it, and telling him wouldn't do her any good anyway. It would just mean that he was worrying about it as well as she was. And Zachary could take worry to a whole new level.

Kenzie made spaghetti and then pushed it around on her plate, not feeling up to eating. If that was how Zachary felt every day, she could certainly sympathize with him. Especially with being told every day by her and by his doctors that he had to eat more. Looking at the food that she should have enjoyed just made her feel slightly sick. And how could anyone enjoy spaghetti if they were already feeling nauseated?

Zachary looked up from his own plate, which was still just as full as hers. "Are you okay?"

"I'm fine. Well, maybe feeling a little under the weather. But okay, really. Not contagious." She grimaced about letting the word "contagious" slip. *Thanks, Freud.* She needed to be more careful.

"You don't have to eat if you're not feeling well," Zachary pointed out. Unlike him. He did have to eat whether he felt sick or not. She had the option of waiting until she felt better.

But she had a feeling she wasn't going to be able to shake the knot of dread in her stomach until they had the results of the tests. And until she was sure that they had everything under control. And how long was that going to be? A few days? Weeks? What if the virus was more widespread than they had feared? There was nothing to say that there weren't other people dying of the virus, in other facilities, in other jurisdictions. Just because their lab had picked up the RNA signature on the virus, that didn't mean that all labs would.

Why had Dr. Savage sequenced the RNA? Had he known that there was something to be found? Was it strange enough to find HHV-4 in the brain that they wanted to find out more about it and why it was there? Or had he seen other cases already that he wasn't telling them about? Maybe he hadn't been surprised by the results at all. Maybe they had just been watching for more cases in the wild. Maybe he was gradually gathering the data that he would need to present his findings to the authorities and make a case for them to take action and lock down the nursing home—and wherever else the virus had shown up.

"Kenz? Do you want to lie down? I can clean up here. Take care of that for you." Zachary nodded to her plate.

"Sorry... I'm only half here. I'm not very good company today."

"It's okay. Understandable if you aren't well. Why don't you go have a nap? You might still be overtired from when you had to get up early the other day. It can take a while to recover from a lost night's sleep."

"I'd rather put something on TV and distract myself from—" Kenzie barely caught herself in time, "—from my stomach. If I have something else to focus on..."

He nodded. "Yeah. Sure."

He stood up and reached his hand toward her. It wasn't like she needed help up. But she accepted it anyway. Zachary put his arm around her and kissed her cheek lightly. He escorted her out to the living room and turned on the TV. He picked up one of the throw blankets that they mostly used during the winter and draped it over her, fussing like a mother hen. "What do you want to watch?"

"Here, give it to me." Kenzie held her hand out for the remote control. Zachary hesitated, then put it into her hand.

She was certainly capable of paging through the menus and finding something to watch. She didn't know what she wanted to watch, but she would find something. Zachary watched her for a moment, then moved out of the way and went back to the kitchen to clean up.

"You still have to eat," Kenzie reminded him.

Zachary stopped and looked at Kenzie through the doorway, his face disappointed. Kenzie shook her head firmly.

"Don't forget who you're talking to. You don't get out of eating just because I'm not up to it."

He leaned against the doorframe, rolling his eyes.

"You pretend that you don't like me making you eat, but I think you really enjoy it," Kenzie said. He liked to be mothered. After losing his own mother so young and then losing Bridget, who he thought would be there for him forever, why wouldn't he want that? Someone to take care of him. Kenzie didn't exactly see herself as a nurturer, but she had been a good big sister and mini-mother to Amanda, and she did care about Zachary and wanted to help him.

"What if I eat later?" Zachary negotiated.

"When?"

"I don't know." He looked at the clock on the microwave behind him. "Maybe... in a couple of hours."

Kenzie couldn't see any good reason to make him eat at a specific time. Other than the possibility of getting more calories in him before the day was over. "On one condition. You have a granola bar or other snack now, and then have your spaghetti—or another meal, but not just a snack—in a couple of hours."

Zachary considered this for a moment, then nodded. He went into the kitchen and rattled and banged dishes until everything was cleared away and the dirty dishes were in the dishwasher. He joined her in the living room with a granola bar, which he brandished dramatically to make sure she knew he was keeping his end of the bargain.

"Don't get crumbs on the couch."

He pulled his computer table over. His laptop was put away, so the table was clear, and he ate over it carefully, brushing all the crumbs carefully into his hand when he was done. He was clean and tidy when he was paying attention. But she had seen how he could get when he was distracted or severely depressed.

He brushed his hands off into the kitchen sink, ran water over his fingers for a few seconds, and dried them on a dishtowel. He returned to sit with Kenzie on the couch, cuddling up close to her and trailing his fingers through her hair as they watched the movie.

47

Although Kenzie had the whole weekend off, they didn't visit Lorne and Pat again. They wouldn't normally make the trip again so soon unless there was something to be concerned about. When Zachary had been investigating the disappearance of Pat's friend. When he'd been there to meet his siblings or Pat's family. Or even if Pat needed some help painting the house or Lorne with cataloging photos on the computer. They were family. Zachary tried to keep in close touch with him, so he tried to at least call most weeks. Lorne was almost a pro at video calls now.

"How are things with you and Kenzie?" Kenzie could hear Lorne's cheerful voice over the speaker even though she was in her home office on the computer.

"We're pretty good," Zachary told him. "Kenzie's fighting some kind of stomach bug, but other than that, we're fine."

"There are some things going around right now," Lorne agreed. "Of course, they never declare it an epidemic until it's practically over, but everybody else knows what's going on."

Which was exactly what Kenzie was worried would happen with the novel HHV-4 virus. No matter how much effort they put into tracking infections, the authorities wouldn't consider it a threat until far too late. Either when it was already on the decline, or when it had put too many people into the hospital and morgue to deny it any longer.

"I might be fighting something too," she heard Lorne say a few minutes later, distracting her from her mail. "I've been so exhausted lately. Just want to sleep all day. And it isn't like I've been doing a lot of extra. If this is what getting old feels like, I think I'm going to opt out!"

"I don't think that's actually an option," Zachary said, chuckling. "If you're tired, then make sure you get enough sleep. That's what your body needs."

"Like you do?"

"Do what I say, not what I do. I try to sleep. It isn't by choice that I don't."

"I know," Lorne agreed warmly. "You have plenty of challenges. But you'll get through it."

"I'm not actually going to get over it, though. Ever." Zachary's voice was low. Confiding. Kenzie stopped typing and listened intently. Maybe it wasn't right for her to be listening in on Zachary's conversation without his inviting her. But he could have put on earphones or gone somewhere private to talk. Or asked Kenzie to shut her bedroom door.

"Zach, I don't think you realize how far you've come over the years," Lorne responded. "You're not the ten-year-old boy who came to us all of those years ago. You've grown up and become a successful business owner. You're in a committed relationship. You've been reunited with three of your siblings. Those are things that... back when you were a teenager, you would have told me were impossible. Things that you would never be able to achieve."

"But I'm still... *broken*," Zachary protested. "You remember how much trouble I had sleeping when I lived with you. I had to have meds to even get a few hours of sleep. And I still have those issues now. And I will for the rest of my life!" At the end of his words, there was a blankness that Kenzie mentally filled in, hearing what he didn't say. *However long that is.*

She moved to get up. To go talk to Zachary and reassure him that things would get better. Maybe not one hundred percent. Maybe he would never act or feel like everyone around him. But the cyclical depression he was experiencing now would recede after Christmas. Of course he knew that. He'd been through it many times before.

"You're depressed," Lorne acknowledged. "And you do need to make sure you get enough sleep. Are you taking a sleep aid? At this time of year, you need to be especially careful to get enough sleep."

"I don't like to take them," Zachary said stubbornly.

"I know that. But sometimes they are necessary. For your mental health. For your physical health. Have you talked to your doctor?"

"I already know what he would say. That it's okay to take them occasionally." Lorne started to reply, but Zachary spoke over him. "But I know it wouldn't be occasionally. It would be every night. Because I know I can only get a few hours of sleep without them. The more I take them, the more I would rely on them and not on my own abilities."

"Okay." Lorne's voice was calm and reassuring, even though Zachary's had risen in both volume and tone. "So what do you want to do? How are you feeling right now—and don't just tell me 'fine.'"

"I'm f—" Zachary cut himself off, swearing under his breath. She could hear him take a few deep breaths, and when he spoke again, his voice was flat and even. Shutting off his emotions. Pulling away from himself and his feelings. "I know it's that time of year and the depression is setting in. I go through this every year. It's only temporary. I know that in my head. But I don't believe it. And my body is telling me this will never end."

"Does Kenzie know how you're feeling?"

"Of course." Zachary's words were clipped. "She sees me every day."

"Have you talked to her about it?"

"Sort of. Sometimes."

"Are you suicidal? Do you need to go to the hospital?" Lorne had learned to ask, not to hint around. Not to use careful euphemisms, but just to put it out in the open. If someone were having appendicitis or a stroke, they wouldn't be expected to speak of it in veiled terms. Zachary's mental health had to be treated the same way. Matter-of-factly. Not as if it were a dirty secret that had to be hidden away.

"No." There were several long seconds of silence. "Not yet."

"Okay. You make sure that you tell someone if you start having suicidal thoughts."

"I have *thoughts*," Zachary clarified. "But no plan."

"Talk to Kenzie. She can help you to be safe. And talk to your therapist about it. What about your meds?"

"I don't want to do a med review. I can't switch meds right now. I wouldn't be covered properly by... then."

By Christmas. He could barely even stand to say the word.

"Right. Talk to both of them. Make sure they know exactly what you're thinking and feeling. And if it changes."

"Yeah."

"And you know that you can come here any time. Any time, Zachary. If you need to be with someone and Kenzie is at work. If you just need to vent or go for a walk together. Or binge on ice cream. Come. You're family. We're there for you."

Zachary cleared his throat a few times. Kenzie stayed where she was, knowing that she couldn't go out there now and interrupt, telling him that she had heard the entire conversation and putting her two bits in. Lorne had said what needed to be said, and Zachary needed to know there were other people in his support network. Plenty of people were willing to step in and help if he just gave the word.

He sniffled. Kenzie listened for Lorne's voice, hoping that Zachary hadn't disconnected the call when it got too emotional for him.

"Thanks," Zachary said eventually, his voice shaky. "Thank you. For everything."

"Of course. And I mean it. Those aren't just words."

"I know."

There were a few minutes of quiet while Zachary pulled himself together again. "How's Pat?"

"I told you we're both good. Pat is already into Christmas preparations. Decorations and baking to put in the freezer and all kinds of plans."

"Are you having his family over again this year?"

"I think they want us to go there. But it won't be until Christmas Day, probably in the evening. You'll be starting to feel better then."

Zachary didn't say anything.

"You know you will," Lorne said. "It's the same every year. You know that once you get past Christmas Eve, you'll start to feel better."

"I don't know."

"Then just trust me. I've seen it before. Even the worst years, you've been better after the anniversary."

"Okay."

"Come by any time. Including Christmas Eve. And if you are up to visits on Christmas Day, you can go with us to see Pat's family. They'd love to see you again."

"I don't know if I made that great an impression the first time."

"You solved a case. How is that not impressive?"

"But I bombed out on dinner. I was rude."

"They understood you were working on something important. Gretta and Suzanne ask after you all the time. They didn't have any hard feelings toward you."

"You're sure?"

Kenzie knew that both Pat and Lorne had repeated this several times in the months since Zachary had met Pat's mother and sister for the first time. His anxious brain wouldn't accept their reassurances that it was just fine. But hopefully, with enough repetition, he would eventually stop worrying about it.

And move on to something else.

Kenzie grimaced and went back to her computer work.

48

The weekend seemed interminably long. Kenzie didn't tell Zachary that she was anxious rather than physically sick, so he continued his ministrations. Promising to get whatever food she decided her stomach could handle. Making sure she slept in and didn't stay up too late at night. Just generally cosseting her and treating her like an invalid for the rest of the weekend.

Kenzie thought of Bridget and what it would be like to have a cancer diagnosis and Zachary hovering over her every day, sure she was going to break. While she could never approve of how Bridget had kicked Zachary out of her life when she got sick, she could understand not wanting him to smother her.

It was a relief to get back to the office. She did her usual Monday-morning sweep of all the rooms and surfaces in their suite. Making sure that everything was properly logged and recorded.

What she really wanted to do was to check the office email for any reports from the virology lab on the additional testing for HHV-4. But she promised herself that she wouldn't look at the report until she reached the point in her schedule that she usually checked the email. During her time at the Medical Examiner's Office, she had learned that if email was the first thing she looked at in the morning, her day was far less productive. She ended up taking much longer processing it, and it was likely to take all morning instead of Kenzie being able to zip through it in half an hour or an hour. She would reward herself for dealing with the weekend full of anxiety and not breaking down and telling Zachary what was going on by checking to see if the results were in.

Eventually, she sat down at her desk and opened her email. "Come on," she coaxed. "Be there. If this testing was so important, you should have stayed there all weekend to do the processing and sequencing. Show me what you found."

Dr. Wiltshire arrived at the office at his usual time. Kenzie guessed that, he didn't want to jinx the results by being too impatient to get them either. Though she knew it was magical thinking, her brain was convinced that if she just did things the way she did every workday, they would find the rest results in email as hoped for.

Dr. Wiltshire looked at Kenzie, an awkward approach that said he was as afraid to ask for the test results as she had been to look for them.

"They came in," she told him quickly, reaching out with the printed copy of the report.

Dr. Wiltshire didn't pretend not to know what she was talking about. He took the stapled report from her. "Did you look?"

Kenzie nodded. "I couldn't really not look when I was printing them... I hope you don't mind."

"Summarize."

"Five more cases, including Mr. Sexton."

"Five." He rubbed the bridge of his nose under his glasses. "Over what period?"

"Going back six weeks. Before that, nothing from the samples we sent."

"So we didn't miss a whole bunch of cases. That's helpful, at least."

Kenzie nodded.

"And any mention of how they are doing at the lab? Back-tracing it to the source of the contagion?"

"No, no word on that. I guess they didn't think we needed to know."

"Not necessarily," Dr. Wiltshire said with a forced smile and a slight shake of his head. "I'm sure it is long, tedious work. And not just a search that can be done on the computer. They'll have to do a lot of interviews to figure out each transfer point. And any labs or scientists that didn't follow proper protocol and might have been an infection point aren't going to want to talk to anyone. Not without a subpoena or some kind of order from public health."

"But we can't afford for it to take a long time. People are dying."

"So far, it doesn't appear to be widespread. Champlain House is currently the only known outbreak."

"As far as we know. But most doctors are not going to do a test for HHV-4 or to collect brain samples when a patient comes in complaining of memory issues or vertigo," Kenzie snapped back.

"No. You're absolutely right. No one is going to know what to look for until it is announced. But an announcement cannot be made based on what we have so far. We're going to need to find out any commonalities of the six victims. If they were all in the same part of the unit, all played poker together, or had something else in common. We don't know yet how the infection is spread. Person to person contact. Surface contact. Large droplet. Aerosol. Epstein Barr is typically spread through saliva. But the new variant could be different. We need to get a better idea of whether those patients all knew each other and were in close contact with each other. Or whether... I don't know... it's in the heating ducts or the shower heads. Or on the doorknobs."

"Okay... I'll give them a call and see if I can get anywhere."

"Good. And I will call and see if I can get any more information from Dr. Pascal Savage."

49

Kenzie hadn't gotten advice from Dr. Wiltshire as to how to go about talking to the staff of Champlain House without letting the cat out of the bag about the possibility of an outbreak. Exactly how was she supposed to gather information on those six particular residents without the staff wondering what was going on? It had to be clear that Kenzie was not just being nosy and using her position with the Medical Examiner's Office to ask idle questions.

She tried to play down the six deaths and any connections between them as much as possible.

"We're doing an audit of a random selection of cases we have received from Champlain House over the past few weeks," she told Nurse Summers. "Just to make sure that everything has been handled correctly by the Medical Examiner's Office. We have to perform self-checks to ensure thoroughness and consistency of results."

"This seems like make-work," Summers objected. "I and my staff are very busy. We don't have the time to be answering a bunch of unimportant inquiries. We have quite enough work to do without your office adding their own requirements into the mix. I don't think there's any legal requirement for us to answer your questions when they aren't even connected to a case."

"They are connected to a case. We have six different cases that we are examining. I realize it's an inconvenience. It is for me too. Believe me, I don't want to be wasting my time and adding extra busywork into my schedule either."

"Yet here you are," Summers said acidly, "taking up my time on the phone."

"Would you prefer that I come there in person? It would probably be a good idea if I do anyway. Then I can talk to everyone who is in and see the various rooms and common areas in the unit." She thought about the various potential points of infection.

"No, I don't need anyone poking around here, either."

"I will probably need to do a quick walkthrough, at the very least. But I'll start with the phone interview. The more information you can give me, the quicker it will all be over."

"Now is not a good time."

"What time would you like me to call you back?" Kenzie tried to pin her down. "What time are you off? Maybe that would work better."

"No, I'm not spending my off-time dealing with this."

"Whatever time you prefer, just let me know..."

"How about never?"

"Nurse Summers," Kenzie let some of her frustration and impatience into her voice and formed the words very precisely. "If you are impeding a legitimate investigation by the Medical Examiner's Office..."

"What? You're going to throw me in jail?"

Kenzie had no idea what the penalties might be for something like that. She strongly suspected that the penalties for refusing to talk to an ME's office were not very harsh. "Do you really want to find out?"

Nurse Summers sighed. "Fine. What exactly is it you want to know?"

"I have a list of patients here. The first thing I am going to need are the room numbers for each."

"The room numbers?"

"Where their living quarters were?" Could a nurse really be that dense?

"Fine."

Kenzie ran through the list of six, and on each patient page, noted the room they had slept in. "Great, that's very helpful. And now, I don't know what the options are for food. Does everyone eat meals together in a common room? In their own room? Are they allowed to bring in outside food?"

"A combination. Most of the residents in our room take meals together in the common room. They like to socialize. Some residents prefer to take meals in their rooms, or have occasional outside meals brought in by family or friends. But that is less common."

"I have the same six patient names and would like to know where they took their meals."

Nurse Summers listed a few off before stopping to ask, "And who else? I didn't catch them all the first time."

Kenzie mentioned the additional names. She wrote the responses on each of the sheets of paper. As Summers had said, most preferred to take their meals in the common room, but a couple took some or most of their meals in their rooms. There wasn't an obvious pattern. But from what Kenzie could interpret from the nurse's answers, everybody went to the common room to eat at least sometimes.

"Extra-curricular," Kenzie announced next. "Did these patients play games together? Visit with each other? Keep to themselves?"

"With each other?" Nurse Summers tapped her nail impatiently on the phone. "No, they weren't all a secret club, if that's what you mean. They might play a game together now and then, but not regularly."

"What kind of games do you have? How are they sanitized?"

"How are they sanitized?"

"Disinfected. Are they wiped down after the residents use them?"

"No. Of course not. That would be a lot of extra work for the staff, and I'm not sure you could wipe down cards or puzzles. I don't understand what you are looking for. Do you think one of these patients had Hep B or staph? The residents are responsible for their own hygiene. We haven't had any lockdowns due to infections in this unit. Not even flu or pneumonia."

"That's a great record. Please don't take these questions as a criticism of your practices; that's not my intention. I'm just trying to learn what I can about these patients we have selected and how thoroughly their deaths were investigated."

"It sounds more like you want to check on our practices than yours."

"Let's move on to contact with staff. I know that this is the independent living unit, so they do not require significant nursing care, but they must still have some contact with the nursing staff and housekeeping."

"Of course."

"Can we go over each patient and the extent of the care they had from the nursing staff? None of them were assigned any particular nurse, is that right?"

"No. All of the nurses are available to deal with residents as needed. Some might need a bit of help with showering, or need someone to give them their pills so they don't get mixed up, that kind of thing."

"Can you go through each of these patients and tell me what kind of assistance they needed?"

"I don't know if this is appropriate for me to be talking to you about under the privacy laws."

"They are dead and this is part of our investigation into their deaths. You are not required to get any consents to communicate information to the Medical Examiner's Office."

"So you say."

Kenzie waited. Nurse Summers sighed in exasperation and began to list each of the patients to describe what care they needed or may have had with the nursing staff before their deaths.

"Is that everyone?"

"You haven't mentioned Mr. Sexton yet."

Summers summarized Sexton's information briefly.

"That's great. Now, what about contact with the housekeeping staff?"

"The residents don't have any contact with the housekeeping staff."

"Housekeeping enters their rooms to clean, don't they?"

"Not while they're there. If they are in their rooms, they are asked to go for a walk until housekeeping is done."

"And they pick up their laundry. And what else? I assume they wear gloves to avoid contamination with soiled clothing?"

"I don't know. I suppose so."

"Do they change their gloves between rooms? What is the protocol for handling soiled items?"

"I don't know what their practices are. That is all dictated by administration, not nursing. Of course they will protect themselves from contaminants."

"And are the residents' laundry items all kept separate from each other, or all washed together?"

"They are kept separate, just like washing at a laundromat or at your house. They are removed from the resident's room in a marked laundry basket and returned to them washed and folded in the same basket."

"And is the basket sanitized?"

"I don't know. You would have to talk to housekeeping about that part."

Kenzie looked for other areas she might have missed. "And they disinfect all high-touch surfaces in the residents' rooms?"

"I assume so."

"How often?"

"Residents' rooms are cleaned once a week unless there is a specific problem requiring the housekeeping staff's attention."

"Do residents visit each other in their rooms? Or only in the common areas?"

"They are allowed to visit with each other privately. We don't supervise interpersonal socialization unless there are known to be problems."

"Like what?"

"What do you mean?"

"What kinds of problems?"

"Just like anyone else, residents don't always get along together. Some of them, they have disagreements or don't like each other. As much as we try to provide a good environment, we can't make everyone like each other."

"Are we talking about arguments or physical altercations?"

"Most of them are too old for a physical fight... but we have had a few of them." Nurse Summers blew out her breath. "Some men... you would think their testosterone would be low enough by the time they get here that we wouldn't have fights. But there you are."

"And have you had any problems with any of the patients on my list? With physical altercations?"

"Well... I feel like I'm telling tales out of school. You know what they say about not speaking ill of the dead..."

"We're not making any judgments about them. Just talking about how they got along together, what the interactions between the patients were like."

"You really need to know this for your report? What does this have to do with how your office investigated these deaths?"

"Well, I know I was the one who came and talked to you about Mr. Cartwright. But I never thought to ask whether he had been in any fights with other residents there. Now that we're having this conversation, I can see that's an area that should be addressed in the future."

"I suppose so," Nurse Summers agreed grudgingly. "But your Mr.

Cartwright wasn't in any fights during the week before his death, so I don't think that was a contributing factor."

"Not in the week before his death? So he was one of the patients that did sometimes get into fights?"

"He had, in the past, been involved in the occasional argument that got physical. Old military man, you know, they have been conditioned to react physically to what they perceive as a threat."

Kenzie jotted down this note on her page for Willie Cartwright. "Does that mean that he had PTSD?"

"PTSD? No, men his age were never diagnosed with PTSD. But I can tell you... if he perceived a threat, he would react."

"Physically. By attacking someone."

"By defending himself. Yes."

"And the other patients that we picked out? Any of them have any physical altercations in the past?"

"I don't think so. Margaret Ashbury, that nice old English lady, she was a spitter. Cross her and see where it got you! A big loogie straight to the eye, if you didn't watch out."

Kenzie made a note of this too. They knew the virus was likely to be spread through saliva. "That's great. Thank you for all the details. Anything else that you can think of with any of the other residents we talked about that I should know about? Health problems? Psychiatric or neurological symptoms, negative interactions with other residents?"

"No. I mean, they all had health problems. They were old. They needed to be in assisted living. But most of them were in pretty good physical condition. Until they died."

Kenzie rolled her eyes. "Maybe we can just quickly run through each of them and you can let me know if they had any diagnosed issues or if there was anything that you noticed that you think should have been diagnosed."

"Is this the last question?" Summers asked in a long-suffering tone.

"I think so. Unless it triggers another thought."

"Well, let's hope it doesn't." Summers ran through each patient briefly to discuss any conditions that they might have had before they died. There were many issues with blood pressure, weight, diabetes, and other issues for being a relatively healthy lot. Kenzie scribbled them all down quickly so that she wouldn't have to ask again.

"Now, if that's everything, I would like to get back to my actual work."

"Of course. If you could just email me a floor plan of the unit so I can see where each of the rooms was in the unit. That would be very helpful. Aside from that... I guess I'll let you know if anything else occurs to me. And I'll probably stop by in the next day or two to touch base briefly with the other nursing staff and housekeeping. Just to make sure that we haven't missed anything."

"You have been very thorough," Nurse Summers said, and Kenzie didn't think it was meant as a compliment.

50

Kenzie was logging in test results received via email and was surprised to see one that had come from a lab she was unfamiliar with. She opened it to scan through the information and was also unfamiliar with the doctor's name. She looked to the patient name, pretty sure by now that it had been forwarded to the wrong Medical Examiner's Office. She started to type a reply to the email to let them know of the error when the pieces began to fall into place.

Lola Canine was, of course, not one of the bodies that they had dealt with, but she was certainly part of their ongoing investigation into the deaths of Cartwright, Sexton, and now four other subjects. Lola the dog, from the care center. She didn't recognize the doctor or lab names immediately because they were veterinary rather than those she usually dealt with. She deleted her reply and paged down into the report to see what they had discovered.

She didn't even remember tapping Dr. Wiltshire's name into the phone keypad, but she had the phone to her ear and was waiting for him to answer.

"Kenzie?"

"Dr. Wiltshire... I just got in a report from the veterinary lab on Lola, the dog at Champlain House."

"Oh. Anything interesting in the results?"

"Well, yes... it says that she is positive for HHV-4, as well as a couple of other viruses."

She heard Dr. Wiltshire put something down with a clack. Maybe his coffee mug or his fountain pen. "She's positive? You're sure? For HHV-4?"

"Yes. That's what the serology shows. I didn't even know that dogs could get HHV-4. I mean, it is *Human* Herpesvirus 4. Can dogs get it?"

"Apparently, they can in this case. I would have to look at the research to see if it is common. I'm afraid I'm not up on my canid virology."

"Maybe it's just this novel variant. I'm really surprised. Once we identified the possible culprit as HHV-4, I assumed that the dog was out as the source of the infection." Kenzie shook her head at herself for not looking into it further.

"Did you find anything out about her history?"

"There was a bit of back and forth. I guess she was a friend of a friend's dog or something like that, they couldn't take care of her, she needed somewhere stable to live, Nurse Ellie who took him couldn't have dogs in her building... blah, blah, blah, so Lola ended up being the mascot of the independent living center."

"You're going to need details. We still don't know how *Lola* got HHV-4. She might have contracted it *from* one of the patients rather than giving it to them. Most viruses don't jump between families of the animal kingdom. We still need to find out where the virus came from, if it came from some laboratory, so that we know what has been done with it, its transmission pathways, and what the mortality rate is."

"Right." Kenzie jotted down notes on her computer scratchpad. "I will start getting names and addresses and see if we can find any association with a lab."

"I will call Champlain House and advise them that the dog is to be isolated from patients. And whoever is caring for her should be extra careful about contact. Wear gloves and mask, frequent hand-washing, keep feces away from anyone else and don't dispose of them in the general garbages."

"Okay. I'll forward this email to you in case there is anything else in it that is important. It doesn't look like they did any PCR, so I should probably get them to send samples over to Dr. Savage so his lab can map them. See if they are the same variant."

"Definitely. He's going to want to run his own tests and factor it into their investigation tracking the virus."

"Can I ask a really ignorant question?"

"Fire away," Dr. Wiltshire invited, a smile in his voice.

"Exactly how does a virus escape a lab? I mean... how shoddy do their isolation protocols have to be if they are accidentally letting it out into the wild?"

"It happens. Each time, if we can identify how it got out, we can add to our knowledge of how to properly keep them isolated even when doing testing. But take a look at history—there have been several cases where plague has escaped labs to contaminate and sometimes kill unsuspecting people."

"Plague? Really?"

"Don't quote me, but I believe there have been three accidental releases since the seventies. Labs worldwide are still running tests on the plague virus to unlock its secrets, whether it is to develop new defenses against virulent plagues, bioterrorism research, whatever. And unfortunately... it would seem that even the most careful lab can make mistakes. None of them are bulletproof. Sometimes it is wastewater, sometimes a ventilation shaft that wasn't properly sealed from the rest of the building. Suddenly you've got someone in the same building dropping from the plague, probably after infecting members of their own family. There have been some fatalities and some recoveries. It isn't something we ever want to see in the wild again."

"But something like HHV-4 is so endemic to the population... so many people already have it in their systems... how could we track it and control one variant? You can't isolate everybody positive for HHV-4. That is half the population in North America. And we don't have a test for just this variant, so it would just be... trying to sequence every positive HHV-4 result... it would be impossible."

"If there is an outbreak, scientists will have to come up with a rapid test for it and treat it pretty quickly."

51

Kenzie double-checked the address that she had been given and looked at the doors of the buildings, trying to sort out which she was looking for. Ellie, the nurse who had taken Lola in, told her that it wasn't an apartment building, but there were living quarters over several businesses. The numbers on the buildings were difficult to make out from the street, so she pulled into the parking lot and found an empty stall. She walked along, checking all the numbers. It was a few buildings down from where she had thought it would be.

She opened one of the glass doors and was able to walk up the stairs, but the door at the top of the stairs was locked. Kenzie rattled the doorknob, knocked, and tried the phone number that Ellie had given her. No luck. Kenzie went back down the stairs and tried a couple of the ground-floor businesses, asking if they knew any of those who lived in the building, or if there were a building manager around.

Receptionists flashed smiles but shook their heads. *No, can't help you, would there be anything else?*

Eventually, she had to give up. She would keep trying to call. Sooner or later, Lola's former owner had to answer.

Kenzie was sitting in her car looking at the GPS map and trying to decide whether to run over to Champlain House to have a face-to-face chat with Nurse Ellie and look at the unit with new eyes, or whether it was just too late in the day and she should get something to eat and tackle the matter again the next day when she was fresh.

Though she was worried about the virus spreading, they didn't yet have confirmation that it was even the same virus as Lola had. Dr. Wiltshire had called the nursing home to isolate Lola, so there wouldn't be any more opportunities for infection on their end.

Her stomach was growling loudly just thinking about the possibility of getting food, so she broke down and admitted to herself that she wasn't going to be any good getting anything else done on the case. She needed to go home, eat, and spend some time with her boyfriend. She didn't like to leave Zachary isolated for too long. He could go out and do things with other people at any time, of course, but he tried to be there for supper. And when he was depressed, he didn't want to leave the house or reach out to others, even if it would help him feel better about himself.

Kenzie picked up her phone and tapped Zachary's avatar. Of course, he would tell her he didn't care what kind of cuisine she bought, but she wanted to ask him anyway. Show him that respect. Show him she cared about his opinion, even if it were just on something unimportant.

"Kenzie?" Zachary sounded out of breath; his voice unusually intense.

"Hi. Are you okay? Did you have to run for the phone?"

"There's someone here."

"What? Who is there?"

A client? Someone he was entertaining? One of his siblings? And why was he out of breath and sounding so strange?

"I don't know who it is. Someone has been parked in front of the house for... at least half an hour now. I don't know who it is. An older man. Dark car. Lexus."

"Someone is parked in front of the house? One of the neighbors?"

"No. I don't know who it is. He's been sitting out there. He's in his car. Waiting."

"You think he has the house under surveillance?"

"Yes."

Who would be watching her? Kenzie had lived a pretty quiet life since she had gone back to school. She hadn't gone out with anyone but Zachary in the last year. So it wasn't an ex-boyfriend. She hadn't exactly been out painting the town red every night when she was younger, but she had been out a lot more, interested in a lot of different men without being able to commit to one. She could understand if someone held that against her. But that had been a long time ago.

It didn't make sense that it was anything to do with work. It wasn't like she was investigating live people. She helped out with the forensics when she could, but it wasn't like she was the one putting people behind bars.

Her mind flashed back to Micah. *They came to my house. They assaulted me. They kidnapped me.* The true horror of Micah's words hadn't really sunk in before.

They had gone to her house.

And now someone had come to Kenzie's.

A chill ran down her spine, raising goosebumps on her neck and arms.

"I don't know who it is," Kenzie told Zachary. "Are you sure he is watching the house? He's not there for the neighbors... or a delivery man or something like that?"

"If he was a delivery man, he wouldn't still be sitting there half an hour later."

"But if it was someone who was surveilling the house, he wouldn't be so obvious, would he? I mean, just sitting out there in his car? People are bound to notice."

"People are blind to their surroundings," Zachary dismissed. He'd been on enough surveillance jobs to know the truth of that situation. On TV, people noticed someone sitting in a car on the street for ten minutes. But in real life? There wasn't much reason for people to watch the street and pay attention to whether vehicles were occupied. "He doesn't exactly blend in, but I haven't noticed anyone else paying him any attention. People out walking their dogs or coming and going to their houses... they just walk on by."

"Well... does he have a camera or anything? Is he filming? What would he want from me? I don't exactly live an interesting life."

"Do you want me to go out there and ask him who he is?"

"No, don't do that." Kenzie was immediately protective of Zachary. He didn't carry a gun. He wasn't one of those macho hard-boiled detectives like on TV. He was a small man without a weapon and she'd seen him hurt before. She didn't want him walking into a dangerous situation. Especially if it were because of her.

Then again, maybe it *wasn't* because of her. Perhaps it was something to do with Zachary's private investigation business. Surely there must be people who were not happy with him for proving that they were stepping out on their spouses, committing insurance fraud, or stealing from their employers. There might even be friends or lovers of the men he had put in prison out to get revenge.

Or the human trafficking ring he had managed to rescue a couple of teenagers from. They might have thought that the kids were dead, as they were supposed to, or they might have somehow figured out it was a con. Luke could have decided to go back to them and spilled the beans.

"It could be dangerous to go out there and confront him," Kenzie told him firmly. "I don't want you to do that. If you think it's someone who shouldn't be there, why don't you call the police, have them check it out?"

"I don't want to do that if it's someone who has a legitimate reason to be there."

"Well, you're the private detective. You figure it out. But don't go out there and expose yourself to someone who could be dangerous."

"Nothing is going to happen," Zachary said, chuckling slightly at her naïveté. "Don't confuse what you see on TV with real life. Everyone isn't walking around with guns, trying to get the jump on everyone else."

"You're the one who brought up guns. And since you don't have one, I don't want you walking into someone who might. If he's just sitting in his car, he's not doing any harm. Just watch and see what happens."

He breathed in her ear for a few seconds, considering. Still out of breath because his anxiety was pumping up his heart rate.

"Are you coming home?"

"Yes. I won't be long. I was just trying to decide what to pick up on the way home."

"You could come straight home. There's stuff in the freezer."

Kenzie mentally reviewed what was in the freezer. Mostly burritos and stuff she didn't really want for supper. She weighed her own cravings against the fact that Zachary was obviously anxious and wanted her to be home as soon as she could be. He might not be having a meltdown yet, but she didn't want to send him into a full-blown anxiety attack because she was taking longer to get home than he thought she should and he thought something had happened to her.

"Okay, fine. I'll heat up something in the freezer. You'll hang in there until I get home? Don't do anything stupid like running out there to confront this guy?"

"No, I won't."

"You're not going to change your mind?" She knew how impulsive he was. And something might occur to him that seemed like a good reason to go charging out there by himself. She wanted him to promise he would stay inside.

"You'll drive straight into the garage, right?" Zachary checked, more worried about Kenzie than about himself. "Don't open the garage door until you're right in front of it, and then shut it right away, so no one can slip in. Then come in through the house, so you're not exposed."

"Okay. I will. I'm coming from across town, so it's going to be a few minutes longer than you expect. Okay? Don't panic when I'm not home right away. I'm not at the ME's Office."

"All right." Another quick, anxious breath. "See you soon."

52

Kenzie knew that it probably wasn't the best idea, but she approached from the direction that would require her to drive the street in front of the house to catch a glimpse of the stranger surveilling her house.

Even though she had told Zachary that the watcher might be dangerous, it was hard to make herself believe that. There had to be a good reason for someone to be sitting in front of her house. And the chances that he would have a gun? Zero to none. Kenzie had rarely met anyone but police who carried guns. That she knew of.

She saw the car that Zachary had referred to immediately and took a look at the driver as she drove past. She did what she had promised and went straight into the garage and shut the door. She went into the house, where Zachary hesitated between running to meet her and keeping an eye on the car through the front window.

"Hey, it's okay," she told him. "Everything is fine."

"He's still out there. Did you see him?"

"I saw him. It's okay. It's nothing to worry about."

"I should have called the police. I shouldn't have waited until you got home. What if he—" Zachary broke off, looking out the window, his anxiety rising. "He's getting out of the car!"

"Calm down. Nothing bad is going to happen. I know who it is."

"You know?" Zachary had been walking back over to the window to get a better look at the stranger, and froze where he was. "You know him?"

Kenzie nodded. "I do. And you don't need to worry. It isn't anyone who wants to hurt me. Or you."

"You know who it is. Someone from work?"

"No."

Kenzie walked to the front door and flipped on the switch for the outside light, as dusk was beginning to fall. She tapped in the burglar alarm code for the front door and opened it as the man walked up the sidewalk. Kenzie reached out and gave him a hug, which was returned. It felt good to be held, to be in his arms again. Even though neither of them was demonstrative, she had missed that.

She turned back toward Zachary, jerked her head for him to join her. "Zachary, this is my dad."

Zachary looked stunned. He looked at Kenzie as if he wasn't sure if she were telling the truth. She had not invited him over to her mother's house or to any family events. She had preferred to keep her parents and Zachary separate and not to have to deal with both of those worlds at the same time. It wasn't because she was ashamed of Zachary—or ashamed of her parents, for that matter. She just didn't want to mix those two worlds and have to deal with them both simultaneously.

But, as she should have expected would happen sooner or later, her father had broken down that wall all by himself. As far as Walter Kirsch was concerned, there were no walls. Only doors to be opened, one way or another. He would knock, phone, pound on the door, ring the doorbell, find a key, or pick the lock, but one way or another, he would get through every locked door that was placed in front of him.

"Dad, this is my boyfriend, Zachary Goldman. Zachary, Walter Kirsch."

Kenzie sighed, realizing she couldn't just leave her father standing on the doorstep, so she stepped to the side to let him in. Walter had been at the house once or twice before. Not very often, and always, as he had this time, just showing up when he decided he needed to see Kenzie about something. She hadn't invited him into her sanctum.

Once they were all in the living room, Walter held his hand out toward Zachary, extending it in greeting. Zachary took it hesitantly.

"Nice to meet you, Zachary," Walter greeted pleasantly. Then silence hung in the air when he should have said, "Kenzie has told me a lot about you."

Because, of course, Kenzie had told him as little as possible. Her personal life was none of his business.

"You too, sir," Zachary responded. Again the awkward pause, because Kenzie hadn't told him much about her father either.

The two men continued to shake hands for another second or two, and Kenzie hoped that her father wasn't squeezing the life out of Zachary's hand in a show of male dominance. Eventually, the two dropped the grip and shifted away from each other slightly.

"Dad." Kenzie wasn't going to wait for him to work his way through the entire spiel this time. "What's up? Why are you here?"

Walter took his time, sitting down on the couch and pinching the sharp crease in his pants. Kenzie didn't want to sit down with him and be forced to exchange pleasantries. She stayed on her feet. She needed to make supper. And to figure out how to get Walter out of there as quickly as possible.

"I can't just stop in to see my little girl?" Walter asked, smiling at her.

"Zachary said you've been sitting in front of the house for an hour. You're making him think you're a stalker. What's going on?"

Walter chuckled. He looked Zachary over, evaluating him. Kenzie didn't like the smirk on his face, the suggestion that he was somehow more superior because he had made Zachary worry. That he was superior because Zachary was clearly smaller and more fragile than he was. She hated him looking down on her partner that way.

"No need to worry," Walter assured them. "I just wanted a chance to talk to Kenzie. I was in the area, so I thought I would stop by. I didn't want to bother you at work. So I thought I would hang out here while I did a little work in the car and catch you after work."

"A lot of nights, I don't get home until late. You could have been out there for hours."

"Oh, I would have called you if it looked like you weren't going to get back in good time. I had plenty I could do while I was waiting."

Of course he did. He was always schmoozing with someone, pressing his agenda and trying to negotiate for whatever bill he happened to be lobbying for at that particular time. All he needed was his phone and his golden tongue.

"So what did you want?"

"Do I have to want something to come and see my own daughter? It used to be that people were happy to see their parents, to take a little time out of their day to visit."

"You could have called me. No need to make this trip."

"I could have. But I wanted to see you face to face. It's important to see your children every now and then."

Except now, he only had one child, and Kenzie couldn't help blaming him partially for Amanda's loss. Of course, nothing would have saved Amanda. They might have been able to get a few more months for her. But not years. However lucky they had been in keeping her alive, she wouldn't still be alive now. Not with another kidney. Not with five new kidneys. She had just been too fragile.

"It's nice to see you too," she said through her teeth. And she waited. She had already asked what he wanted. Sooner or later, he was going to have to come out with it.

"I wondered if you had decided to go to the masquerade ball."

"The masquerade ball? No. I don't know why you and Mother are so intent on me going. I know it is for kidney research, but I'm not interested in going out to these events. I contribute in other ways. Balls have never been my thing."

"You could have a great time there. You could bring Zachary. You could wear matching costumes. Some couples' thing. Dance, enjoy some good food, just be seen there. So people know that the Kirsch family is still there, representing."

"Considering that you and Mother are going to be there, I hardly see why I would need to."

"I'd like you to be there. I'd like to show you off. We don't see each other often enough, honey. You need to get out of that morgue more often. See life instead of death."

"I do get out. I do plenty of things other than just attend autopsies all day. You really have no idea what my job is like. Or what my life with Zachary is like. Don't judge."

Kenzie's face warmed a little as she protested. Because she knew that the truth was, she did spend too much time at the morgue. And she didn't get out very often. With Zachary at home, she didn't even do very much with her girl friends. She couldn't remember the last girls' night out. Maybe sometime when he was out on surveillance, she should give them a call. She didn't want to completely abandon her outside life. She didn't want to get so wrapped up in her work at the ME's office and with Zachary that she didn't have her own life anymore.

She wasn't obsessed with death. Even working with dead bodies, she was really focused on life. What had happened before the person had died. How it could be avoided in the future. By investigating death, they really examined life.

"I'm not judging. I'm saying I would like to see more of you. Is that bad?"

"No, of course not."

They both just looked at each other for a few minutes, studying each other's faces, looking for the familiar tells.

"I was talking to the governor just the other day," Walter said casually, as if there were a natural segue to this topic.

Kenzie's stomach clenched. *The governor?* Walter had his high-powered friends. Everyone who was anyone knew who Walter Kirsch was. And Kenzie had a feeling that her father's conversation with the governor had not been a casual mention of his daughter over drinks.

"You just happened to be talking to the governor?" Kenzie demanded. "And my name just happened to come up?"

"My family is important to me. Of course you came up."

"And what were you discussing?"

Kenzie knew precisely where it was going, and she wasn't going to give him the chance to approach the subject softly. She wanted it up-front. No couching everything in politically correct language. No hints or opacity. Walter frowned. He liked to play the part of the gentleman, who would never say anything to offend anyone, and always knew exactly how to approach every topic.

"Honey..."

"The governor wants Dr. Wiltshire to issue a death certificate on Willie Cartwright," Kenzie said. "Are you telling me that's why you're here? To interfere with the proper investigation of the Medical Examiner?"

"Of course not. I just wondered how it was going. The governor has his concerns about the way it is being handled."

"Why? Doesn't Willis Cartwright's family want to know the truth?"

"The family already knows the truth. Willie Cartwright was an old man. Old men die. Eventually, things just wear out."

"Well, nothing wore out. He had a virus. And we're trying to find out more information about this virus and where he got it and how it developed and led to his death. That takes time. You may think from watching TV that every lab test can be done on the equipment in the autopsy room and that there is never any doubt about any of the results, but that's fantasy. That's not the way things actually work. Tests take weeks, even months to come back. Sure, the families would like everything to be resolved in a day or two, but that's not the way it goes in real life."

"Even if you're waiting for tests back, haven't you already done everything you need to? At least release the body to them."

"If we're not sure that we have all the samples collected and tests ordered that we need, we are entitled to hold the body for longer. It doesn't do us much good if we release the body and then decide later that we need a sample from another part of the brain, or need another liver sample from a different lobe, or find out that we didn't get something else that we needed. By then, it's too late."

"We're just not sure why you're acting like this is such a problematic case. He's an old man who died in a nursing home. It isn't like it was someone in the prime of their life who just dropped dead over his bowl of Cheerios. It isn't like you have some plague that has to be quashed. It's an old man who died in the night."

It was a mistake for him to refer to a plague. Because that's just what Kenzie and Dr. Wiltshire were worried about. If the HHV-4 variant was fatal, they needed to find out how often and trace it back to its source and everyone else who might have caught it. Screen them all for who was positive for the virus and get them quarantined. Watch them for developing symptoms. Keep track of their vital signs so that they would be immediately warned if someone started to deteriorate rapidly.

"You don't know what's going on," she told her father icily. "And neither does the governor. And he doesn't have the authority to tell the Medical Examiner's Office what to do in an investigation."

"No one is telling anyone what to do," Walter said reasonably. "We just don't understand what is going on here. Have you discovered something? If so, you need to report it. Let him know what's going on."

"No, we don't. We have our own reporting lines. As we figure things out, we will report it to the proper authorities." She met her father's eyes. "Not the governor."

Walter shrugged, but she knew from his face that she'd hit her mark. He might act as if her words didn't have any effect on him and he was only casually interested in the matter, but she had seen him in enough negotiations to know the tiny tells. She had spent the years since Amanda had died learning his face and everything she could read from his expression.

Zachary shifted. He had remained quiet during the discussion. It was, after all, something that concerned only Kenzie and her father. But he spoke now, his eyes also fastened on Walter's face, reading him. "You wouldn't let anything happen to Kenzie, would you?"

Walter looked startled at this. He laughed and shook his head, but his face was not amused. "No, I would never let anything happen to her. What are you talking about?"

"The governor has a lot of power. Not just politically. There have been rumors that he has been involved with some... unsavory people. If you thought he was going to take any action against Kenzie, you would tell us, wouldn't you?"

Kenzie looked at Zachary in amazement.

Walter reached over and took Kenzie's hand in his. "Of course. Kenzie is my only living child. I wouldn't let anyone put her in danger." He turned his eyes to hers. "You believe that, don't you honey?"

"Yes," Kenzie agreed faintly.

"Now would not be a good time for rumors of some new virus or disease," Walter said slowly and softly. "Full-scale panic would reverse many of the gains that have been made. There is an election coming up, and the last thing we need is for people to be worried that the government cannot protect them."

"What have you heard?" Kenzie demanded. How could he know about the HHV-4? Kenzie and Dr. Wiltshire had kept it carefully under wraps, just as Dr. Savage had requested. There were more people in the lab who were in the know than in the Medical Examiner's Office, so the leak must have come from there. But who would be talking to the governor about it? Especially before the tests on Mr. Cartwright's tissues had even been completed.

The governor had been pushing back against their investigation even before they knew about the HHV-4 variant.

W alter looked at Kenzie, considering her question. "What have I heard? I hear a lot of things. I talk to a lot of people and I have a pretty good picture of what things are being discussed at the Capitol."

"Why are you talking about an outbreak? An outbreak of what?" Kenzie did her best to bluff, speaking in a tone that implied she didn't have a clue about any outbreak and how it might be related to Willis Cartwright.

"It's a benign virus," Walter said. "You'll get everyone all stirred up over something that isn't even a danger. People carry around these viruses their whole life without being impacted by them. They don't even have symptoms. Maybe sometimes they get stressed out and one of them gets activated, you get a cold sore on your lip or run a mild fever. You get a sore throat. Is that worth getting everybody in a panic about?"

He didn't say he was talking about herpesviruses, but his words testified that he was. Herpesviruses were notorious for hiding out, inactivated, for years. Until stress set in and then the sufferer started to have symptoms. Usually mild, but occasionally... there could be fatal complications. Not usually the brain pathology that they had seen, but liver failure or other serious complications.

"I don't know what you're talking about," Kenzie said with a shake of her head.

"You can't lie to me, Kenzie." He let go of her hand and rubbed his temples. "I know you are loyal to your job and have to respect the confidentiality of the office and of the families of the deceased. And even if you didn't," his eyes were sad, "you wouldn't tell me about it. You think we're on opposite sides, but we're not. I just want what's best for you. And for the state."

"The governor, you mean. You want him to be re-elected."

"No. It's never been about the individuals. You know me and what I do. It's the people I care about. All the people who depend on me to help protect their rights and keep the government and large corporations accountable. That's what I care about. Not the money. Not the governor. All of the people who could be affected."

"You think this is nothing. Just the sniffles."

He nodded. "More or less."

"You don't think it is the cause of death for Willie Cartwright or anyone else."

"No. I don't. If it was that bad, you would be hearing about it before bodies started hitting the morgue. Yes, Mr. Cartwright may have had it when he died, but that doesn't mean he died as a result of it. After all of this, what goes down on his death certificate will likely be natural causes. And if it did have something to do with his death... then it's because he was an old man with a compromised immune system."

Kenzie sighed. So far, she didn't have anything to suggest that he was wrong. They hadn't had time to figure out the way the virus worked and whether it contributed to Cartwright's death or not. And if it had, then, as Walter said, he was an old man and that was not unexpected. Seniors died from influenza too. Thousands every year.

"You've said your piece," she said finally. "I'm not in authority at the Medical Examiner's Office anyway. Even if I wanted to push Cartwright's certificate through, it isn't my job."

"You do have some influence, though," Walter suggested, his eyes glittering. With Walter Kirsch, it was always about influence.

"No. I'm just an assistant. I'm there to answer phones and to learn."

54

After Kenzie saw Walter to the door, she returned to the living room to talk to Zachary. He watched the man get into his car and drive away before he turned back to Kenzie.

"So, that was your dad," he said lightly.

"Yeah. I'll bet you were really impressed."

He shrugged. "Better than mine. Trust me, you wouldn't like him either."

"I don't dislike my dad," Kenzie hurried to clarify. "But I don't trust him. His moral compass... well, you can probably tell, it isn't the same as mine."

Zachary nodded understandingly. He lifted each seat cushion on the couch and swept his hand underneath through all the cracks and crevices. Kenzie watched him put them back down and then shake out each of the throw blankets and decorative pillows. He arranged them again neatly.

This was new behavior. Paranoia? OCD? Probably something that should be reported to Zachary's medical team.

Zachary looked at her sideways. "Bugs."

"What?" Kenzie shook her head. He was concerned about bugs crawling around under the seat cushions?

He finished tidying the couch and went on to check the underside of the side table, then walked out to the front door, scanning the walls and running his fingers around the doorframe molding and picture frames.

"They want to keep an eye on you. You're his window into the Medical Examiner's Office. He knew he wasn't going to make any difference by coming here to talk to you. Would he ever be able to talk you into altering records at the office? Would you be able to talk Dr. Wiltshire into changing his mind on a cause of death determination, even if you wanted him to?"

"Well, no. It would be pretty rare. You got him to reopen a couple of cases. But that's pretty rare."

"Exactly. So he came here because they want to keep an eye on you. Or an ear."

Zachary returned to the living room and opened the soft-sided briefcase that housed his mobile office. He pushed things around until he found what he was looking for, then turned on a device he held in the palm of his hand and extended the antenna on it. Kenzie watched as he began to sweep it back and forth in slow arcs around where Walter had been sitting. As he turned to talk to Kenzie, the device gave a squawk. He started to pass it over her like a security wand at an airport. It squawked a couple more times. Zachary nodded to Kenzie's purse.

"In there, I think. Can I look?"

Kenzie handed it to him. She had come straight into the house and into the visit with her father upon returning home from work. Her purse had been sitting beside the couch while they had been talking. Certainly within reach of the man, but she hadn't seen him touch it.

Zachary removed the contents of Kenzie's bag a few items at a time, passing the bug-finder over them and then reaching back in. When the purse was empty, he felt around the pockets and lining, and eventually came up with a small, round, black device with a pin at one end to make sure it would stay where it was placed and not be jostled around too much by Kenzie putting things into or taking them out of her bag.

Kenzie was stunned. She knew that her father had crossed the line more than once in the past. He always claimed to be on the side of the angels and things had always turned out okay in the end. But bugging his own daughter's handbag?

"He knows that you take it into work," Zachary said. "He didn't just want to hear the conversations between you and me. That wouldn't be very enlightening. He wanted to hear what was going on at the office."

He ran the antenna around Kenzie once more and it didn't squawk. He walked to the front door and back, moving the electronic device slowly until he was sure that there wasn't another bug in the front hall, then returned. He shut it off, pushed the antenna back in, and stowed it back in his bag.

Kenzie sat in the living room as Zachary went about in the kitchen, getting something together for dinner. Kenzie just stared at Zachary's bag. She couldn't believe that her own father would betray her like that. The only reason he had shown up at her house was to be able to put a bug on her? A bug that she would then take with her back to work so that he and the governor and whoever else was putting pressure on Dr. Wiltshire could listen to their conversations. It was unbelievable.

When she had been a little girl, she always saw Walter as a sort of knight in shining armor. The way that he and Lisa described the work they did—how he helped to protect people from big companies that wanted to take their money and big government that wanted to take away their rights—he had seemed larger than life to Kenzie. He was her protector and the protector of everyone else in the state. Kenzie grew up and adjusted to a more mature world view. And then Amanda had died and she had seen him as something else. Someone willing to bend and break a few rules to get what he wanted. He would put his ethics behind him if they prevented him from protecting his family or getting his own way. He had excused his behavior, saying that it had been for Amanda, just as he would justify his conduct in this case, saying that it was for the greater good, but it wasn't.

But she wasn't sure Walter was a bad guy, either. He did what he did out of love and passion and a sense of fair dealing. He really did believe in the causes that he lobbied for. And if he occasionally went a little overboard, out of passion, did that make him a bad person?

But he had tried to use her. To spy on her. She couldn't deny what she had seen. She didn't know how he had managed to slip the bug into her purse without either of them realizing it, but was grateful that Zachary had seen through his mask and had taken the time to check.

"Do you want some dinner?" Zachary asked tentatively, framed in the kitchen doorway.

"Yeah... I need to eat, but I don't know what I want..."

"I heated up some of those frozen burritos. I know it's not a great supper, but..."

"That's just fine," Kenzie said. She forced herself to get up off the couch, even though her body felt so heavy and slow that she could barely move it. She wanted to go to bed. To shut off.

But her feet moved in the direction she pointed them and she walked into the kitchen and sat down in her chair. Zachary had managed to heat a couple of burritos without filling the kitchen with smoke and had even melted cheese over top of hers.

"I thought you couldn't cook," Kenzie teased, giving him a weak smile. "You've been holding out on me."

"I was focused." Zachary smiled, his neck starting to get red. "I knew you needed me to get something ready, so I had a mission and I stuck to it."

"You did good." Kenzie knew how hard that was for him, even if it seemed like a simple thing for her. "Thank you."

Zachary sat down, then bounced back out of his chair to get the carton of milk out of the fridge for Kenzie. "Unless you want something stronger..."

Kenzie thought about it. She wouldn't mind a bit of chemical help to get relaxed. But she shook her head. Zachary always said that he didn't mind her drinking when he couldn't, but she always felt a bit awkward about it anyway. And she needed a clear head to think things through, even though her brain was trying to shut her down.

Zachary poured milk in her glass and sat down again, looking around the table to see if there was anything else he had forgotten. He apparently decided there was not and cut off a bite of his burrito.

"Do you think you're safe?" he asked in a neutral tone.

Kenzie looked at him, shocked. "Am I safe? Of course I am. Why wouldn't I be?"

"If he's working with the governor... there has to be some big money involved. And big guns. When people like that start putting you under surveillance... well, they're probably willing to go farther, if they have to."

"Yeah, like what?" Kenzie laughed, shaking her head. "This isn't a TV thriller. I can't even believe he would plant a bug on me. The only other person who has ever done anything like that was... well... you."

She could remember how angry she had been when she had a mechanic put her car up on a lift to check for any foreign objects, and they had discovered a tracker mounted on the inside of her rear bumper. It was before she and Zachary were serious, and had been such an invasion of her privacy that she had immediately stopped talking to him.

The red flush rose from Zachary's neck to his cheeks and ears. "Uh... yeah. That was stupid, and I'm really sorry about all of the crap I put you through..."

"I understand that you were anxious and that you wanted to protect the people you were close to. But it really was over the line."

"I know." It had been almost two years ago now. They had alluded to it once or twice since getting back together, and Zachary always apologized and looked embarrassed by his own behavior. "But since we changed my meds around, and I started seeing Dr. B regularly... it's been better. I haven't done that—anything like that—since then."

Kenzie didn't actually think that he had. She kept a pretty close eye on his mental state and how he acted around her, and she watched for any signs that he was trying to hide things from her or cover up his activities. Of course, there were many hours in the day when she couldn't monitor what he was doing. He could be having an affair and bugging everything she owned. The bug in her purse could have been his, rather than Walter's. Except then he wouldn't have had a reason to find it there and show it to her.

"What did you do with the bug?"

"I drowned it."

Kenzie looked over at the kitchen sink, filled with water, and grinned. "Well, I guess we don't need to worry about anyone overhearing this conversation, then."

"No. It's just you and me."

"Unless he or someone else has bugged another area of the house."

"No." Zachary's voice was confident. "No other bugs."

"How could you know that? Someone else might have left something here another time. Or I might be bugging you to keep track of you during the day."

He shook his head.

He was so sure about it that Kenzie was unnerved. "How could you possibly know that?"

"Because I check."

"You check?" Kenzie repeated. She thought about the bug detector in his bag. Right there where it was close at hand. How paranoid was he? Did he actually think that she might be bugging him?

"Not every day," Zachary assured her, as if *that* might be considered over the top. "But... every few."

"You sweep this house for bugs every few days."

"Yes."

"Why?"

He blinked at her, as if only realizing now that this might not be considered normal behavior. "To... keep you safe. To protect your privacy. Make sure that no one is watching or listening to us when we're here. After that business with that cartel, especially... it wouldn't be a good idea to assume that they believed what they were told and weren't checking up on us. On me. I don't want any harm to come to you because of what I do. It's just like you having a burglar alarm. An extra layer of protection."

"Well... I appreciate it. But I would have liked to know about it before. I think that's the kind of thing you might want to tell me about."

"Oh." Zachary took another bite of his burrito and chewed, thinking about that. "I just figured... you wouldn't want to know. You'd feel better not having to think about it."

"No, I think I want to know if you think that there are bad guys after you. Or me."

"Hmm." He stared down at his plate, not at her.

"What?"

"I think... are you sure?"

"Am I sure I want to know? Yes, I am."

He scratched the back of his neck. "I think... you should consider... who your father is working with, and what their stakes are."

"Really?"

He didn't say anything. Kenzie poked at her burrito. She cut a few pieces off and worried them rather than putting them into her mouth. Her stomach was roiling. Probably best not to add a bunch of beans to that fermenting mess.

"You think I'm in danger?"

She didn't want to discount his expert opinion. Yes, he was anxious, even paranoid at times. He had PTSD and the least trigger could set him off. She was sure that just having her father parking at the curb for that hour had wound his brain up into overdrive, which might explain why he was so concerned for her welfare. But he'd been right about the bug. And he'd dealt with unsavory characters and criminals who wanted him out of the way before. And Kenzie herself had learned before that just because someone seemed kindly and safe, that didn't mean that they were. She'd been fooled in the past. That was one reason she wanted him to tell her suspicions, even if she did think that they might just be imagination. She needed to know what to watch for.

"Maybe. It's possible. Or, he may want to keep an eye on you to make sure you're *not* in any danger. But that would still mean that you might be in danger from others."

"Yeah. I guess either way... I should take extra precautions."

Zachary blew out a breath, nodding. His shoulders dipped down. He'd been holding himself tense. It was a relief for him that she had seen his point and would consider what she needed to do to protect herself.

"Maybe I could help out for a few days, just to make sure everything is okay."

"Like what?"

"Drive you to work. Or follow and make sure no one is watching you. Maybe put a tracker in your car and in your bag. So I know where you are if there is any trouble."

"Oh, so we're back to trackers now, are we?"

He shrugged. "Only if you said yes. Not covertly."

"I'll think about it."

"And... can I help with this case that you're working on? I know you've been worried about it."

"You do?" Kenzie looked across the table at Zachary. "How do you know that?"

"I can see it. That you're worried. That you're getting stressed about work and trying to figure out what's going on."

"Well, yeah. I am."

"Can I help? Is there any way? I know you can't tell me anything confidential, but if there is something you need. Something I could help with. I'd really like to."

"No, there isn't anything you can do," Kenzie said immediately, discounting the idea.

"Well... think about it. You know I rely on your medical knowledge when I'm trying to sort out a case with medical involvement. Think about whether there are things that my expertise could help with. Skip tracing. Surveillance. Background research."

"I'll think about it," Kenzie agreed. "But I don't think there is anything you can do."

K enzie was trying to read a book sitting in bed to quiet her mind and Zachary, sitting with her, was looking through email or messages on his phone. "You know," Kenzie ventured, "There might be one thing you could do to help me out. With our investigation at work, I mean."

Zachary lowered his phone immediately. "Sure. What do you need?"

"I need to track someone down. I've been trying to call her or get into her building, but I haven't had any luck. It would probably take you an hour, and you'd not only know if she still lives there, but also most of her life story."

Zachary smiled. "Not all of that, but I can probably track her down for you. What do you know?"

Kenzie outlined the details she had on Francine Mudd, the woman who had owned Lola before the dog ended up being given to the nurses at Champlain House. Zachary tapped details into his phone, nodding.

"How long since she's lived at this address, do you know?"

"I don't think it could be long. Maybe a few weeks or months. It was recent."

"I should be able to track her down."

"That would really help. We need to talk to her about something. Related to the case."

Zachary didn't ask what it was. He was very good at not asking her about things that might be confidential. He didn't usually ask her directly about the cases the Medical Examiner's Office was working on, though sometimes he heard things through other channels. Kenzie shared interesting tidbits when she thought it would be okay. Non-identifying things so she wouldn't be breaching anyone's privacy. She didn't actually have any live clients.

"You're careful at work, right?" Zachary asked after finishing his phone notes and setting the phone onto the side table on his side of the bed.

"Careful about what?" Kenzie asked. "I'm not sure what you're talking about."

"Just... your dad was talking about viruses and whether they could kill anyone... I don't want you to do anything that might be dangerous. I can't do anything to protect you from microscopic invaders."

"Oh, that." Kenzie nodded. "Well, he was really talking out of school. It isn't anything that I can discuss."

"That's okay. I don't expect you to. I just hope... you're taking precautions. I don't know. Wearing a mask and gloves. Whatever else doctors are required to do to avoid viruses spreading. Sealing them off or showers or whatever."

"Of course. We are very careful." But Kenzie was mindful of what Dr. Wiltshire had said about viruses escaping from labs. It happened, even when scientists thought they were taking all the proper steps to keep them isolated. The morgue was not sealed from the rest of the building. Not normally. They could take measures if they thought that a case might involve biohazards, but they usually didn't wear hermetically sealed suits or set up air locks between the autopsy room and the outside world.

"Good."

Kenzie put her book down. Even if she wanted to, she knew she wasn't going to be reading anything else. Her eyes just kept going over the same information.

"Let's see if we can get some sleep."

Zachary turned off the light on his side of the bed and waited for Kenzie to turn off her light and cuddle up to him.

Kenzie wondered from Dr. Wiltshire's face the next day if something had happened overnight. A child's death or one of those other heartbreaking cases that made everybody depressed as they handled the body and other evidence. Trying to look past the tragedy of a life cut short and just focus on the evidence.

"Morning, doctor."

"Kenzie... I need you to prep Mr. Cartwright's body for transport. The funeral home will be picking him up later today."

"Oh." Kenzie was surprised. "Have you made a ruling on cause of death, then?"

"We're still waiting for a few tests to come back, so no, I'm not ready... But we've collected everything we need to, and his family is waiting to hold a funeral." He shrugged. "I think that we need to move on to other cases; we've got a few that need to be cleared out. I've been spending too much time on this possible outbreak. There's really no reason to think that this virus is any worse than typical HHV-4. Mankind has been dealing with Epstein Barr for hundreds, possibly thousands of years."

"Okay." Kenzie didn't want to argue with him about it. Maybe if he released Cartwright's body, the political pressure would go away and she wouldn't have to worry about her father or anyone else who might feel like making trouble. "Any... special precautions to be taken? Do you want me to say something to the funeral home about the possibility of contaminants?"

"HHV-4 is not known to be dangerous," Dr. Wiltshire said flatly. "You can tell them he is positive and they should take appropriate action. Wear gloves and a mask, avoid any physical contact with fluids. They would do all of that anyway, but if you remind them... then we've done our duty."

"Is everything okay, Dr. Wiltshire?"

"Yes, of course, Kenzie. Everything is just fine. Take care of that for me, won't you?"

"Sure."

He went on to his office. Kenzie did as she had promised, going into the morgue and preparing Cartwright's remains for pick-up.

Kenzie's phone rang just before noon. Kenzie considered ignoring it, claiming that she was already on her lunch break and wandering down to the vending machine to see if anything edible had been stocked.

Then she saw who it was. Zachary.

"Hey, Zach. How's it going?" She tried to sound as relaxed and unstressed as possible for his sake.

"Good. I have contact information for you for Francine Mudd."

"Already?" Kenzie smiled. "You don't know how much I appreciate that."

Zachary carefully dictated to her the information he had gathered, which was, as Kenzie had expected, a little more than just her phone number and address. The reason she was no longer at the old address was that it had been her boyfriend's apartment, and they had since broken up. She was now back to living on her own—in a dog-free building, Kenzie assumed—and usually worked evenings as a waitress or hostess.

"Perfect. That's really helpful."

"Are you going to talk to her today?"

"Yes, if I can," Kenzie agreed.

Zachary was silent in response. Kenzie tried to figure out if she were supposed to have given him a different answer.

"Okay," Zachary said eventually. "I'll see you later, then."

"See you tonight," Kenzie agreed.

Kenzie decided that sooner was better than later, and if she were to go out, she could avoid eating something from the vending machine. She could stop and get some good takeout, or even just a grocery store salad, and save herself from the questionable sandwiches and other items in the vending machine.

So she headed out right away. She would talk to Francine Mudd and see what information she could offer and still be able to get back to the Medical Examiner's Office to get a few more things done and shut down for the day.

It would probably have been wise to call ahead, but Kenzie didn't want to give Francine an opportunity to offer any excuse for not being able to talk. So she found the woman's apartment and knocked on the door. She hadn't even had to get Francine to let her in through the double set of doors in the vestibule downstairs. A delivery man had been let in ahead of Kenzie. She caught the door and continued as if she belonged there. No-one stopped her.

She rapped sharply on the door, intending for it to sound brisk and businesslike. It was a couple of minutes before a woman arrived at the door. Kenzie looked her over, frowning.

"Are you Francine Mudd?"

"Yes. And you are...?"

Kenzie had expected the woman to say that she was Francine's mother. She had imagined Francine to be a college student, someone just trying to make it on her own for the first time. Living in cheap apartments. Getting a dog and then not being able to take care of it. Breaking up with her boyfriend. Working as a waitress. All those things had predisposed her to think of Francine Mudd as a young woman, not the middle-aged woman who stood in front of her.

"Oh. Sorry. My name is Kenzie Kirsch. I'm with the Medical Examiner's Office."

"Has someone died?"

"No. Well, yes, people have died, but not someone directly connected with you."

"Oh, good. You scared me for a minute; I thought that maybe..."

"I'm sorry. I should be more careful. I'm actually here about Lola."

"Lola?"

"A dog you used to own."

"Oh. That Lola. Well, she isn't dead, is she? And if she was, it wouldn't be handled through your office."

"No. We're looking into a death that occurred at the senior center where Lola is living. I was asked to look into Lola's background as part of our survey of the environment."

"Why would you need to know about Lola?"

"Well, she was with him when he died. It's just routine, ma'am. Do you think I could come in? We could sit down and work through these questions and then I'll be on my way."

"I suppose." Francine opened her door the rest of the way to allow Kenzie in. She led Kenzie to a clean, neat, bright sitting room done in a sort of grandmotherly style. Old furniture with light upholstery or accents, needlework hung on the walls, and smelling faintly of roses or another perfume.

"This is very nice."

"It's comfortable," Francine said, looking around to evaluate it. She acted as if it weren't actually her place, but just somewhere she had landed for the day.

"So tell me about Lola. Did you get her when she was a puppy?"

"No. She belonged to a friend of the family. He passed away, and everyone thought I should take Lola. She wasn't left specifically to me. But no one else could take her. I was living somewhere that allowed dogs at the time, and Jay said he didn't mind, so I took her in. She's not a young dog. She's... mature."

Kenzie nodded encouragingly. "And your family friend? What did he die of?"

"I don't know. I think it was maybe a stroke. Something quick. By the time anyone found him, it was too late. He had a bad heart, you know. He'd always said that. Had this surgery a few years ago to replace faulty valves. He said he was doing better. But then..." Francine trailed off.

"Yes. I'm sorry to hear that. What was his name?"

"Do you need that? It seems to me that you don't need to document the dog's entire life to do... whatever this is. An investigation into a death. You said someone at the nursing home died, right?"

"Yes. This is just background information, but I do need to know who owned her before you did."

"I can't imagine why," Francine muttered. But she was on the move, walking over to a side table with a tiny drawer in it, from which she removed an address book. "Eugene Hopewell. No current address or phone number," she added tartly.

Kenzie smiled. She liked Francine. "Thank you. Much appreciated. And when Lola was with you... was she ever sick?"

"Sick? No, I don't think so. Dogs eat things and throw up sometimes... or eat things and get the runs... or they roll in something or get sprayed by a skunk. But nothing, really, she was a nice dog to have around. Friendly. Never bit anyone even if they deserved it."

"No viruses or infections that you knew of."

"No."

"And where did Eugene live, when he was still alive? Was he in a nursing home? Or in an apartment building or a house...?"

"He lived on his own. In a little bungalow."

"Where was that, do you know? Do you have the address?"

Francine looked down at her address book and gave the address to Kenzie. Kenzie wrote it down along with his name.

"That's really helpful. And when you had Lola, you lived here?" Kenzie looked around at the small apartment.

"No. I was with my boyfriend at the time. Lived at his place. I told you that."

"Oh, of course. And that was at..." Kenzie looked through her notes and read off the address that she had previously visited in hopes of meeting Lola's owner.

"Yes, that's right. Is that everything?"

"Almost done. Does your boyfriend still live there? If I wanted to see the place that Lola lived, do you think he would talk to me? Maybe you could call him and let him know that I'm not some crank?"

"As far as I know, you could be. I'm not really in touch with him anymore. It was a mutual break, but... we didn't stay friends. As far as I know, he is still in the same place, but he could have moved. He wouldn't have bothered to tell me, and we don't have mutual friends."

"Do you have his phone number?"

Francine flipped the pages in her address book to refresh her memory. Kenzie could see that his information had been struck through. But Francine was still able to read it and nodded after she recited the phone number. "Yes, that's his number," she confirmed.

"I really appreciate you taking the time. Thank you so much."

"You're welcome." Francine stood up. "I hope you find everything you're looking for."

56

A s Kenzie left Francine's apartment, her phone buzzed. She looked down at it to see if she had received a text message and saw a calendar reminder that she was supposed to be at couples therapy with Zachary. She swore and double-checked the time. She had completely forgotten that they had an appointment. And Zachary had, she thought, carefully avoided mentioning it or reminding her, maybe testing to see if she would show up this time without any pressure from his end. But it was a thirty-minute warning reminder, which meant she still had time to get there.

She climbed into the car and headed toward Dr. Boyle's office. On the way, she hit her Bluetooth button and called Dr. Wiltshire.

"Kenzie."

"Hi. Uh—I forgot that today is my early day so I can get to therapy with Zachary. I'm sorry. I've left a bunch of stuff up in the air there that I planned to get back to after I talked to Lola's owner."

"I should have remembered this was your usual day."

"Well, so should I," Kenzie said in embarrassment. "If you'll just leave everything where it is, I'll pop back over after I'm done the session and finish up. Is that okay?"

"I can just put your files away and you can pick it up again tomorrow."

"I know, but I really do need to get some of it done today. It's not very good planning on my part."

"We all forget things sometimes. Things have been a little disrupted lately. I'm sure that your files can wait until tomorrow."

"I still prefer to come back in. So just leave them; I'll get them put away tonight."

"Okay," Dr. Wiltshire agreed with a chuckle. "I won't touch anything."

Kenzie checked the time after she parked. It was still ten minutes until the appointment with Dr. Boyle, so she didn't need to rush in, looking all disheveled and apologizing for having forgotten about the appointment. As far as anyone other than Dr. Wiltshire knew, she had remembered all along that she had an appointment. She was a responsible adult. Missing one session didn't make her irresponsible. Just a busy person who sometimes got caught up in things.

She locked the car and walked into Dr. Boyle's waiting room calmly. Zachary was sitting in one of the chairs, elbows on knees, face cradled in his hands. He looked up when he heard Kenzie enter and a smile blossomed on his face.

"Kenzie!"

"Hi." Kenzie made a show of checking the time. "I'm not late, am I?"

"No. Still five minutes to. I'm just... glad you made it."

"Of course. I know I missed the last session, but that's not going to be a regular occurrence. It was just one mistake."

He nodded agreeably. "Of course. You don't forget things like that."

Kenzie let out a breath. No. Of course not. She wouldn't just get busy with something else and forget all about their appointment. Again.

When the session was over, Kenzie was tired and emotionally wrung out, but she had promised Dr. Wiltshire that she would be back to the office, so she explained to Zachary that she needed to spend another hour or two there and then would be home.

"We can have our ice cream today after supper if that's okay with you?"

They had instituted a reward of ice cream following couples therapy to reward themselves for going and doing something that was difficult for both of them. A reward that had been Kenzie's idea. Although Zachary seemed to have taken to it without any difficulty.

"Oh." Zachary looked disappointed, lowering his eyes and fiddling with his key as they prepared to get into their separate vehicles. "Yeah, that would be fine."

"Sorry, I don't mean to screw up the routine. But I really do need to spend some more time at the office today, make sure everything is in order."

"Yeah, of course. Work is important."

"That doesn't mean it's more important than you or our relationship. It just means I need to spend a bit more time there before we can relax."

He nodded.

"I made it here," Kenzie pointed out. "I didn't just work through. That wouldn't have been fair to you, and I've made a commitment to go to these sessions. I'm glad we're doing them."

"Yeah. Well, I'll see you later, then. After work."

Kenzie nodded and suppressed the impulse to apologize to him again. She had explained. He had accepted. She needed to just move on. She would see him again once she was done, and then she could give him her full attention.

The morgue was as silent as... well... a morgue. Kenzie worked through the files she had left on her desk, checked quickly through her email to see what else was awaiting her attention, and decided to tidy up and get on her way. She stowed away the files she hadn't worked on yet and took the ones she had completed into Dr. Wiltshire's office for his review and approval the next day.

His office was in disarray. Dr. Wiltshire was usually pretty tidy, so Kenzie was surprised to see papers on his desk, books and ornaments out of place on his shelf, and his computer screen turned at a different angle from usual, as if he had been displaying it to someone else in the office with him. And maybe he had. She didn't remember him setting up any appointments for the afternoon, but since she hadn't remembered her own appointment, she couldn't rely on her memory.

She spent a few minutes straightening everything back to the way Dr. Wiltshire liked them and looked through the papers and files on his desk. It was going to take longer than she had expected to get out of the office and home. Still, she would rather know she was going back to an environment where everything was tidy and sorted for her and Dr. Wiltshire's arrival than to think about how much work she was going to have to do as soon as she got there in the morning to put things shipshape.

It took half an hour to get his desk put back to rights. Kenzie sighed and turned off his light, then moved on to the autopsy room and cold storage to make sure that if any new remains had been signed in, all the paperwork was in order and she was aware of who their most recent guests were.

As she opened the door, she heard the clatter of sample jars. The sudden, unexpected noise made her jump. Apparently, she wasn't as alone as she had thought.

"Hello?" Kenzie called out, walking into the autopsy room. "Who's here?"

Something was wrong. Surgical tools had been knocked to the floor and not picked back up. There was no body on the table, but there were evidence bins on the counter. Kenzie hadn't left them there, and Dr. Wiltshire would not leave them there when he went home. Only while he was in the process of conducting an autopsy.

"Doctor?"

There was no answer, but there was more banging and movement from the evidence room and the cold storage. Who was there? The night shift could be bringing in some remains, but she hadn't seen or heard anything while she was at her computer to indicate another body being brought in. No texts or messages, nothing in her email. Something could have happened while she was working in Dr. Wiltshire's office, but if a call-out had just been made, they wouldn't be bringing the remains in already.

"Carlos?"

Something was wrong. The space didn't feel right. It didn't smell right, like someone had walked through it carrying their lunch or cut flowers and had left their imprint on the air behind. Kenzie walked across autopsy and opened the door to the cold storage room.

A black shape hurtled toward her and they collided. Strong hands grasped her wrist and shoulder and threw her to the floor. Kenzie tried to catch herself with her hands, but it happened too quickly and she landed on her shoulders and the back of her head, a blow that sent yellow lightning racing through her brain.

"Hey!" Kenzie protested. She tried to get up, but the figure that had hit her was receding, hurrying away from her now. There were shouts, but she couldn't sort out the words. "Stop! Hey!" She couldn't seem to come up with anything more coherent than that. Her knees were wobbly and getting to her feet did not seem possible. If she had a chair, maybe she could use that to get herself up. She felt around herself, disoriented, not sure what might be within reach. Could she reach the counter to pull herself up?

Her fingers encountered a twisted plastic cord, and when Kenzie pulled on it, something came clattering down on her head. A phone. Kenzie tried to orient the phone in the proper position and to focus on it. How many times had she used it to call out to someone in the building? She wasn't sure which end was up, couldn't bring her eyes into focus on the numbers on the buttons. She pushed several buttons in a row, trying to remember where the zero and the nine were on the keypad. There was a tiny voice from the receiver. Kenzie held it up to her ear.

"Trouble in autopsy," she managed to get out a half-ways coherent sentence. "Help. Now."

K enzie was still sitting on the floor, but was upright, with the cabinets behind her back, while she applied ice to the back of her head and tried to sound normal and unflustered as she spoke to Detective Cameron, who crouched beside her.

"Did you get a good look at their faces?" Cameron asked. "Was it anyone you recognized?"

"No. I didn't see anything. Heard noises. Called out. Went to see what was going on. But the one I saw—it was just a shape; I have no idea... no idea who it was or what he looked like."

"That's okay. Perfectly understandable. But this is a secure building. You can't get in without identification, without going through security checkpoints."

"I don't know. Don't know what happened, how they got here. When they got here." Kenzie continued to shake her head, even though it was making her a bit giddy. "I was working late..."

"Were they here when you got in?"

"Maybe. I don't know. Everything was quiet... I decided to close up and get home. Went to Dr. Wiltshire's office. It was a mess."

"Dr. Wiltshire's office had been tossed?"

Kenzie thought about that. It had been disorderly, but not like on TV when there were slash marks in all the upholstery where they had searched for hidden evidence. But Dr. Wiltshire had never left his room in disarray like that before.

"Files and papers that should have been put away were out. Things had been moved on his shelves... things he wouldn't normally even touch during the day. You know, medical texts, ornaments. He might take out one text at a time and then put it away when he was done, but with so much being available online now, there wasn't really even much need for him to look something up on paper."

"Did you call anyone when you saw it had been left in a mess?"

"No. I didn't think... that there was an intruder. I just thought that he'd been... upset or in a state when he left. Something upset him, or he got a call-out. I don't know. He seemed worried this morning, and I just thought... it was a continuation."

"So what did you do?"

Kenzie raised her brows and looked Cameron in the eye. "I tidied up."

He laughed.

Kenzie couldn't say she was sure what there was to laugh about, but she was glad he saw the humor in the situation.

"Of course."

"That's my job."

"You're medical staff, not cleaners." It was half a statement, half a question.

"Yes... but I'm his admin as well. So it's normal for me to file stuff at the end of the day. Make sure that everything has been checked in or out correctly. Just generally... make sure everyone keeps their rooms clean."

Cameron nodded, still smiling. Kenzie shifted the ice pack to find a colder spot. The lump on the back of her head was beginning to throb. She winced and waited for it to settle down again.

"So what did you do after cleaning up the doctor's office?"

"I went to check things out in storage and check-in, make sure all of the tests that were supposed to go out had gone, see if we got any other remains while I was gone, that kind of thing."

"While you were gone?"

"I was out. I had a... personal medical appointment."

"Would anyone have known that?"

"Well... a few people, I guess. Julie covers my desk sometimes, so she knows that some Wednesday afternoons, I have an appointment. Dr. Wiltshire knew; I talked to him on the phone earlier to confirm that. Uh... I don't know. Anyone who works closely with the office probably knows that I am away some Wednesday afternoons."

"What time do you usually get back from that appointment?"

"Usually, I don't. I just go home from the doctor's office. But today, I had some other things I needed to clear up before I could go home."

"So normally, at this time, the suite would have been empty."

"Yes."

"And people know that."

"I guess. Not a lot, but yeah... people do know."

It would make sense that if someone wanted to mess with things at the Medical Examiner's Office, they would pick a time when Kenzie wasn't supposed to be there. When it should have been empty and silent.

Kenzie shifted the ice pack again. "Did they get anything? Take anything away?"

"You'll need to check against your inventory. Things have been rifled. Broken. I don't know if anything has been taken."

"I'd better look." Kenzie moved to stand up.

"Are you sure you should be getting up?" Cameron held out his hand as if to grab her or to steady her. "You should sit until you're sure..."

Kenzie leaned against the counter and waited for the head rush to subside. He was probably right. She should wait for a while longer until she was absolutely sure she was okay and that she was steady on her feet. But once the blobs of color stopped flashing before her eyes, she looked around, scanning to see what was out on the counter and what might be missing from the bins.

She had a growing feeling of dread as she looked at the labels on the sample bottles. The glass was cold against her hands.

"We should probably put these things back in the fridge."

"Can you tell what's missing?" Cameron asked. "Is there anything?"

"Yeah." Kenzie shook her head. "All of the Cartwright samples. And Sexton's." She rubbed her forehead. "Uh... the John Doe. Or former John Doe. And the new one, no identity yet."

"That's a lot of samples."

"It's most of our latest cases. What's left... these are mostly older samples that we needed to retest for something."

"Are all of those cases related?"

"No. Just because they are recent." She didn't tell him that Cartwright and Sexton might be related. "Most of them... I think we still have the remains, so we'll be able to get new samples." Kenzie looked toward the cold room. "Do you know if they... took any bodies?"

"If you could have a look; I don't know your cataloging system and don't want to screw anything up."

"Yeah. I'll see."

"Kenzie! Kenzie, are you all right?" Dr. Wiltshire hurried into the room. It was a tight space for two people, a long, narrow room with a counter, designed for one person to work at a time. Dr. Wiltshire squeezed himself in anyway and took Kenzie by the shoulder. "Are you okay? What happened? There was a break in?"

"Yes. I don't know who it was," Kenzie told him. "Or how they got in."

"We'll leave that to the police to sort out. I just want to make sure you are okay."

"Just a bump." Kenzie indicated her head. "Nothing serious. They took samples. We have to make sure they didn't take the bodies too."

"Who would do that?"

"I don't know. I don't understand it..." Kenzie's thoughts were still so scattered from the attack that she couldn't come up with an explanation. "I don't understand why anyone would want to break into the morgue."

"I'll check the inventory. Don't you worry about it." Dr. Wiltshire turned to Detective Cameron. "Has someone looked at her? Checked to see if she has a concussion? Sometimes these things are more serious than they look at first."

"There were a couple of paramedics here. They cleared her. Said she could go to the hospital if she wanted to, but everything looked fine."

Dr. Wiltshire squeezed Kenzie's shoulder again, looking worriedly into her eyes.

Kenzie was reminded of her father holding her hand to comfort her at the same time as he was putting a listening bug in her purse. Was Dr. Wiltshire just acting? Pretending to be concerned and searching her face to see if she had any suspicions?

But that didn't make sense. He had known that she was coming back. He was the one person who had known that she would return to spend a couple more hours clearing files. If he had arranged a break-in, he would have known to make it later at night.

"They were in your office too," Kenzie told Dr. Wiltshire. "You should look to see if anything is missing. I didn't realize... I thought you had just left stuff out. I cleaned up and didn't even know that someone else had been in the room. I should have realized."

His face paled. "In my office? What are they looking for?"

"I think... anything to do with Willis Cartwright. The samples that were taken from here were all taken since his intake. Somebody outside the office wouldn't know how the numbering system worked. It looks like they just went by the dates on the samples."

"But Cartwright..."

He didn't have to say it. Kenzie could see exactly where he was going. "We released Cartwright today," she finished for him.

"Yes." He swore and hit the heel of his hand to his forehead. "I should have known! I should *not* have released him!"

"He'll just be at the funeral home. Even if they have started the embalming, we can still get some samples. And everything that has been done so far is on the computer, all documented."

Cameron looked back and forth between Kenzie and Dr. Wiltshire. "What's going on? You think this Cartwright was the target of the break-in? What is he, mob?"

"No." Kenzie shook her head. "An old man who died at a nursing home."

Cameron's nostrils flared. "Why would anyone be interested in him?"

Kenzie looked at Dr. Wiltshire. He shook his head. "We'll tell you when we're in a more secure location."

Cameron looked around at the various law enforcement officers who were moving around the suite. "I don't think you can get much more secure than this."

"It will have to wait," Dr. Wiltshire said firmly. "Kenzie... can you call the funeral home? Confirm that we need a hold put on the body. I'll check in with the lab and let them know there has been a breach. They'll want to increase their security as well. If this is about the pathogen, they may be the next target."

5 8

Kenzie walked slowly out to her desk to sit on her own chair and be surrounded by her familiar things while she made the call. She didn't want to search for the phone number on her phone while leaning against the counter in a place where she had just been attacked, trying to keep her balance on shaking legs while her head whirled with disconnected thoughts and vertigo.

She sat for a few minutes, just trying to regain her equilibrium. Then she pulled up her electronic contact list and checked to see which funeral home had picked up Mr. Cartwright's remains.

After talking to the funeral home, she tried to call Dr. Wiltshire, but his phone rang through to voicemail. He was probably on the phone with the lab. Or talking to one of the cops there. He would either call her or come find her when he was ready. She opened her email to work through a few other chores while waiting for him to free himself. She should call Zachary and let him know that she would be later than expected. Except she didn't know yet how long she would be and she didn't want him freaking out over her having been assaulted in the midst of the robbery. She wasn't badly hurt. When she could see him face to face, she would tell him about it, when the evidence that she was okay would be right in front of his eyes.

She logged in to her email, but the system kept asking for her password and then not accepting it. She had a strong suspicion there was a problem with the server, which she couldn't fix. The tech guys would have to fix it in the morning. Kenzie probably wasn't the only one locked out.

She tried to get into the file system and ran into the same problem. Definitely the server, then. There would be a lot of people screaming by the time the techies got it sorted out. Kenzie didn't know if the problem was localized to their own space on the server or whether it would affect all the law enforcement in the building. She hoped the techies got a good sleep, because they would need to use all their brain cells in the morning.

So she played solitaire on her phone until Dr. Wiltshire made his way out to her desk.

"Oh, there you are. How are you managing?"

"Fine. I should head home soon. I don't want Zachary worrying, especially if word of this leaks out before I can get there."

"Yes. You should be able to be on your way in a few minutes. I'm hoping that you talked to the funeral home and they agreed to hold the body until we can get more samples?"

"I got the funeral home—"

"Good. That's a relief!"

"There is a problem, though."

"They wouldn't argue with the Medical Examiner's request to hold the body, would they?"

"It's too late. He's already been cremated."

Dr. Wiltshire's face looked long and drawn, worse than Kenzie had ever seen him on his worst days. He shook his head, looking at her with eyes as hollow as Zachary's.

"What is it?" Kenzie asked. "The lab still has samples there. And we have all of the imaging and test results in our file system."

"I talked to the lab." Dr. Wiltshire shook his head. "Kenzie... they were broken into as well. A security guard is in serious condition. All of their physical samples are gone."

It was no coincidence, then. It wasn't a coincidence that the body had been cremated and all the samples burgled the same day. That left them only the electronic files and the print copies that were in Dr. Wiltshire's office. Kenzie looked at her computer. She wanted to reassure Dr. Wiltshire that not all was lost. They still had access to everything they needed in the file system. Only she couldn't log in. There was a computer glitch that wouldn't be solved until the morning, at least.

"We still have our files."

"When you cleaned up my office, did you see any of the Cartwright reports?"

"No. They would be in your..." Kenzie trailed off as Dr. Wiltshire shook his head.

"Everything couldn't be gone," Kenzie insisted. "There's no way anyone could wipe everything out. What about back-ups? Offsite storage?"

"The lab is going to check theirs. I'm going to give tech support a call tonight to have them look at the system." Dr. Wiltshire nodded to Kenzie's computer. He had apparently tried to log in as well and come to the same conclusion as Kenzie. "If they can't get it up and running... I'll ask them to restore what they can from backup. Assuming that hasn't been destroyed too."

They just looked at each other, unwilling to believe that any third party could have had the audacity to do what had apparently been done. A brute force attack on the Medical Examiner's Office, both physically and electronically. Wiping out everything they had on the Cartwright case.

"What did the lab say about their backups?" Kenzie asked tentatively.

"Savage is quite sure that they have everything saved to several physical and cloud drives. He says that everything is backed up multiple times in multiple places. They've been working hard to map out the virus's genome, figuring out where each piece of RNA originated. He said this may slow them down for a day, but they'll have everything up and running soon. Even without the physical evidence, they still have the raw genome data."

Kenzie walked slowly out to the parking garage. She was feeling more unsteady than she would like to admit, though the lump on her head wasn't throbbing anymore. She still didn't know what to think of everything that had happened. It seemed absurd, like something that would happen in a Jason Bourne movie on TV, not in real life. Fantastical and far-fetched.

"Dr. Kirsch."

"Hi." Kenzie gave the guard a nod and kept walking.

"Dr. Kirsch, wait."

Kenzie waited. She supposed that they had higher security protocols in place than usual after what had happened. They would want to make sure that everything was buttoned down and no one else could walk out with evidence. She turned to Frank, the guard, expecting him to demand to see her security card or to wand her with the metal detector. He got closer to her, what felt like uncomfortably close, but maybe that we just because of what Kenzie had been through that evening. She didn't want anyone getting too close to her.

"I have a message for you."

Kenzie blinked. "A message?" She frowned, thinking about her father and now the men who had attacked her and stolen evidence from the office. Now someone wanted to warn her off? Someone else?

"Your... friend. He said that you should call him."

"What friend?"

"That private investigator." The guard pulled a business card out of his shirt pocket. One of Zachary's. "Him."

Kenzie pulled her phone out to look at it. Zachary hadn't sent her any messages or tried to reach her, even though it was getting late enough that she had been expecting to hear from him. Was her phone dead? In airplane mode? Had they messed with her stupid phone too?

"He said he didn't want to worry you," Frank explained. "He said that if you knew..." He went slowly, trying to get it right. "If you knew *he* knew what had happened to you, then you would be worried about him, so no one was to tell you until you were out."

Kenzie gave a weak laugh. Just like she had avoided calling Zachary because she didn't want him to be worrying about her. He had known what was going on but had let her think that he didn't.

"How did he know?"

"He's a private investigator." Frank shrugged. "Don't ask me where he gets his information."

"So I'm supposed to call him?"

"Yeah. Before you get into your car."

Kenzie case a nervous glance toward her baby. "Why?" she asked tentatively, "What's happened to my car?"

"Nothing, nothing," he held up his hands for her to stop. "Your car is here, safe and sound. But he didn't want you driving."

"Of course." Kenzie tapped Zachary's picture on her phone and waited for him to pick up. Usually, she had to wait for a few rings, and sometimes he didn't even hear her call and she had to try him several times before he was able to pull himself from what he was doing to realize she was trying to get him.

But this time, it was only one ring. "Kenzie?"

"Hey. I'm done. And Frank says I'm supposed to call you."

"Uh, yeah." Zachary gave an uncomfortable, coughing laugh. "I hope you don't mind. I didn't think you should drive."

"I'm fine. And it's not far."

"I'm parked on the street. Just come out, I'll drive you home. I'll drop you in the morning, and Frank will make sure your baby is fine tonight."

"You don't need to do that."

"I'm already here."

Kenzie stood there, stymied. It wasn't really that she even wanted to drive, just that she had planned to, and she was finding it remarkably difficult to change directions. She was usually a flexible person who could weigh all the solutions and pick the one that worked best at the moment, even if it weren't her original plan. But apparently, when she was traumatized and had been hit over the head, it wasn't so easy. Maybe that gave her some insight into Zachary or others she knew who could be very rigid about their plans or routines and had difficulty changing direction when another avenue opened up.

"Where are you?"

"In front of the building. I would have parked at the back entrance, but I didn't want you walking into the alley where it is dark. Nice and bright out front."

"Yeah. That's probably a good idea."

Kenzie waved to Frank and changed directions, exiting out the front of the building instead. There were more guards there, and since she usually entered and left via the parking garage, they didn't know her as well as Frank. Her ID was checked several times. The guard who appeared to be most senior knew who she was.

"You were injured, Dr. Kirsch?"

"Just a bump on the head," Kenzie explained, slightly embarrassed. "He knocked me down."

"You're not driving home, are you? Do you need a cab? You should have taken the ambulance to the hospital..."

"It isn't that bad—just a bump. And my boyfriend is picking me up. He didn't want me driving either, apparently."

259

"Where is he?"

Kenzie indicated the front doors.

"I'll walk you out," he told her.

"You don't need to do that. I'm quite able to walk out on my own."

"I'll walk you to your ride," he insisted.

"Fine." Kenzie let him walk her out of the building. She pointed to Zachary's white compact and the guard walked her slowly down the stairs, watching for any sign that she was unsteady and might need him to swoop in and catch her.

Kenzie made it to the car without mishap. Zachary didn't get out of the car to consult with the guard, as Kenzie had been afraid he would. He just leaned over and kissed her on the cheek after she got in. "How are you? Is everything okay?"

Kenzie pulled her car door shut and waved at the guard.

"Yes. Everyone is overreacting. I just got knocked down. Bumped my head, and not even hard. The paramedics were not concerned. No concussion."

"Good." Zachary waited while Kenzie fumbled with her seatbelt. Eventually she managed to get the metal tongue into the buckle and snap it into place. Then he pulled out and drove toward her house without any further argument about her physical condition.

59

When they got home, Kenzie noted that Zachary disarmed the burglar alarm after unlocking the door.

"I didn't think I'd be long, but I figured... we don't need any unexpected guests around here."

"No," Kenzie agreed. "I don't have a clue how they got into the office. We have security. They shouldn't have been able to."

"I think it must have been through the ambulance bay."

That made sense. There were guards at all the public entrances, but for the loading dock, you had to be let in from inside or have the special clicker to get in, so there were no guards checking IDs. But that meant that they'd somehow gotten ahold of someone's clicker or they had fooled the system into thinking they had one. Forcing the door would have set off alarms.

"You're probably right," she agreed.

Zachary steered Kenzie to the table to sit down. He hadn't prepared anything for dinner and Kenzie didn't have the energy to make anything. They would have to order in.

But as she watched Zachary, he placed two bowls on the table, followed by the ice cream. A couple of half-pint containers with their current favorite flavors. He put glasses in front of each place setting and pulled an unopened bottle of wine out of the fridge.

"Ice cream and wine? Is this dinner?" Kenzie demanded. "A bit... bohemian, don't you think?"

He poured her a glass of wine and got a cola out of the fridge for himself. He poured it into his glass. "I don't know what that means."

"Oh... well, sort of free-spirited and nonconformist."

"Ah." He waited for his drink to stop fizzing and then topped it off. "Then yes. Tonight, we are being bohemian."

Kenzie picked up her glass and had a sip before even dishing up her ice cream. She closed her eyes and tried to relax, letting the stress of the day go.

"Thank you for this. And for picking me up." She opened her eyes and looked at him. "How are you not having a meltdown about this?"

"You need me." He shrugged, studying her closely. "I'm worried, but the most important thing is for me to be there for you. That makes me... stronger. When the problem is just in my head, it's easier to get over-whelmed by my own thoughts and feelings. When it's an actual crisis, someone needs my help... It's different."

She remembered how he had been with Madison, Luke, and Rhys when they'd had people shooting at them and several medical crises on their hands. Zachary had been focused and planned things out. He hadn't freaked out and panicked. The same was true of when Lorne and Pat were in danger or when he had been looking for a bug that Walter might have planted. He was a different person when he was protecting someone else. He didn't disappear into himself. He had laser focus.

She tipped her glass toward him, toasting him. "Good job."

Zachary smiled. He scooped a curl of tangerine ice cream into his bowl. "You want chocolate?"

"Yes. As if you need to ask."

He scooped a couple of balls of double chocolate fudge swirl into Kenzie's bowl. Kenzie picked up her spoon and had a couple of bites of cold deliciousness.

Best supper ever.

While Kenzie couldn't tell Zachary any confidential details about the cases she was working on, she could tell him what she knew about the break-in and what she had or had not seen. She told him about the theft of the recent samples, files from Dr. Wiltshire's office, and the possible hacking of their computer systems.

"I can see how they could break in through the loading dock," Zachary said. "There is a weakness in security there. You don't generally have people trying to break into the morgue. It's not an area that's targeted. But the computer systems..." He thought about that and shook his head. "You've got good security. I think... you would need a pretty heavy-duty hacker to break into that."

"I would hope so. I always thought we had all the firewalls and encryption and everything to protect the Medical Examiner's Office and the police systems. It's kind of scary to think that someone could break into it." Kenzie took another sip of her wine. "Everything should be backed up, unless they've somehow been able to break into that too. I think it is at another location, with some security company."

"It should be."

"Yeah. Well, we've all seen system fails before. Usually on the human end." She breathed out heavily. "They broke into the lab too, and I guess... they had injuries over there. At least one of their security guards in critical condition at the hospital." Kenzie rubbed the bump on the back of her head.

"You're lucky that all you had was a bump. If he'd decided to pull a gun on you or to make sure that you couldn't follow or identify him... You're always telling *me* to be careful. Who would have guessed that you would be in danger in the Medical Examiner's Office?"

"Not me. I thought I had a pretty safe job. I haven't even heard of anything like this happening before. People don't... people just don't break into a Medical Examiner's Office like that. Even on TV."

"The way that this was coordinated, it couldn't all have been perpetrated by just one person. This is a group acting in concert. And a pretty powerful group. You need money and influence to pull something like this off." Zachary ticked points off on his fingers. "Break in at your office, taking both samples and files, break in at the lab around the same time, with more violence, breaching your server and the lab's server. The kind of person you hire to do a smash and grab is not the same kind of person as you hire to hack sophisticated computer systems. Even if one person hacked both systems, that is still at least three teams coordinated to act at once."

"And with the body being cremated today... I mean, that just doesn't happen. The funeral home doesn't usually cremate a body the same day that they pick it up. And I had the feeling..." Kenzie trailed off, not sure how much she should say. She was only speculating, and she might be building the situation up to be worse than it was. She didn't need to make it worse. It was bad enough without her blowing it up.

But Zachary leaned forward, his eyes searching her face. "What? What is it?"

"I got the feeling... I know Dr. Wiltshire wasn't really ready to release the body yet. I know he was being pressured by the governor's office. And then my dad trying to talk me into influencing him. He talked about the governor too. And then Dr. Wiltshire just decided to release the body when he hadn't yet made a determination. Just the timing of it... do you think he was threatened or coerced somehow?"

"If you think he was, then you're probably right. You know him. You know how he usually works. If this was unusual, and he was under that much pressure.... then you're probably right."

"What are we going to do?"

"Do you have other avenues of investigation you can pursue while you wait to see what can be recovered from the lab and the computer backups?"

"No... not really."

"What about the woman that you were looking for? Have you talked to her?"

Kenzie thought about Francine Mudd. It seemed like a long time ago. "Yeah. I talked to her today. But I would still like to talk to her ex-boyfriend as well. It's his place that the dog lived at before. I can't go back any farther to the previous owner, because he passed away. But I should probably at least take a look at the place Lola lived at before the nursing home, see if there is any obvious source of infection. If we've got a zoonotic virus—a virus that can be passed from animal to human—then it is possible that the dog got it from another human in the first place. That could be Francine's boyfriend."

"Why don't we see if we can track him down tomorrow, then?"

"We?" Kenzie repeated with a smile.

"I could help you with that. I've already done half of the work, tracking Francine down. I have most of the background I need to start with."

"Well... since it's probably going to take at least a day before they've been able to restore whatever information they can from the backups, I guess we might as well. You don't have anything else you have to do tomorrow?"

"Nothing I can't reschedule. I've got a pretty good relationship with the head boss of Goldman Investigations."

60

K enzie had a restless night. Even after a couple of glasses of wine, her mind was still whirling as she tried to make sense of what had happened and tried to predict how things would unfold over the next few days. And the bump on the back of her head hurt. It wasn't bad, but it reminded her every time she moved. She couldn't lie on her back comfortably. Not that she was usually a back sleeper, but knowing that she couldn't made her hyperaware of her position and she couldn't get comfortable on her stomach or sides either.

She jumped at every sound in the house, even though the house's night noises were familiar to her. Zachary stayed with her for a couple of hours, but then she was aware that he was gone, and every time she awoke, she listened for him, trying to discern where he was in the house and what he was doing. He was quiet, either working on his computer or sleeping on the couch where he wouldn't be disturbed by her tossing and turning.

She fell into a restless sleep full of dreams early in the morning, just as she gave up on being able to get any sleep before it was time to get up.

Kenzie shut off her alarm when it buzzed and went back to sleep. Dr. Wiltshire wouldn't be expecting her in with all that had happened, and they probably wouldn't be able to do any work until at least the afternoon, maybe the next day. She slept for another hour and a half and then got up, feeling sore all over and still exhausted, but she was too restless to sleep anymore. She wandered out to say good morning to Zachary before her shower.

"Hey, hon'." Kenzie covered a big yawn.

"You look like you could use some more sleep."

Kenzie rubbed her sticky eyes and looked at him. "Well, to be honest, so do you."

"I slept okay."

Of course, his "slept okay" was different from the average person's. He regularly survived on less sleep than a hyperactive squirrel.

"You still want to go looking for Francine's ex today?" Kenzie asked.

"Yeah. I've done some background. Shouldn't be too hard to find him. He is at the same address as you checked already."

"Doesn't help much if he doesn't answer the door."

"We can still scout around. You said you want to see if there are any obvious sources of infection nearby. We can do that, and hopefully be able to raise Jeremy by phone, find out what time he will be home... meet him somewhere so you can ask your questions."

Kenzie nodded. She ran her fingers through her hair, which felt coarse and sticky. "Okay. I'm going to have a long shower. Then something to eat, and then we can go."

Zachary nodded his agreement and went back to his work.

"Jeremy?"

Zachary was going through the cryptic-looking notes in his notepad when Kenzie got out of the shower and walked into the living room, towel-drying her hair, another towel wrapped around her torso.

After a moment, Zachary looked up. "What?"

"You said Jeremy, we would try to get a hold of Jeremy."

He nodded. "Right. Francine's ex."

"She said her boyfriend was Jay."

"Nickname. Full name Jeremy..." Zachary flipped through the pages of his notepad to find it. "Jeremy Salk."

The name sounded familiar to Kenzie, so it must be right. "Oh, okay. I'm going to get ready now. Have you eaten breakfast?"

He opened his mouth to answer and Kenzie shook her head. "Of course you haven't. Why don't you brew some coffee and pop a couple of pieces of bread in the toaster? You can tell me what we know about this Jeremy, and then we'll go over to his building. If he's got a nine-to-five job, he's still going to be working, so it's sort of a waste of time, but it isn't like I have a lot else to do right now, until the office is back up and running."

She had emailed Dr. Wiltshire before getting into the shower, and he had confirmed what she had already suspected. That he wasn't expecting her in and they couldn't work until the police had cleared the area and the techs had the computers working properly.

Zachary nodded and Kenzie went back into the bedroom to dress and make herself look presentable. She suspected that Zachary was too involved in what he was doing to get the coffee and toast started, but she wasn't in a hurry, so it didn't matter. For once, they could have a long, relaxed breakfast if they wanted to.

Kenzie was feeling somewhat more like herself when they reached the building she had previously visited in trying to reach Jeremy Salk. She looked around, unsure why she thought she would be able to find anything significant by just looking at the building. But Zachary's eyes were bright and alert, looking around for anything that was out of place.

"Were you able to get into the building?" he asked.

"No, everything was locked up. I mean, the glass doors are unlocked, but there is a hall door at the top of the stairs, and that's locked."

"Did you try to get anyone to buzz you in?"

"No... I just tried reaching Jeremy. Or rather, Francine. But I couldn't get her."

Zachary nodded. He pulled out his phone and placed a call. To Jeremy's number, she assumed. He walked toward the glass doors that she had previously used. Kenzie followed him in. There was a panel near the door, but it wasn't quite like the electronic directories Kenzie usually saw at apartment buildings. Only four buttons, and none of them were properly labeled. Some numbers and names had been struck through, but Kenzie couldn't make out who the current residents were or which apartment Jeremy lived in.

Zachary pressed each of the buttons, a long press on each of them.

One of the residents answered over the speaker. A woman's voice, mature. Slightly suspicious or irritated.

"Yes?"

"I have a delivery for Jeremy Salk."

"Then ring his doorbell."

"I have, but he's not answering. He's not answering his phone, either. I can't stand around here all day. Can you buzz me up and I'll just leave it outside his door?"

Kenzie had no idea what Zachary was planning to do if the woman said yes and then wanted to know where the package they were supposedly delivering was. Maybe it was a ploy he had used other times in other cases, but she would think that he would at least want to carry a generic parcel around and put it down in front of the door if someone let him in.

"No, you can't leave it outside his door."

"Can I leave it with you? Would you give it to him?"

A deep sigh. "*Who* are you?"

"Delivery."

"Come up."

There was no buzz. There was no vestibule to go through like there was at Francine's building. They both climbed the stairs and tried the door at the top, and this time there was no resistance. It was unlocked and they were able to let themselves through. Kenzie looked down the corridor and saw a woman looking out one of the doorways. She was an older woman, brunette turning gray, jowls starting to sag, wire-rim glasses, and a knotted housecoat.

"You're not a deliveryman," she said accusingly.

Zachary handed her one of his cards. "Private Investigator." He looked at the door down the hall from her. "Do you know what time Jeremy gets off work? He isn't answering his phone."

"What would you be investigating him for?" She shook her head. "And he doesn't go by Jeremy, he goes by—"

"Jay. Yes, I know. I'm not investigating him. I have some questions that he might be able to answer about a consumer transaction."

Her brows lowered. "What?"

Kenzie wasn't sure what that was supposed to mean either. Did he mean the sale of the dog? Except that it hadn't been a sale, it had just been Francine taking the dog when its previous owner had died.

"Do you know what time he gets off work?"

"I don't think he's even in town."

Zachary looked at Kenzie and then back at the woman.

"You think he's out of town? Did he tell you that?"

"He hasn't been around for... at least a week. More. Maybe two."

"Oh." Kenzie was disappointed. "Do you know if he's having his mail forwarded somewhere else? Or where he might have gone? Was it a vacation?"

"I don't know. Why would he tell me? We're not close. He's just a neighbor."

"Is there someone else we can talk to? Maybe he is friends with someone else in the building?" Zachary looked at the other doors in the hallway. "Or is there a building manager who would be in charge of sorting mail that might know something?"

"You can call the building man," the woman shook her head. "But he isn't going to be able to tell you anything."

"How do you know that?"

"Because he was asking the other day if I knew anything about where Jay was. He missed paying his rent."

"So he's just disappeared. No one has any idea whether something is wrong or whether he's just gone on vacation."

She shrugged. "What could be wrong?"

"He could be sick, hurt, who knows?"

"He could be dead," Kenzie pointed out. Since that was her wheelhouse. Then she had a sudden feeling of vertigo. *He could be dead?*

Jeremy Salk.

Zachary held Kenzie's arm to keep her from falling over. "Kenz? What is it?"

Jeremy Salk.

"I thought that name sounded familiar."

"Yeah." She could see him nodding even though she couldn't focus on anything in the present. "Because that's the name of Francine's ex-boyfriend."

"Francine? Oh, I remember her," the old lady said approvingly.

"No," Kenzie said, shaking her head slightly. "Because that's the identify of our John Doe."

K enzie was leaning against the wall for support. Zachary held on to her to steady her, but he wasn't following her train of thought. "What?"

"The one who was in the news. You remember? You looked at his picture and said that he wasn't homeless. And you were right. Once they stopped looking for him in the homeless shelters and community, they were able to identify him. And his name was Jeremy Salk."

Zachary looked at her, then looked at the woman in the doorway. "How long has he been gone?"

She was tentative, uncertain in the face of this news. "Maybe two weeks."

Zachary looked back at Kenzie. "If it's been two weeks and he's been identified, then why doesn't anyone here know? There should have been someone to get his personal effects. Clean the apartment out. And inform the landlord that he's passed."

"No. Next of kin is out of state. They have to make arrangements to travel here, get his things, arrange for the body to be cremated and shipped, all of that. It will be up to them to clear out the apartment and let the landlord know."

"So Jeremy Salk is dead." Zachary considered this. "What did he die of?"

"Alcohol poisoning." Kenzie swallowed and gave a little bit of a head shake. "Not a virus or unexpected death."

"Alcohol poisoning?" the neighbor demanded. "Jay? He wasn't a big drinker. Every now and then, he'd have a beer, but I don't think he ever had much more than that. How would someone like that get alcohol poisoning?"

"I don't know. But that's definitely what he died from," Kenzie told her firmly.

"How would you know that?"

"Because I'm with the Medical Examiner's Office."

The woman looked a little taken aback by this. She looked at Kenzie and Zachary, then shrugged her thin shoulders. "Well, if you don't have anything to deliver, and now you don't have anyone to talk to, then I assume you'll be leaving now." She shut the door firmly.

"Yeah," Kenzie said. "I guess I am. Leaving. Now."

"Just take a minute," Zachary said. "You're very pale. Are you sure your head isn't bothering you?"

"No. Just a bit. I'm fine. It was just a bit of a surprise to realize that the man we are looking for is... the man we were trying to identify."

"Quite the coincidence."

"Yeah. I guess it is. That's very weird."

Kenzie peeled herself away from the wall. "I'm okay. And we don't have any reason to stay here now."

Zachary walked beside her, watching her for any sign she was dizzy or faint. They reached the stairs that led down to the main level and he paused, considering.

"You're sure you're okay. Not going to get dizzy on the stairs?"

"I'm fine. Quit treating me like I'm made of glass."

He nodded and started down the stairs. Kenzie stayed close behind him, watching his feet go down the steps one at a time, keeping pace with him easily. She had a feeling that he was going more slowly than usual to make sure she didn't have to hurry to catch up. They reached the bottom and headed toward the car.

"So, we can't get into the apartment," Zachary said, reminding Kenzie of why they were there in the first place. "But we can at least have a look around the building, the neighborhood, see if we can find anything that might suggest how Lola got the infection in the first place."

Kenzie sat against the hood of the car, nodding. She was a little bit unsteady despite all her protests and didn't want him to see that her legs were shaking. She looked at the businesses on the main floor of the building again. They were not the kinds of places a person would go to eat or shop. Instead, they were light industrial offices, most of them with names she had never heard of before. Places that took care of things behind the scenes and were not usually in customer-facing positions. She went through the names in her head, parsing them and trying to predict what each of them was. She had gone into some of them the last time she was in the area trying to find Francine. She didn't much feel like going to each of them now to see if they had known the late Jay Salk.

Virutek Labs.

Kenzie blinked at the name and studied the shape of the logo. She'd never heard of Virutek Labs before. As far as she knew, it was not a medical lab that drew blood or did ultrasounds or other work for living patients. And likewise, not one of the labs that she dealt with as a representative of the Medical Examiner's Office.

"There's a lab," she said quietly to Zachary. Like they might overhear and all run for cover. Like they might slip out of her grip as Jay Salk just had.

"Do you know them?" Zachary asked.

"No."

"So they probably don't have anything to do with Salk."

"No," Kenzie agreed, pushing herself away from the car and walking toward it.

The V in Virutek appeared to be a double-helix strand of DNA separating into two single strands at the vertex. DNA? Or a double strand of RNA? Or were they using single-strand RNA viruses to modify DNA? Did the logo tell a story, or was it just designed by someone who had no idea what the difference was?

Zachary followed a step or two behind Kenzie, letting her take the lead this time. He was good at finagling his way into a locked building and talking to neighbors. She was good at talking to medical people.

Kenzie pushed her way through the glass door with frosted lettering. There was a small, sterile-looking reception area, where there really wasn't anywhere to sit down. A larger brushed-aluminum copy of the logo was the focal point on the wall to their right. To the side were several pictures in a grid and a plaque with a corporate name on it. The counter was polished white resin and the woman sitting at the computer looked at Kenzie as if she must be lost.

"May I help you?"

"Can you tell me what this company does, please?"

"I beg your pardon?"

"What does Virutek do? It looks from your logo like maybe you're a medical research lab?"

"Yes."

"Does Virutek mean 'virus technology'?"

The woman's penciled eyebrows rose. "It sounds like you already know all of the answers. Who are you, again?"

"Did Jeremy Salk work here?"

"Jeremy Salk?" She shook her head. "No, there hasn't been anyone by that name here."

"Jay, I mean. Jay Salk."

"Still no."

"He lives in this building. In the apartments down that end..." Kenzie motioned.

"No one from Virutek lives in the building. I'm sorry. You must have been misdirected."

"No, I'm just checking. I need to talk to one of your researchers. Is there someone who could spare a few minutes to talk to me?"

"About what?"

"About what experiments they are doing. Whether they are doing anything with HHV-4."

The woman gave her a puzzled look, frowning and shaking her head. "And who are you? Why are you asking these questions?"

"I'm with the Medical Examiner's Office. My name is Dr. Kenzie Kirsch."

"The Medical Examiner's Office."

"Yes. We've had a number of cases lately that have had lab-engineered HHV-4 infections."

The woman blinked. She started to stand, then sat and reached for her phone, but couldn't seem to complete the action. "We don't do human studies," she said flatly.

"That doesn't mean you haven't had a virus escape. If you are doing any work with HHV-4, you'd better get me in to talk to someone ASAP." Kenzie was already standing against the counter, but she leaned over it toward the woman, deliberately getting into the woman's personal space.

The receptionist looked at her for another minute longer, her eyes wide, then seemed to overcome her inertia. She tapped a few buttons into the keypad. It didn't look like 9-1-1 from where Kenzie stood. But it could still be internal security. She waited for an answer.

"Dr. Ducros?" she asked, her voice high with anxiety that hopefully, Dr. Ducros could hear clearly. "There is a woman here from the Medical Examiner's Office demanding to speak to someone about your studies."

"Dr. Kenzie Kirsch," Kenzie repeated. Not some woman. She was a doctor and she was there to get answers.

A few more words were exchanged between Dr. Ducros and the receptionist, with Ducros apparently doing most of the talking and the woman giving one- or two-word answers, keeping the content of the discussion from Kenzie.

"Dr. Ducros will be out to get you in a moment," the woman eventually said as she pressed a button to hang up. Her eyes strayed toward Zachary, wondering who he was and why he was there, but Kenzie didn't fill him in on any details.

It was sort of awkward that Zachary was there when she was trying to do her job. But on the other hand, it didn't hurt to have someone backing her up and acting as a witness to what she discovered. He was staying quiet, not interfering or trying to give her any advice.

A man entered behind them and looked startled to find someone else in the small reception area. He smiled and raised his eyebrows questioningly. He had a sweet, woodsy-smelling cologne or aftershave on, and it quickly filled the small, warm area.

"Oh, Mr. Fisk," the receptionist smiled and nodded at him. "We are expecting you." She shot a look at Kenzie as if to point out that people didn't just barge in at Virutek. They made appointments. "I'll just make sure everything is ready."

She turned away from them for privacy and spoke quietly into her headset.

"Aaron Fisk," the man introduced himself, holding his hand out to Kenzie.

"Dr. Kenzie Kirsch."

"A pleasure to meet you. Are you here for the..." he indicated the receptionist and trailed off.

"Oh, no. We have some other business."

"Oh...?" he leaned forward, head cocked slightly, waiting for more.

"What company did you say you are with?" Kenzie asked.

He smiled pleasantly. The receptionist took off her headset and stood. "I'll just take you in." She led him to a door on the left and swiped her card to unlock it. Aaron Fisk nodded at Kenzie and Zachary and followed his escort.

Kenzie had thought that Dr. Ducros might play power games and keep her waiting before coming out. And if he did, she was prepared to take the discussion to the next level. But he entered the reception area from behind a door behind the reception desk that blended in with the rest of the wall. Kenzie wouldn't have known it was there if she hadn't seen it open. He was younger than Kenzie would have expected, wearing a long white lab coat. He had round, black-rimmed glasses and smudged shadows under his eyes like he regularly worked too late or worried too much.

"Uh, Dr. Kirsch, is it?"

"Yes."

"Come with me, if you would."

He frowned when Zachary followed, but didn't try to stop him. Neither did Kenzie. It might not be Zachary's area of expertise, but as she was swept into the lab behind the door, she was glad she wasn't there alone.

62

Ducros led Kenzie to a small meeting room, and they sat down. The walls of the room were glass with some frosted striping that afforded little privacy. The table was shiny white, as was pretty much everything else she could see. Miles of shining white counters covered with experiments that might take months or years to complete. Or which might quickly discover the cure to some disease they currently had no purchase on. Kenzie recognized much of the equipment, but of course, she couldn't tell what they were working on.

"Now, explain to me..." Ducros said slowly. "You are from the Medical Examiner's Office, and you came here because..."

"This is where my investigation led me," Kenzie said honestly. "We have come across a number of deaths that have all had one thing in common. A lab-engineered HHV-4 virus."

"That doesn't make any sense. How would that lead you back here?"

"Is that what you are working on? Some experiment with a modified HHV-4?"

"That may be one of the things we are working on," he said carefully. "But I don't see how that could have anything to do with your deaths or how you would trace it to this lab."

"It would appear that your virus has escaped into the wild."

"Impossible. No."

"It isn't impossible. Do you know how common escapes are from laboratories that should have had all the best isolation features known to the scientific world? Look at plague just as an example. There have been three escapes from supposedly sealed laboratories." Kenzie looked around her. "I don't see a lot of isolation protocols being used here, actually. None of you are in biohazard suits. I see samples in open containers. I don't know what kind of ventilation system you have, but you realize that if there is even one vent that isn't properly isolated, you could be venting your virus into this building."

"It isn't possible. No. We are very careful. There have not been any escapes."

"You wouldn't know until we connect up the deaths with this lab. And then... it's too late to keep arguing."

"If you had the proof, we wouldn't just be sitting here. You would have... a subpoena or a court order. You'd have the CDC behind you. But I don't see anyone but this..." He looked Zachary over, trying to classify him. "This assistant with you."

"Oh, we'll be calling in the troops. You can bet on that." Kenzie stopped talking and waited for that to sink in. "Now is the time to talk about what you are doing and to mitigate any damage before any accusations can be made."

"It seems like you're already making them."

"I can come back here with the Medical Examiner and the CDC if that's what you want."

He considered that and shook his head, lips pressed tightly together. "Why are you here, then?"

"I'm investigating."

"What do you want to know?"

"First of all, confirmation that you are working with a variant of HHV-4."

"We are doing several different studies here. One of them might be HHV-4."

"What are you doing with it? How have you changed it?"

"That's proprietary."

"What are you trying to do with it?"

"Really, we do have the right to trade secrets. Considering the fact that we are not doing any human studies, I don't see how you think this could have infected any of your... patients."

"A man in this building has died. With lab-engineered HHV-4 in his brain." Of course, that might be a stretch. Kenzie didn't have evidence that Jay Salk had HHV-4 in his brain like the four victims from the nursing center. Not yet. And they couldn't even prove that it was cause of death for those whose brain tissue did test positive. It certainly wasn't Salk's cause of death, as she was implying.

"That..." Ducros shook his head. "That really doesn't make sense."

"Somehow, it got out. Has anyone in the lab been sick? Or died?"

"No. Of course not. Colds, maybe, certainly nothing that we have been studying here."

"You haven't had anyone who has shown... unusual symptoms?"

Ducros raised his hands palms-up. "I don't know what you're talking about."

"A number of the victims we have seen were showing signs of dementia before they died. Not far in advance, just a few days before death. You haven't had anyone who is... I don't know... being forgetful, erratic... incontinent?"

Salk gave a sharp bark of a laugh. "What?"

"Have you had anyone who has been behaving strangely lately? Altered personality. Unable to find the right words when describing something. Emotionally labile."

Ducros sat back abruptly. He looked at Kenzie, his face a blank mask.

As if that weren't a big tell.

Kenzie watched him, waiting for him to think it through and tell her what he was thinking. Now he was worried. Maybe he was starting to see that Kenzie could be telling the truth. It might not be some fantastic tale.

"We had one employee who was feeling a lot of stress. He was... advised to take a vacation. He hasn't shown up at the lab again since."

"So he's missing?"

"He's not missing. He was told to take some time off and he did. It certainly would have been better if he had arranged his schedule with us first, but..." Ducros shrugged. "Scientists can be a funny bunch. We don't always have the best social skills. You tell him to take a break, he takes a break, and then wonders what you're going on about when you complain that he didn't make the proper arrangements. No one is missing. No."

"Where did he go? Does anyone know?"

"No."

"And you don't know when he's coming back."

"No. But he will."

"What was going on with him? You said he was stressed? How was that manifesting?"

"He was very anxious. Accusing others of stealing his equipment or changing his results. He had a couple of blow-ups, getting angry over nothing. Everybody kind of had enough of him, so he was asked to... please take some time off."

Kenzie nodded. It was a possible fit. But of course, it could just be a scientist getting stressed out and having a bit of a breakdown because he needed a rest. What were the chances that he was at home, dead in his bed? Or in the street? Another John Doe in her morgue?

"What's this guy's name? And description?"

Ducros frowned, looking at her. "Why?"

"I think someone should make sure that nothing has happened to him. If you haven't heard from him, it may just be that he's taken some time off like he was told to. But it could also be because something happened to him. He could be in the hospital. Or at home, sick, in need of assistance. Or he could be..." Kenzie trailed off and didn't finish her sentence.

Ducros didn't like the question. Kenzie could see his indecision. Did he give a description of his missing employee, hoping that nothing had happened to him? Or hold it back? If something had happened and he withheld information, could he be held responsible? It wasn't like Kenzie was a cop.

"He's... late twenties, I think. Medium height, slim. Brown hair. Too long, but not in a ponytail. Pretty average."

Kenzie thought through the bodies that she had in the morgue or had seen recently. "What's his name?"

Ducros hesitated.

"Really," Kenzie said. "I need to know."

"Abernathy. Joe."

Not the name of anyone who had been through the Medical Examiner's Office recently. Kenzie would have remembered that name. She let out a breath of relief. Maybe he was just taking some mental health time.

Unless it was another John Doe. She was a little paranoid about that, seeing as how Jay Salk had ended up being in the morgue as a John Doe. It was pretty much impossible that the same could be true of Abernathy. The only current resident who was unidentified was the DB from the motel. And Abernathy was local. There wouldn't have been any reason for him to be in a motel.

"Did Abernathy know Jay Salk, who lives in this building?"

It was a stretch, of course. How would the two men, who were probably decades apart and with totally different lifestyles, know each other? Just living and working in the same building wouldn't do it. The apartments were completely separated from the lab. Although they might have shared ventilation.

"No, Abernathy wasn't friends with any of those people."

"Do you know any of them? Did they ever have reason to come in here to make an inquiry? Maybe you run into each other at a convenience store close by?"

"Sometimes you run into people you recognize. But that doesn't make you friends or mean that you're close enough to each other to pass a virus on to someone." He shook his head. "A virus that is only transmitted through *bodily fluids*, not through the air."

"Which people from this building have you seen outside or other places?"

"I don't know. People come and go. I don't remember faces very well, couldn't tell you what someone's face looked like if my life depended on it." He paused. "There was that woman with the dog."

Kenzie drew in her next breath with difficulty. She tried to continue the conversation without any change in her expression. Not to give away that she was about to fall apart completely. "What woman with a dog?"

"I don't know if she even lives here anymore. I don't think I have seen her for a while. Older woman. Had a dog, very friendly. The dog, I mean. The woman was friendly enough too, but the dog always wanted attention. Everybody's best friend."

"Was the dog's name Lola?" Kenzie asked, her voice breaking slightly.

Ducros considered. "Yeah, that might be right..."

"So you would see them outside the building or around the neighborhood somewhere, and you would pet the dog?"

"Sure." He shrugged, not seeing how this could be a problem. "Friendly dog. Why not?"

"Because you're working with viruses and not following a proper isolation protocol. It could be clinging to your clothes, your hands, your face. And the dog comes, and you pet her, and maybe transfer it to her fur. Or she licks you." Kenzie felt a certain amount of revulsion at the thought. She had never been one of those people who was okay with dogs licking people. Especially on the face, even the mouth.

What better way to spread a virus?

"We always use gloves and a mask when handling the virus," Ducros said uncomfortably. "So there is no chance that someone was contaminated when they left here."

"You don't know that. You hope so, but you don't know that."

He shook his head in disagreement but didn't say anything.

"I think you need to call this Abernathy. Let him know you're concerned about his mental health and just checking in. If you can't get through to him, then you should at least notify the police. Do you have a next of kin?"

"I don't think so. He lived by himself, didn't have anyone in the area."

"Maybe you could... give him a call now. I'd feel a lot better about it if I knew he was okay."

Ducros rolled his eyes. He tapped away on his cellphone, looking for the number, then tapped it and waited. After waiting a few seconds, he shook his head at Kenzie. "It just goes to voicemail."

"Right away? Or is it no answer and then to voicemail?"

"Right away. He's probably still ticked off with us and doesn't want to talk. So he's rejecting it when he sees my number."

Or something had happened to him. "Leave a message, tell him that you need him to call back or you will be in touch with the police to do a welfare check."

"Seriously?" Ducros made a face. "You deal with your employees how you think is best and leave me to deal with mine."

Kenzie shook her head, irritated. "So tell me... what were you doing with this HHV-4 virus? What were you hoping to achieve? And what kind of results have you had?"

"We are only in the beginning stages of development. It is solely in vitro at the moment. No live hosts, human or animal. We have been... editing it. Hoping that we will be able to use it to insert certain information into human cells, which will allow them to combat disease from the inside out."

"Which cells?"

"Neurons. We are hoping to be able to reverse the course of brain cell degeneration in Parkinson's Disease and a number of others. The same principles apply. If we can cure one, we open the door to curing the rest."

"Huntington's Disease?" Zachary suggested.

Ducros looked at him in surprise, as if he had forgotten that Zachary was even in the room. "Possibly."

"So you have engineered these viruses to cross the blood-brain barrier," Kenzie said.

"Well, they have to get into the brain to do their work."

"What are they supposed to do once they get in there?"

"We are still working through the processes. It's not like programming a computer, you know. We have a lot of theories right now. Putting them into practice will be a different story." Ducros looked at Kenzie. "When we start testing out different scenarios, it will be on genetically altered mice, not humans. There is no way we are ready for human studies."

"You may have unintentionally started human studies already. And the results are not looking good."

63

When they eventually made their way out of Virutek, Zachary looked at Kenzie. "So, you found the source of your virus."

"It looks that way. I can't believe they are working with viruses without proper isolation protocols in place. If they have an employee with this virus and he's out there spreading it around..." She put her hands out in a pleading gesture. "Even if Abernathy doesn't have dementia from the virus, any of the employees could be carrying it. The whole place needs to be shut down until they can be tested and cleared."

"Do you think... do they have the ability to shut this down now? It hasn't spread too far 'into the wild'?"

They got into the car. Kenzie immediately started rifling through her purse. Zachary started the car and watched her, clearly ready to drive wherever she wanted to go next, but waiting to make sure she wasn't going to be disrupted by the movement of the car. Kenzie held up a finger to make him wait.

"Are you looking for your phone?" Zachary suggested.

Kenzie was already holding it in her other hand. Not that she hadn't ever caught herself looking for her phone when she was already holding it.

"No, just for..." Kenzie found the small bottle and pounced on it. She squirted a generous amount of alcohol-based gel cleanser into her palm, then passed it to Zachary. "It may not be one hundred percent effective, but it's better than nothing."

Zachary took the bottle and followed Kenzie's example, working the gel around his hands, between his fingers, into his fingertips around the nails. Kenzie put the bottle back into her purse. Hopefully, that would keep the heebie-jeebies at bay. Her skin had been crawling ever since she had realized how lax the protocols were at Virutek.

"And now... I'd better talk to Dr. Wiltshire. I'd go to the office to meet him, but he probably isn't even there."

"So do you want to go somewhere? Or just sit here for a few minutes?"

"I think we'd better go to the nursing home." Kenzie thought about Lola wandering around to meet all the patients. Licking their hands or faces. They had asked the nurse at Champlain House to keep her isolated away from the patients until they had things sorted out, but they would have to be more aggressive than that. Lola should be in quarantine in a lab somewhere while they ran tests on her.

Zachary nodded and pulled out. Kenzie tapped Dr. Wiltshire's cell number on her phone screen and put the phone to her ear.

Kenzie didn't even waste time on greetings. As soon as she heard the click that told her Dr. Wiltshire had picked up, she started talking.

"Doctor, I think I found the source of the viral infection. Lola and her previous owner lived in a building that leases space to both residential and commercial businesses. There is a lab on the main floor called Virutek. They are working with viruses, including HHV-4, which they have modified to make it easier to penetrate the blood-brain barrier."

"Virutek." Dr. Wiltshire said the name slowly, so Kenzie knew he was writing it down. "And you've talked to them?"

"Yes. I was in the lab, and believe me, I wish I wasn't. I've disinfected my hands, but..." She trailed off. "Anyway. They are handling the virus with mask and gloves and believe that the only way for it to be transferred is via bodily fluids. The guy we talked to said that the ventilation is sealed off from the rest of the building, but who knows if that is true? Or how well-sealed it is? He was familiar with Lola, remembers running into her outside or around the neighborhood. That she was very friendly, liked contact with people. I assume that includes licking people who pet her. If not, at least licking her own fur, which people then touch..."

"So you think the dog picked it up through contact with someone at Virutek or through the shared ventilation."

"Yeah."

"And it sounds like it could be the right form of the virus. But we'll need to check with Dr. Savage. His team will need to compare the virus obtained from Cartwright and the others to whatever virus strains Virutek started with and has developed. They'll be able to tell if it has the same origin."

"You'll have to see if you can get Virutek to cooperate on providing samples of their work product. I have a feeling... it's not going to be that easy."

"It never is," Wiltshire sighed. "But this is good work, Kenzie. Well done."

"Thank you. That's not everything, though."

"What else?" he asked cautiously.

"You remember that I said Lola's former owner used to live there?"

"Of course."

"Well, the owner's boyfriend stayed there when she moved out. And he is—or was—Jeremy Salk."

"Jeremy Salk." Dr. Wiltshire took a moment to place the name, but was faster than Kenzie had been. "The John Doe? Alcohol poisoning?"

"Yes."

"Well, that's... bizarrely coincidental."

"If we didn't have such a clear cause of death, I would wonder if he died from the virus."

"We didn't test him for it. We had no idea that there was any connection to the nursing home deaths. I suppose we can go back and test the samples now." Dr. Wiltshire stopped speaking abruptly.

Kenzie tried to finish his thought process. "Were those among the samples stolen or destroyed?"

"Yes. They were."

Kenzie swore. "I thought that they just didn't know which samples were Cartwright's. But what if all the samples they took were from victims who were positive for the virus? What if the cover-up is... much bigger than we thought?"

"How would anyone know that Jeremy Salk was positive for the virus? Or had at least been exposed to the virus?"

"There's no way, is there? That is... *we* don't have any evidence that he had contracted it. Maybe someone else did. If he was acting strangely, and someone recognized the symptoms as those that this virus causes..."

"No," Dr. Wiltshire said firmly. "That would mean that they had seen enough other cases to recognize the symptoms as a pattern. And for that... there would have to be a lot more cases."

"There were others at the nursing home. Maybe there were other outbreaks that we don't know about. Another pocket somewhere in the city that they could trace back to Virutek. And we only went back three months at the nursing home. How long has this virus been spreading? It could be longer."

"This is all wild speculation." Dr. Wiltshire's tone told Kenzie he wasn't going to allow it to go any farther. And she knew he was right to pull her back. It was too easy to get wrapped up in conspiracy theories and to see proof of it wherever you looked. "Any outbreaks would have been identified by the authorities. We have nothing to suggest that there were any. Salk's death was alcohol poisoning. We don't have any evidence to the contrary. We don't know if he contracted the virus or not."

"It's a pretty wild coincidence that he died at the same time that the rest of this stuff was going on."

"This life is full of coincidences. It is our nature to see patterns and connections, even where there are not any. You're aware of that through your studies of medicine. Similar theories and medicines being developed around the world from each other, with no apparent connection between them. Constellations of symptoms that are similar between diseases with different causes. Scientific advancements that started out as mistakes. There is not necessarily a connection."

"Will you see whether Salk's body is still available or whether he was cremated?"

By his hesitation, Kenzie knew what he was going to say. "I don't have any reason to do that. The Medical Examiner cannot just make demands willy-nilly. He needs to have reasons and follow the evidence."

"You need to be able to get the evidence."

"We already pushed our luck on the Cartwright case. If I am seen as wasting taxpayer money and investigating conspiracy theories, I'll lose my job."

Kenzie sighed. "Okay. And... there's more."

"Something worth looking into? Or more theories?"

"Do you buy into the theory that the engineered virus was probably contracted by Lola from Virutek?"

"I am willing to consider it as a possibility. To check into it farther."

"When I asked about any employees who might be showing symptoms of dementia, Dr. Ducros identified one employee who had been showing increased emotional lability, anxiety, and paranoia."

"What did you advise him?"

"The man is currently missing."

"He's been reported missing?"

"No. He stopped showing up at work. I asked Dr. Ducros to call him, and he didn't answer."

"Did they report him missing?"

"No, they figured he just took some time off. I suggested they at least call for a welfare check, but he declined. I don't think he's going to. They said he lives alone and they don't know of any family in the area, but he wasn't convinced."

"Maybe that's one action we could take without raising any red flags. What's his name? Do you have a phone number or address?"

"Just the name. Joe Abernathy."

"Phone number is in my notebook," Zachary said.

Kenzie looked at him. "What? How did you get his phone number?"

"I watched him dial it."

Kenzie reached into Zachary's pocket and withdrew his notebook. She hadn't even seen him write it down.

"Who is there with you, Kenzie?" Dr. Wiltshire asked.

"Zachary. He came along to be my driver and to see if we could get into the building. I guess he watched Dr. Ducros dial the number and took it down." Flipping through the notebook, Kenzie found the phone number and read it to Dr. Wiltshire.

"Okay. I'll get the police to do a welfare check."

"And what about calling in the CDC to look into Virutek and whether they have accidentally released this virus into the wild?"

But she knew what Dr. Wiltshire's answer would be before he gave it. "Not enough evidence, Kenzie. We need actual proof before we can call the authorities in."

"There's a lot of evidence."

"There's not enough. They won't listen and I'll end up with egg on my face. I don't want to be branded a conspiracy theorist by the CDC. I want them to listen when we have something."

64

They were at Champlain House, but Kenzie wasn't yet ready to go in. She needed to talk to Dr. Savage first and run her theory past him. He was the one who had all the data about the virus. He was the one who would be able to trace where it had come from, who was already working on tracing where it had come from.

"I'll just be a minute," she told Zachary.

He gave her a wry smile. "Take however long you want. It doesn't make any difference to me."

It was, after all, her case, not his.

Kenzie nodded, a bit embarrassed, and scrolled through her contacts to find Dr. Savage. Hopefully, he wouldn't be too busy to talk with her. He could be sitting around because all his data had been corrupted and he was waiting for it to be restored. Or he could be deeply involved in the restoration of the data and not want to take the time to deal with someone who really didn't know as much as she thought she did.

There were a few rings, and then the call was answered.

"Savage."

"Doctor, it's Kenzie Kirsch. I don't know if you remember me—"

"Of course I do, Dr. Kirsch. How are things going over at your office today? And how are you feeling?"

"I'm out in the field today, since there were still police in the Medical

Examiner's Office and our server hadn't been sorted out yet. And I'm feeling okay, thanks. Just a little tender. Nothing but a bump on the head, but you'd be amazed at how many times during the day you rest the back of your head against something..." In fact, Kenzie was leaning slightly forward in the car, keeping her head off the headrest.

"I was certainly sorry to hear about your trouble. And I gather you heard about ours."

Kenzie shook her head. "It sounds like it was much worse. You had guards injured? Someone in the hospital?"

"Critical condition," Savage agreed. "Who would ever have thought that this type of... thuggery would happen in our offices?"

"Not me."

"So, what can I do for you today?"

"You may not have your data restored yet, so I don't know if this will be something that you can act on right away...?"

"We have restored almost full functionality at this point. One thing I have always been very cognizant of is the need to make multiple backups at different locations. And the ability to remotely access at least one of those backups without any specialized software, equipment, or tech support."

"Wow. That shows great foresight."

"You only have to lose critical data once to have the point driven home. I'm no smarter than anyone else."

"So I may have found the source of the escaped virus. I thought I would run it by you, give you what we know, and maybe you would be able to go farther with it."

"Really? That's great detective work. I'm afraid that the tedious process I have been going to was likely to take at least another week to trace it, unless I was lucky."

"We traced the dog that we think is the source of the virus being spread at the nursing home. Before the nurse who has her now owned her, she lived in an apartment above a virus laboratory."

Savage blew out his breath with a triumphant "ha!"

"No kidding. What is the name of the lab?"

"It's Virutek." Kenzie started to spell it out for him.

"I'm familiar with them. They are on my list of labs to talk to. Have you talked to anyone over there?"

"A Dr. Ducros."

"And I expect he told you that it is impossible that the virus escaped from his lab."

"Yes. But I walked through a part of the lab... and they had no containment protocols. Gloves and mask. Maybe a sealed ventilation system. That's it."

Dr. Savage snorted. "Unbelievable. And where exactly *does* their air system vent? Into the alley outside the building, I'll wager."

Kenzie hadn't thought about that. Even if there was no shared ventilation between the apartments and the lab, what were they doing with the exhaust air? Were they scrubbing it? Was it even possible to make sure that it was virus-free before venting it outside?

"Dr. Ducros remembered the dog. Volunteered it when I asked him who he would recognize from the neighborhood. He said she was very friendly, liked people. They would see her when she was out for walks or around the neighborhood."

"And all it takes is a small transfer of saliva..."

"Yeah."

"Do you have access to this dog?"

"Yes, I'm just going to go talk to the nurse at Champlain House. I didn't know whether to tell her to take the dog to you, or some facility where she can be isolated...?"

"We do have animals in isolation cubes here, so if you can get her here or we can pick her up, we can make sure that she's safe. Or that everyone else is safe. And we have decontamination here for you if you need it. Best to handle her with as much protective gear as you can, just to be safe, and we can help ensure that you're clean of the virus once you get here. Start you on an antiviral protocol as well. You've already been in contact with the virus in your morgue, so you should consider the antiviral protocol even if you aren't in contact with the dog."

"Yeah. So this Virutek place, you agree that they are probably the contamination point?"

"Yes, you're probably right, but we'll need to test to be sure. I was actually expecting it to be a place that does live animal trials, not just in vitro."

"But if it came from a dog, does that explain any anomalies?"

"One of the large viral segments that the virus gained from recombining with another virus is porcine. So I was expecting pigs to be involved."

"Pigs?" Kenzie echoed. She tried to think of any way that pigs entered into the equation. She hadn't seen anyone walking a potbellied pig around the lab. There hadn't been any meat-packers close by. If there had been any kind of live pig farm nearby, they would have been able to smell them. Kenzie had only been around pigs a few times, but they always had that distinctive smell. Maybe one of the scientists in the lab had a pet pig? "What kind of sources would you look for?"

"Like I said, I expected a live animal trial to be involved somehow. That's why Virutek is way down my list. I know that they got an early version of the engineered virus for use in their studies, but they are not supposed to be doing any live trials. So I didn't think the source would be them."

"Anywhere else?"

"One of the people who was in contact with the dog might have already been in poor health. While humans do not generally get porcine viruses, it is still possible, especially if their immune system is compromised. In that case, someone in your dog's circle might have picked up a porcine virus... somewhere."

"But the victims at the nursing home all live there. There wouldn't be a lot of opportunities for transmission of a porcine virus."

"Maybe from a visitor or a nurse. It's impossible to say. We see strange things happening with viruses. They are rather unpredictable."

Kenzie thought through what she knew about Lola and her history. Where had she picked up a pig virus? "Could she have picked it up from food? Being fed pig scraps?"

"They would have to be uncooked, of course, and most people know that pork carries nasty parasites and would not give it to their pets raw. I wouldn't say it is impossible. But it seems unlikely. Viruses don't generally live long without a live host."

What other way could Lola have been exposed to someone or some creature with a porcine virus? Maybe one of her doggy friends at a dog park? Another animal that had been sick, like a squirrel?

What about...?

Kenzie's heart dropped to her stomach. She didn't even want to think of other possibilities. That was one area of medicine she wanted nothing to do with.

"Dr. Savage... what about a xenotransplant?"

"**A** transplant of another species?" Kenzie could hear the surprise in Savage's tone as he considered the possibility. "There are very few cases where xenotransplants are successful. Pigs are certainly high on the list for xenotransplants since their organs are largely compatible with humans and develop to full size within months rather than years. Pig hearts, lungs, kidneys... but they don't generally last for more than a few weeks."

"Except in a case where it is a tissue transplant rather than an organ transplant," Kenzie amended. "People sometimes get porcine heart valves instead of artificial valves. Particularly if they are old, so the heart valves may outlast them and not need to be replaced."

As much as Kenzie disliked the field of transplantation, she knew her stuff.

"Yes. It's possible that someone at the nursing home has porcine valves," Savage agreed. "They are supposed to be disinfected in an antiviral solution before transplant to avoid just that problem. And as you can imagine... not everyone remembers, or there could be confusion over who on the team is supposed to do that step. Or just plain sloppiness. Third world transplants are notorious for transferring diseases along with the transplanted tissue or organ."

"So I've heard," Kenzie agreed tonelessly. Zachary gave her a sympathetic look and squeezed her knee gently. "My point is, the dog's previous

previous owner, before she lived above the Virutek lab, died of heart issues. The woman who got Lola from him said that he'd had surgery a few years earlier to replace his valves."

"Indeed." Savage's voice was impressed. "Dr. Kirsch... I think you've nailed the source. That explains both the genetic tag of the lab-manipulated HHV-4 and the large porcine segment."

"Virutek was designing a virus that they hoped to use to cure brain degeneration like Parkinson's," Kenzie told him. "It has been designed to go through the blood-brain barrier. What effect would the pig virus have on the brain of a human?"

"We have no way of knowing. Except to say... you have already seen some symptoms repeated across several victims. Those symptoms are probably not just coincidental."

"You mean the protein deposits and dementia?"

"That is what I fear."

"Yeah. Me too."

They were both silent for a moment. It was Savage who broke it.

"If you will get me the dog, I will see if I can do some magic and talk Virutek into giving me a sample of their re-engineered HHV-4."

"Do you think they will agree? They seem pretty possessive about it."

"That's why I said it will take some magic. We will see."

Kenzie sat in the car after hanging up with Dr. Savage, thinking it all through. The pieces were gradually coming together and, while she didn't like the picture, she was happy to be making progress. If they figured out enough details, maybe they could stop the virus's spread before it became an epidemic. She hated to think of all the people whose lives could be lost if they didn't manage to stop the novel virus.

"Are you okay?" Zachary asked.

"Yes. Just... it's a little overwhelming. Finding out these details while everyone else in the world still has no idea of what's going on. Even though we can see the virus spreading, causing deaths, the situation potentially getting worse and worse... but no one else knows."

Zachary nodded. "Imagine what the world looks like to a paranoid schizophrenic."

Kenzie raised her eyebrows, thinking about it. Seeing conspiracies and connections everywhere and having no one believe them. Even if they weren't yet satisfied that there was enough evidence, Dr. Wiltshire and Dr. Savage at least didn't think she was crazy. Just that they needed to gather more information before they could take any action. "Sheesh. Can you imagine? What a horrible world it would be for them."

"Very scary."

"Very," Kenzie agreed.

She dug around in her purse again. She really needed to organize it a bit better so that she could lay her hands on what she wanted to quickly. Zachary was quiet this time, not asking her what she wanted. Kenzie pulled out a plastic zip bag with gloves and a mask inside it.

"You keep those in your purse?" Zachary asked.

"You never know what you're going to run into. Stopping to give someone first aid beside the road... best to be prepared. I should have put them on before going into Virutek. I had no idea what we were walking into over there."

"I'm sure we will be fine."

"Probably. I hope so." Kenzie put on the mask and gloves. She touched the door handle. "Do you mind staying in the car? I probably should try to maintain some level of confidentiality here. I should be pretty quick in and out." She looked into the back seat. "Do you think we have enough room for a large dog kennel back there?"

Zachary looked. "Well... I can lay down the seats. That gives a bit more cargo space. But it really depends on the size of the kennel."

"Okay. Put them down. I will try to be quick."

"Take the time you need to. We don't want to mess anything up because we are rushing."

"True. Thanks."

Kenzie left him there and went into the nursing home. The receptionist didn't seem to remember or recognize her, so Kenzie showed her identification and gave her name. "I'm going in," she said, without asking for permission. Act as if being the Medical Examiner's assistant gave her the right to just march in there, and no one would stop her.

And she was right. The receptionist looked flustered but didn't try to stop her or run after her or call security. Kenzie went to the nursing station in the independent living unit. She took a quick glance around.

"Where would I find Nurse Ellie?" she asked briskly.

It was not Nurse Summers at the desk, and Kenzie hoped that if she again confidently demonstrated her authority, it would not be questioned. It was a break, Nurse Summers not being there, because Kenzie had a feeling she would have objected to what was about to happen.

"Nurse Ellie? She's not here."

"Where is she? And where is Lola?"

"They're not here."

Kenzie focused on the nurse's name badge. Camille Jackson. "Nurse Jackson. Please tell me where she is. I understand she wasn't able to keep Lola at her apartment, so are they out for a walk? Visiting one of the other units? Where would they have gone?"

Nurse Jackson's face folded into a scowl. "Just who do you think you are? You can't come marching in here and demand to know details of where everyone is. How is it any of your business?"

"I am with the Medical Examiner's Office, and that dog was supposed to be under quarantine. Where has Nurse Ellie taken her?"

"Oh, you're the one who's been making all of the trouble? The one everyone keeps talking about? You don't have the right to know where Nurse Ellie and her dog are. You can't interfere in their freedoms as citizens."

Lola was a citizen? Kenzie suppressed the urge to laugh at the statement.

"Nurse Jackson, please. I'm not here to make trouble. I'm here to help to protect your patients. That dog is carrying a dangerous virus and needs to be examined. You don't want her killing off any other patients, do you?"

"The dog doesn't kill patients. She helps them. She can sense when they are sick and dying, and she helps to make their last moments more peaceful."

"I'm sure she does."

"You and your kind can't come around here and do whatever you like. That dog is not yours! She is smarter than you will ever be. She knows what's going on, and she wouldn't let you near her. Neither will I!"

Kenzie shifted uncomfortably. The conversation had rapidly gone to a bad place. Nurse Jackson was not just being obstructive and provoking, but she sounded paranoid. Kenzie tried to remember what she and Zachary had just talked about. How scary the world would be to a person who had paranoia.

"I'm sorry if I scared you," Kenzie said soothingly. "I didn't mean to do that. I'm not here to do anything to hurt Ellie or Lola. They will both be very safe with me. I'm a doctor, you know, and we promise to do no harm."

"You're not a doctor. You're with the coroner's office."

"Yes. I am an assistant to the medical examiner. I am a doctor. Do you want me to show you my credentials?"

Nurse Jackson drew back suddenly when Kenzie reached into her purse for her wallet, cringing as if Kenzie had pointed a loaded gun at her. "Stop! No!"

Kenzie glanced around herself. Others were watching, puzzled and concerned. Kenzie looked at Nurse Jackson, cowering back as if Kenzie had threatened her. When Kenzie saw Nurse Summers coming down the hall at a quick clip, she was actually glad.

"What is going on here?" Summers demanded, looking at Nurse Camille Jackson and Kenzie with a scowl.

"I was just asking Nurse Jackson about where Lola and Ellie are," Kenzie said. "I'm sorry, I think she has misunderstood me..."

Nurse Summers looked at Nurse Jackson. "What's the matter?"

Nurse Jackson slapped her hand down on the counter with a loud crack. "That's enough! No one is going to touch me!"

Summers's eyes were wide. She glanced uncertainly at Kenzie as if she might have the explanation for Nurse Jackson's behavior.

"How long has she been like this?" Kenzie asked.

"Like this?"

"Confused, paranoid, emotionally labile."

"I... don't know." Summers shook her head. "There's got to be something wrong. This is not... she's never behaved this way before."

"I think... she's got it."

"Got what?"

"The virus that Lola is carrying."

Kenzie wanted to say, "The virus that killed Mr. Cartwright," but she didn't want to cause panic. That would probably be enough to send Nurse Jackson right over the edge if she hadn't already crossed it.

"The virus?" Summers repeated.

"Yes. That's why we called and gave instructions that the dog was to be isolated and anybody who had anything to do with her should be gloved and masked." Kenzie motioned to her own face. "Because we don't want anyone else catching this."

"What virus are you talking about?"

Kenzie didn't have the time to walk Nurse Summers through it. "A novel variant HHV-4 virus that causes dementia." She looked at Nurse Jackson. "Dementia that appears to develop very, very quickly."

Nurse Summers swore. She looked at Nurse Jackson as if trying to convince herself that it was true. Then she looked at her watch. She looked back at Kenzie, her mouth opening wide.

"What?" Kenzie demanded.

"The dog... there was a big write-up about her in the news. She was a celebrity."

"Yes."

"Well... she was invited to the Halloween Masquerade Ball."

Kenzie remembered the article that Zachary had sent her.

It took a few more seconds for everything to click into place. The ball. The one her mother and father were going to. That they had begged her to go to. All the people who would be there. Politicians, celebrities, the wealthiest and most influential people in the state. All jammed together in one room, with a friendly, hero dog carrying a deadly virus.

Kenzie swore. It wasn't under her breath and she didn't stop swearing. She just kept swearing over and over, like a mantra, as she hurried away, leaving Summers to deal somehow with Nurse Jackson. Kenzie swore all the way back to the car, one final time as she sat down in the passenger seat and pulled her door closed.

Zachary looked at her. "She... wasn't there?" he guessed.

Kenzie swore again. "Okay. I'm stopping now."

And then she swore again.

"She's gone to the ball."

Zachary's head tipped slightly to the side as he tried to understand what she was saying. "Who has gone to what ball?"

"Lola. The dog. And her owner. You remember you saw the article...? They have gone to the masquerade ball. The big fundraiser that my dad and mom were trying to get me to go to. That place is going to be packed, and Lola will be the star of the show. Do you know how many people are going to want to pet her or shake a paw? Or how many will let her lick their faces? Especially for a well-placed photo in the big magazines?"

"Oh." Zachary repeated Kenzie's swear.

"Exactly," Kenzie agreed.

"What do you want to do?"

"Go to my office."

"Your office?"

He had clearly been expecting other directions from her. Such as to go to the ball so they could get Lola before she infected everybody of importance in Vermont.

"Yes. As quickly as we can safely get there. And not get pulled over for speeding."

Zachary was happy to comply. He pressed the gas pedal down and focused on the road ahead.

Kenzie called Dr. Wiltshire again. "We have a problem."

"Kenzie." The sigh that carried down the line let Kenzie know that her call was not cause for celebration. "What problem? What do you mean?"

"I went to Champlain House to get Lola."

"To get Lola?"

"Dr. Savage said that they could properly isolate her while they ran tests to find out if she carries the virus. So I went to pick her up."

"Okay."

"She's not there. They did not isolate her as we instructed them. Instead, they have sent her to the big masquerade ball to meet all the celebrities."

There was silence from Dr. Wiltshire. He didn't swear. But Kenzie knew he wanted to.

"Not only that, but when I got there, one of the nurses freaked out. She wasn't making any sense. She was making accusations, acting paranoid. Inappropriate emotions. Confusion."

"She's got it."

"Yeah. So it isn't just old, sick people who can get it. And it progresses very fast. Everyone kept telling us that the victims had only had symptoms the last few days, and we thought that they had just missed the earlier symptoms. But maybe... it actually does progress that rapidly. That once it gets a foothold, there are only a few days until it is fatal."

"What did you do about this nurse?"

"I called you. I am going to the masquerade. I get that the CDC won't act that fast, and I'm going to go get that dog out of there before she infects half the state. I'll leave dealing with the nurse to you. Her name is Camille Jackson. Nurse Summers is there if you want to give her a call. She might have already called for an ambulance."

"Where are you now?"

"Heading back to the office to get geared up. Then we're going to Burlington."

"Okay." Dr. Wiltshire didn't say anything for a minute. "I have news for you too."

His tone of voice indicated that it wasn't good news. Kenzie wasn't sure she could take any more bad news. Maybe she should hang up and pretend that they had been disconnected accidentally. Her phone had died, so she couldn't talk to him until later, when they had dealt with the dog and everything was okay. But she couldn't do that.

"What did you find out?"

"The police did a welfare check on Joe Abernathy. When they couldn't raise him on the phone, they tracked down his address and sent someone over there."

Kenzie had a growing sense of unease, her chest and stomach muscles tightening. She was suddenly nauseated. When was the last time she had eaten? Was she going to be sick?

"Tell me he's not dead." She pictured them finding Joe Abernathy in his bed, dead from the virus. His body lying there, putrefying while Ducros waited for his eventual return to the office.

"He is dead," Dr. Wiltshire agreed.

Kenzie let out her breath and held one hand to her forehead, as if by doing so, she could keep her brain from exploding.

"He was a competitive swimmer a few years ago," Dr. Wiltshire said, seeming to go off on a tangent. What could being a competitive swimmer have to do with his death from the virus?

"Oh. Was he?"

"So there were pictures of him in his home, dressed in swimming trunks."

"Uh-huh?"

"He had a large port-wine birthmark along the outside of his right thigh."

Kenzie swore under her breath. Zachary glanced over at her, one eyebrow cocked, wondering what she was upset about.

"He is our other John Doe. The one from the motel room."

"Yes."

Kenzie's head whirled. "Why would he be checked into a motel? He had a house or apartment in town, right? So why would he check into a motel?"

"According to the manager the police talked with, his behavior was erratic. He was grumpy, didn't want anyone to talk to him. Had requested a room that was farthest from the motel office. Insisted that there couldn't be anyone in the room next to his. Yelled at passersby for spying on him."

"So he had the virus."

Of course he had the virus. She knew from the start that was why he had been so paranoid and moody when he was at Virutek. Not because of the stress of his job. Not because he needed a vacation. But because he had the virus.

"He was paranoid about people being after him, so he left his house," she offered, not waiting for Wiltshire's confirmation. "He thought that by going somewhere else, he could escape... whoever he thought was after him."

"Whoever he *thought* was after him?" Dr. Wiltshire repeated.

And then the full implication of that statement hit Kenzie. Abernathy hadn't just been paranoid. He hadn't, as she had imagined, died in his own bed after the virus had clogged up his brain with tangles of proteins. He had been tortured. His face was beaten in. So that not only could he not tell anyone what was going on at Virutek, he couldn't even be identified.

"Do you think Dr. Ducros is involved?" Kenzie asked. "He is the one who should have asked for a welfare check. If someone silenced Abernathy, isn't it most likely someone at Virutek?"

"It's... worth considering. The police will be looking into it. They'll look into Virutek and anyone else who might have threatened Abernathy. Because *his* death was clearly not accidental or natural causes."

Zachary pulled up to the building. It might have been quicker to go in the back way, but Kenzie didn't have a clicker for the ambulance bay door and her electronic pass card for the parking garage was in her car, not Zachary's. So he pulled into the loading zone in front of the building.

"Do you want me to come in?"

"You'd better stay here to make sure we don't get ticketed or towed. That would really put a crimp into our plans. I'll get everything we need. I know where it all is, so it really wouldn't be any faster for you to come in than it is for me to just grab everything myself."

"Okay. Is there still security around down there?"

"I don't know. Dr. Wiltshire didn't say."

"If there isn't... maybe you should get someone to escort you down. Just to make sure that you're safe."

"There isn't going to be anyone there after what happened yesterday. They already got everything they needed. And the police have been there and still could be. Someone would have to be stupid to go back there."

"Don't discount it. And they didn't get everything."

"What do you mean?"

"It sounded like you said this body that has been identified as being Abernathy is still in your morgue."

Kenzie stilled and thought about that. "Well... yes. We didn't know until now that he was part of this."

"But you can bet that they do."

"Who is *they*?"

"Ducros. Or the person or people who killed Abernathy."

"How do you know it was homicide?"

Zachary shrugged. He could read her, even if he hadn't been able to hear everything that Dr. Wiltshire had said to her on the phone. She had to be pretty careful if she wanted to keep him from seeing what she was thinking and feeling. He'd cultivated his ability to read people not just as a private investigator, but also as a child in the foster system, having to evaluate strangers every time he was transferred to a new home or school. To get a feel for who was safe and who was a threat. To read all the hidden undercurrents that ran through a family.

He was very good at what he did.

Kenzie put her hand over Zachary's, still resting on the gear shift after putting the car into park. "I'll make sure someone walks me down."

"Good."

Kenzie got out and entered the building. After being admitted through the security checkpoint, she told the guard that she was hoping someone could escort her downstairs just to make sure everything was safe and secure. "I'm not going to be there long; I just need to pick some things up. But I'm kind of nervous after the break in. I was attacked, you know..."

He looked sympathetic. "We've got a guard down there already. He's stationed outside of the Medical Examiner's Office, but you show him your ID and he'll go in with you. I'll call ahead."

"Thanks. I appreciate it. I suppose... it's going to be a while before I feel safe down there alone."

"Well, usually there are other people around. No one today because of all of the problems."

"Yeah. That's true. I probably won't be staying late, though. Until I feel like all of this is behind us."

"We have beefed up security. You can no longer get in through the loading dock without showing your identification to the camera first. So we know exactly who is there. No more clickers."

"That's good." And anyone coming in through the front had to go through the security checkpoint. "How about the parking garage?"

"We have a guard down there like we always have. And someone doing a regular walk around to look for anything suspicious."

"Good. Thanks."

Kenzie did as he had instructed and met another guard when she got down to the office. He checked Kenzie's identification and walked her in. "I've been here all day, and there hasn't been anyone else in," he assured her. "And they've changed the ambulance bay protocol."

"Yeah, he was telling me upstairs."

"Let me go ahead of you."

Usually, a man would stay back a step to allow Kenzie in ahead of him. But he did the opposite this time, motioning for her to stay back. He unlocked the door and walked in with his hand on his firearm, looking around alertly for anything that was out of place.

"Looks all clear, doctor."

"I'm going to need some gear from the supply room."

He led the way, again opening the door first and peering around to make sure that everything was safe. "Clear."

Kenzie went into the room and started to pick up everything she needed. The guard watched her for a moment and then withdrew into the autopsy room. Ten minutes later, Kenzie was headed back up the elevator to Zachary's car.

They didn't discuss what they were going to do in detail. Their main goal was obvious, to get Lola out of the ball, away from where she could contaminate people. Put her in the car and get her over to Savage's lab to be properly isolated until they were finished running all the tests they needed to. Kenzie didn't anticipate that it would be difficult to get into the ball. Her mother and father had both been begging her to attend. All she had to do was drop their names. Even though she hadn't responded that she would go, there were always last-minute cancellations or appearances at such an event.

"We don't have a kennel for the dog," Zachary pointed out.

"No. But if we can talk Ellie into it, she must have a kennel in her car. She had to transport Lola there somehow."

"But some people just let their pets roam free in the car."

"If that's what she did, then that's what we'll have to do. And she must be used to riding. So she shouldn't get all wild because she's not kenneled."

"Unless she has doggy dementia. Why hasn't she been affected by the virus?"

"That happens sometimes. The same virus can cause a bunch of problems in one animal family, and yet have practically no effect in another. So this one causes dementia and possibly death for humans... but dogs seem to just be carriers. If you can judge from just one case, which is pretty presumptuous."

"Or maybe she's just like... what's that expression? Typhoid Mary?"

Kenzie nodded. "Yes. She wasn't affected by the typhoid pathogen that she carried, but she passed it on to dozens of other people. Because she wasn't sick, she didn't believe them when they told her that she could make other people sick."

"So what if Lola has been to a dog park and passed it on to a bunch of other dogs?"

Kenzie shook her head. "Don't make any more suggestions, okay? I'm pretty freaked out about this already."

"Okay. Sorry."

"It's okay. There's nothing wrong with suggesting it, but I'm going to shut down the conversation anyway. I just don't want to talk about it."

He nodded. He stared at the road ahead, and she wondered whether she had upset him. But Dr. Boyle had encouraged them both to share their feelings to be fair to each other. Hiding their emotions was bad for the relationship. If Zachary were bothered by her asking him not to discuss it any further, he would get over it.

It didn't take too long to get to Burlington. Nothing in Vermont was too far and Zachary tended to have a lead foot out on the highway. He usually tried to curb it when he was with her, but Kenzie had made it clear that they were in a hurry. She wanted to limit Lola's exposure to all the other guests as much as possible. She didn't think she would be able to get there before the event was in full swing, but she would sure try.

They pulled up to the conference center. Kenzie got out and separated the gear into two piles. She suited up, showing Zachary how to get into the protective coveralls, and to put on the gloves and the helmet-like face mask with integrated breathing apparatus.

"Aren't you worried about what people are going to think when we walk in there?" Zachary asked. "Your father's warning about not panicking people...?"

Kenzie smiled. "This is a costume ball. Aren't these great costumes?"

Zachary's eyebrows went up as he struggled to get everything properly fastened. "I pictured... big ball gowns and those little decorative eye masks on a stick."

"I'm sure we'll see that too," Kenzie agreed. "And tuxedos. Vampires. But other people will have plain old Halloween costumes too. Not everybody goes for the highbrow masquerade stuff."

"Then I guess we'll fit right in."

Kenzie finished fastening her mask and checked her breathing. Then she helped Zachary with his.

"How does that feel? Good?"

Zachary nodded, testing his movement and range of vision and taking a few experimental breaths. "Yeah, it's okay."

"No claustrophobia?"

"No."

"All right. Let's go in. Follow me."

They walked together, drawing some looks and pointing fingers, but pretty much everyone was getting the same as everyone checked out each other's outfits. As Kenzie had predicted, there was a full range of costumes, from superheroes to French ballgowns. Kenzie stopped at the check-in counter.

"Do you have your invitation?" the elderly woman at the desk asked, peering at Kenzie through glasses on a chain and then looking down at her list.

"No, I didn't get a printed invitation. My name is Dr. Kenzie Kirsch. My parents are Walter Kirsch and Lisa Cole Kirsch. I'm sure you have us all on your list."

The woman checked it slowly, flipping through pages. She nodded when she reached the K's. "Walter and Lisa, yes. I see them here."

"I don't know if there is space at their table or not. We can sit somewhere else if not."

The woman had to check. She stood up to discuss the matter with one of the event planners circulating behind the check-in counter. Kenzie sighed and rolled her eyes at Zachary. It was difficult to see facial expression behind the face shields, so she tipped her head to the side slightly and shrugged dramatically. "I'm sure they'll sort it out."

Zachary's posture was less confident. He shrugged his shoulders slightly. "If not, you can show them your ME identification."

"I'm not sure that would gain me admittance anywhere."

The man the name-checker had whispered to approached the counter, smiling a cultured smile at Kenzie. "Miss Kirsch?"

"That's Dr. Kirsch," Kenzie corrected sharply. She rarely corrected people on her title, but the circumstances warranted it. She wanted to put the man off-balance, if he weren't already.

"I'm sorry, Dr. Kirsch. I don't have your response on our official list...?"

"No. I didn't expect to be able to be here today. But things were fluid, and I found myself available. It's such a good cause. I'm sure you know that my younger sister died of kidney disease. Our family is very passionate about raising awareness for kidney research. And funds, of course. I was told the governor would be here tonight?"

He looked startled by this. "Uh, yes, certainly. We're hoping that he will be available."

"It will be great to talk to him again. Are my parents here?" Kenzie mimed looking at her watch. If she had been wearing one, it would have been under her coveralls, but the gesture was just to nudge him forward. "They're always very prompt, so I'm sure they made it ahead of me. I cut it a little closer than I meant to. You know how doctors' schedules are."

"Yes." The man looked toward the dining room. "They are just going to make sure there is room at the table for you... and your guest?"

"Yes. Zachary is here as my plus one. He's looking forward to meeting the governor."

"I will go check on that seating. Feel free to mingle for a few minutes while we arrange everything."

Kenzie nodded politely. She looked back at Zachary, and they broke away from the check-in counter, walking into the ballroom without any problems from security.

"We're in," Kenzie told him with a smile.

"I can see that. Well done."

"I've attended enough of these things. I know how they work. As long as you have money and know the right people, you can get in anywhere, no matter how exclusive the invitation list was or how late you are in responding. They don't care about pushing extra chairs up to the table. They want your money."

"So, will you make a donation tonight?"

Kenzie was a little surprised by the suggestion. They were only there for one reason, and that was to get Lola. But Zachary did have a point. She had made out that she would make a donation, and her family name was well-known. And kidney research was important. "If I don't get a chance tonight, I'll mail them a check."

6 8

They looked around the ballroom at the chattering crowds. The helmet of the protective gear limited their range of vision. Kenzie found it necessary to turn her whole body, rather than just her head. Zachary was doing the same. They were both scanning for Lola or the nurse. Kenzie didn't know if the nurse was costumed or would be recognizable. The dog, however, would be a dead giveaway.

"Mackenzie!"

She turned right into her mother, dressed like some fairy godmother out of a Disney movie, with a pretty blue eye mask obscuring part of her face.

Kenzie's mouth dropped open. Even though she had known that her parents would be there, she had not expected to run into them. She was so focused on getting Lola and getting her away from the crowds that she had tunnel vision, everything else forgotten.

"Mother! Hello."

Kenzie stooped slightly to hug Lisa gently around the shoulders and blow air kisses past her cheeks. Was that really necessary when she was wearing a biohazard suit?

"Why didn't you tell me you were coming?" Lisa gushed. "It's so good to see you. I'm so glad that you came."

"I didn't think I would be able to. It was all very last-minute. And there is someone here that I need to see... I don't know how long I will be able to stay."

"Nonsense, of course you must stay. There are people I need to introduce you to."

"Another time. I really do need to find someone."

"And this..." Lisa turned to Zachary. "Is this your young man? Is this Zachary?"

"Hi, Mrs. Kirsch," Zachary said politely, his voice muffled behind the protective gear. "It's so nice to meet you."

Lisa peered at him. She lifted her eye mask so that he could see her face and peered into the depths of the protective suit. "You need to take that off so I can see your face!"

"Not now, Mom," Kenzie insisted. "You know we're not supposed to remove our masks until the end of the festivities."

"Well, you won't be able to eat with those on!"

"We have a plan," Kenzie promised.

She spotted a cluster of people at the end of the ballroom, laughing, bending over, surrounding something of interest that was closer to the ground. Kenzie recognized the clustering behavior. It had to be Lola. One dog at an event where one didn't usually see any pets, Lola would be sure to garner lots of attention. Everyone would want to pet her. Especially since she had been labeled a hero.

"Over here, I think," she told Zachary, steering him in the right direction.

Zachary walked beside her at a quick clip, nodding his head as he saw the crowd around the dog too. "That has to be it. Your mom seems nice."

"Oh, she is. Being nice was never an issue. She's very gracious. I'm sure you'll like her. But another day. When we're not trying to save the world."

"Is your dad here too, then? Did they come together or would they have been separate? Each coming from their own direction?"

"Separate. Unless Dad is staying over at the house."

Kenzie pushed past a few people who didn't move out of the way fast enough. "Excuse me. I'm sorry. Sorry."

Zachary stayed close behind her, not letting the crowd close back in around him. The guy could use his elbows when he had to. Kenzie broke through into an open space where she caught a glimpse of Lola and her adoring crowd for a moment. She swore under her breath at how close people were to her, how they reached out to pet her or to let her smell and lick their hands. All of them just begging to contract the virus and head quickly into dementia and an early grave. Kenzie put on an extra burst of speed.

"Ellie. Nurse Ellie, we need to talk to you."

A few people looked over at her curiously, but most didn't hear her over the conversations going on. Kenzie stepped firmly forward, pushing waiting fans aside.

"Ellie! Hey!"

The nurse was dressed... like a nurse. She had on a nursing smock as well as an old-style nurse's cap, just in case anyone wasn't sure what she was supposed to be. She had on a white Zorro-style eye mask.

"Yeah?"

"Dr. Kirsch from the Medical Examiner's Office. Do you remember me?"

"Well... yes, I guess so. You came and talked to everybody that one day. I didn't expect to see you *here.*" Her tone was questioning.

"Move back, please," Kenzie said in a raised voice, speaking above the hum of voices. "Everyone, please step back from the dog."

"What's going on?" Ellie asked.

Others around them were grumbling and complaining, not eager to move out of the way and lose their chance of saying hello to the hero dog.

"You were told that this dog was to be in isolation."

"Lola got an invitation to attend the masquerade ball. From the governor himself. You don't turn down an invitation like that."

"You do if you are infected and don't want to make everyone in the place sick!" Kenzie raised her voice still more, making sure that everyone around her understood. "This dog was quarantined for a reason. The governor does not have the right to override the Medical Examiner's directions."

There were a few whispers and laughs from the crowd, thinking that Kenzie was putting on a show. Acting in character.

"I don't know what you're even talking about." Ellie shook her head. "What is all this? You don't have any jurisdiction here."

"I have been authorized to pick this dog up." Kenzie didn't know how that would play when she was in another city, but she wasn't going to take the time to find out. "I'm to put her into isolation until they've had a chance to run all of the necessary tests on her and to ensure she is no longer a danger to *everyone around her.*"

People were starting to back off a little. Beginning to realize that maybe it wasn't just a joke or an act. There really was something going on.

"You can't just come barging in here and take Lola away from me. She's my dog."

"Do you know that her previous owner is dead in my morgue? And that her owner before that is dead? Do you think you won't catch this virus too?"

Ellie shook her head. "What are you talking about? Dead? Francine isn't dead."

"No, but Jay is. Francine's ex. And they lived in an apartment over the lab. The lab that engineered this virus and was stupid enough to let it into the wild. Do you understand me? This virus is killing people at Champlain House. People like Willie Cartwright and Stanley Sexton. And others over the past few months. Nurse Jackson is showing symptoms. You couldn't see what was happening right in front of your own eyes. Lola doesn't sense which people are going to die and give them comfort. She gave her favorite patients the virus that killed them!"

Ellie's mouth hung open. She was no longer protesting, her face draining of color.

"How stupid is it to take a dog to a ball with hundreds of vulnerable people when you've been told by a medical authority to keep her isolated?" Kenzie demanded. All conversation around them had now ceased. The room was silent and hanging on her every word. People were scurrying away from Lola now. Backing up, spreading out in a wave around her as each consecutive ripple moved farther.

"Mackenzie!"

She should have known that her father would be there to interfere. As soon as he realized she was causing trouble, of course he would be there at her side to gently pull her away and see that she quieted down.

He was dressed as a cowboy. White hat, of course, declaring his status as one of the "good guy" lobbyists acting to protect the people.

"Dad. You need to stay out of this."

"Mackenzie, what's going on here? What are you shouting about?"

"I'm here to do a job, Dad. This is work. So butt out."

"What are you talking about." He looked baffled. "What about work?"

"This dog is infected with a deadly virus. She was supposed to be quarantined. Instead, she's exposing all these people, including you, to a nasty virus that could cause your death within days."

People continued to flee, leaving the ballroom altogether. Pretty soon, they would be alone—Kenzie, Zachary, Ellie, and Lola. And Walter, who was undeterred.

"You don't want to make a scene here," he said reasonably. "Couldn't this wait until tomorrow? What's the difference now, really?"

"I don't want hundreds of people's blood on my hands. That's the difference."

He seemed stymied for a moment. He looked around him, trying to find someone in the crowd that had dispersed, leaving the rest of them an island in the room.

Someone was striding toward them now, wearing a Phantom of the Opera mask, black cape, and white gloves. One of the event planners, no doubt, getting ready to throw them out.

"Walter. What's going on here?"

"Some misunderstanding," Walter assured him. "I'm just talking to my daughter. I'll get it straightened out."

"No, you will not," Kenzie said firmly. "I'm taking this dog." She reached for the leash and pulled it out of Ellie's hand. Ellie was confused enough by this point, worried enough that what Kenzie said could really be true that she allowed it to be pulled out of her hand. Lola whined and looked back and forth at them, wondering what was going on. But she was a happy dog, a friendly dog, and she would go with Kenzie if that was who was holding her leash.

"You can't do that," the man snarled. He stepped forward abruptly and shoved Kenzie. It took Kenzie off guard and she nearly fell over, as she had during the break-in. But she managed to catch herself and Zachary reached out and steadied her. He stepped between them, trying to keep the Phantom from touching Kenzie again.

"Stay out of this," Zachary warned. "She's here on official business."

"Official business? There is no official business," the Phantom asserted. "She's not a real doctor. She assists in the morgue. That's not a *real* doctor. You don't have live patients. You aren't a doctor any more than this dog is." He reached out for the leash.

Kenzie jerked it back. The three of them danced around, the man trying to grab the leash away from Kenzie. Zachary pushed the Phantom back once, and the other man swung, hitting Zachary somewhere in the side of the head. Kenzie wasn't sure whether he connected with an ear or the face shield or another part of the apparatus. It wasn't good for the isolation suit, though. They weren't made for roughhousing.

"This dog is contagious," she told the Phantom forcefully, hoping to get through to him. "If you contract this virus, it could kill you. Why do you think I'm in this protective gear?"

"You're just making this up. I don't know who sent you, but this is completely ridiculous. The dog is safe. She's perfectly safe. If she had this virus, she would be dead months ago."

He had admitted there was a virus and that he knew something about its incubation period. Something about his voice was familiar. Kenzie tried to see his face under the mask, to reconstruct the part that was covered so that she could recognize him. "Who are you? I don't understand why you would interfere with a case like this. Do you want to get sick? Do you want everyone here to get sick?"

"That's not the way viruses work. Even with the most virulent virus, it isn't a hundred percent. It isn't ever *everybody*. Someone will always survive even direct exposure. What is more important? A few people dying, or being able to cure terrible diseases like Parkinson's and Alzheimer's that thousands die of every year?"

Kenzie glanced over at her father. Was this who had been whispering in his ear? Was Walter of the same opinion? That it was okay if a few people died from the virus, as long as the Virutek studies were allowed to go on?

They wanted to keep it all quiet, hush it all up so that they didn't have a virus outbreak to distract everyone from the upcoming election. The governor was bringing in all the goodwill he could with the masquerade ball, schmoozing and making people feel like they were making a difference and that he was helping to advance medicine and the well-being of his population.

The announcement of an outbreak would ruin that illusion.

"Mackenzie," Walter said quietly. "I think this has gone far enough. You've made a scene. There's going to be talk. I don't know if this event can be salvaged. Why don't you just quietly take the dog and go? We'll smooth things over here."

"No!" the Phantom shouted. "She's ruining everything. That dog is the best thing that happened to this ball! Do you know how many more people responded when we started to publicize that he would be here?"

"*She*," Ellie corrected, looking angry. Like maybe she'd already had to correct people on the dog's gender half a dozen times.

"They're here," Walter pointed out. "But after this scene, they're not going to want their pictures with the dog. They'll leave if it stays. So let Mackenzie just take it."

"*Her*."

They both looked at Ellie in irritation.

Kenzie tugged on Lola's leash and took a step back. If both Walter and Ellie were no longer fighting it, Kenzie could get out of there. She could get Lola to the lab and properly quarantined and stop the spread from dog to humans. There was still the human-to-human spread to be concerned with, but Typhoid Mary had to be stopped.

The Phantom grabbed Kenzie's arm and held on tightly. Zachary moved in. He was no ninja, but he didn't quail before the bigger man. The first thing he did was grab the edge of the Phantom mask and pull it away, snapping the elastic.

69

Kenzie swallowed. She stared at the face, trying to sort out all the conflicting images crowding into her brain. His iron grip on her arm and the smell of his body and his aftershave sent her hurtling back to the attack in the morgue. This was the man who had attacked her there. She hadn't seen his face during the attack, but she recognized that smell, the shape of his body, and his hands on her.

But before her stood Aaron Fisk, the pleasant man from the lobby when she had visited Virutek. He had seemed so cultured. A great addition to any board of directors. Maybe a family guy, sort of like her dad.

Like Walter.

The two of them clearly knew each other. So who was Aaron Fisk? Why did he care about Lola? About the Virutek studies? Why had he been at Virutek earlier?

Kenzie tried to jerk her arm out of his grip. Zachary gave Fisk a shove back, but didn't manage to dislodge him. Zachary drove a hand toward Fisk's face, fingers bent into claws, going straight for the eyes, and that did cause a reaction. Fisk stepped back, flinching out of the way and releasing Kenzie.

Kenzie's relief at being released lasted for just a split-second. Her shoulders dipped and she looked down at Lola for an instant, regrouping, ready to make a dash for the door.

Then Fisk was on Zachary—hitting him, Kenzie thought, until she saw the blossom of red on the protective coveralls. She registered the fact that Fisk was armed and had attacked Zachary with some kind of weapon. Then Walter went hurtling into the fray, his white hat flying off. There were shrieks from the other side of the ballroom where partygoers were crowded in the doorways watching from a safe distance away. Kenzie reached out a hand toward Zachary.

"Are you okay? Let me see."

He covered his side and shook his head. "Just a graze. Your dad—he's going to get hurt!"

Kenzie forced her attention away from Zachary and the blood on his suit to her father and Fisk, rolling around on the floor, both trying to get control of the knife in Fisk's grip. "Dad! Be careful!"

She didn't know what to do. If she joined in the struggle, she might be hurt or make things more dangerous for Walter. She looked around for some kind of weapon, but there was just open space intended for visiting and the dancing that would come after dinner and the fundraising pitches.

"Dad!"

And then, as quickly as it had begun, the struggle was over and they were both still. Kenzie looked at the two men on the floor in horror, unable to take it all in.

Walter rolled over, off of Fisk. Fisk didn't move. His white shirt was also turning red. Kenzie looked once more at her father to make sure that he wasn't hurt. She didn't see any sign of injury. But Fisk's condition was grave.

Kenzie put her gloved hand directly over the wound and pressed hard. At least she was protected by her gear from any blood-borne disease. She leaned close to Fisk's face, watching for the rise and fall of his chest, listening for his breath.

"I had to protect you," Walter said breathlessly.

"Put your hand here," Kenzie ordered, gesturing to the wound. "Press down. Zachary, are you okay?" She looked over her shoulder to him.

"Fine," he said. He was still on his feet, not looking any worse.

"Call 9-1-1."

He nodded and looked for his phone, zipped away into one of the pockets of the coveralls. Kenzie adjusted Fisk's head and neck and started chest compressions.

"I don't know what happened," Walter said. "I've never seen him like that. So... unreasonable. I don't understand. He's tough and hard-nosed, but this was... animal-like..."

Kenzie continued the chest compressions, feeling breathless herself. "This virus... it changes people. It causes rapid dementia. Personality changes, confusion, emotional lability..."

"But... like this?"

If Fisk had somehow contracted the virus, then Kenzie's chest compressions were probably less than useless. A stab wound in the belly. No pulse or respiration. That was bad enough. The chances of bringing someone back from that with just chest compressions were extremely remote. Add in the virus, and his brain was probably so clogged with proteins that he would have been dead within hours anyway.

But Kenzie continued the compressions. She had committed to the rescue; she had to continue until Fisk was declared dead.

K enzie realized suddenly that she had another patient, one who might benefit from her attention, unlike Fisk. She looked around for Zachary as she continued compressions.

"Zachary? Are you okay?"

He was slightly out of her line of sight due to the limited field of vision of the face shield. He moved closer, where she could see him. His hand was still pressed to his side.

"I'm fine," he assured her.

Kenzie remembered another private investigator, years before, and the stab wound that he had sustained. She remembered the blood pumping out under her hands as she screamed for help. Was history repeating itself?

But what she could see of Zachary's face through the shield was still a healthy color. As healthy as Zachary's face ever was. Pale, but not blue or gray. He seemed to be steady on his feet, not weak or staggering.

"You're sure you're okay?"

"Yes. It burns, but that means it's just a surface wound. It's not bleeding much."

Lola nosed at Fisk, whining. Kenzie didn't know what to do about the dog. She would still have to take Lola into the lab for quarantine. After she was done there. Despite the little bit of wrestling, her suit still seemed to be intact, so she was protected from the virus.

The integrity of Zachary's suit, on the other hand, had been compromised. He was now exposed to Lola and the virus. The risk wasn't significant because he was still breathing clean air and had his gloves on, but the wound in his side did offer another entry point for the virus.

"You need to stay back from Lola," she told him. "I don't want you to be exposed."

"Okay."

The chest compressions seemed to go on forever. But eventually, an ambulance arrived. The paramedics were shown through to the ballroom. Everyone else stayed back, mindful of Kenzie's raving that Lola was a deadly contamination risk. But apparently, no one told the paramedics of the danger and they approached without any concern.

"I don't think there's anything you can do for him, but I have been keeping up compressions," Kenzie told the first paramedic to kneel down at her side. "And you need to treat this patient as a biohazard. He may have a virus that has caused several deaths recently."

He looked at her in disbelief. "Is this some kind of joke? Because of the costume?"

Kenzie shook her head. "No. I'm wearing the biohazard gear because of the virus. It's not a costume. I came to take the dog," she nodded toward Lola, "to put her into quarantine, because she is carrying the virus and has spread it to a number of people already. We need to get her into isolation."

"I can't do anything about that."

"I don't expect you to. I have a place to take her to. But you need to treat this patient very carefully, even if he's dead."

The paramedic already had gloves on in preparation for examining the patient. He put on a second layer of gloves and motioned to his partner to do the same. He opened up his case and pushed things around to find a face mask, which he put on.

"Could you look at Zachary?" Kenzie motioned to the other paramedic. "He was stabbed, but he says it's not bad."

The second paramedic approached Zachary to attend to him. The first knelt over Fisk, feeling for a pulse. As Kenzie had expected, there was no sign of a pulse.

"Keep up the compressions until I tell you to stop."

Kenzie nodded. "I will."

"Let's have a look at the wound." The medic motioned for Walter to give him access to the stab wound. Walter lifted his hand and moved out of the way. The paramedic poked around, pulling Fisk's shirt back to have a look. Walter stood and looked down at his hand.

"Uh, Mackenzie...?"

Kenzie looked at Walter staring down at his bloody hands, her stomach tightening in a knot. She wanted to swear, but kept it to herself. "Go straight to the nearest restroom and wash up. Don't touch your face. Keep the water on a low stream. You don't want it splashing back in your face or aerosolizing any contaminants. Warm water, soap, wash for two minutes, making sure you get in between your fingers, under your nails, everywhere. Okay?"

"Okay. You don't think...?"

"No, unless you have open wounds on your hands, your skin should protect you. It can be spread through bodily fluids, but you shouldn't be able to absorb it that quickly with the natural barriers that skin provides." And once she had a chance to talk to Savage, they would work out what antiviral protocol to give the people who had been exposed to the virus. Zachary, her father, the other residents and staff at the nursing home. Anyone who had petted Lola. The Virutek people. The list was not going to be short.

Walter nodded and walked toward the nearest restrooms. Kenzie was happy to see that he was walking, not running in a panic. The chances that he would follow her instructions to the letter were much greater if he stayed calm.

"There's no point in continuing the compressions," the paramedic advised. "There's not going to be anything we can do for this patient, and if there really is a biohazard here, we need to focus on containment rather than pursue extreme measures. Exactly who are you and how do you know about this virus?"

Kenzie sat back, relaxing her shoulders and massaging her arms. "Dr. Kenzie Kirsch with the... I'm from the Medical Examiner's Office in Roxboro. We've had some deaths that may or may not be related to a novel HHV-4 virus that escaped a lab. The lab virus is designed to cross the blood-brain barrier and we've seen cases of very rapidly progressing dementia, leading to death within a few days."

"Good grief. Where is the CDC on this?"

"We're still in the evidence-gathering stage. We don't have enough for them."

The paramedic looked around at the ballroom, Lola, and all the people peering in at the doors. He swore. "I'm not doing anything without bringing in the infectious disease experts. Let's lock this down."

Kenzie let the paramedic make the calls their protocol dictated. She went over to Zachary and the other paramedic. "Is he okay? Really?"

"Should get stitched up, but it's clean and didn't go in deep," the paramedic said. "If he'll let me access it properly, I can bandage it up temporarily, and they can suture it at the hospital."

Zachary blocked the paramedic, and Kenzie realized the man wanted to cut the suit or for Zachary to take it off. Kenzie was with Zachary on that note. "No, he needs to keep the suit on, for whatever protection it will still give him. We need to get the dog into quarantine."

"The dog isn't leaving here, and neither is anyone else," the first paramedic said firmly. "When I say lockdown, I mean lockdown! Until we have someone with authority clear the site, no one is going anywhere. I'm not going to be responsible for releasing any carriers."

Kenzie looked at Lola, then back at Zachary. "Well... I guess we're here for a while. Do you mind if we find a place to sit down? My legs are shaking."

Zachary nodded, looking happy to comply. "Yeah, I think we could all use a few minutes, after all this..." He nodded toward Fisk's body.

"I can't believe it."

Walter was walking back from the restroom. He gave Kenzie a weak smile. "All okay now. Washed off the first two layers of skin. And it looks like you're finished." He glanced over at his friend's form. "Or Aaron is, anyway."

"Yeah. I'm sorry, Dad. There wasn't anything I could do."

"Of course not. I had to protect you..."

"We were talking about finding a place to sit down. I don't suppose they're going to want us in the dining room or around anyone else now."

"There are bound to be private rooms available. Let me find out."

Walter strode toward the crowd watching through the doorways. People backed away, giving him space to pass, definitely nervous about the talk of a contagious virus. Walter was back a minute later with one of the venue staff. "Mackenzie, Zachary, come this way."

The two of them followed, and the employee led them to a private room where they could meet. Kenzie looked at the engraved plaque next to the door. *The Champlain Room.*

It started and ended with Champlain.

Kenzie sat down in one of the soft, comfortable leather chairs arranged around the heavy boardroom table. Zachary fell into one next to her. He gave a sigh. Kenzie was sure he was just as glad to get off his feet as she was. Probably more so, since he was injured. He didn't want to show her any weakness, but she knew he must be shaking worse than she was. All the adrenaline from the day, peaking at the point that they were attacked. Walter sat in one of the chairs on the opposite side of the table. He leaned forward, examining them, looking eager to begin a long list of questions. And Kenzie wasn't up for more questions. She needed an answer.

"How do you know—did you know—Aaron Fisk?"

Walter looked surprised that she had beat him to the punch. "I've known him for many years. He's a lobbyist."

"I thought he was some kind of scientist. We saw him at a laboratory."

"No." Walter shook his head. "But he does a lot of lobbying on behalf of medical corporations. Big pharma. We've been on opposite sides of the table more often than on the same side."

"So what was he doing there? And what was he doing here?"

"Medical studies have to be funded. You know anything about the funding that this laboratory receives?"

"No." Kenzie wished that she could take her suit off so that she could scratch an itch. But she didn't want to take any chances. It was safer, for the moment, for her and Zachary to remain in the biohazard suits. "I never thought to ask. I guess I just saw them as a little independent lab studying whatever it was that interested them."

"Not really the way it works. Studies need to be funded."

"There was a sign on the wall at Virutek," Zachary said. "A plaque that had a name like Something Gesundheit GmbH. That's like a German corporation, right?"

"That's right," Walter agreed. "AFG, maybe? They're very big. Or it could have been a smaller one. Aaron hired out to a lot of those companies.

He had a reputation for succeeding when others had only run up against roadblocks. A troubleshooter."

A troubleshooter. Someone who was prepared to go above and beyond to clear the way for a big corporation. For a nice chunk of money, Kenzie assumed.

"He was the one who broke into the Medical Examiner's Office," she told them. "The one who knocked me down."

"Are you sure? I thought you didn't see who it was!" Walter demanded.

Kenzie hesitated before answering. She was pretty sure she hadn't told him that. So who had he gotten it from?

"Not to describe him, no. But he was the same size and shape. And he has a certain scent. His deodorant or aftershave. It's distinctive. I recognized it when he grabbed me."

"I don't know if something like that would hold up in court," Walter observed skeptically.

"It's not going to court. He's dead."

"Well, yes," Walter agreed uncomfortably.

"If he's the troubleshooter," Zachary said slowly, "the one who pushes things through and makes them work, the one who broke into the office, then the police might want to look into the possibility he was involved in Abernathy's death."

Kenzie frowned. "You don't think that he was killed by someone unrelated to Virutek? It could have just been a mugging..."

"In his motel room. Where he was hiding out."

"Well... maybe. That's only a guess."

"Fisk is clearly not someone who is opposed to violence. To solving things with force instead of negotiation. Not above breaking the law."

Kenzie looked at Walter for his opinion. Her father gave a reluctant shrug. "He was known for being... kind of a cowboy." Walter brushed his fingers over his own hat, which he had retrieved at some point. "Getting things done his own way. If you can make some headway... these difficult cases can bring in a lot of cash."

"Wow. But all of that... killing Abernathy, breaking into the ME's office and stealing evidence... that would mean that he knew there was a problem. He knew the virus had escaped from the lab and was helping to cover it up."

"Yes," Walter agreed. "I suppose it does."

"And it means that he should have known to wear protective gear. If he knew the virus was out there, that maybe Abernathy had it, that the samples he stole from the morgue might be infected, he should have worn something to protect himself."

"You can't exactly walk into a motel room wearing something like this without attracting attention." Zachary indicated their protective gear.

"Not to this extent, but he could have a least put on gloves and a mask. The blood splatter in that motel room was... extensive. He basically aerosolized the blood. He was breathing it in. Right along with the virus."

They had been isolated, been put through decontamination procedures, had extensive medical examinations, and Zachary's knife cut had been stitched up. Kenzie lifted Zachary's shirt and checked out the sutures, touching the wound lightly to reassure herself that the injury was minor and she wasn't going to lose him as she had Lance.

Zachary gave a shiver and hugged her to him, giving her a comforting squeeze. "It's all over. Everything is going to be okay."

"I hope so. But what if the CDC doesn't find the same things as we did? What if they think the virus doesn't have anything to do with the dementia and deaths? I mean... my whole career could be down the crapper if they come back and say that I acted without reasonable proof that there was a danger."

"You were acting under Dr. Wiltshire. So... it would be his career down the crapper."

"And mine too."

He held her more loosely so that their bodies were just lightly touching. "What would you tell me?"

Kenzie thought about it. "To stop worrying about what's going to happen. Quit catastrophizing it."

Zachary nodded and rested his head against hers. "I'm glad that you're okay. That you and your dad didn't get hurt."

"And I'm sorry that you got hurt. But glad it wasn't serious. Now you just have a cool scar to show your buddies and say 'yeah, I got this protecting my girlfriend from a maniac with a knife.'"

Zachary grinned. "That *is* pretty cool."

"Everybody's going to want one." She looked around. "I can't believe that the CDC went all-out. Dr. Wiltshire said that we would need more proof before they would do anything."

He gave a shrug. "Well, if you can't get proof, get publicity."

One of the staffers came into the hospital room that Kenzie and Zachary had been assigned to. She was wearing a protective suit similar to the ones that they had worn to the ball. She handed them each a bag of their personal possessions. Anything that they had been able to properly disinfect.

They each sat down on one of the hospital beds. Kenzie turned her bag around to survey the contents inside. Zachary immediately delved into his to retrieve his phone. Kenzie preferred not to look at her phone yet. There would be calls from her mother and father, from Dr. Wiltshire, and who knew how many others. She wasn't ready to deal with it yet.

She looked over at Zachary to say something to him, but the remark fled her lips. He was scrolling through a screen, looking worried.

"What's up?" Kenzie asked.

He passed the phone across to her. Kenzie took it, unsure what she was going to see. A worrisome message from Rhys? Bad news about Bridget or her babies? Another break-in at the lab or at the house?

She saw a column of texts from Lorne Peterson, asking for one of them to call him as soon as possible. But specifically asking not for Zachary, but for Kenzie. Lorne probably didn't have Kenzie's number handy, as he always talked to Zachary.

Rather than pulling her own phone out, Kenzie just tapped Lorne's name and 'Call.' The phone started to ring through. Kenzie put it on speaker so that she and Zachary could both hear and talk.

"Hello? Zachary?"

"We're both here, Lorne," Kenzie said. "Is everything okay?"

"Well... I'm sure it's all right, but I wanted to talk to you, Kenzie, to see what you thought. Seeing as you're a doctor..."

So something was wrong. They hadn't just seen Zachary on the news or heard that he'd been injured. "What is it?"

"Pat's been fighting this bug," Lorne said. "The same one I had. Or that's what we figured, anyway. He was dragging around tired all the time, kind of cranky and depressed. You know how a sick toddler behaves!" Lorne tried to joke, but the concern in his voice was clear.

"Is it his meds?" Zachary asked. "Have they adjusted the dosages lately?"

"No. I don't think it's anything to do with his meds. But... he fell down today—said that he just tripped—and he's asked the same questions several times... I know it's nothing, but I'm worried. He doesn't have any of the symptoms for a stroke; I looked them up on the computer..."

Kenzie's eyes met Zachary's. Zachary swore.

"I'm sure it's nothing," Lorne said apologetically.

"Actually... it might be," Kenzie admitted. "Lorne... I was exposed to a virus before I came down to visit you guys last. And I might have passed it on to Pat."

"Then it isn't anything to worry about. If you've already had it."

"I didn't get any symptoms. But sometimes, people are just carriers or are asymptomatic. This is... a brand new virus, and we don't know yet how it might behave"

"So what should I do? Rest and fluids? Like the flu?"

"You need to get him to the hospital right away. I'm going to call someone so they will be expecting him when you arrive. Go to the emergency room doors, but wait there and don't get out of the car. They'll come to get him. They'll be wearing protective clothing, like HAZMAT suits. Don't open the doors to anyone who isn't wearing protective gear."

"Kenzie?" Lorne's voice shook. He had been worried when he called, now he was clearly frightened. "Is it that serious? Is it the plague?"

"It's not the plague. It's something new. It has... it has caused some deaths. I'll convince the doctors to treat it aggressively. I'll get them to treat all of us, you too. The earlier we catch it, the better our chances."

"Do you and Zachary have it too?"

"Neither of us has been showing any symptoms. But we're already in isolation because we were exposed. We'll just have to take it up a level and not wait to see if we test positive for it. If I passed it on to Pat, then I have it for sure. Maybe Zachary too. Maybe you."

Lorne swore, worried. Kenzie had never heard him swear before. "Pat? Pat, you need to get ready to go. Come on. Pull on a jacket and your shoes. We have to go to the hospital."

They could hear Pat grumbling in the background, obviously not wanting to take the trip.

"I talked to Kenzie, and we have to go. Get ready." Lorne spoke back into the phone. "I'll let you know when we're there."

"Okay. Remember what I said and only open the doors for someone with proper protection. I'm going to light a fire under someone now."

72

Neither of them could look at the other. Zachary took his phone back after Kenzie hung up, but he didn't look at it like he normally would, diving into his email or messaging apps to see what else he had missed. He just held it in his hand, looking blankly in front of him.

Kenzie hit the emergency call button, which brought a couple of nurses hustling into the room within seconds, unlike in a regular hospital ward where they usually didn't show up for a while.

"The emergency button is not for—"

"This is an emergency. We just got word that a family member is showing symptoms," Kenzie snapped. "That means I am a carrier, because I'm the only vector between him and the outbreak. And if he's showing symptoms already, he needs aggressive treatment or he might not survive."

The nurse looked at Kenzie for a moment, then nodded. "I'll get the doctor."

The two of them retreated.

The beds were close together. Kenzie reached and took Zachary's hands, holding them out in front of her, the two of them sitting facing each other with their clasped hands in the center.

"It's going to be okay, Zachary. We caught it before the symptoms got too bad, and we'll throw everything at it that we can. He's going to recover. It's going to be okay."

"If anything happens to them..." Zachary's voice was rough. "They are... the only family I had for years. I can't lose them."

"It's going to be okay."

73

From the chair beside his bed, Kenzie watched Zachary sleep. His chest rose and fell in a steady rhythm.

He slept so little when he was well that she'd rarely had the opportunity to watch him sleep. Or she hadn't taken the opportunity when she'd had it.

He looked younger. The lines on his face and bags under his eyes were less pronounced. She could imagine what he had looked like as a little boy. She'd seen a few pictures that Lorne had taken over the years, but she'd had a hard time reconciling the young Zachary's face with the one she knew, all angular and frequently unshaven, a man who had been through a lot in his life that no one should ever have to.

He stirred and opened his eyes. He lay there for a moment, eyes glazed and unseeing before he focused on her face and smiled.

"Kenz."

"Hey, Zach. How are you feeling?"

"Ugh."

That was pretty much how he felt all the time, and Kenzie was glad they were nearly at the end of the treatment protocol and they would be able to get back to their lives soon.

"Do you think you could eat something?"

"I'll try."

Kenzie raised the head of the bed. Any time he was awake, they tried to get him to eat. Zachary was already thin and nauseated from his depression and medications, and the side effects of the Acyclovir and the chemo drugs that they were using to fight the virus off made it hard to keep anything down. They didn't want him to lose more weight.

Kenzie reached for the snacks on the bedside counter. "Jell-O?"

"Yeah."

She tore the sealed top off a new Jell-O cup and handed it to him with a spoon. He took a couple of bites and closed his eyes. Kenzie nudged him. "Hey. Stay awake. Have some more."

He focused on the gelatin again and had another bite.

"Heard from Lorne today," Kenzie said. "He's back home."

Zachary's lips twitched. "He is? That's good. He didn't get any symptoms?"

"Nope. And he handled the protocol like a champ. No trouble."

"We'll be done soon."

"Yep," Kenzie agreed. "And then back to work. Dr. Wiltshire says that he's tired of me lazing around on vacation when everyone else in the office tested negative and is hard at work. And your family has all been calling. Heather says she's running out of work and needs you to send some more files her way."

"Yeah." Zachary nodded. "Be good to be home again."

Kenzie didn't tell him that she'd already finished her protocol. Zachary's viral load had been much higher, so he was on higher doses and had not yet completely cleared the virus, though they figured he would be done in another day or two.

"Let's see if we can get Lorne on the tablet," Kenzie suggested. Zachary's eyelids were starting to droop, but she knew that if he could talk to Lorne, he would make an effort to stay awake longer.

"Yeah, okay."

Kenzie pulled the wheeled table across Zachary's lap and set the tablet on it, propped at an angle. She tapped the buttons on the screen until a call started to ring through to Lorne Peterson's account, and then they both watched to see if he would answer.

After a few rings, Lorne's round face fringed with white hair appeared on the screen as he bent down to answer the call. He smiled tiredly, happy to see his former foster son, and sat down.

"Zachary! How are you managing?"

"Good," Zachary proclaimed, though he obviously wasn't well. "Going to be done here soon. Then I can go home and get back to work."

"You might need to take it easy for the first little while," Lorne warned. "I thought I would be back to normal when I finished, but I can still barely walk from one room to another without getting out of breath."

Kenzie made sympathetic noises. The chemical cocktail that they had been on had left her tired too. A couple of days off it and she was starting to feel more normal, but not quite ready to go back to her usual routine yet.

"And it's so quiet around here," Lorne said.

Zachary's head was starting to nod. Kenzie nudged him and tried to keep him awake for a few minutes longer. Another bite or two of Jell-O to keep up his strength.

Pat's head appeared over Lorne's shoulder. "The reason it's so quiet around here is that whenever I put on the music, you say your head hurts and you want a nap, old man," he teased.

Lorne turned his head to smile at his partner. Pat put his hand on Lorne's shoulder, and Lorne put his hand over it and gave it a squeeze.

"Well, that might be true," Lorne admitted. "Don't ask me how he's so full of energy and bouncing around here when he was the one who had symptoms," he complained. "Weren't so bouncy a couple of weeks ago, were you?"

"It's those green drinks," Pat said. "If you want me to whip you up some wheatgrass shots..."

"No!" Lorne made a face. "You don't need to go to all of that bother. I'll just lie down for a nap when we're done talking. If you'll keep your music down."

Zachary's head sank into his pillow and Kenzie couldn't shake him awake again. She took the Jell-O cup and spoon out of his hands.

"I guess that's it," Kenzie said softly to Lorne and Pat on the tablet. "We'll call again tomorrow. Take care of yourselves."

"We will," they both agreed.

"Look after that boy," Lorne said.

"Sure will." Kenzie gave a little wave to the camera and ended the call. She rested her head on Zachary's pillow, just touching her forehead to his head. "Sweet dreams, Zachary."

Did you enjoy this book? Reviews and recommendations are vital to making a book successful.

Please leave a review at your favorite book store or review site and share it with your friends.

Don't miss the following bonus material:
Sign up for mailing list to get a free ebook
Read a sneak preview chapter
Other books by P.D. Workman
Learn more about the author

Sign up for my mailing list at pdworkman.com and get Gluten-Free Murder for free!

PREVIEW OF DOSED TO DEATH

CHAPTER 1

How's it going?" Kenzie asked Zachary, poking her head into the bedroom to see whether he had finished packing.

Zachary was sitting on the bed looking at his duffel bag. It didn't look as if he had made much progress since the last time she had seen him. She cocked her head to the side.

"Tired?" she asked sympathetically.

Zachary raised his head to look at her. His face was painfully thin, eyes dark hollows. He attempted to hide how sunken his cheeks were with the dark stubble, but she could still tell. The antiviral protocol that the two of them had been through had been much harder on him. Kenzie was feeling pretty much her old self. She just tired a little faster than usual. But Zachary had already been sinking into his annual depression and didn't sleep or eat well, so it had really taken its toll on him.

But better thin and tired than dead.

"I just don't know if I can do this," Zachary said.

Kenzie had already taken care of everything else. The only thing left for Zachary to do was to pick out the clothes he wanted to wear for the holiday and throw anything else he wanted to take along into the bag. Once they were at the resort, he could rest and sleep as much as he needed to. They had a cabin to retreat to that was separate from anyone else, so they didn't have to worry about thin walls or people being aware of their comings and goings. They would have both the privacy they needed and socialization activities to boost their spirits.

Rather than criticizing him or telling him to just focus and get it done, Kenzie entered the bedroom to see if there was anything she could do to help.

"Do you know what you want to wear?"

He looked at his flat bag listlessly. "No."

"Does that mean you don't care? Can I just pick some stuff out for you?"

Zachary rubbed the back of his neck. "Yeah. Sure."

Kenzie went through Zachary's drawers and his side of the closet to pick out a few outfits, folded them neatly, and set the piles into his bag. "There. What else? Do you have your meds?"

"Yes."

Kenzie opened the toiletries case to see what was in it. Comb, toothbrush, razor, and a few bottles of pills. She checked the names on the sides of each, and didn't think he had everything he needed. She left the bedroom and went down the hall to the main bathroom, which was the one that Zachary usually used, leaving the ensuite bathroom to Kenzie. She opened up the medicine cabinet and looked through the remaining pill bottles, picking out a couple more that Zachary probably couldn't go without for a week. She grabbed his deodorant and toothpaste and glanced over his toiletries for anything else he might need that the resort wouldn't have on hand.

She returned to the bathroom and added the items she had picked out to his toiletries bag. Zachary watched her and didn't comment.

"What else are you taking? Your computer and phone? Anything else?"

"Computer," Zachary echoed.

"It's in the living room? Let's go grab it and you can tell me if there is anything else you need."

She picked up the duffel bag. Zachary took a few extra seconds to consider this, then pushed himself to his feet. He took the bag from her as they walked to the doorway, and Kenzie let him. She didn't know whether he was being chivalrous or just didn't want someone else touching his stuff, but it didn't matter. It was good he was taking some part in the preparations, however small.

In the living room, he put his bag down on the couch and picked up his laptop computer, which was sitting closed on his mobile desk and put it into his soft-sided briefcase beside the couch. He picked up the cord, unplugged it from the wall, and carefully coiled it up to add to his gear. Kenzie stayed back and watched him gather the peripherals he wanted. An external drive and mouse. A couple of notepads. He stood there looking at his desk, again grinding to a stop.

"Is that it?" Kenzie prompted.

"I don't know if I can do this," Zachary said again.

"Do what?" Kenzie had assumed that he meant he couldn't do the packing on his own, but since he was now packed, she wasn't sure what he meant.

"Just... this whole thing. Going to this place. Being around other people. Leaving my business behind when I've already been neglecting it because of this virus protocol..."

"You wouldn't be able to do it if you were here anyway. You still need more time to recover. Just because you're out of the hospital, that doesn't mean that you are on hundred percent better. What about after your car accident? You couldn't go right back to work a couple of weeks after that, could you?"

"No. But that was different. I had a lot of rehab to do... I couldn't physically do the work."

"And how is that different from now? You're not being weak or lazy. You're recovering from a virus and treatment protocol that could have killed you. Just like that car accident. Your clients will understand that you can't service them right now. They will wait, or go to another private investigator, or Heather will help them out with what they need. And when you're feeling better, you can get back to it."

"Heather can't do everything. She's not trained. She doesn't do field work."

"I know. I said that they could go to another PI if they need to. If they just need backgrounds or skip tracing or other computer stuff, Heather can do that."

He scratched his head. "Yeah."

"You can't work like this. And if you're out of town, people will get that. Everyone takes vacation now and then. It's not healthy to work all the time. Most jobs will wait a couple more weeks, until you're ready."

"I thought this vacation was only a week."

"Yes, the vacation is only a week. But I don't think that's going to be enough time for you to recover enough to work cases again."

"I can do some. Maybe not everything, but I can start doing some work, can't I?"

"I'm not the one dictating it. That will depend on your body."

Zachary started to sit down on the couch. Kenzie stepped forward and picked up the duffel bag. "Don't get comfortable. Let's get the car loaded up."

He took the bag away from her firmly, then bent down and picked up the laptop bag as well. "Which car are we taking?"

It was always a fight to see who got to drive. Zachary enjoyed driving, especially on the highway, where he was able to zone out and let go of his usual anxieties. Kenzie loved getting out in her baby, a sporty red convertible. But she had decided they would take Zachary's nondescript white compact instead. It was better in the fall weather in Vermont, which was supposed to be taking a turn for the worse in the next few days. And she wanted to give Zachary that time to drive, to get out of himself and be in the zone for a while. It would help him as much as any vacation. She also preferred not to have her baby sitting outside unprotected when they were at the resort. It as safer in her garage.

"Yours. But you have to watch the speed limit."

Which meant that he'd better not go more than ten miles or so above the speed limit. Zachary preferred to way too fast for Kenzie's comfort. At least, when they weren't racing against time to stop a viral outbreak.

Zachary brightened a little at this news. He hefted his bags higher and headed to the front door. Kenzie grabbed the food bags from the kitchen and her suitcase from the hall and followed him out to his car.

Zachary had the trunk open and carefully stowed his bags, then took Kenzie's from her and fit them in.

"You aren't taking a computer?" he noted.

"I'm on vacation. I've got my phone and tablet for simple emails or looking things up, I've got some books I intend to read, and I'm going to participate in some of the group activities and spend time with you. No work."

He considered this. "They do have Wi-Fi, right?"

"Yes, they have Wi-Fi. I don't know how fast their internet service is, being up in the mountains like they are, but there is internet. And you could always hotspot to your phone."

"Maybe I should have bought some extra data..."

"You can do that later if you need to. You don't have to be home to do that. Now, is there anything else? Last chance."

Zachary gazed back at the house, but his eyes were far away. She didn't know what he was seeing or remembering. "Yeah. I'm fine. Got everything."

CHAPTER 2

K enzie kept an eye on Zachary as he drove out of the city and settled into highway driving. He gradually became more relaxed, the lines in his face softening and his hands loosening on the steering wheel. Kenzie gave him a while to enjoy the drive before trying to start a conversation.

"Now are you happy to get out of town?"

Zachary nodded. "Yeah. You're right. Some time away from work will be a good thing, even if I have already been off for a couple of weeks. There's money in the bank and I don't think I would be able to do much in the shape that I'm in right now."

"I think you'll feel a lot better once you've been able to relax for a while. Lorne says this resort is really nice."

"Did Pat take him there?"

Kenzie grinned. Patrick Parker had previously taken his partner, Lorne Peterson, to a day spa as a Christmas gift. While Lorne had said that he enjoyed it, it really wasn't his type of thing. Pat was far more concerned about healthy living and taking care of his body. Lorne was more of a pizza and beer guy. Zachary was clearly trying to set his expectations of the resort based on which of the men had first suggested it.

"No. It's run by an old friend of Lorne's."

Zachary nodded, understanding it was more of an indulgence than a health spa. Somewhere he wouldn't be expected to be fit or to eat clean.

"Sounds nice... Do you think..." Zachary trailed off.

Kenzie gave him some time to rethink his question and tell her what she wanted to know, but he fell silent and didn't finish the question.

"Do I think what?"

"It's just stupid."

"It's not really fair, deciding you know my answer without asking the question. How do you know what I'm going to say?"

"I'm not. I just decided it was a stupid question and I don't want to ask it."

"Ask me anyway."

Zachary pulled out to pass a few cars. Kenzie watched the speedometer to make sure that it settled back into place once he pulled back into the right-hand lane.

"Okay. But it is stupid. I was just wondering if we could not tell people what I do for a living. People find out I'm a private investigator, and suddenly they're telling me their whole life story and asking my opinion about cheating spouses and Poirot and Monk and if I could help them find a long-lost family member..."

Kenzie laughed and nodded. "Like when people find out I'm a doctor and want to know what I think of their mole or if there really are untraceable poisons."

Zachary smiled. "Exactly like that."

"Well, I'm game. What do we want to tell people we do instead?"

"I can be unemployed. Then no one will ask me any questions requiring my expertise in any other area."

"Okay. Then I'd better be something that makes money. But something really boring. How about... an accountant. Hmm... not just an accountant..."

"How about an IRS agent?" Zachary suggested. "No one will ask you for your opinion on any creative accounting if they think you might turn around and audit them."

Kenzie nodded, pleased. "Great! I'm an IRS agent. An auditor. If anyone starts a conversation, I don't want to be a part of, I'll just start asking them questions about their income and whether they have ever been the subject of a detailed audit."

Zachary chuckled. "You are evil."

"It was your idea. I'm putting the blame on you."

Dosed to Death, Book #2 of the *Kenzie Kirsch Medical Thriller* series by P.D. Workman can be purchased at pdworkman.com

ABOUT THE AUTHOR

Award-winning and USA Today bestselling author P.D. (Pamela) Workman writes riveting mystery/suspense and young adult books dealing with mental illness, addiction, abuse, and other real-life issues. For as long as she can remember, the blank page has held an incredible allure and from a very young age she was trying to write her own books.

Workman wrote her first complete novel at the age of twelve and continued to write as a hobby for many years. She started publishing in 2013. She has won several literary awards from Library Services for Youth in Custody for her young adult fiction. She currently has over 70 published titles and can be found at pdworkman.com.

Born and raised in Alberta, Workman has been married for over 25 years and has one son.

Please visit P.D. Workman at pdworkman.com to see what else she is working on, to join her mailing list, and to link to her social networks.

If you enjoyed this book, please take the time to recommend it to other purchasers with a review or star rating and share it with your friends!

facebook.com/pdworkmanauthor

twitter.com/pdworkmanauthor

instagram.com/pdworkmanauthor

amazon.com/author/pdworkman

bookbub.com/authors/p-d-workman

goodreads.com/pdworkman

linkedin.com/in/pdworkman

pinterest.com/pdworkmanauthor

youtube.com/pdworkman

Lightning Source UK Ltd.
Milton Keynes UK
UKHW020032070223
416579UK00003B/711